IN THE
SHADE
OF THE
JACARANDA

REGALO GRANDE

IN THE
SHADE
OF THE
JACARANDA

NIKKI ARANA

Revell
Grand Rapids, Michigan

© 2006 by Nikki Arana

Published by Fleming H. Revell
a division of Baker Publishing Group
P.O. Box 6287, Grand Rapids, MI 49516-6287

Printed in the United States of America

Library of Congress Cataloging-in-Publication Data
Arana, Nikki, 1949–
    In the shade of the jacaranda / Nikki Arana.
        p.   cm. — (Regalo grande ; bk. 2)
    ISBN 0-8007-3049-6 (pbk.)
    1. Mexican American women—Fiction. 2. Married women—Fiction.
  I. Title.
PS3601.R35I5 2006
813′.6—dc22   2005020817

Scripture is taken from the New King James Version. Copyright © 1982 by Thomas Nelson, Inc. Used by permission. All rights reserved.

Information on pages 170–71 is taken from Robin Elise Weiss, LCCE, "AFP & Triple Screen Testing," *Your Guide to Pregnancy/Birth*, http://pregnancy.about.com/cs/afp/a/afptesting.htm; Robert G. Resta, quoted in "Counseling, Genetic," *Talk Medical*, http://www.talkmedical.com/medical-dictionary/3470/Counseling-Genetic. Information on page 188 is taken from Kendall Powell, "Ultrasound Scan Spots Down's Syndrome," *news@nature.com*, December 20, 2002, http://www.nature.com/news/2002/021216/pf/021216-14_pf.html.

To all who have followed the Lord where He leads and have found His ways are mysterious and beautiful.

For by one Spirit we were all baptized into one body—
whether Jews or Greeks, whether slave
or free. . . . Now God has set the members, each one
of them, in the body just as He pleased.

The First Epistle to Corinth

Prologue

Near Guadalajara, Mexico

THE OLD WOMAN rose. Slapping the dust from the creases of her tattered skirt, she stepped out of the shade of the jacaranda tree. It was time to go to the stream. Shading her eyes with her hand, she scanned the fields that stretched before her. In stark relief against the cloudless sky, she saw her daughter's back curved over the plow that dug furrows into the hard earth, the dry ground as unyielding as the hunger that plagued them.

Behind the plow, her nine grandchildren carefully pressed seed into the narrow ditches. The smallest ones were at the end of the line, squatting as they walked, one foot on each side of the furrow, hands patiently brushing loose dirt back into the shallow trough.

She would not bother them. Time was short to work the land that fed them . . . and it was better that she go alone.

Ducking back under the branches of the tree that was

their home, she returned to the spot where she had been sitting and knelt beside the baby. She took her shawl, made a pouch, and strapped the crying child to her back. Using the tree for support, she stood. She crossed herself and began the long walk to the river's edge, where cool water would quiet the feverish child, if only for a short time.

As she walked a breeze picked up, cooling her bare feet and face. She whispered a word of thanks to God.

She stopped. Hesitating. The baby had become quiet. All thoughts left her as a sense of dread surged within her. She willed herself to move faster. When she reached the stream, she hurried along the rocky bank until she found a flat spot of ground surrounded by stones, where the water pooled.

She untied her shawl and lifted the infant from it. The child whimpered. The fever that had burned within the baby for days now threatened its life. She knew. She had seen much in her seventy years. She had seen sickness that came to provoke the body, to teach the body to fight, and she had seen sickness that destroyed, that came to steal the life the Creator had given.

But she also knew the God of heaven and earth had provided a way to strike the powers of darkness. In her time with Him, He had revealed His consuming love and mercy and grace. And He had taught her that faith alone gave life to prayers. Making them living things, imbued with the power of the Creator.

She believed. With that faith, with certain knowledge, she knelt and lifted the crying child above her, to heaven. She felt His presence. "If it please You, Lord," she whispered.

As she surrendered to the Spirit of God, all things of the earth fled from her, and she was but an empty vessel, filled with the Spirit.

And so the prayer of healing was prayed. Not with the

words of the old woman but by the groanings of the Spirit, so His will might be done. And in that moment, dead to the flesh, transfigured by faith and the glory of God, there in the desolate field, unseen by the eyes of man, her prayer was answered.

Under the arc of the wings of a legion of angels, amidst the worshipping praise of one accord, the child was made whole.

ANGELICA AMANTE PEREZ looked at her watch again. Thirty seconds had passed. The next two and a half minutes could change her life forever.

She walked to the living room, staring at the plastic stick from the pregnancy test kit, her heart racing. One minute had passed. No line. No red line to stamp across their lives, canceling everything they'd worked toward.

She laid the plastic stick on the coffee table and walked to the large window that faced the street of the little subdivision. The roses her husband had planted to climb the archway framing the small entry to their home in Valle de Lagrimas were in full bloom. She could see the pruning shears half hidden at the base of the arch. Since the day the bush had first bloomed, Antonio had never failed to rise before she awoke, cut a rose, and put it on the little table next to her side of the bed. It was often the first thing she saw when she opened her eyes. He loved her with a purity and devotion the first year of marriage had only deepened.

She thanked God every day for the man He had brought into her life. Angelica walked back to the couch.

The sound of the phone ringing jarred her. *Mother*. She hadn't returned either of the calls that her mother had left at her work the day before. She put her hands over her ears. If only she'd turned the answering machine on before she'd started the test.

She counted the rings. If she didn't answer, and the machine didn't pick up, her mother would show up on her doorstep in twenty minutes. . . . She ran to the kitchen.

Mixed emotions surged through her. "Hi, Mom."

Her parents didn't understand why she'd chosen to marry Antonio instead of the bright, young attorney who'd pursued her. Even now, after almost a year and a half, they still didn't accept him. Thankfully, they kept their thoughts to themselves when he was present, but she'd heard the rude comments of others who moved in their circle—how the Mexican was lucky to marry the only daughter of the wealthy heart surgeon Benito Amante. Angelica knew the truth. She was the lucky one. What Antonio gave her, money couldn't buy. A rock solid partner. A man of honesty and honor. A man who understood her . . . a man who loved her. He didn't deserve their ignorant judgments, but the arrival of a baby would surely lead some to whisper how Antonio had trapped her and managed to tie himself to her family forever.

"Angelica, I was getting worried. Didn't you get my messages?"

"Just a second, Buddy's barking to get in." Angelica stepped to the glass slider and pulled it open. The tricolored sheltie looked at her, waiting for permission. "Hurry up." She nearly caught his tail in the door as she slammed it shut. Taking a deep breath, she returned to the phone.

11

"Sorry. I should've returned your call. But I haven't had a free moment since we got back from Mexico." Angelica turned, leaning her back against the counter, her eyes taking in the big kitchen. The down payment on the house had been a wedding gift. At least that's the way her parents had presented it. It was really their way of reminding her she was still a white, upper-class Amante, even though she'd married a Mexican. Reminding her appearances mattered. Reminding her that somehow their love for her was tied to her meeting *their* expectations for her life. She was their only child—born years after they'd been told her mother couldn't have children. It was almost as if, after waiting all those years, they wanted what was due them.

Antonio had recognized the gift for what it was and refused to accept it. He was determined they would make their own way. Angelica agreed with her husband. His wisdom and integrity were the very things that had drawn her to him, but she also loved her parents and knew it had hurt them when she'd married. Finally, to keep peace, Antonio had agreed to accept the money, not as a gift, but as a loan. The difficult compromise between her proud husband and her demanding parents had left both parties dissatisfied. It had also left her to figure out how to make the payments until Antonio's business created income. She clenched her jaw.

And now this. A possible pregnancy. She hadn't breathed a word of her fears to her mother. It would only upset her. Instead of seeing it as the early arrival of the most precious gift a married couple could receive, her mother would see this as interfering with her daughter's promising career. She would see it as an unplanned and unnecessary financial obligation the young couple was in no position to take on. Her mother would see the red lines as pointing the way to a downward spiral.

Angelica rubbed her forehead. "I've got twenty cases stacked up on my desk, and I'm trying to finish fixing up the guest room for Maclovia. She arrives tomorrow. I was going to try to get to the office for at least an hour today and review some depositions."

"If you'd accepted one of those offers you got from the big San Francisco firms, instead of taking that job at the public defender's office, you'd have an assistant." Her mother let a few seconds pass before continuing. "And there's no reason for you to be bothered with that guest room. If you would've let me send Maria down there to help you, you could've taken a nap this afternoon and been rested for our dinner tonight." Angelica waited through another carefully placed pause. "Why isn't your husband helping you? He doesn't have anything else to do, and it's *his* grandmother."

Angelica could hear the disapproval in her mother's voice. Her stomach knotted. Why couldn't her parents be happy for her and accept Antonio as the man she'd chosen to spend the rest of her life with? "He went to the community center to his English class." Her grip tightened on the phone. "He's studying hard to learn enough English to find work." She looked at her watch. Three minutes and fifteen seconds. "Mom, I've got to run. Anything you want me to bring tonight?"

"No, honey. Just yourself."

"Love you, Mom. We'll see you in a little while."

Angelica put the phone in the cradle, then turned and walked to the living room. As she reached for the plastic stick, her hand was shaking. She felt like she was observing her own life from some distant place.

Two lines.

One in the control window, one in the result window.

"A baby. I'm going to have a baby." She sank down onto

13

the couch, staring at the stick. Two red lines, as clear as two red flags.

She picked up the little white paper that came in the early pregnancy test. "Over ninety-nine percent accurate."

She sat in lonely silence. It wasn't that they didn't want children; it was just that the timing couldn't be worse. She was pursuing her career as a public defender for Sierra County. Her boss had assured her, one more year of work as impressive as her last one, and she would be promoted; she would begin litigating felonies. Experience she needed. She straightened her back and ran her hand over her stomach. Eventually, she hoped to open her own firm and specialize in advocacy for the poor. Something she was passionate about after being fired from her job in New York when she had refused to exploit a legal loophole that allowed big produce companies to deport Mexican laborers like Antonio without fair compensation for their labor. Although she had lost her job, she'd never regretted the career-ending decision. But it had left her financially strapped, and she and Antonio had agreed—children would come when they were financially stable. That was how it was supposed to be.

Now what would Antonio say? He had just received his permanent visa and was trying to start a gardening business. It was important to him to be able to provide for his new family. He'd grown up in Mexico with nine brothers and sisters and had lived in abject poverty. He'd vowed to give his children the life he'd never had.

She knotted her hands together. "Oh, Lord God, where are You? Why this? Why now?" A flood of emotions washed through her. "A baby." She whispered the words again.

As gentle as the brush of an angel's wing, a sweet joy swept over her. She blinked a few times. For a split second she seemed to be looking through a gossamer veil. She rubbed her eyes, probably just the blur of tears. "A baby!" She slowly closed her eyes, pressing her hand lightly on her stomach, imagining for a moment what lay beneath her fingers. The darkness that had shadowed her vanished, and something encircled her, luminous but elusive, something powerful and pure and beautiful. She wanted to open her eyes, but she didn't want to move, to intrude on the magical moment. Ever so slightly, she lifted her lids, half expecting to find someone present with her. But she was alone in the room. A smile came to her lips, and warmth glowed in her cheeks. She was suddenly filled with peace.

Antonio. She needed to find him, to talk to him. Angelica grabbed her purse and keys. "Buddy, watch the house."

As she pulled the door shut, she saw Buddy, still standing facing the couch where she had been sitting, his bright, shoe-button eyes focused on the empty space, wagging his tail, as if greeting some unseen visitor.

Angelica paused. His ears were quivering as they sometimes did when he heard something before she could. "Buddy?" He turned at the sound of his name. "See you later."

She hurried to the car. Antonio would be on his way home by now. She'd driven him to the class and helped him register, but they'd agreed he'd walk home since she needed to spend some time in her office.

About a mile from the house, she saw him. Pulling up, she opened her window. "Need a ride?"

He bent down and rested his arms in the opening. "*Sí, señorita.*"

His deep tan accented his even, white teeth and broad smile. A few strands of black hair shadowed one eye. She brushed them away from his handsome face and smiled at him. "Love you."

He pulled her hand from his face and kissed her fingers.

15

"I love you too." He spoke the words carefully, deliberately, trying to hide his accent. It touched Angelica. He wanted so much to fit into her world, to make her proud of him. Everyone had been shocked when she had married the illiterate, Mexican man who took care of her father's horses. But she hadn't wavered. She knew this was the man God had for her. And though Antonio didn't know of the Bible's commandment for husbands to love their wives as Christ loved the church, it was a truth in their marriage.

She straightened. "Get in."

As she watched him walk around the car, her mind began to race. The enormity of what she was about to tell him gripped her. She shouldn't just blurt it out sitting in a car stopped in the middle of the street. She gripped the wheel, trying to gain control of her emotions. The oaks. She would take him to the oaks. The place on her parents' ranch, Regalo Grande, where he'd first held her in his arms.

The door slammed. Antonio put on his seat belt and turned to her. "*Qué pasa?*"

"What do you mean, what's the matter?"

"You come for me."

"I just wanted to go for a ride." She put the car in gear, avoiding his eyes.

"Really." He studied her face. "Nothing more?"

She tried to keep her voice casual. "No. No. Nothing more."

"Your hands white." He touched her knuckles.

Even though he pronounced the words carefully, she could hear concern in his voice. "Let's drive up to the oaks."

He raised his eyebrows, then nodded.

Angelica stepped on the gas. "How did you like the class?"

"Difficult." He opened his binder.

She glanced at the page. She could make out large, uneven letters. He'd never had any schooling. And after her trip to Mexico, where the government required him to go to get his visa, she'd learned the exacting price of poverty in his country. The poor had no education, no opportunities, no way out.

She'd hoped to help his family. But her father's failed business venture the previous year, to develop a new transplant drug that would stop organ rejection, had drained the family's assets, including most of her trust account. Her father still practiced as a heart surgeon and had managed to salvage their big home and twenty-five acres of the ranch, but she had given up most of what she had been gifted through the estate over the years. She hadn't minded. She was glad her parents could maintain their lifestyle. At twenty-six, having graduated from Hastings College of the Law magna cum laude, she'd felt perfectly capable of making her own way. That seemed like a lifetime ago. Now she was committed to a demanding job, to being a wife who supported her husband, a partner in a fledgling business, and the mother of an unborn child. She swallowed the lump in her throat.

"Looks like you're making progress." She nodded toward his binder.

When he saw her looking at the page, he closed the cover. "I will." His face filled with resolve, his voice certain.

"Just think, your *abuela* will be here tomorrow."

Antonio's expression softened. "I am the first child. She help care for me. Now I help care for her. I will find work soon."

Lord, please help him. Antonio was a proud man, and she knew how important it was to him to find work. Especially now. They'd decided yard work would be his best option. His job on her father's ranch had disappeared when her father sold his breeding stock as part of the liquidation of his assets. Then her father had made it clear Antonio should find other work. Even though he spoke little English and had no transportation, Antonio had started looking the day they returned from Mexico. When she'd returned home from her job that first day back, she had found he'd visited both of their neighbors to see if they wanted to hire him. Though they had expressed no interest, he'd learned from one of them that she had hired a gardener in the past but was dissatisfied with his work. He had convinced the neighbor, Mrs. Dupre, to let him maintain one of her front flowerbeds free for one month. If she liked his work, he thought perhaps she would hire him. Angelica smiled, remembering his confidence. "Soon I have a good business," he'd said.

"Monday, you can start looking for work again. We'll keep studying for your driver's license. Maybe you can try the test one day next week."

"*Sí, señorita.*" He gave her a salute, then winked at her.

They were nearing the ranch. She could see the red tile roof of the big hacienda she'd grown up in atop the ridge. Just where the long, winding driveway intersected the road, she pulled over.

Antonio looked at the dashboard gauges. "*Problema?*"

She switched the engine off, leaving her hand on the key longer than necessary. Right now, Antonio's life was full of their dreams. He was still in the free and benevolent place of hope and a future. As soon as she took the key out, all that would begin to change for him—for her. She drew a deep breath and pulled the key from the ignition.

"Come on." She unfastened her seat belt and opened the door. "I don't want my parents to know we're here."

Antonio's eyes narrowed ever so slightly, but without a word, he got out.

"We'll see them later tonight. Follow me." She could see her horse, Pasha, through the oaks, prancing around the pasture and whinnying. His standard greeting for Angelica. "Pasha must have heard my car. I hope he doesn't give me away."

Angelica grabbed Antonio's hand, and they walked down under the oaks. She led him along the stream to the place where they'd sat late one night when he'd first come to the ranch—where she'd fallen asleep in his arms—where she'd fallen in love with him.

"Please. Sit right there." She pointed at the big oak branch that had fallen by the water.

He sat on the branch and pulled her onto his lap. She felt the heat of his body, the muscled firmness of his arms locked around her. "What is it, Angelica?" His eyes rested on hers, attentive, intimate, giving her just what she needed.

She hesitated. The words she chose would change all the plans they had made over the past year and a half. Her toes curled in her shoes. "We're going to have a baby."

"Baby?"

He drew in a sharp breath, and she dropped her head, not wanting to see his face as grim reality set in.

"Say it again," he whispered, pulling her to him.

"We're going to have a baby." She turned her face into his shoulder and bit her lower lip, fighting for control.

He stood, scooped her into his arms, and spun in a circle. "*Dale gracias a Dios.*" He looked at her. "God is good." He set her on her feet and kissed her. "Thank you." Then he knelt down in front of her and put his hands on her hips. Speaking directly to her tummy, he said, "Welcome, little one."

Angelica began to giggle and covered her mouth with her hands. Antonio's love for his unborn child brought tears to her eyes. What more did a child need to thrive? A weight lifted from her shoulders, and she became aware of her surroundings for the first time. The oaks, the stream, the sunny spring afternoon . . . a man who adored her. They would work through this, together.

Antonio stood, then placed his hands on her shoulders and held her away from him. Looking at her, studying her. Then tenderly he ran the tip of his finger over her cheekbone and down the oval of her jaw line, as if tracing fine art. He tilted her chin toward him and kissed her. Deep emotion always moved him to touch her face . . . on their wedding night . . . now.

"Antonio, the timing's all wrong. We don't have much savings, and you've just started your business."

He put his finger on her lips. "Shh. This is the way of life, my Angel. No worry, God is with us."

As they drove home to get ready for dinner with her parents, clouds began to fill the April sky, and the bright day became somber. The joy she'd felt began to fade. She looked at her watch. In three hours they would be having dinner with her parents. She dreaded telling them. Would they accept that this was just the way of life? A drop of rain splashed on the windshield.

Antonio stepped out of the shower, wiped the steam off the mirror, and tied his towel around his waist. "Hi, Papa," he said to his reflection. He shook his head slowly. "I can't believe it. I'm going to have a son." He picked up his razor and began shaving.

He thought back to the moment when Angelica had told

him. When she'd first said it, he'd felt an impression. He couldn't say why or how, it was just a knowing. God was giving him a son. When she'd said it the second time, he was filled with certainty. It would be a boy, a special boy. But he had felt a check in his spirit. . . . He should not tell Angelica yet.

He had known what his wife meant when she'd said the timing was wrong. Angelica knew his heart and his desire to provide for his children. It was his responsibility. He respected her need to work and achieve. It was part of who she was. But it didn't absolve him of his duty to his family. This news meant he would spend every free moment looking for work and he would study harder. He would begin tonight. *Dios, I trust You. Give me the strength to accomplish what is before me.*

Angelica stuck her head around the door. "You about ready?"

"*Un momento.*" He splashed aftershave on his face.

"I'll put Buddy out for a minute, then we'll go."

Antonio watched Angelica walk from the bedroom. "That woman is strong with men and have no patience." A grin tugged at his lips.

"You about ready?"

He could hear Angelica calling from the living room. He fastened his belt buckle and grabbed his blazer.

"Wow. You look handsome, *señor.* That was worth waiting for." She gave him a peck on the cheek, then ran out the door in front of him.

On the drive to the ranch, Antonio thought about his in-laws. They were good people. They'd given him a job when he'd desperately needed one. And though he knew they did not think him worthy of their daughter, they still included him in their family.

Surely a baby would change everything. Angelica's mother would probably want to care for the baby every day. He hoped that wouldn't cause a problem with *his* grandmother. It sometimes did in Mexico, with the first grandchild. Later, when there were many, all eyes and hands were needed, and everyone was happy.

As they headed up the drive of Regalo Grande, Angelica pushed the button in her visor. The massive, black wrought-iron gates swung open. As they neared the house, Pasha began to gallop up and down the fence line. She honked her horn. Two short beeps. He pranced and tossed his head in response.

She pulled in front of the arched stucco entryway and parked. As Antonio reached for the door handle, he felt her hand on his arm.

"Antonio."

There was something hidden in her voice. He turned to her, watching her as she spoke. "I'm so excited about the baby."

He nodded, waiting, studying her beautiful face as she struggled to find words. "Um . . . it's just that I'm not sure if my parents will be as excited as we are."

Why would she say this? "Of course they be happy. Very happy. This big news."

"It's just that we haven't been married very long. We didn't plan children so soon. They might think we should've waited."

There was something she wasn't saying. As if this were a wrong thing and they should apologize. "We did wait. God no wait."

Tenderness filled Angelica's face. She leaned over and kissed him on the cheek. "Maybe you're right. I'm just being silly. Let's go give them our big news."

They got out of the car, and as they walked through the entryway to the front door, he wrapped his hand firmly around hers. His thoughts returned to her face, to her eyes cast down, the unnecessary fingering of her hair, the tone of her voice, the tenseness in her shoulders, as she had spoken of her concern. He knew her well. She often expressed her feelings without words. She was quick to reveal her mind but slow to reveal her heart. This was one of the reasons he loved her.

What wasn't she saying? The kiss on his cheek . . . there was something more . . . something . . . it was him. This was not about the baby, it was about him! He felt a wave of heat sweep over his face. Angelica's parents did not think *him* worthy.

Angelica opened the front door and called out. "We're here."

"Come on in. I'm in the living room."

They walked down the hall to the spacious front room. Antonio stepped aside as Geniveve Amante embraced her daughter.

"Ben, they're here," she called down the hall. "Your father's opening the wine." She gave Antonio a quick smile.

"Have a seat."

Antonio turned at the voice behind him. Benito Amante had two bottles of wine tucked under his arm. The big man's steel gray hair, penetrating eyes, and the self-assuredness that came with his medical degree could be intimidating.

"Good evening, *patrón*." Antonio extended his hand.

"Good evening, Antonio." As they shook hands, Antonio noticed the man's eyes were on his daughter. It was obvious her father loved her deeply, yet Antonio rarely saw him hug her or her mother. Perhaps his many years as a doctor

23

had taught him not to show people what he was feeling for them.

"Drink?"

"I'll have a Diet Coke, Dad."

"What about you, Antonio? A beer?"

"No. *Gracias*. Nothing."

Angelica took a seat on the couch that faced the big picture window and its expansive view of the Sonoma Mountains and the valley they embraced. The lush green of the spring hills could be seen, even at twilight. Her mother sat down beside her. "Here, Ben. Sit by me." Mrs. Amante patted the empty cushion next to her.

"Let me get Angelica's Coke."

Antonio took a side chair.

Mrs. Amante poked Angelica with her elbow. "Look at Pasha tearing around down there."

"He's excited I'm here. We haven't been riding in ages."

"He's been excited all day. He was doing that this afternoon."

"Really?" Angelica shifted in her seat.

Benito handed Angelica her drink and took the seat next to his wife. "So, Antonio, have you found work yet?"

"Dad, he just got his visa so he *can* work."

Antonio waited for his wife to finish speaking. Answering for him was a habit she'd developed when he couldn't speak English. That wasn't necessary now, and he gently reminded her by answering himself. "I look for work, and I go to school, learn English."

"Antonio's planning to start his own landscape maintenance business. I'm going to do the books. I've got QuickBooks on my computer at home."

24

"Angelica, don't you have enough to do with your job?" Mrs. Amante looked at her with impolite eyes.

"It's easy, Mom. I keep our checkbook and bills on there anyway. We figure he can get started with about three thousand dollars. We're going to invest our savings in his business."

Antonio nodded proudly in Angelica's direction, then glanced at her parents. They stared at their drinks with frozen faces. Before they noticed him, he looked casually away, out the window, his heart heavy.

The visit continued. Antonio didn't understand everything that was said, but he joined in when he could and tried to use only English words he was sure of. Finally, Maria announced that dinner was served.

Antonio spoke in Spanish to the woman who kept the house and cooked for the Amantes. "Good evening, Maria. I've been waiting all day for your good food. Thank you." She and her husband lived on the ranch, in what had been the bunkhouse when Benito Amante still had breeding stock and show horses.

They ate in the formal dining room. The *patrón* took his place at the head of the table, and Mrs. Amante sat at the opposite end. Antonio and Angelica sat in the middle, facing each other. Gold-rimmed plates and tall, thin glasses that sparkled in the candlelight were part of each place setting. Antonio never felt comfortable with all the extra forks, spoons, and knives that were a part of these formal meals. He knew each one had a special purpose, and he managed, but he couldn't help thinking of Maria working in the kitchen and having to wash them all, late at night.

"So, Antonio, your grandmother arrives tomorrow." Benito buttered a roll.

"Antonio was her first grandchild." Angelica answered for him.

"Now many grandchildren, and their children," he added.

"Well, I'm glad you two are waiting to start your family." Mrs. Amante smiled at Angelica.

Under the table, Antonio slid his foot over and tapped Angelica's toes.

"Yes, that was the plan." Angelica took her knife and began to cut her meat.

"Was?" Benito looked at her and laid his fork down.

Mrs. Amante's eyes widened. "Angelica?"

Seconds seemed like minutes. Angelica raised her head and looked at Antonio.

She needed him. . . . Antonio stood up. He walked quickly around the table, stood behind Angelica's chair, and put his hands on her shoulders. His mind was racing. What could he say? He didn't know much English. What if he said something stupid and embarrassed her? He closed his eyes a moment. *Dios, give me words.*

"Mr. and Mrs. Amante." He nodded at each of them.

Benito folded his arms across his chest.

"You are my father- and mother-in-love."

Angelica reached up and patted his hand.

"This is my wife, and I love her. We are proud to tell you we are having a baby . . . a boy." He kissed the top of Angelica's head, then walked back to his chair and took his seat.

Caught up in the joy of the moment, he lifted his water glass. Then he tipped his head, first to the *patrón*, then to Mrs. Amante.

No one moved. No one spoke.

2

"MEXICANA FLIGHT 253. Guadalajara to Sacramento, now boarding. Rows 26 to 15."

The frail, old woman rose and stepped into the line of people forming in front of the door. She wrapped the black shawl over her white hair and across her narrow shoulders and smoothed her thin, cotton dress. It was important she look her best so her grandson would be proud of her.

For the hundredth time Maclovia fingered the primitive cross around her neck, seeking the Lord, wanting to feel His presence, needing His reassurance that she was in His will. She had seen many things in her life, floods, drought, starvation, and death. But all were governed by the laws of nature and the unfathomable mind of God. None were as mysterious as the huge, heavy, metal tube she saw outside the window, which was supposed to lift her into the air as though it weighed no more than the fog that floated through the air in the fields of her home. This was the greatest test the Lord had ever given her. She fingered the cross again. She would trust Him.

Her thoughts returned to her grandson and the American girl he'd married. When he had brought his wife to visit, word had spread rapidly. Many thought, and many more whispered, the polished and charming lady with the beautiful face was a movie star. Rumors flew far and wide that Antonio had married well and was now a millionaire. But Antonio had explained to his family that she was a lawyer and was as smart as she was pretty.

Maclovia carefully refolded the top of the paper bag she carried, making sure all her possessions were secure. The missionary who had brought her to the airport had told her to keep the bag with her at all times. She pressed her hand against the side of the bag, feeling the outline of her passport. The line moved forward.

"Ticket, please." A young man plucked the paper from her hand. "Mrs. Regosa, you're in seat 6A. It isn't time for you to board yet."

Maclovia's heart began to pound. She had done something wrong. There were so many people. Everyone was getting on the plane. She looked at the people in front of her. They carried handsome leather boxes with handles, not paper bags. Maybe the important people got on first. Quick heat rose in her cheeks.

She looked back at the young man. Suddenly, he tore off a piece of her ticket and handed it back to her. "Give this to the attendant when you board the plane." He waved her toward a long chute. She followed the man in front of her and found herself carried along with the crowd of passengers moving toward the plane, her ticket clenched in her hand.

A woman in a crisp white blouse and dark blue skirt stood at the opening of a big metal door. This must be the attendant the young man had told her about. She raised her gnarled hand toward the woman so she could see the torn piece of paper.

"Welcome, *señora*. Is this your first time flying?"

She smiled up into the woman's kind eyes. "Yes, I'm going to America. Please call me Maclovia."

"Very well. Let me help you to 6A." The woman gently touched her elbow.

Maclovia looked around at the chairs, straps, and low ceilings as the young woman led her to a big, deep seat next to a window. Not once, in the many seasons of her life, had she thought she would see God's creation from the heavens. When she'd learned He was calling her to America and she would be traveling in a plane, she had asked the Lord, if it would please Him, to allow her to see His marvelous works from a place in the clouds. But now, as she stepped toward her seat, fear pricked at her, trying to rob her of her trust in the Lord. She immediately took the thought captive and rebuked the darkness.

"Can I put your bag in the overhead storage?" the attendant asked.

"No, I will hold it." Maclovia folded both arms across the bag, pressing it to her chest.

"It would be best if you put it under the seat in front of you."

Maclovia did as she was asked, then put her foot on top of it.

"Can I help you with your seat belt?" The attendant pointed to the straps.

Maclovia felt around and pulled them onto her lap. "You don't need to strap me in. I will stay in my seat if that is the rule."

"It's for your safety, *señora*. For takeoff and landing and in case we hit turbulence." The young woman showed her how to make them fit together and how to tighten them, then she stepped away to help others.

Turbulence. This was a word Maclovia had never heard. It sounded dangerous. She hoped the men flying the plane would watch for it and not hit it. She pulled her belt tighter.

Maclovia leaned into the circle of glass next to her. Her brows knitted together as she watched the frenzied activity outside her window. The scene was void of trees and fields, just machines and metal and men hurrying to somewhere and from somewhere. It was strange and unnatural. She tilted her head until she caught a glimpse of the sky, a sliver of blue, a tiny piece of home. She put her hand over her cross and closed her eyes.

Someone dropped into the seat next to her. Black pants, black shirt, white collar—she smiled at the balding man.

"Good day, *señora*." He fastened his straps.

"Good day, Father." *Thank You, Lord.*

The plane was moving. The young woman who'd helped her was standing in front of the aisle speaking. She told everyone about the straps and small cups that might appear if the cabin lost pressure. While the young woman spoke loudly about terrible things that could happen, Maclovia looked around. The priest seated next to her was reading a magazine. No one was listening. She leaned forward, wanting to catch every word.

As Maclovia folded her hands in her lap, the plane picked up speed. A roaring noise surrounded her, and a great force pressed on her. She felt a clunking sound from somewhere below. Had they hit a cloud . . . turbulence? Without moving her head, her eyes sought the window . . . then widened. Everything had vanished. She gripped the armrest with one hand and with the other pulled on the strap in her lap.

Help me. Oh, help me. Please. She closed her eyes and

30

immediately felt the presence of her Lord. Into that quiet place came images. A bolt of light sent through a torrent of rain splitting a tree. A blanket of light sent through a torrent of tears healing a child. Reminders of the kingdom and the power that were His alone. She drew a deep breath, filling herself with His peace. She was in the will of God, and He would care for her. He had called her to America, of that she was sure . . . though she had no idea why.

"Don't be afraid, *señora*." The priest patted her arm. "There's nothing to worry about. You can trust Mexicana to keep you safe. The men who maintain these planes are well qualified. This airline has an excellent safety record."

Maclovia smiled sweetly at him. "Thank you for telling me. I'll remember that." Somehow putting her trust in the men who maintained the planes didn't appeal to her. She'd stick with the God who created the men who maintained the planes.

A voice suddenly came from overhead. "Thank you for flying Mexicana. We will arrive in Sacramento one thirty local time. We will cruise at an altitude of thirty-five thousand feet. The forecast is clear skies all the way. When we have reached our altitude, the seat belt sign will be turned off, and you may move around the cabin." Then the voice began to speak words she did not recognize. She listened carefully. Not one word was familiar, except Mexicana and Sacramento. English. She knew a few words from the missionaries. *God, bless, pray, believe, faith*. She whispered each one carefully, deliberately.

"Really, there's nothing to worry about." The priest patted her arm again.

As the hours passed, Maclovia could not take her eyes from the window. Not only had she seen the earth from the clouds, she was now above the clouds. Could this be heaven's doorstep? She smiled. As was His habit, He had provided for her far beyond what she asked. She loosened the strap holding her to the seat. God was with her.

She glanced at the priest, who, she was relieved to see, had dozed off and wouldn't be offering any more of his explanations about the plane. She noticed the half-finished glass of water on the tray in front of him begin to jiggle. Maclovia watched the glass inch forward. She knitted her brows together, then looked toward the window, just as the shaking began beneath her feet. The plane was heading down. Tubes and cups dropped from the ceiling as a voice began speaking from overhead. The priest sat straight up and gripped the arms of his seat. "Put on your masks and fasten your seat belts. Please, stay in your seats." She recognized the choked voice as that of the young woman who'd helped her. Maclovia pressed her back into the cushion.

Looking above her head, she could see her mask had not dropped down. Trembling, she reached up and grabbed it and did what she'd seen the attendant do at the beginning of the flight. She should have listened more carefully. She looked at the man next to her.

The priest fumbled with the tubes, one moment straining to get out of his seat and the next flailing for the mask. Maclovia reached for his mask and helped him get it on. The plane was dropping. Food trays crashed into the aisles. People were screaming. The child in the seat across the aisle began to cry and reached for his mother.

As the plane continued dropping, the cabin became quiet. Fear replaced by terror. She glanced at the priest. His hand clenched the cross hanging from his neck; his eyes were closed.

Oh, my Lord. Where are You?

Luminous, but elusive, like the flash of a knife blade,

32

something cut across her line of vision. It seemed to separate her from everything else, speaking to her spirit, cutting away man's truth, to reveal God's truth. *His truth. Not man's truth.* There was nothing to fear. God had called her to America . . . and He would deliver her there. God's plans and purposes were not subject to the whims of fate. Remorse gripped her as she realized her absence of faith encouraged the presence of the enemy. *Forgive me.*

No one spoke. Only the muffled cries of children could be heard as parents tried to comfort them. Maclovia glanced at the child across the aisle. He'd wrapped his spindly arms around his mother's neck, his head against her chest. She could see his hair was extremely thin, missing completely where an ugly scar slashed through it, and his gaunt face was unnaturally pale. The child was ill. Hadn't he endured enough? She could feel fear spewing its hot breath all around her, filling the air with despair. *Lord, if it please You, pierce this darkness and give them Your peace.*

Maclovia laid her hands in her lap. With her palms and her face turned upward, she began to hum, seeking the Lord. The melody made its way through the cabin. As the sound of it touched each ear, it calmed each heart.

Someone from the middle of the plane, a woman, began to sing. The most beautiful, high voice filled the cabin. Even though the plane still angled down and shuddered under the force of the descent, fear was forgotten. Strained faces relaxed, and calm settled among the people. Maclovia closed her eyes, listening to the beautiful voice and the words of praise being lifted to heaven.

The sound of the captain's voice was again overhead. "We lost pressure in the aircraft and have taken the plane down to eight thousand feet. We've leveled off now, and we'll remain at this altitude until we reach Sacramento. We're about forty-five minutes out. We declared an emergency, so fire trucks and ambulances are waiting on the runway as a precaution. At this altitude you can take your masks off. We will be able to reach Sacramento and land safely."

People began to talk, their voices filled with relief. "That was the most frightening thing I've ever been through."

A lady across the aisle asked, "Did you hear that woman singing up in the front? What a voice. But I couldn't quite make out the words."

A few rows behind Maclovia, a man spoke out. "She wasn't in the front. I'm sitting in the middle, and *she* was definitely sitting in the back."

A teenager walking up the aisle stopped. "I was in the back." He spoke American Spanish. "That voice came from the middle of the plane. She sang in some kind of foreign language."

The little boy across the aisle chimed in. "She was singing about God. I heard her, and I wasn't scared anymore."

It was the sick little boy who'd clung to his mother's neck. Maclovia drew a breath. The color in the boy's cheeks, the light in his eyes. *Glory to You, God.* Yes, he had heard the voice . . . and he needn't be scared anymore. Maclovia lifted her hands just a few inches from her lap, her crooked fingers straining upward. *Glory to You, God.*

As the plane continued to Sacramento, Maclovia quietly listened to the passengers debate the whereabouts of the woman with the beautiful voice.

She knew where the voice had come from. She'd heard it before. On her knees, in prayer by the stream.

Airrrpooort. Antonio silently sounded out the word on the freeway sign.

"Off here for airport," he announced to Angelica.

"Whoa. That's impressive."

Her sweet smile and the delight on her face made all the studying worthwhile.

"How come you're so sure?" Angelica looked at him.

"About the airport?"

"No, what you said last night, after you made that toast. You said our baby is a boy."

"I feel it . . . here." He touched his heart. He had noticed this about the Americans. They seldom talked about the truth in their hearts. Didn't they hear the things that were whispered there?

He turned toward his wife. "What do you feel?"

"About if it's a boy or a girl? Umm." She tapped her fingers on the steering wheel. "I don't know. But the doctor can tell us, if we want the test." Angelica looked in the rearview mirror. "Buddy, sit down."

"Why would we want to test our son? He's just a baby."

Angelica's face filled with a wide smile. "The doctors give the babies tests to see if they're okay. To make sure they're perfect. And they can tell if it's a boy or girl too."

"Of course my son is perfect. God made him for us." Angelica's certainty about all of this caused him to keep his thoughts to himself. He did not understand the ways of the Americans. Disturbing a baby as it grew within its mother to see if it was perfect. Didn't they know all things from the hands of the Creator were perfect?

"You sure got my dad's attention, saying it was a boy." Angelica slowly shook her head. "I couldn't believe it when he told us he'd kept a baseball mitt in the back of his closet all these years."

"He said he bought it when your mother expecting you. Didn't they have the test?"

"They didn't have it back then, I guess." She raised her eyebrows. "That's the first time I ever heard he wanted a boy." Angelica's cheeks were flushed and her eyes dancing. "And now he's going to get one, if you're right. For the first time since we've been married, I feel like we're family. You know, parents and grandparents."

Her words touched his heart. Perhaps this was God's way of answering his daily prayers that someday he would become acceptable to Angelica's parents.

"When I was turning the car around to head home, I saw my dad running down to the storage shed behind the house." She hesitated, catching Antonio's eye. "That's where he keeps his fishing gear."

They both burst out laughing.

Antonio stifled his laughter, not wanting to disrespect the *patrón*. "He is good man." Antonio admired all Angelica's father had achieved, and he adored the daughter the man had raised. If only he could be the son-in-law they'd wanted. He'd seen the way the *patrón* and his wife had looked at him when they'd announced the news. But what hurt most was the way they'd looked at their daughter. He could do nothing but trust that God would make a way.

As Angelica pulled into the parking lot, she suddenly became serious. "I'm kind of scared." She turned off the engine and picked up her purse. "This happening right now. What if your business doesn't go? What if we can't make our payments? What if we can't . . ."

He put his finger on her lips. "Shhh, my Angel. No borrow trouble. You are not alone. I am with you. My business *will* go, and . . . I will get a bigger wheelbarrow."

Angelica leaned into him, and he stroked her hair. "Come.

36

It's time to go meet our grandmother." She straightened. "Should we bring Buddy?"

"Of course. He doesn't want to sit in the car." Antonio grabbed Buddy's leash.

They walked hand in hand to the Immigration building where international passengers deplaned, Buddy prancing, leading the way with his head held high above his beautiful, white fur collar, as excited as his master and mistress to meet Grandmother.

"Look at the crowd." Angelica slowed her steps.

Antonio pulled Buddy in. Something wasn't right. People were waving their arms and talking excitedly. A lot of people were talking on their cell phones. Antonio could just pick up a few words and phrases. He looked at Angelica.

"Something happened on the plane." She listened to the conversations around her. "Sounds like they had some kind of mechanical problem."

Fear gripped Antonio. "Is my grandmother alive?"

"Is everyone okay?" Angelica asked one of the people holding a suitcase and a child.

"Everyone's fine. But I've never been so scared in my life. I'm still shaking."

They moved as close as they could to the exit door. One by one people continued to emerge. Finally, a young man opened it and held it so an elderly woman could pass through.

"There she is." Angelica jumped up and down.

Antonio looked where his wife was pointing. He blinked rapidly and took a steadying breath. His grandmother. She was safe. Everyone had told him there was nothing to worry about. Flying was safer than driving. He hadn't believed it then, and he certainly didn't believe it now. The whole thing was unnatural. He handed Angelica Buddy's leash and made his way through the crowd toward his beloved *abuela*.

"Grandmother. Welcome." He took her bag and kissed her cheek. She patted his arm. With his free hand he touched her elbow and guided her gently toward Angelica, matching his steps to hers so she wouldn't feel rushed.

"Is very good to see you, Maclovia. *Mucho gusto.* Are you all right?"

Antonio hoped his grandmother could understand his wife's heavily accented Spanish. It had improved a lot since their marriage, even though Angelica often spoke her words out of order. There were many things Antonio hoped his grandmother would understand. America was a great country in so many ways, but in matters of God and family, it was very different from their homeland.

Maclovia looked toward Antonio. "What is she saying?"

"*Abuela*, we heard the plane almost crashed. Are you all right?" he translated.

Her wise eyes looked into his. "That is what they tried to tell me. But it isn't true. The plane took the path God intended. Nothing more and nothing less."

As she spoke, Antonio was reminded of his grandmother's great wisdom. His time in America had dimmed that memory.

Angelica tapped his arm. "What is she saying?"

He looked into his wife's concerned face. Angelica knew nothing of his mysterious and wonderful grandmother. "No worry, my Angel. She says she is fine. God was with her."

Angelica's face relaxed. "Well, let's get her home. She can tell us all about it in the car." She touched Antonio's arm. "Look at Buddy."

Buddy sat, not moving, eyes focused on Maclovia's face.

The old woman stooped down and cupped her hands

38

behind his ears. She whispered to him. Buddy danced in place, his tail wagging in big, fluffy sweeps.

"He didn't even bark. You'd think he knew her. They say animals can read people." Angelica laughed. "Buddy's bilingual. He probably understood every word she said."

Maclovia slipped her arm into Antonio's, and the four of them walked to the car to begin the trip home.

"Antonio, she's so frail." Angelica glanced in the rearview mirror at Maclovia. "She needs to see a dentist. I think she's lost more teeth than she's kept. And those clothes. That dress is so thin you can see through it. Let's stop on the way home at the factory outlets and buy her a few things. Then she'll be dressed, and we can take her to a restaurant for a nice, big meal. That would be the perfect time to tell her about the baby."

Antonio watched how animated Angelica appeared, delighting in the idea of doing good for his grandmother and giving her their wonderful news. Still, he gave silent thanks to the Lord that Maclovia didn't understand a word of English. "Honey." He turned toward her. "My *abuela* never eat in restaurant, and she never shop in factory outlets. It is much better to wait. In time I take her. But first I ask her."

"Oh." Angelica's cheeks reddened.

"But it was a good thought. If you don't want us to cook, we can stop and get takeout," he added, to soften his correction of her. "Then we can tell her about the baby, at dinner in our own home."

This was so like his wife. Charging ahead, not looking right or left, sure of herself. This was what made her good at defending people in court. But it was not necessarily a good way to handle family matters, particularly with elderly members. They had lived long and knew many things. They were to be respected.

For the briefest moment, sadness touched him. His grandmother was not acceptable to Angelica in the same way he had not been acceptable to her parents. He looked at his wife again, the color still in her cheeks. Perhaps she was thinking the same thing.

They chatted in broken English and improvised Spanish all the way home. Antonio was proud that there were few words he was unable to translate. Maclovia told of her frightening plane ride and gave updates on each family member. As Antonio listened, he realized how his new life was taking him away from his loved ones. He missed them.

As they pulled into the drive, Angelica pressed the remote clipped to the visor, and the garage door opened. Before she pulled in, she stopped, and Antonio helped Maclovia out.

"Grandmother, come this way."

He led her up the walk and stopped by the arbor. Taking the shears, he cut two roses and handed her one. "We will put this in your room."

He opened the front door with a flourish. "Welcome."

Maclovia's eyes widened. She lifted one foot and carefully set it down on the carpeted floor. As if unsure of the stability of the strange material, she waited a moment, then completed her step. She slowly looked around the room. Without moving her feet, she leaned right and left, looking down the halls. "How God has blessed you." Her voice trembled. She squatted down and began unfastening her sandals.

Antonio was proud of the beautiful things Angelica had furnished the house with, some from her parents' home, some they had purchased themselves. But he didn't want his grandmother to feel uncomfortable. "No, no. Leave your shoes on. Come and see your room."

His grandmother looked up at him, tears brimming in her

40

eyes. He helped her to her feet. "Yes, Grandmother. God *has* blessed me, and I want to bless you."

He took her hand, and they walked to the little bedroom Angelica had fixed for her. Lace curtains framed the window that looked to the backyard. White sheets with tiny, deep pink roses peeked out from behind a large, soft pink comforter scattered with more roses. Two big pillows rested against the wicker headboard. Antonio repeated with confidence to his grandmother what he'd heard Angelica say. "Your sheets have a 230-thread count." He beamed. "And your bed skirt matches your comforter."

Maclovia slowly turned in a full circle, looking at everything.

"Here, sit." He turned the large, wicker rocker by the window toward her.

She perched on the edge of the chair, still holding the rose, just below the bloom.

Antonio put her paper bag on top of the small dresser, then took the rose from her. "I chose the most beautiful rose on the bush for you, *Abuela*. Even the leaves are perfect." He laid it on her pillow. "Do you want to rest before dinner?"

"No. No." Maclovia took off her shawl and shoes. "I'm hungry. Can we eat now?"

"Let's go see what Angelica is planning."

As they stepped into the hall, Maclovia tapped Antonio's shoulder.

"I need to go to the bathroom," she whispered.

Antonio stopped, unsure of himself. His grandmother did not know the habits of the Americans. He wasn't sure she'd ever seen an American-style toilet or tub. Should he call Angelica? This seemed like something the two women should work out.

"I didn't see anyplace outside when we got here or from that window in the room."

Antonio felt heat in his cheeks. He turned and walked a few steps, opened a door, and turned on the light. "This is our bathroom." He stepped to the side.

Maclovia looked at the toilet . . . the tub . . . the sink . . . Antonio.

Antonio reached over and flushed the toilet. They both looked into the bowl, watching the water swirl.

When it emptied, he glanced at his grandmother. Her face was filled with concern.

Antonio ran his hand through his hair, then pointed to the toilet paper holder.

"But where do you put the paper?" Her brows knitted together.

He looked down at the bowl. "There. Then you push that thing." He touched the handle.

Maclovia pressed her hand to her chest. "Oh my."

Antonio backed out the door, speaking through the crack as he pulled it closed. "I'll be in the kitchen helping Angelica."

Angelica had the refrigerator open and a package of chicken on the counter. "Here, Antonio. Would you skin this and fix it for baking? I want to go change my clothes. I'll be right back."

Antonio got out a baking dish, set the oven to 350, and began to prepare the chicken. He stopped and tilted his head toward the hall. Nothing. He took a few steps, listening . . . nothing . . . a few more steps . . . nothing. Finally, he heard the rush of water going through the pipes. The sound of the bathroom door opening sent him dashing back to the counter.

"Let me help you." Maclovia stepped into the kitchen.

"Show me where the fire is, and I will cook the chicken. The way you like it."

Antonio pointed to the oven. "The fire is in there, and the oven will cook it."

Maclovia walked over and looked at the front of the oven. "I don't see a fire. I don't smell a fire." She put her hands on her hips.

Antonio reached around her and opened and shut the oven door. A little puff of warm air escaped.

Maclovia's hand flew to her lips. She shook her head.

"I can finish." Angelica's voice came from behind them. "Go ahead and visit with your grandmother. Why don't you sit at the kitchen table so I can hear? It'll be a great way to practice my Spanish."

Angelica put the baking dish in the oven, then got out the silverware and set three places. When she'd finished, Maclovia asked Antonio, "Where is the other person?"

He thought a moment. "What other person?"

"The one who opened the door to the house you made for the car."

Antonio rested his hand on his lips, hiding his smile. He'd forgotten how strange everything had been to him when he had first arrived in the United States. "Grandmother, a machine did that. We have a button in the car, and it tells the machine to open and close the garage door."

Maclovia raised her eyebrows.

As Angelica prepared dinner, Maclovia watched with fascination. When Angelica used the microwave, she accused Antonio of trickery. There was no possible way the food could heat that fast. The whole concept made her uneasy. And the beans that had been cooked there were left untouched on her plate.

After the dishes were put in the dishwasher and the kitchen

cleaned up, they went into the front room. Antonio and Angelica sat on the couch. Maclovia sat in a side chair at the end of the coffee table. Buddy lay at her feet.

"Grandmother." He paused. "We have a surprise." Antonio took Angelica's hand. "We're going to have a baby."

Maclovia clapped her hands together. "It's about time. When's the baby coming?"

"We don't know yet." Antonio looked at his wife. "Angelica will go to the doctor, and he will tell her."

Maclovia stood and leaned across the coffee table. She took Angelica's face in her hands. "God's blessings on you, dear one." Then she stepped back, studying Angelica's face. She sat down. "Six months. The baby will come in six months."

"What'd she say about six months, Antonio?"

"She said, 'God bless you, and the baby will come in six months.'"

Angelica giggled. "Oh, I think it will be a little longer than that."

"We make baby room in your room." Angelica tried her Spanish, then looked at Antonio. "Did I say that right?"

"The baby is staying in my room?" Maclovia's weathered face became a mass of wrinkles behind her smile.

"No, Grandmother. Angelica meant the baby's room will be next to yours."

Maclovia laughed at the misunderstanding. "Well, I'm glad I brought my sewing hook. I will make the baby some clothes. Do you have thread?" She looked at Angelica.

Angelica looked at Antonio. "What'd she say?"

"She said she brought her, uh, um. *Aguja para tejer*. Thing to sew. Do you have any, any *hilaza*. Uh, string. You know." He waited patiently for her answer.

"All I saw her bring was the paper bag. What could fit

44

in there?" Angelica thought a moment. "Do you mean a needle?"

Antonio slapped his hand on his leg and turned toward her, pointing his finger. "Close, close." He bit his lower lip. "Yes, a needle. But different." He held out his hand and crooked one finger. "Like this."

"Oh, a hook." Angelica made a hook with her finger. "A crochet hook?"

Antonio slapped her knee. "Yes. I think that's it." He looked at Maclovia.

She was leaning forward, straining to pick up the words. Looking at Antonio's hand, she pointed at his finger. "Yes, yes."

"Good. Good." Angelica nodded her head up and down.

"That is it then," Antonio announced.

Everyone smiled and nodded. The room became quiet.

Angelica slowly turned toward Antonio. "Er, exactly what did we just say?"

"She going to make clothes for the baby with hook and string," he summed up with confidence.

The phone rang. "Excuse me a second. I'll get that." Angelica ran to the kitchen.

Antonio heard his wife talking. It was something about work. Her voice dropped. Her tone, her short sentences—something seemed wrong.

Maclovia stood up. "I'm tired, my son."

Angelica returned to the living room. "Just a call from work."

Antonio observed his wife. There was a trace of concern around her eyes.

He stood. "Our grandmother wants to go to her room now."

"I so glad you here. Tomorrow." Angelica gave her a kiss and a hug.

Antonio winced at his wife's Spanish as he and Angelica watched Maclovia shuffle to her room, Buddy at her heels.

Angelica snapped her fingers. "Buddy. You get back here. You know your bed's in the laundry room."

As soon as his grandmother disappeared down the hall, Antonio turned to Angelica. "A problem at work?"

Angelica tilted her head and looked into his eyes. "You don't miss a thing, do you?" She let out a sigh. "I'm not sure. My boss wants a meeting with me in the morning. Something's up."

Maclovia closed the door behind her. The room was dark, but light shone through the window. She stood still, waiting for her eyes to adjust.

She took a few steps and ran her hand lightly across the bed coverings, being careful not to make any impression. She moved to the head of the bed, and without touching the comforter, she lifted a pillow from its place against the white backboard. She carried it to the rocker and placed it against the back of the chair. She returned to the bed and picked up the rose Antonio had cut for her.

She sat down and looked out the window. Her eyes wandered over the backyard. There was the faint outline of another house across the fence. She got up and pulled the chair closer to the window. When she sat back down, she turned her head to one side, resting it against the chair. Now she could see the moon, right where God had placed it. Its shape was the same as it had been the night before, when she'd sat by the stream and sought Him. When she'd thanked Him for the beautiful life He'd given her in Mexico, the years He had cared for her. She had asked Him why He was sending her to America, but He had not answered her. She trusted the Lord. He would answer her in His way, in His time. And He had.

"Grandmother. We have a surprise. We're going to have a baby." The same sense of certainty that she'd felt when she'd first heard the words filled her. She put her hands in her lap, her palms up, cradling the flawless rose, the most beautiful rose on the bush. "I am here, Lord, as You have asked." She raised her hands, lifting her offering to the Creator. "Lord, if it please You, as You knit this child together in the womb of his mother, ordain a life that will bring glory to You. If it please You, make him perfect. Perfect for Your plans, perfect to accomplish Your purposes."

Luminous but elusive, something powerful and pure and beautiful encircled her. Then disappeared.

3

Angelica watched Antonio in her rearview mirror as she pulled away from the drive. He was on his way to the house next door to talk to Mrs. Dupre about taking care of her yard. *Oh, Lord, bless him today.*

As she merged onto the freeway, her thoughts turned to her boss, Dave McMahon, and his phone call of the night before. He'd sounded concerned, but it was obvious he didn't want to go into any detail on the phone. He'd been instrumental in helping her get the public defender position and over the past year and a half had become a friend. He would be delighted with her news about the baby.

Baby names and the pastels of pink and blue wallpaper filled her thoughts. By the time she pulled into the parking lot of the Sierra County business complex, she was seriously considering a bunny border for the baby's room.

"Good morning, Fronie." Angelica stopped at the front counter. She lowered her voice. "Can you go to lunch today?"

Instant interest filled the face of the pretty receptionist.

"Yeah, what's up, girl?" She pushed her earpiece into the mass of thick, black hair that framed her face.

"Tell ya then." Angelica gave her a wicked smile. "Got to get to work if I'm gonna take time off for lunch."

Fronie Phillips was the only one of Angelica's co-workers Angelica saw outside the office. They'd struck up a friendship when they'd recognized each other at the Faith Community Church Wednesday night Bible study. Their friendship had deepened when Fronie had confided to Angelica that her father was the powerful Senator Davis from New York. It was something she preferred not to have widely known, especially at work, where local politics sometimes came into play. Fronie'd never enjoyed the high-profile life of her childhood. She'd found happiness with her husband, whom she'd met when he interned for the senator in Washington, D.C. She loved the quiet lifestyle of Valle de Lagrimas.

As Angelica headed toward her desk, she passed her boss's office. Low voices filtered from behind the closed door. She slowed her steps but couldn't make out a word of the conversation. Something was up.

Angelica turned on her computer, seated herself, and pressed the intercom code for Dave McMahon's assistant. "Good morning, Anne. Dave said he wanted to meet with me this morning."

Angelica opened her calendar and scanned her schedule. With as many as four hundred new cases being opened each month in the office and only eleven attorneys, she was swamped. She glanced at the stack of replies from the DA's office that her discovery motions had generated.

"He's in a meeting right now with Max Jaeger."

Max Wolfgang Jaeger. Angelica bit her lip. He was referred to as "The Wolf" by the women in the office. Married twice, he was on the prowl once again. Not that it seemed to matter if he was married or not. It was always hunting season for him. It was common knowledge around the office that he thought the best work women did . . . wasn't in the workplace.

Angelica'd had more than one run-in with him. Somehow, whenever she was alone in the coffee room, in the storage room, even in the parking lot, he seemed to show up. She always ignored him, even when he stood so close she could smell his aftershave. She didn't want to give him *any* encouragement. Thankfully, she didn't have to work with him.

"When Dave gets out of his meeting, please tell him I'm in and will be all morning."

"I'll tell him."

She hung up, fanned through her Rolodex, picked up the phone, and dialed. Dr. Gremian didn't have an opening until May. When Angelica explained to the nurse why she was so anxious to see him, she told Angelica they would work her in Wednesday afternoon. Angelica hung up the phone with a sigh. Two days before she would be absolutely certain.

The morning passed quickly. Angelica prepared for her upcoming cases and met with clients. It was noon when Fronie tapped on her door.

"Is it lunchtime already?" Angelica looked at her watch. "I always feel so guilty taking a lunch break."

"Come on. I told Gayle I wanted to take an early lunch and switched with her. I'm dying to find out what's going on with you."

"Let me tell Anne I'm leaving." Angelica pressed the intercom. "Anne, were you able to set up some time with Dave for me?"

"He's still in a meeting."

"I'm going to lunch now. I'll be back by one, and then I'll be here all afternoon."

Angelica and Fronie walked across the street to The Carrot Patch, a small vegetarian restaurant that had quickly become their favorite meeting place for lunch. Not only was it close to the office, but the menu offered lots of choices that kept their size 8 skirts and pants in the front of their closets. They took seats at a table by the window.

"Tell me." Fronie put her elbows on the table and her chin in her hands.

"We haven't even ordered." Angelica looked casually at her menu.

"Stop it. You know you're ordering spinach roll-ups with lime chutney and raspberry tea. Tell me." Fronie plucked the menu from Angelica's hands.

Angelica folded her arms on the table and leaned toward her friend. "I'm going to have a baby."

Fronie's squeal brought the waitress running. "Is something wrong?"

"When's your due date?" Fronie's dark eyes were wide with excitement.

"As near as I can figure, early November." Angelica turned to the waitress and smiled at the young woman.

"No, nothing's wrong. Nothing at all. We're ready to order."

As they ate, the exciting news of Angelica's pregnancy dominated the conversation.

"How much time are you going to take off for maternity leave?" Fronie put her fork down and pushed her plate to the side.

"I hate to ask for any time off. Remember when Kit had her twins? It threw everybody into a tailspin, trying to cover her cases while she was gone." Angelica took a sip of tea. "Besides you, Dave is the only other person in the office I'm going to tell right now. I want him to know my pregnancy won't affect my work in any way. I'll only have to miss a few hours for doctor's appointments." She hesitated. "I need this job more than ever now."

"I know." Fronie's deep brown eyes filled with compassion. "It will work out. I bet Antonio's business thrives. He's such a hard worker." She brightened. "You going to Bible study Wednesday? Can't wait till they hear the news."

"I plan to." Angelica's face softened. "They're such an awesome group of ladies."

"They'll be praying for this baby. I guarantee that." Happiness glowed in Fronie's sweet face. "Just think, Angelica, the Word says God knew us in our mother's womb. He knitted us together there." She shook her head slowly. "Can you believe it? God knows your baby right now."

Angelica stared at her friend. She'd never thought of it quite that way. She put her hands to her lips. Suddenly, it was real. She was a mother. Joy bubbled in her laugh. "Fronie, I'm going to have a baby. A sweet, precious little one."

The two women walked back to the office, and, in spite of Antonio's insistence that it would be a boy, Angelica was still listing her favorite girl names as they approached the front desk. "Yep, Antonia. That's my first choice."

"There you are."

Angelica turned to the voice behind her. "Dave."

He took her by the elbow. "Let's go to my office."

Angelica took a seat. She couldn't help but reflect on the first day she'd sat across from her boss, desperately needing a job, her résumé far more impressive than his. He could easily have perceived her as a threat and chosen one of the many other applicants, just out of law school. But he'd understood her desire to make her life count, by being an advocate for the poor, and hired her. They'd formed an unspoken bond. She knew he'd share in her happiness and be supportive in every way he could when she told him her good news. She was counting on it.

Dave rolled his chair up to the desk. "I wanted to catch you before you heard it from someone else."

Angelica's mind went blank. "Heard what?"

"I'm leaving." His voice was matter-of-fact.

"Leaving? Why?" She sat motionless.

"I'm burned out. The county commissioners won't approve my request for a budget increase. I've been trying to get more staff for the office, trying to resolve some of the inequities in the pay scale. I just can't do it anymore. And . . ." His eyes held hers.

Angelica felt her stomach knot.

"Max Jaeger will be taking my place."

Antonio watched Angelica's car disappear around the corner at the end of the street. He stepped onto his neighbor's front porch and knocked on the door. He listened for the squeaking. The door swung open.

He took off his broad-brimmed hat. "Good morning, *señora*."

Mrs. Dupre locked her wheelchair and took off her glasses. "Good morning, Antonio."

He tipped his head toward her. She was holding a green pencil. The last time he'd talked to her, she'd had a blue pencil behind her ear. "I come to see if you like my work."

Mrs. Dupre's face broke into a dimpled smile. "Let's go look. I'll meet you by the flowerbed. I'll go through the garage."

Antonio had seen the ramp in the garage while he'd been working in the yard. Her house had been tailored for her wheelchair, the van in the garage was too. Yet she never seemed to leave and seldom had visitors, except for a young woman with a child and a man who Angelica had said worked for the builder. He stood by the flowerbed, hat in hand.

"I was wondering when you were going to get in touch with me." She shaded her eyes as she looked up at him.

He quickly stepped to the side, so the sun wouldn't be in her face.

"I wanted to call you, but I didn't have your card."

A card? Antonio's mind raced. The real estate man had had a card. She must mean a card like that. "I no have card."

"You should get some, young man. You're going to need them. You've done a beautiful job. With all the new construction going on around here, you'll do well." She glanced at her flowerbed again. "I've never had a gardener who could weed with a hoe. Do you know how to trim hedges?"

She liked his work. He wanted to throw his hat in the air and shout. Instead, he asked, "Do you want a gardener with a hoe to take care of this yard?"

She smiled. "What are you charging?"

He'd thought a lot about what he should charge while he was weeding her flowerbeds. "Twenty dollars a week. I mow and clean flowers and trim bushes."

"And the backyard too?" the *señora* asked.

"Front and back. Yes."

The *señora* put her hand out, and they shook. "Can you start next week?"

"I will." Antonio spoke his words carefully, hiding his accent.

He watched the woman motor back into her garage and shut the door. He threw his hat in the air three times on the way back to the house.

54

"*Abuela*," he shouted as he barged through the front door. He ran down the hall to Maclovia's room. "*Abuela*." Her room was empty. He looked in the kitchen. Empty. "Buddy." He stood still, listening. Nothing. He noticed a bag on the kitchen counter and looked into it. Neatly packed were a bag of tortillas, eggs, and a frying pan. They were still cold to the touch. Next to the bag was an empty orange juice glass.

Antonio looked out the kitchen window. He could see the back of his grandmother, with Buddy at her heels, as she dipped a towel into a bucket of water. She was cleaning the barbeque. He looked back at the bag and winced. This could be touchy.

Antonio opened the slider. "*Abuela*. Let me help you."

Maclovia looked up, her bottom tooth showing as she spoke. "This is filthy, son." She turned back to her work.

Antonio took the rag from her hand and squeezed it into the bucket. "We aren't using this right now. We will use it when the sun is hot. I'll clean it later."

"Not using it?" Maclovia stepped back.

Antonio didn't want to offend his grandmother. He weighed his words carefully. "We don't have anything to start the fire with, and it's much easier to use the kitchen." He picked up the bucket. "Let me fix you something to eat."

"No, I had some juice. I was going to cook something for you." Maclovia looked longingly at the open barbeque, then at her grandson. "Perhaps you know best."

Her words didn't sound convincing to Antonio. He quickly announced, "I have a job."

Maclovia's eyes shone, and her fingers flew to the cross at her neck. "A job. How wonderful. Where?"

He guided her toward the kitchen, giving her all the details of his agreement. They sat at the kitchen table going over every word of his conversation with Mrs. Dupre.

Maclovia sat back in her chair and folded her arms. "She must be a rich woman."

Antonio shrugged his shoulders. "Many Americans have gardeners."

Maclovia rubbed at a smudge of barbeque grease on her skirt. "She didn't bargain with you." It was a statement, not a question.

Antonio thought a moment. "I don't think Americans bargain. When Angelica and I go shopping, we just pay what they ask."

"Don't you think she would have told you if you asked too much? Whenever I buy my thread in Mexico, I tell them if they ask too much. But if their price is good, I buy more."

And the backyard too? The *señora*'s words echoed in his mind. He stared at his grandmother. "I'm not sure what people charge for yard work. But twenty dollars is a lot of money. I plan to do ten houses a day." He tapped his finger on his lip.

Antonio jumped up and opened a drawer. He set the phone book down on the table. He'd seen Angelica use the yellow pages many times. He put his hands on his hips and stared at it.

"I'm a *gardener*." He said the word in English, then sounded out the letter. "Guh. Guh." He looked at Maclovia. "I have to know what that letter is to look in this book. Guh. How do you spell *gardener*?" He ran his hand through his hair.

Maclovia raised her eyebrows. "Guh." The sound choked out over her front tooth.

"I've never seen the word in my *Ejercicios de inglés*."

"Guh." Maclovia stuttered out the syllable. "Guh . . . guh . . . God."

Antonio's mouth dropped open. "Grandmother, that's it. G-O-D." Antonio stamped his foot. "It's a G." Buddy jumped up and barked, waving his big tail like a victory banner.

Maclovia sat up in her chair and squared her shoulders.

Antonio sat down and opened the big book to the yellow part. "There is a certain order to these letters." Antonio sighed. "It starts with A, B, C, D. But after that I'm not sure. There is just so much to learn."

His grandmother scooted her chair close to his. Buddy circled around, put his front paws on Antonio's leg, and nosed himself up under Antonio's arm, his black button nose just inches from the book.

Page by page they went through it, looking at the big black words printed at the top edge of each yellow sheet for the letter G.

At last, they found it.

"G-A-M-E-S." Antonio chewed his lower lip. He began looking at the pictures, turning the pages slowly, going over each box. Finally, his finger rested on a picture of a lawn-mower.

"*Con permiso*, Buddy." He got up, grabbed a pen and paper, copied down the number, then stepped to the phone and dialed.

A friendly voice spoke. "Gardening supplies. If we don't have it, you don't need it."

"Good morning." Antonio waited a moment, but the man did not respond. "I need a gardener."

"Huh?"

Antonio cleared his throat and spoke slowly. "I . . . need . . . talk . . . to . . . a . . . gardener."

Again, there was a long pause.

"Um, all we have here are some cards pinned up to a bulletin board up front."

Bulletin board. Antonio wasn't sure what that was. He'd seen a board with papers pinned on it at the grocery store. Maybe it was like that. "Yes, I need a card from there."

"You can come and get one, they're free." The voice seemed clipped.

"I no have a car. Can you tell me what the card says?"

Another pause. "Are you from customer service? Is this one of those random checks?" Suddenly, the voice was friendly again. "Just a sec."

In a moment, the man was back. "B.J.'s Lawn Care, 555-3489."

Antonio marked the numbers down. "He do good work?"

"Yeah, he does the lawns here at the store. We just hired him recently, but so far, so good."

"*Gracias, amigo.*" Antonio hung the phone up. Giving Maclovia a wink, he dialed the number for B.J.'s Lawn Care.

A woman answered. Antonio told her he wanted to know what they charged to do a lawn like his. She promised someone would be out later in the day to tell him. Antonio turned to his grandmother. "Now I find out. The Americans, they're good people."

"Antonio, I wonder, can you do something?" Her face was a mixture of curiosity and respect.

"Anything, *Abuela*."

"You said the letters of God. Could you write them for me?"

Antonio took the pen and wrote the word, then tore off the paper and gave it to her.

Maclovia looked at it, studying it, then put it in her pocket.

Antonio reached around her and took the bag from the counter. He began to empty it.

Maclovia tapped his arm. "*Hijo*. Show me how to heat those tortillas."

Antonio stepped to the stove and put the electric burner on low. He took his grandmother's hand and held it on the knob, turning it on and off. "I'll show you how a Mexican in America does it." He grinned at her. "But don't let Angelica see you. She'll insist you use that pan."

He took a tortilla from the sack and laid it directly on the burner. In a few seconds it bubbled. He took the edge of it and flipped it to the other side. He flipped it back and forth until it was steaming. He handed it to Maclovia.

She spread it out on her palm, then, with her other palm, she curled the edge, and in one sweep, rolled it into a small tube. She stuck it in the side of her mouth and bit off a piece.

"Ahh." Maclovia closed her eyes and chewed.

Antonio got a plate, and for the next thirty minutes, they cooked tortillas on the electric coil and talked about Mexico.

As the morning passed, Antonio showed his grandmother how some of the appliances worked and where things were kept. He let her wash their dishes in the sink, since he couldn't convince her that the dishwasher would do a good job. She was fascinated by the washer and frightened by the dryer; conjuring up heat and wind in a metal box was not something she wanted to be a party to. He showed her how to answer the phone but told her never to answer the door, since she was too short to look out the peephole Angelica's mother had demanded be put in. And he showed her how to operate the lights, the television, and the portable radio. They found a station with Mexican music.

Antonio moved the radio to her room and set it up on the little table next to the rocker. By the time he plugged it in, Maclovia was sitting in her chair with her eyes closed.

He glanced around the room. He noticed the bed had not been touched. He looked toward his grandmother: her wizened face, mottled with age spots, her crooked hands in her lap, thick socks pulled up to her knees, the torn paper with the name of God clutched in her hand.

Stepping quietly toward her, he kissed the top of her head, then tiptoed from the room.

Antonio looked at his watch. He didn't want to look for more work until he was sure about the pricing. The woman had said that someone would come out later in the day. He got his books and sat at the kitchen table. As morning turned to afternoon, he decided to take a break. He'd just stepped out on the front porch when a pickup pulled into the drive. He could see "B.J.'s" printed on the door.

The man walked toward him, his hand extended with a card. "I'm Bill. So you want a bid?"

Antonio took the card. "I need you to tell me how much you charge to do a yard like this."

"What exactly would you want done?" The man stepped onto the grass.

"Cut grass, clean weeds in flowerbeds, make bushes look nice."

"Backyard too?"

Antonio nodded.

The man walked around the yard looking at everything, then returned to Antonio. "Don't do no beds. Takes too long to weed. All handwork is extra. Mow, edge, and blow, thirty-five dollars."

Antonio pursed his lips.

"That's very competitive." The man shifted on his feet. "I do lots of houses in this area. And with phase two under construction, I'll be getting a lot more. I can give a price like that because I'm already in the neighborhood." B.J. hooked his thumbs in his jean pockets. "You want me to do it?"

Realizing what the man meant, Antonio felt concerned. "No, sorry. I'm just asking what you charge. I look for job like this."

The man stepped back and guffawed. "You're kiddin' me, right? This is a joke."

Antonio smiled back at him. "No. No joke."

The man's face darkened. A minute of silence passed. "You beaner. You wetbacks coming in here, takin' jobs from hardworkin' people like me."

For a moment, Antonio thought the man was going to spit on him. He stepped back.

"I suppose you're gonna wait for me to leave and then knock on that door and tell the people who live here you'll do it for thirty-five dollars."

Antonio could feel the man's anger. "No. I live here." If only his English were better, he could clear up the misunderstanding. He hadn't meant to offend the gardener.

"You lying thief. In your dreams." He snatched the card out of Antonio's hand and strode back to his truck. As he backed out, he rolled down his window and shouted, "You won't get no work around here if I can help it."

4

Angelica pulled into her drive and honked. She looked at her watch, then at the front door. She honked again. Antonio came bounding out, putting on his jacket as he ran, the car already moving before he shut the passenger door.

"*Sí, señorita.* I see you come into the drive, and I grab my coat. I come fast as I can." He looked at her with mock humbleness, while using the tone of voice he'd used when she was the *patrona* and he wanted to know if he'd done a good job cleaning the stalls of her Arabian horses.

Angelica cut her eyes to him. The sight of her big, handsome husband in a blue blazer and dress slacks, speaking to her like he was reporting for duty as a ranch hand, brought a smile to her face.

"Stop it." She gave his knee a playful slap. "I'm just feeling stressed. After going in at six this morning, so I could carve out a few hours this afternoon for myself, I feel like I'm more behind than ever with my case load." She grimaced, remembering how the fresh cut rose by her bed had awakened her with a wave of nausea that had plagued her the rest of the morning. "I'll have to go back tonight."

Antonio reached over and rubbed her shoulder. "It work out. Soon I have my driver's license, and I can help you more."

"Yep, sooner than you think." She glanced at his face. "Remember when I asked you if you had any yard work to do today?"

Antonio gave her a tentative nod.

"It's so hard for me to get away from work that I decided after our doctor's appointment, we'll go to the Department of Motor Vehicles. I've got your birth certificate and papers in my briefcase, and if you pass the written test, you can take the driving test right after."

She saw the color creep up Antonio's neck and turned her eyes to the road. He was a proud man. It was hard relying on her for almost everything while he became integrated into American society. He didn't know she'd seen the sheets of paper in the trash on which he'd practiced printing the letters of his name the day after he'd had to make an X on the closing papers for the house, with her parents sitting across the table. And many a night she'd awakened to find him missing from their bed, having looked for work all day, unwilling to give up study time for sleep.

"You'll do great. I've quizzed you on that *Driver Handbook* so often, you answer me before I finish the question. Besides, the old pickup from the ranch is just sitting in our garage. It needs to be driven." She glanced at him again. He was looking out the window. "Remember I told you Dave, my boss, was leaving?"

Antonio nodded. "He very good to us when you need time to help me get my papers."

"They made the official announcement today. Max Jaeger moves into Dave's office on May first." She tapped the steering wheel with her fist. "This is so political. He's been instrumental in raising money behind the scenes for the campaigns of the county commissioners for years. And in the case of Commissioner Sally Rand . . ." Angelica drew a deep breath, slowly shaking her head. "And she was married at the time. For that matter, so was Max."

Antonio shifted in his seat. People's private lives were something he never encouraged her to discuss. He even observed a certain decorum toward her private life, never pressing her about issues she didn't want to talk about. Always patient and supportive.

The conversation turned to plans for the baby's room and evolved into plans for the baby. By the time they arrived at Dr. Gremian's office, in the Women's Health Center, they were talking about private kindergarten and preschool soccer teams.

Angelica checked in with the nurse, then she and Antonio took a seat in the waiting room. Suddenly, she had butterflies in her stomach. She took Antonio's hand.

He put his arm around her, pulling her toward him, and kissed the top of her head. Angelica closed her eyes, breathing in the scent of her husband, feeling the hardness of the muscles beneath his jacket and the tenderness of his lips on her hair. She felt safe and secure, with her unborn child, in the arms of the man who loved them more than life itself.

A nurse opened the door between the waiting room and the exam rooms. "Angelica Amante."

Angelica glanced at Antonio as she got up. When they'd first married, she'd explained to him that she wanted to use her maiden name in her professional life. Sometimes cases in the public defender's office ended up in the newspaper. She didn't want to subject their family to that kind of controversy. He'd reluctantly agreed. She'd made a point of asking the receptionist at Dr. Gremian's office to change the name on her chart during her last visit. Obviously, someone had dropped the ball.

She smiled at the nurse. "I'm Angelica Amante Perez, and this is my husband, Antonio. Would you mind changing my name on the chart?"

"Oh, I'm sorry." The nurse wrote on the file's tab. "Your husband can wait here. I'll come and get him after the exam."

Antonio looked at his watch again; Angelica had been gone forty minutes. He hoped nothing was wrong. He was the oldest of ten children, and he'd never known his mother to go to a doctor. His grandmother had given a prayer covering while his mother carried her babies, and other women had helped when the babies were born. Even he had helped one summer, when his mother had fallen behind the plow. His little sister Allegra had been born, arriving without warning, and later that day, quietly slipped away.

A nurse called his name, interrupting his thoughts. He followed her to a small room where Angelica was sitting with a man in a white coat.

"Dr. Gremian, this is my husband, Antonio." Her face was flushed with excitement.

Antonio studied the man. Gray, straight hair framed an oval face, and scruffy, coarse hairs sprouted from his chin. Everything was neatly trimmed, as if the man took pride in his appearance. Yet, in spite of the careful manicure, it reminded Antonio of his family's goat.

Dr. Gremian was smiling, but his eyes were formal and cool, resting on Angelica as one might look at a stranger, closed to the joy that shone about her.

"Good afternoon, *señor*." Antonio's strong grip completely covered the doctor's long, thin fingers.

"Congratulations, you're going to be a father."

A broad smile spread across Antonio's face. "I know."

"It looks like the due date is November 11."

"Here, sit, Antonio. I want you to hear what Dr. Gremian has to say." Angelica patted the chair next to her.

Dr. Gremian handed Angelica a small white paper and a large, thick one. "I've written a prescription for your prenatal vitamins and an order for blood work. I've ordered a standard pregnancy panel, CBC, blood type, HCG quantitative. You're at about ten weeks. I want to see you again in four weeks."

"What happens then?" Angelica leaned forward in her chair. "Will it be possible to hear the baby's heart?"

Antonio looked at his wife with surprise. He patted her arm. "Honey, you hear our baby's heart when he born. He—"

"Yes, you'll be able to hear the heartbeat." Dr. Gremian ran his forefinger over the hair growing from his chin.

Angelica grabbed Antonio's hand. "I can't wait. Won't that be exciting?" She turned back to Dr. Gremian. "You'll be able to see if it's a boy then, won't you?"

Somewhere in the distance, Antonio heard the doctor answer, "When we do an ultrasound . . ." His mind was reeling. Amidst a mixture of excitement and concern, he was trying to process all the things he was hearing. This was a mystery of life, to remain unseen by the eyes of man, until God called the child into the world. Yet this doctor and his wife spoke of hearing his son's heart and "seeing" if it was a boy. It *was* a boy. He didn't need Dr. Gremian to tell him. Why did Angelica doubt him? Why did they burden the baby with their demands?

Angelica tapped his arm. "What do you think, Antonio?"

"Sorry." He focused on her. "About what?"

"Dr. Gremian is saying that on my next visit they can do a test to check for abnormalities."

"Abnormalities? What is that word?"

"You know. When something's not right. Something's abnormal." Angelica's voice was matter-of-fact.

All of this made him uneasy—intruding into things that were God's alone. "My baby is not abnormal. My baby will be as God has made him. God no make abnormal things."

Antonio saw the color rise in Angelica's cheeks. Had he used a wrong word? Somehow, he had embarrassed her.

"This isn't a decision you have to make now." Dr. Gremian rose. "You are young, and there is no family history to indicate your child is at risk. It's an option we offer." He turned toward Angelica. "We can talk more about it next time. Stop at the front desk on your way out. The nurse will give you a folder with a list of over-the-counter medications you should avoid and a list of those symptoms I talked with you about, which are highly unlikely to occur, but if they should, call immediately." He glanced at Antonio. "Also, if you'd like information about prenatal classes in the area, our nurse can provide some."

As they drove to the Department of Motor Vehicles, Antonio turned to Angelica. "You not talking. I say something wrong?"

"No, not really. It's just that you don't seem to understand all the wonderful things that are possible for our baby. To make sure that he is born healthy."

Antonio listened as Angelica explained that all American babies were cared for by doctors before they were born, and she wanted their baby to have every advantage that modern medicine offered. "In Mexico lots of babies either die in childbirth or in the first five years of life."

"I know." Antonio looked at his wife. She had spoken the words without feeling. Sentences far removed from the world she lived in. *Allegra*. He shifted in his seat.

Angelica's face brightened. "Good. Then you agree. We *should* do everything we can to make sure our baby is born healthy?"

"Of course." Antonio patted his wife's hand. He *would* do everything possible. He and Maclovia would pray for the baby and for the doctor, that he might have wisdom.

"Oh look, it's not too crowded. When I called they said no appointment was necessary."

Antonio looked at the imposing gray building. He got out of the car and waited for Angelica to get the papers he needed from her briefcase. When they approached the counter, Angelica spoke to the woman. "My husband would like to take a driver's test."

The woman spoke to him. "Your application?"

"We haven't filled it out yet." Angelica answered for him.

The woman handed Antonio a paper. "Take this and bring it back when you've finished."

The two of them stepped to an empty counter. Antonio put his finger under the first word on the first line. "Naamme."

"Let me help you." Angelica took the paper and began filling it out.

His wife was going into her "helpful" mode. He clenched his teeth. It could be very annoying, especially when they were with other people. And this was a government matter. The book said the state gave you the license . . . a driving privilege. He took a deep breath and let it out slowly. She meant well. "Shouldn't I do that?"

"I'm just helping you to save time. Put your signature there." She pointed to a line at the bottom of the paper.

Antonio took the paper, laid it on the counter, and smoothed it carefully. He took the pen and set the point down just above the line. With slow, deliberate strokes, he formed each letter. Some of the letters went below the line, and the *A* should have been bigger than the *n* next to it. Still, it was one of the best "signatures" he'd ever written. When he finished, he lifted the paper to the light, checking for errors.

Satisfied, he carried the paper back to the counter and handed it to the lady.

"Here's the test. Step over there." The woman pointed to a counter at the side of the room. "Mrs. Perez, you can wait on one of the benches."

Antonio looked at the front and back of the paper as he walked to the counter. He recognized the numbers one through thirty-six. But there were so many words. Lines and lines of small words. Suddenly, he felt too warm and wiped his forehead with the back of his hand.

He examined the first sentence, trying to sound out each word, trying to make sense of it . . . but he couldn't.

Fronie rushed up behind Angelica. "Hey girl, I'm glad you made it. When you didn't come back to work, I was worried. Everything okay?"

Angelica and Fronie walked up the steps to the church's second-floor Sunday school classrooms that were used for Bible studies during the week. "Everything is fine. I'm officially expecting."

Fronie grabbed Angelica's hand and squeezed it.

"I got held up because after my appointment, I took Antonio for his driver's test."

"And?" Fronie tilted her head.

"He just couldn't read well enough to take the written test."

"Oh, dear. I know you're both anxious for him to start driving."

"Fortunately, they had an alternative testing method. He was allowed to take the test orally. He got a hundred percent and then passed his 'behind the wheel' test with flying colors." She gave Fronie a thumbs-up.

"I bet he was proud of himself."

"That's putting it mildly." Angelica winked at her. "He ended up driving me home and, when I left to come here, he told me he was taking his grandmother to the mall in *his* truck."

They took their seats around a big oval table. Angelica opened her Bible to First Corinthians. The sight of the wobbly, handwritten notes and marks on the page brought an ache to her heart. Poppy. The man who'd been like a grandfather to her had left her his Bible when he died. That had been over a year and a half ago. Being in the Word was like being with him again. If only he had lived to share this day with her. *Poppy, I'm going to have a baby.*

"Are you announcing your big news tonight?"

The sound of Fronie's voice pulled her from the peaceful, safe place that remembering Poppy always created. "Uh. Yes. Can't wait to share."

Angelica looked around the room. There were about fifteen ladies in her Bible study group. They'd been meeting for over a year at Faith Community Church and had become close friends. Natalya Lohrer, a Russian Jew who'd escaped from the repressive Soviet Union before *perestroika*, led the study. The dynamic woman's testimony of her dramatic escape touched the heart, but the stories of her many dangerous return visits to distribute Bibles in her homeland touched the soul. Angelica considered her a spiritual mentor, especially since Poppy's death. "This is such a great group of women, so supportive."

Natalya raised her voice. "Ladies. Ladies." When the room quieted, she continued. "Fronie?"

Fronie stood and took a few steps back from the table. "Hmm. Let's see." She started to tap her foot. "You ladies ready?" She began to snap her fingers. "I feel a song comin' on. . . . Go tell it on the mountain."

And as was the group's custom, Fronie led them in an opening song, her rich, powerful voice filling the room. "That Jesus Christ is born."

By the time she reached the last bar, many of the group were clapping their hands and singing with her.

"God bless you for that. Thank you so much." Natalya waited for Fronie to return to her chair. "Let's open our prayer circle. Any praises this week?"

Several ladies reported on previous prayer requests, giving praise and thanks where they had seen God move and seeking Him again for those petitions they believed had gone unanswered. The group was delighted to learn that Martha's dog had survived the neutering procedure but disappointed by the dark prognosis the doctors had pronounced on Sylvia's eighty-seven-year-old grandmother. Several women offered new prayers of hope and encouragement.

"Any more praises or requests this week?" Natalya acknowledged Angelica. "Yes?"

Angelica stood. She paused a moment, gathering her thoughts. "You know how we've been studying about spiritual gifting?" Several women nodded. "And how, as awesome as that is, without love our gifting is nothing." There were murmurs of agreement from around the table.

"Natalya, in your closing prayer last week you asked God to work in our lives, providing us circumstances to

71

love others as He loved us, so the world might know Him through us." Natalya gave Angelica a sweet smile.

Angelica felt tears welling up in her eyes. "God is so good. He's given me the best way in the world to practice His commandment." Angelica saw understanding flicker across Natalya's face, as she realized what Angelica was about to say. "Today I found out my husband and I are expecting our first child."

Screams, laughter, and applause filled the room. Fronie moved her chair to the side so the ladies could hug and congratulate Angelica.

Finally, Natalya tapped the table with her pen. "We'll certainly be praying for you and your baby." As the women settled back into their seats, she continued, "Is there anything else before we close the circle and start our study?"

Jan Wilcox raised her hand, and all eyes turned to her. "I've got a prayer request for my sister's son-in-law, Billy. My sister and I have been praying that he'd come to know the Lord. He's just started a gardening business, and he's gotten some good accounts, but they have four children and just aren't making ends meet. He desperately needs more work. My sister told him we were praying for him, but he told her not to waste her time. He said he would get the business going with hard work, not by waiting on God." She hesitated. "I know what's said here stays here." She cleared her throat. "The financial pressure is taking its toll. Their marriage is in trouble."

Natalya looked around the circle. "Anyone want to start?"

Stephanie Scott gave a strong prayer, peppered with Scripture, calling on the Lord to move in a mighty way. Mary Smith followed with a simple prayer, asking God to bless Bill's business and to send a laborer in his path who would reveal God's love to him.

Angelica felt moved to pray for the man, his business situation so like Antonio's. As silence settled in after Mary's prayer, Angelica closed her eyes and tilted her face upward. "Lord, I ask You to give this man favor in his business and soften his heart so he might hear Your voice. And Lord, I ask a special blessing on his wife and children during this difficult time."

A few minutes of silence followed, then Natalya led the group in a closing prayer, ending by thanking God for the special gift of love He'd given to Angelica and her husband. She raised her head. "We'll continue to pray over these things this week. Now let's turn to First Corinthians and start our study."

It was eight o'clock by the time the meeting broke up and Angelica got in her car. She looked at the clock on her dash. She hated to go back to work, but the memory of the morning's nausea convinced her she needed to put in a couple more hours at the office. She'd already told Antonio she'd be late.

As she pulled into the parking lot of the Sierra County business complex, she noticed there were two other parked cars. One was Max Jaeger's black Lexus. She chose a spot as far from it as she could, which meant the back of the parking lot. She hurried into the office.

"Hey, you're working late." Jonathan Cantrall, whose office was next to hers, came out just as she was going in. He held the door open for her. "See you tomorrow."

"See you." Angelica watched the door close behind him, then pulled it to make sure it was locked. She looked right and left as she walked to her office, trying to see where Max was. His office was dark. Maybe he'd gone out to dinner with someone from work and had left his car in the lot. She took a quick look in the copy and resource rooms. They were empty. Convinced she was alone, she went to her desk and pulled a stack of files in front of her.

She'd lost track of time when the direct line on her phone rang.

Her face eased into a smile. Antonio. She pressed the speaker button. "Hi."

There was no response. "Hello?"

She suddenly felt uneasy. Her eyes instinctively went to the window. The vertical blinds were closed.

"Hello." Still no answer. She hit the speaker button again, disconnecting the line. She sat still, listening, unable to shake the feeling that something wasn't right.

She picked up the phone and dialed her home number.

Antonio answered on the first ring. "*Sí?*"

A rush of relief flooded through her. "Did you just try to call me?"

"No. I studying my *ejercicios* and waiting for you."

She stood, the phone still to her ear, stretching the cord as she walked out past her office door. She looked up and down the darkened hall. Nothing. "I'm at the office, and I'm going to work for awhile. I'll call you just before I leave."

"You okay?"

She could hear concern in his voice. He knew her so well. Something in her tone had signaled him she was upset. "I'm fine. Fine. Had fun announcing our news at Bible study." There was no need to worry him. She lightened her voice. "Be home soon. Bye." She hung up.

"I'm being silly," she told the empty office, then closed and locked her door.

She returned to the work on her desk, but the ordinary sounds of the office somehow seemed threatening, and she found her concentration continually broken by a phone ringing down the hall or the heat going on and off.

She glanced at the small clock in the right-hand corner of her computer screen for the umpteenth time. Ten after ten.

She rubbed the back of her neck. "Time to go home."

After organizing her desk and prioritizing the next day's work, she rose, picked up her purse, and opened her office door. The little rush of air caused by the opening door carried the faintest scent of aftershave. Max.

She put her hands on her hips and reflected on the anonymous, unresponsive phone caller. He'd probably wanted to strike up a conversation and then thought better of it. Still, it made her uneasy. With everything going on in her life, she didn't need the additional stress of having to watch out for her boss.

Wanting to pinpoint his whereabouts so she could avoid him, she snapped her light switch off and tiptoed down the hall toward his office. As she neared the corner, she could see a shaft of light stretched across the hall carpet. Slowing her steps, she leaned forward to peek around the corner.

The light vanished. She could hear Max's footsteps coming toward the hall.

Doing an about-face, she made a beeline to the front door, thankful her steps were soundless on the carpeted floors. *Oh, brother. What would he think if he caught me peering into his office at this hour of the night?* She burst through the office entry looking in the direction of her car, heels clicking loudly on the cement as she quickened her pace.

"Angelica." Max's voice came from behind her. "Wait up."

With no way to avoid acknowledging she'd heard him, she turned and smiled.

He fell into step beside her. "Let me walk you to your car. It's late and it's dark." He glanced around the parking lot. "Why on earth did you park way in the back?"

"I was just wondering that myself."

They walked in awkward silence.

"You're working late." Her words were stilted.

"Just catching up. I was gone this afternoon. Closing on my house. I've been in an apartment for the last three years." He gave her a boyish smile.

It had been rumored in the office that Max had married his second wife on the rebound after his first wife and child had been killed in a car accident. Then a few years later, she'd taken most of his assets during a messy and bitter divorce, when she'd left Max and married his brother, who hadn't had a steady job since he dropped out of high school. Those who had known Max during his first marriage said he'd been a devoted husband and father. But the tragic loss of his family, followed by the humiliating and very public dissolution of his second marriage, had changed him. She tried to glimpse his face in the shadowed moonlight.

He turned toward her. "The new house has a wet bar in the family room."

Angelica turned her face away. Max's breath hinted that perhaps he'd been breaking it in earlier in the evening. Angelica didn't have the slightest interest in talking about his wet bar or his personal life. It made her uncomfortable. She was sorry for the loss he'd suffered, but he'd apparently chosen to live the swinging single life now.

As they approached her car, she felt in her purse for her keys. "Thank you, Max."

Angelica slipped the car key into the door lock and turned it. As she took the key out, Max reached around her and pulled the door open. "You're welcome, Angie."

Max watched Angelica pull out of the parking lot.

As he walked back to his car, he remembered the first day he'd seen her in the public defender's office. The beautiful young attorney had been in a spirited discussion with Jonathan Cantrall over a case that was being appealed. Fully informed, articulate, and quick, she made her point and did it with a sophistication and polish that promised more than a career as a deputy public defender.

When Max had taken the top position in the public defender's office, he'd looked in her personnel file and pulled her résumé. He wasn't surprised to see she'd graduated at the top of her class in law school. But he was surprised to see she'd listed her hobby as reading and her favorite book, the Bible.

He'd also checked her marital status.

The truth was, she reminded him of his first wife, his high school sweetheart, the love of his life, Angie. Not that Angelica looked like her. It was something else. An air she had about her, confident, yet not overbearing. She had natural leadership qualities that drew others to her, yet a compassionate manner that he admired. He'd found himself thinking about Angelica often.

Regret and guilt smothered him. Angie. He'd never really appreciated what they'd had together. He could discuss the most complicated law case with her in a lively exchange and then, an hour later, sit on their deck sharing the beauty of a sunset, holding hands, no words necessary. If only the clock could be turned back.

As he watched Angelica's car disappear into the night, he sighed. A woman like that could have any man she wanted. Had she married one of her Hastings classmates?

He gave a resigned shake of his head. If only he'd met her at a different time in her life. Before she'd married and settled into an easy life.

5

WITH ONE SMOOTH swing of Antonio's hoe, the weed, half hidden between the rocks of the small, decorative wall of the Jessicks' house, flew through the air and landed on a nearby tarp.

Over the past month, Antonio had learned that his expertise with a hoe was a novelty to the Americans. Most gardeners didn't do handwork because it was so time consuming. He'd won many a bid by giving the homeowner five minutes free, clearing the weeds out of an area of the person's choice, while they watched in disbelief. He offered a standard package. Thirty-five dollars for weekly service. Mow, edge, and blow . . . weeding free!

All the new construction in his neighborhood had given him a reservoir of potential clients, but he'd learned that most homeowners requested multiple bids. The competition was intense. Still, he was careful as he went door-to-door. If he saw the lawn was being maintained, he moved on. He didn't believe in taking another man's job. He didn't want people to do it to him, so he didn't do it to them.

He and Angelica had designed his cards, and she'd printed them with the computer. The discussion of what to name the company had gone on for days. He'd wanted "Perez and Son," but Angelica had said it was too soon. She'd finally convinced him that "Affordable Lawn Care" was a better choice.

Antonio stood up, arching his back, then shaking out the cramp in his hand. He watched the forklift across the street raise a big load of roof tile into the air. He was keeping an eye on the progress of these new model homes for the next phase of the development. Someone maintained the lawns of the models that were used now, but he hoped the developer would take bids for lawn maintenance when these were finished.

He glanced down the street. From his place behind the rock wall, he could make out a slight, hunched figure walking in the distance. Maclovia.

It must be lunchtime.

His grandmother had fallen into a routine over the past few weeks. She spent the mornings in her room. He didn't question her about what she did there, but he had seen a tiny sweater laid out on the bed once. And he suspected she found the quiet solitude of the room an open invitation to be with God.

At about noon every day, she made him a lunch. If he didn't come home to eat by one o'clock, she and Buddy walked the neighborhood streets until they found him. She still refused to use the oven but had learned how to make a fire in the barbeque with scrap wood. Antonio knew the grocery bag she carried was full of warm tortillas, cheese, and fruit. He turned back to his weeding, wanting to finish before he stopped to eat.

"Hey, Fred, it's that old bag woman again. The one with no teeth."

Antonio raised his head, stress lines forming on his brow. The voice had come from a man on the roof of the unfinished model home across the street.

A young man stepped out of the garage of the unfinished house, biting his cigarette as he talked. "Yeah, the one we saw taking wood off the site last week. We sure gave her a scare when I let Skip off his leash. Too bad he knocked her down."

Antonio laid down his hoe, not taking his eyes off the men. His grandmother hadn't said anything about this.

"Go get Skip outta the truck. This'll be fun. She's walkin' right this way. And look, she's got somebody's dog with her." The man leaped off the edge of the roof with the casual confidence of someone who did it every day. "Skip'll make a meal outta that fancy puppy. Hurry up."

Antonio jumped over the low wall and strode toward his grandmother, meeting her in front of the models, placing himself between her and the men.

"Fred, wait a sec, looks like she's got a friend. That Mexican that was pullin' weeds over there."

Antonio could hear disappointment in the voice.

"Whoa. He's a big guy. No point in causin' ourselves trouble."

Antonio looked their way, barely able to control his anger. Not wanting to alarm Maclovia, he took her arm and guided her to the backyard of the Jessicks' house. He gently took the bungee cord his grandmother used when she walked Buddy and hooked it on a patio chair leg. He'd been unable to convince her to use the leash with the diamonds on the strap. Not nearly as practical, she'd insisted. Besides, it was too hard for her to open the clasp with gnarled hands.

80

"Please sit, *Abuela*." Antonio pointed to a chair.

She took a seat, then handed him the bag.

He opened it and held it under his nose. "Um, umm, smells good." He winked at her.

Her leathery face broke into a smile.

Buddy sat at attention, his nose quivering, his eyes pleading.

As Antonio ate, he asked his grandmother about the men across the street and what he'd heard them say.

"Don't worry, my son. God takes care of me."

He noticed she ran her hand under her shawl and up her arm as she spoke.

He leaned toward her and gently lifted the fabric, exposing an ugly gash, surrounded by a deep purple bruise.

He started to rise.

Maclovia put her hand on his arm. "No, *mi hijo*. It is better to suffer wrong than to do it."

Her words transported him to his childhood, to him standing at her knee in tattered clothes, tears streaming down his cheeks. He, the poorest of the poor, enduring the taunts of other children whose families found status in their hovels and lean-tos, while he lived under the branches of a tree.

Then, he had not questioned her wisdom; now, it seemed unreasonable. Still, he respected his *abuela* and sat back down.

Maclovia looked with interest around the yard. "Is this one of the secret houses?"

Antonio searched his thoughts, then broke into a smile. "Yes. They pay me cash for my extra work. They leave my money under the front mat if they're not going to be home." He reached into his shirt pocket and pulled out three bills. "I scrub oil off their driveway last week. Angelica knows nothing of it."

Maclovia clapped her hands. "When will you have enough?"

"I have one hundred and five dollars. The lady at Wal-Mart told me I need one hundred and fourteen dollars and eighty-seven cents. Then I can bring the crib home. I'm hoping next week."

"Will you put it in your room?"

"No, in my son's room. He will be proud of his room." His face darkened. "But I found out I don't get the one they show you in the store. It comes in a box."

Maclovia waited for further explanation.

"You have to build it. They only sell you the parts."

"No!" Her hands dropped to her sides. "That's a lot of money for parts."

Suddenly, there was a deafening crash. Antonio felt the vibration under his feet. Buddy jumped up, barking.

Antonio and Maclovia ran to the front yard.

Across the street at the models, the forklift was tilted at an odd angle, and roof tiles were scattered everywhere. Two men were shouting into cell phones. A third man knelt beside a body partially visible under broken tiles.

Maclovia ran ahead of Antonio with a quick, shuffling gait. When she reached the men, she slipped between them and knelt with the man beside the body. As Antonio approached, he could see that the man sprawled on the ground was the one who'd been on the roof.

"Lady, you shouldn't touch him. An ambulance is on its way."

Antonio looked at the man who had choked the words out; it was Fred, the man whose dog had chased Maclovia. He was trembling.

"He was just trying to unload the tile. Oh, God, don't let him be dead."

The terror on Fred's face filled Antonio with sorrow. He knelt beside him and put his hand on the man's shoulder. "She pray for him."

Fred looked at Antonio, then lowered his eyes. "Yes, please."

A distant siren began to grow louder. Fred jumped up and ran to the street. The other men ran after him.

Antonio watched his grandmother's hands move across the ashen face. Her lips moving, she rested her fingers over the man's heart. She began to moan, almost wail. Antonio glanced toward the men on the street directing the ambulance to the site.

A whisper escaped the man's lips. "Mother?" His eyes flickered open.

He looked directly at Maclovia. Confusion filtered across his face. Holding only the faintest spark of life, his eyes moved past her, over her shoulder to the cloudless sky.

Moments passed. He closed his eyes. "Father."

"Move. Move." The people from the ambulance pushed through.

Maclovia rose and stepped to the side, watching. Antonio stood behind her, his hands on her shoulders.

Many things were brought from the ambulance, and at one point a *médico* breathed into the man's mouth and pounded on his chest.

Finally, the man's body was placed on a board and covered with a sheet. Not even his face was visible as they put him in the ambulance.

The *médico* returned to the small group and spoke to Fred in a low voice. "I'm sorry. We did everything we could." Then he turned to Maclovia. "I'm sorry."

She looked up at Antonio.

He translated for her. "He is dead."

She answered him, her face serene. "No. He is not dead."

Max Jaeger was a hard guy to figure out.

Angelica sat on the edge of her bed and slipped her foot into her tennis shoe.

During the two weeks since Max had officially taken the position of chief public defender, he'd been extremely cordial and professional toward her whenever their paths had crossed. Particularly when they had ended up in the office alone at night, which seemed to happen often since her bouts with morning sickness kept her from accomplishing anything until around ten o'clock. Maybe she'd read too much into the incident in the office. Perhaps the phone call had been nothing more than a wrong number. She'd been stressed out that whole evening. Work, Antonio's driver's license test, a doctor's appointment, pushing herself to go to Bible study, then more work. It had never bothered her before to fill her days with eighteen hours of pressure, but now it seemed to wear her down. She smiled to herself; this was the kind of thing that gave pregnant women a bad name in the workplace. Her smile widened. For that matter, Max must have been pretty stressed out himself, calling her Angie. She shook her head—probably his latest conquest.

She put on her other shoe. Maybe Max was trying to clean up his act.

"You ready?" Antonio interrupted her thoughts.

She looked up from tying her tennis shoe. "Is Maclovia coming with us?"

"She said she very tired and going to bed early." Antonio patted his pockets, looking for his keys.

"Well, I'm not surprised after that horrendous accident

you two witnessed." Angelica sat up and brushed her hair away from her face. "That was so sad."

The sound of Antonio picking up the truck keys from the dresser brought Buddy thundering down the hallway.

Angelica stood and gave herself a once-over in the bedroom mirror. "You can't come with us, Bud. They don't allow dogs in Wal-Mart."

"I go put him in the backyard." Antonio slapped his hand on his thigh. "Come on, boy."

Angelica smiled, watching Buddy try to snatch the keys from Antonio's hand as they walked down the hall. She looked back into the mirror, studying herself. Where were the five pounds she'd found out about at her fourteen-week appointment with Dr. Gremian that afternoon? She turned sideways, raised her hands parallel with her shoulders, and craned her neck toward the mirror. Her stomach looked just as flat as it ever had.

"What you doing?"

Antonio's voice startled her. "Uh. Nothing."

He stepped behind her and put his arms around her waist, pulling her to him. He spoke to her reflection in the mirror, his eyes intent upon her. "You are my perfect wife."

Seeing him in the mirror, his black hair falling across his forehead, his muscled arms gently holding her against his broad chest, she felt her heart turn over. But even more than his incredible physical presence, she was drawn to his beautiful spirit; there was no guile in him. She was blissfully happy he was the father of her child. *Thank You, Lord, for bringing him into my life.*

Angelica took his hand and stepped away from him. "It's early. Why don't we run up and visit my parents before we go shopping?"

She'd tried to avoid Antonio's repeated request that she

go with him to look at baby furniture at Wal-Mart. She'd never shopped at Wal-Mart before she'd married Antonio. She and her mother went to Saks, Gucci, and designer boutiques for serious shopping. Wal-Mart didn't carry any of the brands she was familiar with.

He pursed his lips, then gave her a patient smile. "*Sí, señorita*. But just a short time."

"Deal." She jumped up on her toes and gave him a quick kiss.

Antonio insisted they take the truck, and not the fire engine–red Expedition her parents had given her on her birthday.

"I am so thankful for this baby. It's caused Mom and Dad to see us as a family." Angelica looked out the window, enjoying the drive through the beautiful Sonoma Mountains. "They've really opened up about how much they want grandchildren. . . . Antonio?" She sought his eyes. "You know I think my dad is hoping we'll name our child Benito, if it's a boy. You and I *have* talked about it."

"Yes, and I think about it." Antonio laid his right palm faceup on the seat between them, inviting Angelica to give him her hand. "A lot."

"And?" Angelica felt his strong fingers wrap around hers.

"I like my boy to have a Mexican name." His voice was so gentle, she couldn't be offended. "That his blood." He paused, then continued. "But your father is good man, and you his only child. Maybe this his only grandboy." Antonio looked at her. "So I am thinking for many days."

She squeezed his hand. "And?"

He turned the truck into the long, curving drive that led to Regalo Grande. "And I think Benito Crecencio is a good, strong name."

Angelica drew her breath. "Yes. How perfect. The two grandfathers. I love it."

Antonio pulled up in front of the entryway and turned off the truck. He unfastened his seat belt and faced her. "I no can give you many things. But I can give you this thing."

Angelica felt a warmth flow through her. "Oh, Antonio, let's tell them right now."

He gathered her into his arms and held her tightly. "I am so in love with you," his voice broke into a husky whisper.

The intensity of his voice brought tears to her eyes and a flash of heat to her cheeks. "I love you too."

They walked hand in hand through the beautiful, arched entry of the big hacienda. The bougainvilleas were in bloom, framing the portico with pink and purple. Before they reached the rough-hewn double entry doors, the doors swung open.

"Hey kids, come in. Dad and I were just having our after-dinner cocktails in the living room when we saw you drive up." Angelica's mother stepped to the side, ushering them in. "Honey?" She looked at Angelica with concern. "You look flushed. You feeling okay?"

Angelica turned her head just enough so her mother couldn't see the intimate wink she gave Antonio. "Yes, Mom, I feel great. Got any iced tea?"

The four of them settled into the living room with their drinks.

"I forget how beautiful this view is at sunset." Angelica leaned toward the window. "I can just make out Pasha tearing around down there." She tapped her husband's knee. "Look, Antonio. He's pacing back and forth in front of the gate. He knows I'm here."

"Didn't you have a doctor's appointment today, dear?"

Angelica could tell by the rushed tone of her mother's

voice that she'd probably been waiting to ask since the moment she saw the truck out the window. At least she was making an effort not to pry.

"Yes, I saw Dr. Gremian this afternoon." She grimaced. "I gained five pounds."

"It'll be a battle all the way." Her mother took a sip of champagne.

Her father chuckled. "Don't worry about that. How's work going with that new boss? You didn't seem too excited about the change."

"You mean Max." Angelica set her tea down. "It's kind of funny. I may have misjudged him."

Her father's eyebrows shot up. "You didn't have one good thing to say about him last time we talked. I think you even referred to him as 'a womanizing predator.'"

She folded her arms across her chest; she hated to admit she'd been wrong. "I haven't made up my mind yet. He only took the position a couple of weeks ago. I'm starting to think he's decided to clean up his act and not risk any problems with the board of supervisors." She caught her father's eye. "Especially now that there's talk of reopening the Vasquez drug case."

Angelica had been living at home, looking for work, when the case had been in the headlines on a daily basis. It had been controversial because many in the local Mexican community believed that the young Mexican national, Miguel Vasquez, legally seeking work, thought he'd been hired as a laborer to work in the vineyards. Instead, he found himself held hostage by armed guards in a remote area, forced to work marijuana crops. She and her father had had many spirited discussions regarding the case. She, convinced Vasquez had been duped. He, convinced Vasquez was an opportunist who'd been caught.

Her father leaned forward in his chair. "Why is it being reopened?"

Angelica couldn't help feeling smug. "Max told me that a new witness has come forward."

"Oh, boy. That'll be a feather in somebody's cap if they get Vasquez off. Especially with elections coming up. It'll cinch the Hispanic vote."

Angelica nodded. "It sure will, but that's not the point." Her voice began to rise. "The point is, they may have sent an innocent man to jail. I almost volunteered to work the case for free when I first heard about it. Want to take bets Max takes the case himself? He said—"

"Angelica, tell us what the doctor said."

Her mother's clipped words reminded Angelica how annoyed her mother had become when the original case had dominated every dinner conversation for weeks. Her mother saw no reason why the trial of some ethnic minority should intrude on her privileged life.

Angelica lowered her voice. "Everything was fine." She gave Antonio a quick glance. "In fact, Antonio and I were talking about the baby on our way over. We'd like to make an announcement."

"What?" her parents asked in unison.

"We've decided, if it's a boy . . . which Antonio has assured me it is . . . we're naming him Benito Crecencio."

Angelica saw the play of emotions on her father's face. First surprise, then disbelief. He blinked rapidly and cleared his throat. "This is one of the happiest days of my life, Angel." The words were filled with emotion.

Angelica's mother leaned over and gave him a kiss. "How wonderful. When will you find out for sure if it's a boy?"

"Probably on my next visit. I'm supposed to get an ultrasound." Angelica gave her husband a sideways glance. "If it's okay with Antonio."

Her father's face became serious. "Why wouldn't it be? Don't you want your firstborn to have every advantage modern medicine has to offer, Antonio? I know I certainly want that for my grandchild."

"It not my idea, and it not my *decisión*." Antonio held her father's stare, his jaw set.

The two couples sat in awkward silence.

"It's all going to work out." Angelica stood. "We'd better get going. We've got shopping to do."

Antonio set his glass down and rose. "Good evening, *señor . . . señora*. I go start the truck." He tipped his head and left the room.

Angelica's mother frowned. "I hope he's not going to stand in the way of that baby getting the best care possible."

"Don't worry, Mom. When he understands what it's all about, he'll be fine. He wants his child to have the best of everything."

"Oh, that reminds me." Her mother ran to the magazine basket next to the couch. "Look here." She pointed to a page of beautiful, handmade cribs. "This one has a white antique finish with end panel caning. And look, you can get the matching French armoire for only fifteen hundred dollars." Her face was filled with excitement. "Perfect for a boy or girl. It's an heirloom piece, honey. You'll want to keep it for your children's children."

Angelica felt her stomach knot. "It's beautiful, Mom." She searched for the right words. "But we really haven't decided just how we want to decorate. Let's wait for a while." *Please.*

Her mother's smile froze. "Of course, dear."

Angelica let herself out and walked quickly to the truck. She got in and turned to Antonio. "You okay?"

His face softened. "I'm fine. No worry." He put the truck in gear and headed down the hill to the valley.

They found a parking spot and walked hand in hand into Wal-Mart.

The baby department was filled with merchandise. They looked at strollers, then car seats. Antonio seemed preoccupied with the cribs.

"This one looks nice." He was standing beside a cheap, generic crib that was on sale. She stepped next to him and tried to look interested.

Antonio held up a large, white ticket that hung from one of the corners. "Sol-id wood." He gave her a proud smile.

Her heart went out to him. He never missed a chance to read something to her, and his appreciation for the barest necessities touched her. "It's lovely."

She didn't want to tell him about the custom baby furniture her mother had shown her and continued to look around the department to please him. The more he examined the crib, the more uneasy she felt.

"Antonio, I think my parents are planning to help us with furniture. It'd be nice to save that expense." She tried to sound casual.

He knelt down and opened and shut the trundle drawer of the solid wood crib. "They help us enough. I no like any more help."

Maclovia rocked slowly in her chair. The low hum of Antonio's and Angelica's voices drifted through her bedroom door. Her thoughts went to *señora* Craig, the missionary in Mexico who had told her about God's love . . . become man. She said His name was Jesus. Maclovia had perceived it as truth when she heard it, tucking it into her heart. Many times since then, and on this day, she had felt the presence of Truth. Whenever she surrendered to the power of God and called upon His healing love, she called the presence by its name, Jesus.

As she'd kneeled by the man who lay under the tiles, she had been aware of the hedge of fire that had encircled them, its light stripping away the things of the earth. Wherever her fingers had moved, there had been streaks of light, like tongues of fire, laying bare before her the pain and suffering of the young man's life. She was but an observer, a silent witness to the years of abuse and wounding. His heart scarred and broken. Hardened so it might be fashioned into a sword by the hands of the enemy.

But the presence had been there with them. Jesus. And the man had seen Him. Father.

Though his loved ones would bury the body, though they thought him dead, for the first time since his birth . . . he was alive.

She rubbed her arm where the painful cut and bruise had been. The skin was smooth, unblemished. In the presence of the Spirit, all things were made new.

6

ANGELICA SAT, HUNCHED over, with her head on her desk. *And this too shall pass. And this too shall pass.* It had been two weeks since she'd seen Dr. Gremian. If she was still this sick at her next appointment, she was going to ask him if there was something he could give her. She closed her eyes and concentrated on taking slow, even breaths. If she could keep it together until ten o'clock, she knew she could get through the rest of the day. Her phone rang.

Without raising her head, she felt her way across the desk to the speaker button and managed to push it.

"Angelica, could you come to my office?"

It was Max.

As much as she'd wanted to keep her pregnancy a secret from the office for at least the first few months, word had gotten out soon after she'd told Fronie. Still, she'd done everything she could to conceal her morning sickness from her colleagues. She felt guilty knowing they'd have to cover for her when the baby was born, and she certainly didn't want her workload to fall on anyone else before then. She'd managed to keep up with everything by staying late most nights.

With all the strength she could muster, she turned her head toward the phone. "I'll be in as soon as I finish what I'm doing." A wave of nausea rolled over her.

"See you then." The voice was warm and friendly.

She heard the phone click and dropped her hand on the face of the phone set, then wiped it across the buttons to be sure she hit the one that turned off the speaker.

She pulled her wrist in front of her eye. 9:40. Time to sit up.

For the next twenty minutes, she alternately sat still, counting ten breaths, and paged through the stack of papers on her desk. By eleven o'clock, she'd determined what had to be done and felt well enough to do it. She decided to see Max before continuing. She picked up a yellow pad and made the short walk to his office.

Angelica paused in his doorway. "May I come in?"

"Sure. Take a seat." He turned away from his computer screen and pointed to the chair next to his desk. "I was just looking up some recent appellate decisions that might help in the Vasquez case."

Angelica set her pad on the edge of his desk. "I followed all the coverage of the Vasquez trial last year. In fact, I was interviewing here while it was going on."

He looked directly in her eyes. "So Dave told me before he left. We had a few discussions about you."

Angelica felt herself stiffen. She sat back in her chair. "Oh?"

"He really admired you. Thought you were one of the brightest young attorneys he'd ever worked with."

Angelica studied him. There was nothing about his manner, his tone, or his body language that signaled anything

94

other than a professional discussion between the chief public defender and one of his deputies.

"Do you still have an interest in this case?"

Her heart skipped a beat, and she straightened. "As a matter of fact, I was just discussing this with someone a few nights ago. I believe Vasquez is innocent." She tried to keep the excitement out of her voice.

Max settled back in his chair, his face serious. "So do I."

She waited for him to continue.

"Would you mind closing the door? I'd like to discuss this with you in detail."

Angelica knew, whatever her personal opinion of Max Jaeger, she needed to put it aside. This was serious business. A man's freedom hung in the balance. She closed the door and took her seat.

"Dave and I talked about this quite a bit before he left. As you know, a new witness has come forward."

Angelica nodded. "Do you think the person's credible?"

"I think a jury would believe him."

She put two and two together. "A snitch."

Max looked amused. "You're as sharp as Dave said you were."

Angelica folded her arms across her chest. "They make the worst kind of witnesses because they're looking for something in return."

"And that's why I want the sharpest person I can get to work with me on this case."

She felt herself blushing and resented it. There was nothing in his words that should make her feel self-conscious. If it had been Dave, she would have thanked him for the compliment. "I appreciate your confidence in me."

"You're going to get some great experience, but it's going

to be time consuming and challenging. I'll give you as much of a break on your caseload as I can."

Angelica couldn't believe her good fortune. She was fully aware few young attorneys moved up to felonies, and this would position her to make that move. A promotion that would help her career as well as her finances. But it was the thought of having fewer cases to focus on, less time in court, less time going to the jail, and fewer appointments with clients, particularly now, that made her weak with relief. "When do I start?"

"Would now be too soon?"

She saw the mischief in his eyes, inviting her to make this a private joke. She ignored it. "That would be fine."

He rose and reached across his desk and picked up a stack of papers. "You can start reviewing these transcripts."

She stood and took the stack from him. During the shift of papers from his hands to hers, she felt the brush of his fingertips across her knuckles. She pulled the papers to her chest and took a step back.

Max casually seated himself. "I'll give all new assignments to the other deputies. But bring me your calendar, and we'll go over what you're working on now. If there are cases that should be reassigned, I'll take care of it."

His smile was benign, and Angelica couldn't detect any subtext to his words or actions. She chastised herself for her suspicions. This case could have political benefits for Max, and he wanted competent help pursuing it. Advancing his own career was driving his decisions . . . just like it was driving hers.

"I'll get started on these." She hesitated. "And thank you, Max, for giving me this opportunity."

He nodded toward her and turned back to his computer screen.

Angelica returned to her office and focused on her scheduled work, anxious to finish and get a look at the transcripts.

When she glanced at her watch, it was two o'clock. She sat back in her chair and rubbed her forehead. She'd worked through lunch and felt exhausted. As much as she hated to take the time, she knew a short walk to The Carrot Patch across the street would do her good. She could bring the food back to her desk and keep working.

She rose and picked up her purse, then reached for the desk to steady herself. She closed her eyes, something wasn't right. She'd make a quick stop in the ladies' room.

Taking unsteady steps, Angelica made her way down the hall. She shouldn't have pushed herself. Tomorrow she'd bring a lunch. She opened the door of the bathroom. Feeling shaky, she decided to use the handicapped stall, in case she needed the grab bars. She latched the stall door.

Blood. Spots of blood on her pantyhose. A flood of panic swept over her.

Please, God. Protect my baby.

Antonio looked at his watch. It was almost one o'clock. He blew the last of the grass from the sidewalk, loaded his equipment, jumped into his truck, and headed home.

Maclovia and Buddy were in the backyard. Maclovia had the barbeque grill full of tortillas, cobs of corn, and chicken. Buddy helped by giving her approving and encouraging glances from his place just below the cutting board, where pieces of meat sometimes fell.

Antonio gave his grandmother a kiss on the cheek. "Oh, boy. I'm starved." He picked a piece of crispy skin off a breast that was sizzling. "Nobody cooks like you."

Maclovia's weathered face lit up. She wiped her hands on the towel hanging from the waistband of her skirt and began to load a platter with the steaming food.

Antonio snatched a tortilla from the stack and rolled it up. "After lunch I'm going to go pick up the crib."

Maclovia's eyes widened. "I will go too."

He and his grandmother had secretly visited the store several times to admire the crib. When he'd told her that in America blue was the color for baby boys, she'd begun knitting a blue blanket. Each time they visited the crib, she checked the progress of the blanket to be sure it wasn't too big or too small.

Antonio took the platter from her and carried it to the patio table. Buddy dutifully watched them eat, in case they needed any help. And, as luck would have it, once in a while he was given charge of a piece of chicken.

Antonio stood and began to clear the table. "There's enough here for another meal."

Maclovia followed Antonio into the kitchen. "Let's take some to Fred."

Since the accident, Maclovia had taken Fred a homemade lunch whenever she took one to Antonio at the Jessicks' house.

Antonio began rinsing the dishes. "It's not Tuesday. He probably brought his own lunch."

"Then he'll have it for dinner. The poor boy isn't married." Maclovia shook her head slowly. "God did not mean for him to be alone." She looked at Antonio. "I am praying for Fred."

They finished cleaning the kitchen and packed up the leftover food.

Maclovia handed Antonio the sack. "Wait one moment. I want to change before we go to town."

98

Antonio waited in the front hall, and within moments Maclovia reappeared wearing the dress she'd worn on the plane, her scarf wrapped around her shoulders, and some thick, brown hose that didn't quite reach her knees.

Antonio whistled at her.

Buddy began wagging his tail and dancing in place, his mouth open in a big, doggy smile.

Antonio opened the front door and with a flourish of his hand invited her to step through first. He quickly stepped after her, shutting the door behind him. Buddy's muffled, indignant barks followed him to the truck.

When they drove up to the unfinished models, they saw Fred next to the garage, stacking scraps of building material.

Fred met them as they got out.

"*Buenos días, amigos.*" Fred shook Antonio's hand and gave Maclovia a hug.

Maclovia held out the sack of food.

"You shouldn't have. You're too good to me."

"God bless," she answered him in English.

As Maclovia showed Fred each thing she'd packed, Antonio looked across the street to the Jessicks'. He could see the fertilizer he'd had them put on their grass was finally greening it up.

His eyes wandered to the drive. He could see one of their cars . . . and a truck parked in front of the house. Antonio's eyes narrowed.

The pickup looked familiar. He stepped to the side to get a clearer view. The blue truck had landscaping equipment in the bed and a low metal trailer hitched to the back. Antonio's eyes went over the vehicle. He could make out white letters on the door. B.J.'s.

Antonio shifted back on his heels and folded his arms

across his chest. The man, named Bill, who'd come to his house and given him a price to do the yard had driven a truck like that one. Antonio chewed his lower lip. *"You won't get no work around here if I can help it."* The man's parting words echoed in Antonio's mind. He pressed his lips together.

"Are we going to get the crib?" Maclovia's words broke into Antonio's thoughts.

"Uh, *sí.*" He turned to Fred. "Enjoy."

As they drove to Wal-Mart, Antonio couldn't stop thinking about the blue truck. Surely Bill would not try to take his job from him. It would not be right to question the Jessicks. Perhaps they had called Bill. Maybe they were not pleased with his work. He resigned himself to the fact that he would have to wait and see what happened.

As soon as he parked at Wal-Mart, Maclovia was out of the truck and into the store. He ran to catch up with her. She made a straight line to the baby department.

As they waited for the box to be brought from the back, Maclovia said, "I can't believe that my great-grandson will have such a beautiful bed. None of my children or grandchildren has ever had a bed." Her eyes misted. "God is so good."

Antonio found he needed to look away. His grandmother's emotions brought his own to the surface. This was a proud day for him.

The box was loaded into the truck, and they drove home, talking of different ways to surprise Angelica.

"First I have to build it," Antonio reminded his grandmother as he turned into their driveway.

Her face sobered. "Do you know how?"

Antonio shrugged his shoulders. "I'll figure it out. I'm

going to hide the box in your closet. She'll never find it there."

Maclovia beamed.

"Then I'll work on it when she's not home."

As he dragged the boxed crib from the garage and through the kitchen, Antonio noticed the message light flashing on the answering machine. Had the Jessicks called? He hurriedly put the box in the closet, ran to the kitchen, and pressed the play button.

Angelica's trembling voice came over the speaker. "Antonio, I'm at Dr. Gremian's office. There's something wrong."

Dr. Gremian pointed to the monitor. "Here is the face." He moved his fingers an inch. "Here are the arms. That's the heart beating."

Angelica blinked back tears as she lay on the table watching the miracle of life materialize through the shadows and shades on the monitor. Her baby. No longer unknown and unseen. She wished desperately that Antonio could be by her side. "Is it a boy?" she whispered.

The doctor moved the transducer over her stomach. "A leg is hiding that right now, and besides, it's a little early." He studied the sonogram. "Are you sure about your dates?"

She searched her memory. "I'm reasonably sure, Dr. Gremian. Why?"

"The measurements I've taken show the fetus is small for sixteen weeks." He looked at her. "I want to get a quantitative blood test to determine the level of HCG you have and see if it correlates with your last cycle." He continued to study the monitor. "If you are sixteen weeks pregnant, we should also do an alpha-fetoprotein test. It's optional, but I highly recommend it."

Angelica made up her mind not to give in to the fear his words sparked within her. "Does that mean there's something wrong?" She took a slow breath. She needed to be strong for her child.

"No, it's a pretty standard test to help evaluate what's really going on. It's generally used for detecting neural tube defects, but it can also indicate many other things, like abdominal wall defects, some renal and urinary tract anomalies, Turner's syndrome, and placental complications. A low level of AFP could also indicate Down syndrome."

Angelica thought about Antonio's reaction when the doctor had brought it up on their first visit. Antonio had been completely against any kind of testing. She thought about how he'd resisted the suggestion just two weeks ago at her parents' house. He'd said again he didn't want her to have the ultrasound . . . but he'd also said it was her decision. If only he'd been home when she called.

She closed her eyes, trying to clear her mind.

But that was before the spotting. That was before there was any reason to think something was wrong. She could understand why he would have felt that way. All of these ideas were foreign to him. His family had never had modern medicine available to them.

She didn't have to make up her mind right now. She could wait and talk to him tonight. Explain everything.

What if he still said no? Fiery darts of doubt pricked at her, creating fear. She opened her eyes.

"I want the test."

She would explain it to Antonio if the test showed any abnormalities. If not, she didn't even need to tell him. Her fear began to fade.

Besides, this was a blood test of *her* blood. This wasn't really testing the baby. That's what she would tell him. The fiery darts vanished.

Dr. Gremian put the transducer down. "Go ahead and get dressed." He marked a form and handed it to her. "Go down the hall to the lab and have your blood drawn. When you're finished, come back and tell the nurse to take you into my office. As soon as I can break away from my scheduled appointments, I'll go over with you in detail what the ultrasound showed."

Angelica dressed and went to the lab. As soon as her blood was drawn, she returned to Dr. Gremian's office. Standing at the counter, waiting for the nurse to take her to him, she felt a hand on her shoulder.

"You okay? Our baby okay?" Antonio's voice was low and urgent.

She turned to him. "I don't know." His presence gave her strength. She pressed into his chest and took a deep, steadying breath.

"God bless." The heavily accented English came from behind Antonio.

Angelica looked over his shoulder. "Maclovia." Her heart went out to the old woman in the ragged dress, fingering the primitive cross at her neck. Maclovia's face was filled with concern. Angelica reached around Antonio and squeezed her hand.

"You can see the doctor now." A tall lady, with her hair pulled into a tight bun, spoke in their direction from the doorway.

Angelica turned to the nurse. "My husband will join me."

The nurse looked at Maclovia over the top of her glasses. "Is she with you?"

Antonio answered. "This my grandmother."

The nurse turned toward Angelica, waiting for a response.

"Antonio, could you ask Maclovia to wait for us here? The doctor's office is small."

Antonio rested his hand on his grandmother's shoulder and guided her to an empty chair next to a woman holding a baby. "Wait here. We are going to talk to the doctor and make sure Angelica and our baby are all right."

Maclovia took a seat.

Dr. Gremian was writing at his desk when the nurse seated Antonio and Angelica.

He turned to face them. "Good afternoon, Mr. Perez." He dropped his pen in his pocket, sat back in his chair, and crossed his legs.

"I've reviewed the ultrasound results, and the fetus appears to be small. I've—"

"*Con permiso, por favor,*" Antonio interrupted. His voice was intense and abrupt.

Angelica's eyes cut over to him. His lapse into Spanish was a sure sign he was upset.

Antonio leaned forward in his chair. "What is fetus?"

"The fetus is the unborn child." The doctor smiled patiently.

"Why do you call him fetus and not baby?" His face reflected the question in his voice.

The doctor shifted in his chair. "The unborn child is more correctly referred to as a fetus. It's not technically a baby until it is born. Until it draws a breath."

Antonio's eyes narrowed. "What?"

Angelica put her hand on Antonio's leg. "The word means the same thing as baby. It's just a different way of saying it."

Angelica could tell by the look on Antonio's face that he either didn't believe or didn't understand what she was saying. She would explain it to him later. "Please, Dr. Gremian, tell us what this means."

"It's something we want to watch. I will get the HCG quantitative test results tomorrow. The AFP will take two to four weeks, it has to be sent to the state for testing. The state will then notify me and send you a letter with the results. Once I have those test results—"

"My blood test results." She restated the doctor's words to Antonio.

"Yes, your blood test results, we'll know more."

"More about what?" Antonio was focused on the doctor.

"Mr. Perez, your wife spotted blood. It is a concern when a woman spots during her second trimester. There could be a number of reasons for it. We just want to make sure there is nothing abnormal, that everything is okay. We want you to have a healthy baby."

Antonio settled back in his chair and folded his arms across his chest.

Dr. Gremian continued. "Angelica, when we get your HCG test results tomorrow, they will tell us if you're producing the amount of hormones that would be expected at sixteen weeks. I hope to have the AFP results back in time for your next regular appointment. We'll discuss things in detail then."

"Thank you, Dr. Gremian." Angelica stood. "Is my baby all right?"

He rose and rested his hand on her shoulder. "I didn't see anything unusual on the ultrasound. The fetus looked perfectly healthy. Now go home and take it easy for the next day or two."

Antonio stood. "*Buenas tardes, señor.*"

Antonio stopped in the waiting room for Maclovia, then the three of them walked to the parking lot.

When they got to Angelica's car, Antonio turned and faced her. "Why is there different name for my baby before he is born?"

His jaw was set. There was an air of stubbornness about him that Angelica had never seen before. "It's just another name for the baby. Like I could be called wife, daughter, or attorney. It's still me." She tried not to show her frustration.

Antonio thought for a moment, then seemed to relax slightly. "Oh. It is that simple?"

Finally. "Yes, it is that simple."

"Then I call the fetus 'my son.'" Antonio looked her directly in the eyes. "He is my son now, and he will be my son when he's born." He pulled Angelica to him and kissed the top of her head. He looked into her eyes again. "I'm sorry I don't know my English better." He brushed the hair from her face. "I'll see you at home."

Angelica got in her car. Antonio's words made her uneasy for some reason. He was asking her something she'd never really thought much about. She never thought of her baby as a fetus. It seemed impersonal somehow, but it didn't offend her when Dr. Gremian used the term. Still, there was something about Antonio's manner that told her he didn't completely accept her explanation.

She closed her eyes for a moment. It had been an exhausting day. *Lord, it's Your baby too. I know it's Your will that my child be born perfect. I know You will protect him. I have put my baby in the hands of Dr. Gremian, and I'm trusting You to guide him.*

She looked at her watch. She needed to go back to work. If she didn't, everything that she'd left unfinished on her desk would only create added pressure at work tomorrow. It was

106

an endless circle. She let out a deep sigh, started the car, and turned out of the parking lot toward the office.

She reached for her cell phone and dialed. When Natalya answered, Angelica told her everything that had happened. "Please call the prayer chain and have them pray for me and the baby."

"Of course I will. Everything's going to be all right. The Word says, 'Trust in the Lord with all your heart, and lean not on your own understanding.' I don't know why this happened to you today, but God's in control, and it's all going to work out."

The certainty in Natalya's voice soothed Angelica. Natalya was right. God was in control. "See you at Bible study. Oh, have you heard anything from Jan Wilcox about her sister's son-in-law? I've prayed for him several times, asking the Lord to bless his business. He's struggling with his landscape business, just like Antonio."

"No, I haven't. But I'll be asking for updates next Wednesday night."

After saying good-bye, Angelica called Antonio to tell him she'd decided to go back to the office.

The phone was busy.

Antonio never used the phone. Maybe her parents had called. She waited a few minutes and dialed again. Antonio answered.

"The phone was busy. Did my parents call?"

"No." There was a pause, then Antonio continued. "The Jessicks call me."

Maclovia stood at her bedroom window, her hands clasped in front of her.

Antonio had told her on their way home from the doctor's

office that the doctor had been worried about their baby and had taken some of Angelica's blood to test. He said the doctor had told him that while his son grew within Angelica, somehow he was not really a baby. He would not be a baby until he breathed air.

Maclovia sank to her knees, bowed her head, and pressed her clasped hands to her lips. "Creator of this child, I beg You, protect our baby from the hands of this doctor—a man who does not know that when the child cannot draw his own breath, he breathes Yours."

7

Antonio gently lifted his guitar from the stand in the living room. Not wanting to wake Angelica, he tucked it under his arm and stepped out the front door. The morning sun was just beginning to light the sky.

He sat on the top step of the porch and gently strummed a chord. He hadn't played for weeks. Working to get his business going, studying, and trying to lighten Angelica's load had left no time for himself.

This morning, he felt especially burdened. The visit with the doctor the day before still troubled him, though he couldn't say why. He closed his eyes, seeking God.

"*Dios*, every good thing comes from You. I thank You for my wife and my son. Help me be a man worthy of Your blessings."

He opened his eyes. Directly in front of him, radiant light from the morning sun flooded across the sky. Its fiery beauty touched his heart. "*Dios*, I am a poor man with nothing to give You. Yet You have given me so much."

He gently pressed the guitar to his chest. He closed his

eyes, and for the next measure of time, became lost in the music that flowed from his heart, through the strings of his guitar, to the throne of God. And there, in that dimension of light and love, filled with deep gratitude, he gave his tithe.

As his touch lightened and the music slowed, a peace that passed his understanding settled over him.

"That was beautiful."

The familiar voice brought him back to the present.

"Grandmother! Where have you been? When I got up this morning, I saw Buddy was gone." He winked at her. "So of course I checked your room. But neither one of you were there."

Buddy's ears and tail went up at the mention of his name.

"We have been walking, son. I started as soon as the night sky was in place. I walked toward the mountains." She seated herself beside him.

Antonio waited, respecting his grandmother's desire to tell her story in her own time. This was the way of his people. Important things were not spoken out in one sentence, casting aside all that had gone before.

"I have watched your bride each morning. She can barely hold her head up. This is often the path from childhood to motherhood." Maclovia smiled compassionately, perhaps remembering her own journey.

Antonio nodded. "Angelica's friends have suggested many things, but nothing helps . . . except time."

Maclovia looked at him. "Time is a great healer. But God has filled His fields with many medicines." She slowly looked around the neighborhood. "These people have covered all that He has planted." She shrugged her shoulders. "So I went to the mountains."

His eyes swept over her. "And did you find what you were looking for?"

"No. Not what I was looking for, but what I needed."

Antonio waited for her to explain what she had hidden in her words.

Maclovia opened her hand. In her palm rested two tiny pebbles.

"How can those help her?" Antonio immediately felt shame as he heard the doubt in his voice. In the fields of Guadalajara, he had never questioned her wisdom.

"Time will tell you." Maclovia rubbed the stones with her finger. "First I want to pray for her."

"I'm sure she's awake now. Let's go see." Antonio helped his grandmother up, and they walked to the master bedroom.

The rose Antonio had laid on Angelica's night table was on the floor. Angelica's face was buried in her pillow.

"Angel? You awake?" Antonio knelt beside her.

She acknowledged his words with a moan.

"*Abuela* is here to pray for you."

Angelica moaned again but didn't move.

His grandmother tapped him on the shoulder, and he rose, then she sat on the edge of the bed.

Angelica moved her hand to cover her mouth.

Maclovia waited a moment, then put the pebbles on the nightstand and took Angelica's hands in hers. She began to hum.

Angelica slowly rolled to her back. "I'm so sick," she mumbled.

Maclovia turned Angelica's hands palms up. Then she took Angelica's right forearm and began stroking it just above the wrist.

Antonio watched as Maclovia laid her three middle fingers just above the first wrist crease of Angelica's right hand and

111

then pressed her thumb into the soft flesh over them. She picked up Angelica's left arm and placed her other thumb at the same point above her left wrist.

Maclovia's lips moved in silent prayer. Minutes passed.

Slowly, Angelica opened her eyes. "What is she doing?"

"I no have idea, but she knows many things. It help you?"

"I'm not sure, but it definitely isn't making things worse."

Antonio thought Angelica's voice seemed a little stronger.

Maclovia nodded toward the pebbles. "I need something to fasten those where my thumbs are. Do you have some cloth?"

"I will get some tape."

Antonio ran into the bathroom and got a roll of white tape. When he returned to the bedroom, Angelica was sitting up.

Maclovia took a pebble, and while she held it three finger spaces above Angelica's wrist, Antonio secured it in place with the tape. Then they repeated the process on her other wrist.

"Is it helping?" Antonio asked.

Angelica drew a shaky breath. "Maybe. I don't feel quite as nauseated." She stared at her bandaged wrists, her face a mixture of concern and amazement. "But what on earth is this about? How does this work?"

Antonio translated Angelica's question for his grandmother.

Maclovia stood. "Tell her I do not know how it works. But it is not necessary for me to understand how God works to be used by Him."

Antonio repeated his grandmother's words to his wife.

Inch by inch, Angelica moved her legs off the edge of the bed, resting her feet on the floor. She sat still, waiting.

"Antonio, I think I *am* better." A tentative smile touched her lips. "My stomach still feels touchy, but I think I could actually get up and move around." As she began to rise, Antonio took her arm.

For the next hour, as Angelica got ready for work, Antonio observed her from around corners and through doorway openings, in case she might suddenly become ill again and need him. He had learned long ago that she didn't like any-one near her when she was sick. She called it "hovering." He was not sure what the word meant, but she'd made it very clear he was not to do it.

His independent, stubborn, impatient wife . . . he loved her so. Now if only she'd leave for the office. He'd doubled up his work yesterday so he could have today off. As soon as she left for work, he'd begin to build the crib. She'd been through so much over the past few days, she deserved a nice surprise.

Angelica picked up her purse, then took her cell phone off the charger and put it in her pocket. She wanted to be sure she wouldn't miss the doctor's call. Perhaps she'd been off on her dates. Maybe the baby was not sixteen weeks old yet and was just the right size for his actual age.

"Antonio, I'm leaving," she shouted down the hall.

He suddenly appeared next to her. "Oh, there you are. I'm feeling so much better, I'm going to work." She held her wrists out in front of her. "Do you think it's possible those little rocks could be helping me?"

Antonio took her wrists and pulled her arms around his waist. "*Sí, señorita.* My grandmother is a wise woman." He tilted her chin up and kissed her gently on the lips.

113

She felt herself tense up. "Sorry. I thought that would make me sick."

Antonio's eyebrows shot up. "What!"

Angelica burst out laughing. "Not your kiss, moving my head like that."

She could tell from his expression he didn't find it funny. "Love you." She brushed past him into the garage.

As Angelica approached the freeway exit for her office, she glanced at her watch and saw it was only eight o'clock. She hadn't been to work before nine in weeks. It was going to be a great day.

She noticed the outlines of the tape beneath the sleeves of her blouse. She had to admit she didn't know if she believed that a pebble and some tape could cure morning sickness, or even help, but something was making her feel better. She'd chosen to wear long sleeves so no one would ask her about it.

Angelica wished she spoke "Mexican" so she could get to know Maclovia better. Her job as a public defender was incredibly demanding, and she was seldom home during the day. When she was, she'd tried to draw Maclovia out. But the old woman always declined her offers of shopping or going out to lunch, in favor of sitting in her bedroom by the window or taking Buddy for a walk. Even the clothes Angelica had bought for her remained in Maclovia's closet. Maclovia always wore one of the three or four dresses she'd brought with her in her bag. Still, she seemed content in their home, and there was a certain peace and gentleness that her presence brought to the house. So like Antonio.

A shadow clouded her thoughts. Being peaceful and gentle in America did have a downside when it came to business. Antonio had told her his clients, the Jessicks, had called. They'd told him that another landscaper had come to their home and said they were paying too much for yard work. The man had offered to do their yard for ten percent less than whatever they were paying, and though they were happy with Antonio's work, they'd decided to try the man out.

Angelica's grip tightened on the wheel. She'd told Antonio to go back to them and say he'd match the guy. That would beat him at his own game. But Antonio had said no. He'd said the Jessicks were pleased with his work and had said his price was fair when they hired him. He saw no wisdom in lowering his price and proving the man right. He didn't even seem to hold it against the Jessicks for dumping him. She whipped around the car in front of her. He was going to have to get tough if he wanted to build a business. This wasn't Mexico.

Angelica parked the car and hurried into the office. She stopped at the reception desk.

"Hi, Fronie. I've got to go to court this morning, but I should be back by noon. Then I'll be working in my office for the rest of the day. Did you bring your lunch?"

Fronie took a call, then forwarded it. "Yes, what's up?"

"Why don't you eat in my office? I need to talk. You know, girl talk."

"Sure."

Angelica rarely had time to take a real lunch break, and the two friends often shared a few minutes around noon to catch up on each other's lives. Today she wanted to talk about what had happened at the doctor's office. She hadn't told anyone about it, not even her parents; there was no need to worry them.

Angelica gathered what she needed from her office and made the short walk to superior court. After she handled the arraignment calendar, she pulled the court file on the Vasquez case and made copies of the documents.

115

As Angelica got to the steps of her building, her cell phone rang. *The doctor's office.* She stopped and flipped the phone open. "This is Angelica."

"Hi, honey. It's Mom."

For as long as Angelica had worked, she'd tried to persuade her mother not to call her during business hours. She hated cutting her mother short, but her job just didn't give her the luxury of having lengthy social chats. "Mom, I'm in the middle of a busy day, and I've got to leave my phone line open. Did you need something?"

"I hope you're not too busy for your mother."

Hearing the edge in her mother's voice, Angelica grimaced. "Of course not, Mom."

"Your dad and I wanted to stop by tonight. Would that be okay?"

Her parents rarely dropped by. They had a full social calendar and somehow thought it was Angelica's duty to come and visit them.

"We haven't spent any time with Maclovia, other than that one afternoon you all stopped by." Her mother's voice was firm.

Angelica pulled the phone away from her ear and looked at it. Something was up. "That's a great idea. But I was planning on going to Bible study tonight. Could you come tomorrow night instead? Antonio and Maclovia love to barbeque. It'd be fun."

"Angelica, your dad and I have set aside this evening to visit with you. You can go to Bible study any night."

Angelica knew by the tone of her mother's voice that trying to make her Bible study a priority would only result in hard feelings. She *had* been working late a lot. Antonio never complained or pressured her, and he'd be delighted to see her home early. "How about coming over after dinner then, around seven?" Angelica heard a click on the phone, another call was coming in. "Got to go, Mom. Will I see you at seven?"

"We'll be there. Love you."

Angelica pressed a key to take the second call. "This is Angelica."

"This is Dr. Gremian's office. We have your blood results."

Angelica's stomach flip-flopped. "What did they show?"

"The HCG quantitative indicates the baby is sixteen weeks old."

"Dr. Gremian thought the baby measured small for sixteen weeks." She tried to stay calm. "What does this mean?" She sat down on the steps.

"Your chart shows that Dr. Gremian also ordered an AFP. Those results aren't back yet. We'll call you as soon as we get them."

The nurse's words sounded carefully chosen.

"I know that. But what does *this* mean?"

"Dr. Gremian will go over everything at your next appointment."

Angelica's heart sank. She wanted this phone call to be someone telling her she was wrong about her dates. She wanted this phone call to confirm everything was going to be all right. Instead, she felt helpless and frightened. "What does this mean? Is something wrong?"

"This test doesn't show anything is wrong. Dr. Gremian will go over things with you at your appointment."

"Thank you." Angelica flipped the phone shut. *"This test doesn't show anything is wrong."* What did that mean? Some other test would?

She closed her eyes. *Lord, I know You're in control. I*

know everything will be okay. It just feels scary right now.
She searched her memory for a verse to claim. Something
to calm the uneasiness the phone call had fostered.

"*My peace I give to you; not as the world gives do I
give to you. Let not your heart be troubled, neither let it
be afraid.*"

"That is what You promised, Lord, and that is what I
need right now. Please give me Your peace." She drew a
deep breath.

"Angelica, you feeling okay?" It was Kit Elliott, another
attorney in the office, on her way out of the building.

"Oh. Fine. I'm fine."

Kit smiled at her. "I remember when I was expecting my
twins. Can't tell you how many times I sat on these steps
just to get fresh air. Sure you're okay?"

"Yes, and thanks." Angelica got up and hurried to her
office.

She sat at her desk and stared at the files and papers. She
needed to focus, to trust God and not borrow trouble. She
set her jaw and picked up a transcript from the Vasquez
indictment. For the next hour, she shut everything out and
studied the documents, underlining and making notes.

"Hey, girl." Fronie's voice brought Angelica to the present.
"Ready for a break?"

"Is it lunchtime already?" Angelica glanced at her computer's clock. It seemed like she'd been reading for only a
few minutes.

Fronie held up her red nylon lunch bag. "Sure is." She
slipped into the chair next to Angelica's desk. "How about
helping me with this?"

Angelica watched as Fronie lifted a sandwich, an apple,
and a bottle of juice from the sack.

"I'm not hungry right now, thanks." Angelica set aside

the transcript she'd been reading and rubbed her forehead.

Fronie rested her hand on Angelica's arm. "Why don't you let me get you a glass of cool water?" Before Angelica could answer, Fronie was out the door and on her way down the hall.

"Here you go." Fronie put a cup of water in front of Angelica, then she stacked four thick law books from Angelica's bookcase on the floor by Angelica's chair. "Now, you just kick off those shoes, put your feet up, and talk to me."

This was what had made them fast friends. From their first meeting, they'd had a connection. Each always seemed to know just what the other needed, Angelica giving pointed counsel during a few rocky months of Fronie's marriage, and Fronie giving tempered perspective to Angelica's often intense and analytical responses to the ups and downs of daily life.

Angelica stepped out of her shoes, shut the door, and put her feet up on the books. Then she leaned forward, her elbows on her knees. "Fronie, I'm scared."

Her friend's face filled with compassion. "About what?"

"The baby." Saying it out loud somehow helped.

Fronie set her sandwich down. "Why, sweetie?"

"It just seems that nothing is going right. I've been so sick." She rubbed her hand over her forearm. "And I just found out that the baby is small for sixteen weeks."

"My mom was sick with both us kids for the whole nine months, and I was only five pounds, four ounces when I was born." She spoke with a matter-of-factness that brought a simple reality to Angelica's fears; sometimes pregnancies weren't easy.

"Really?" Angelica's shoulders relaxed slightly.

"We laugh about it now. After I was born, she said she learned her lesson—no more kids." Fronie picked up her sandwich. "Besides, babies grow the most in the last six weeks. You're going to be fine."

Angelica bit her lower lip. "Fronie, I want to show you something. But promise you won't laugh."

Fronie put her sandwich down. "What?"

Angelica hesitated, then rolled up her sleeve.

Fronie's eyes widened. "What's that?"

"Antonio's grandmother put a little rock under that tape." She glanced at Fronie's face. "And somehow it's helping my morning sickness."

"For goodness' sake." Fronie reached over and rubbed her finger across the tape. "There's lots of old-fashioned remedies that work better than modern ones."

Angelica's mouth curved into a smile. "That's true, isn't it? I don't know why it seemed kind of weird to me." She rolled her sleeve back down. "Maybe I will have a bite of your sandwich."

Fronie broke a piece off and gave it to her.

Angelica took a bite and swallowed. "It's been great having Maclovia with us, but she's kind of mysterious. I've tried to get to know her, but there's a definite language barrier. Her Spanish and the Spanish I've learned aren't the same." Angelica shook her head. "There's a cultural barrier too. Even Antonio seems kind of primitive in his thinking about having a baby. He means well, but it seems like he just wants to accept whatever happens."

"Give it time. It'll work out." Fronie gave her a conspiratorial look. "The two of them probably think *you're* strange."

They laughed, and Angelica began to relax. "My par-

120

ents are coming over tonight to visit us. They've only met Maclovia once."

Fronie rolled her eyes. "That'll be interesting."

"Won't it? But that means I can't go to Bible study." Angelica took a sip of water. "Would you please tell the group about the baby being small and ask them to pray for me? Oh, and let Jan Wilcox know that I'm still praying for her sister's son-in-law, Bill, and his landscaping business."

"I will." Fronie picked up her apple. "Don't you worry. God is in control."

"I keep telling myself that." Angelica's eyes drifted to the floor. "I hope it's true."

Antonio slowly nodded his head as he traced the black line to the letter D with his finger. "That is what they mean."

Maclovia stared blankly at the letters and lines that covered the big sheet of paper spread out on the floor. "I don't know how you can understand anything on that paper." She clucked her tongue. "It looks like matted hair to me."

Antonio turned his head to the side, hiding his smile, not wanting to disrespect his grandmother. "I spent a lot of time at Wal-Mart studying how this crib was put together. Look here." He pointed to the big diagram. "If you follow these arrows, they show you how things fit together."

Maclovia shrugged her shoulders and sat on the couch. Buddy took his place by her feet.

"I know I can do this. *Abuela*, would you help me lay out all the pieces on the floor?"

For the rest of the morning, Antonio studied the pieces of the crib and found the matching pictures on the papers that had come in the box. When the phone rang, he was attaching G to H.

He hurriedly tiptoed through the scattered crib parts and got to the phone just before the machine picked up. "Hello."

"Hi, it's me. I was hoping I'd catch you home for lunch."

He smiled at the sound of his wife's voice. "How you feel?"

"I feel good. I've gotten a ton of work done today. I'm calling to let you know that my parents are coming over tonight."

Antonio glanced toward the living room. "Oh? When?"

"They're coming at seven. Mother said they want to visit with Maclovia."

"Why now?" Many times over the past weeks, Antonio had wanted to ask Angelica why her parents never invited Maclovia to their home, or to meet their friends, as would have been proper in his country. He suspected it was for the same reason they rarely included him in their lives, so he'd held his tongue, not wanting to make his wife uncomfortable.

"Who knows? But I'm glad they're finally taking an interest in her."

"I am glad too. She is part of our family."

This was something Antonio didn't understand about the Americans. They separated their families. He had observed that most parents looked forward to the day when their children would leave home and live on their own. And he had never seen any of his clients' parents living in the homes he maintained. He had even heard of people giving their parents away to other people who would take care of them. The Amantes' sudden interest in Maclovia didn't ring true to him. But it would be wrong of him to judge their decision to visit. "When will you be home?"

"In time for dinner. Um, Antonio?"

"*Sí, señorita.*" He waited patiently for her to answer.

"Do you think tonight Maclovia would wear one of the dresses I bought for her?"

Antonio understood his wife's request. It was not a rejection of his grandmother; rather it was an effort to make her acceptable to Angelica's parents. However, he knew his grandmother well, and she would want to be accepted on her own terms. "I will do my best, Angel. You no worry."

"See you tonight. Love you." He heard Angelica hang up the phone.

When he returned to the living room, Maclovia was tightening the bolt he'd inserted in H.

"*Abuela*, Angelica's parents are coming to visit us tonight." He took the screwdriver from her.

Maclovia stepped back and put her hands on her hips. "Then we'd better hurry and get this finished." She looked at him, her eyes bright. "I want them to see how smart my grandson is. And what a good provider you are."

Looking at his precious grandmother, head up and chest out, Antonio suddenly knew one thing. Angelica's parents' absence from their lives had not gone unnoticed by her. "They must think I'm smart." He winked at her. "I chose their daughter for my wife, didn't I?"

"I would say the daughter got the best of that arrangement."

Maclovia's wise eyes, fixed on his, told him in no uncertain terms that she too found the ways of the Americans unusual.

She drew herself up. "And I will wear a special dress. Your wife has given me many pretty things. I have been keeping them in my closet for just the right moment. I've only worn one dress, for a special meeting with God."

Antonio lowered his eyes remembering Maclovia's refusal to return to Faith Community Church after attending one service. Nothing Antonio said convinced her that the casual dress, loud music, hand clapping, and hand raising were just different ways of worshipping the same God whom she approached on her knees in silence and humble awe. "You do not find God by screaming for His attention," she'd told him. "You find God by longing for Him. That is when He draws you to Him." This was her belief, and he respected it. He'd not asked her to go with them again.

Maclovia reached down and picked up the big instruction sheet. "What's next?"

They spent the next several hours putting together, and sometimes taking apart, the crib. It was almost five o'clock when they finished.

Maclovia took the hem of her skirt and polished the crib one final time. "Are you going to leave it here so her parents can see it when they arrive? It is such a fine piece, Angelica might want to keep it here."

"No, let's roll it into the baby's room and shut the door. I want to surprise her."

After the crib was in place, Maclovia got the blue blanket she'd made and laid it over the side of the crib.

Angelica didn't get home until after six o'clock. She and Antonio had just finished putting away the dinner dishes, and Maclovia was still dressing, when the doorbell rang.

"*Buenas noches, patrón* and Mrs. Amante." Antonio stepped to the side.

"Mom and Dad, it's so good to see you." Angelica gave them each a hug. "Come on in. Here, sit on the couch."

Mrs. Amante looked around the room. "Where's Maclovia?"

"Antonio, why don't you go see what's keeping her?"

Antonio found his grandmother in her room, standing in front of her dresser mirror in a simple yellow shift, braiding her hair. "Are you almost ready?"

She wrapped the long braid around the top of her head and secured it. Then she picked up a fresh rose and stuck it in the side of the plaits. "I'm ready."

"You look beautiful." He offered her his arm.

She slipped her arm through his, and they walked together down the hall to the living room.

Antonio seated Maclovia in the side chair next to the couch, then joined Angelica on the love seat. Everyone sat in silence.

"Well, I bet you're wondering why we're here." The *patrón* stood, as if he were about to make a speech.

"Mom said you wanted to get to know Maclovia better."

Antonio's mother-in-law tapped her husband's foot with the point of her shoe. "That's right, Ben. Sit down." She turned to Maclovia. "How are you?"

Antonio quickly translated.

Maclovia smiled around her bottom tooth and tilted her head. "*Bien, señora.*"

"She says she's fine," Angelica informed her mother. "We love having her here."

"Tell her she certainly looks pretty tonight." Mrs. Amante smiled at Maclovia as though Maclovia were a well-behaved child.

Antonio translated for his grandmother.

Maclovia smiled and tilted her head.

Everyone sat in silence.

"Well, she certainly seems like a sweet lady." Mrs. Amante

125

turned toward her husband, her back closing the conversation with Maclovia. "Angelica . . . and Antonio. We have a surprise."

The *patrón* stood. "Your mother and I talked about it. . . ." He glanced at his wife. "And we decided to have a crib custom-made for our grandchild."

Angelica's mother jumped up. "It arrived this morning. That's when I called you, Angelica. It was made in Italy." She started toward the front door, talking over her shoulder. "Antonio. Would you please come get the box out of our trunk?"

The *patrón* rushed past her, reaching the front door first and leaving it open on his way out to the car.

Antonio looked at Angelica.

"Isn't that sweet? I had no idea." Angelica turned to follow her parents outside.

Antonio grabbed her hand. "Wait. I too have a surprise."

Angelica stopped, her voice uncertain. "Can it wait until after my parents leave?"

He shook his head and gently pushed her back down on the love seat. "Wait."

Antonio ran down the hall and opened the door to the baby's room. He carefully wheeled the crib into the living room.

Angelica's hand flew to her lips. "Oh. Where did you get that?"

The sound of the *patrón* dragging something through the front door kept Antonio from answering. He stepped toward Angelica's father and helped him with the big box. They leaned it against the wall.

"What's *that*?" Angelica's mother pointed to the crib standing in the living room.

Antonio saw his wife blinking back tears.

126

He shot his mother-in-law a glance. "I buy for my wife and son. I make it myself." His eyes returned to his wife's face. Was she happy, sad . . . surprised?

"How did you buy it?" Angelica was obviously trying to keep her composure.

"I save money from extra jobs." He rubbed his hand over the crib's side railing.

Maclovia rose and stepped beside Antonio. She moved the blue blanket an inch or so toward the center of the top rail.

"My grandmother make this blanket."

"Why. Uh. It's beautiful. . . ." Angelica turned toward her parents. "Isn't it."

"Very lovely, dear."

Antonio recognized his mother-in-law's tone of voice. Her words were lifeless, hardly strong enough to leave her lips.

The *patrón* stepped toward the crib and took a closer look at it. "That's quite nice. Perhaps you two could put it in your bedroom for when the baby comes home."

"That's a wonderful idea, Ben." Suddenly her words danced in the air. "We can put our little crib in the nursery, Angelica. I've even contacted a man who can come over and assemble it. There are other matching pieces that I can order." She looked toward the big box. "We can do the whole room. My crib is white with carved cherubs and caning. I thought we'd get the French chest to match."

Antonio watched his mother-in-law as she spoke. He did not understand all the words, but it was clear his crib did not have cherubs and caning. And it seemed somehow that she thought it should have; he felt heat in his cheeks. He looked at his wife. She was still upset.

Suddenly, Antonio felt as though he were alone in the

room. The voices became muted, and his thoughts became clear. This was his home, his wife, and his child. He would not be made to feel somehow inadequate. He would not allow Angelica's parents to steal his joy. "*Con permiso. Perdone.*"

All eyes turned to him.

"*Patrón*, you are right. It *es necesario* for two cribs. I am thinking that our baby will visit your house, no?"

"Of course." The Amantes answered in unison.

"Then, if you think your crib is best in our house, we will let you put our crib in your house. For his room there."

Mrs. Amante's eyes widened. Antonio thought he heard the *patrón* make a gulping sound. They stared at him wordlessly.

He looked at Angelica. "What do you think?"

She stepped toward him and kissed his cheek. "I think that your crib is perfect for our nursery." She picked up the blanket and admired the handwork. "And I think we'll paint the walls just this shade of blue."

Then she turned to her mother. "Don't worry about hiring a man to put that beautiful crib together. I'm sure Antonio would be glad to help Daddy."

Antonio's heart nearly burst with pride. He took the baby blanket from Angelica. Turning slowly, he carefully laid it over the crib rail; his eyes lowered, blinking rapidly.

Maclovia rose from her knees and walked the few feet from her bedroom to the baby's room. She had not understood all that had gone on. Antonio had only said Angelica's parents had bought a crib for themselves. She picked up the edge of her skirt and ran it over the railings of the beautiful piece of furniture her grandson had made for her great-grandchild. She was glad Angelica's parents had taken their big box back to their big house.

She began to hum.

The image of Angelica lying on her bed that morning appeared to her. She immediately stood still, focused on the memory. Angelica, with her face buried in her pillow, clearly suffering the early days of motherhood.

She felt God present with her, speaking to her, showing her something special and unique about the baby. Angelica's suffering was for a purpose.

8

ANGELICA LEANED OVER Max's shoulder to read the document on his computer screen. "I agree. That case is right on point for the Vasquez appeal." She straightened and returned to the chair by his desk. "His bail hearing is this afternoon. I've got to run out to a doctor's appointment at eleven o'clock, but I'll be back in plenty of time for the hearing."

Funny how a few short weeks ago she had been leery of being alone with Max in his office. Now she thought nothing of working by his side, even late at night. He had a brilliant legal mind and a great sense of humor, which, she had to admit, helped a lot at the end of a twelve-hour day. He *was* a flirt, and she could see how he got himself into trouble. Still, it took two to tango, and the women who'd fallen victim to his charm were equally responsible for the consequences. He'd never been anything other than a perfect gentleman with her. In fact, they worked with a kind of mutual admiration, two colleagues, driven and focused on a common goal. Justice for Vasquez.

Max clicked on the "Close" command. "It's good to know this appearance will be in your capable hands. I've got to meet with the county commissioners this afternoon."

Hearing his compliment, Angelica felt the heat rise in her cheeks. This would be her first bail hearing. One more step along the coveted path to an eventual promotion. It seemed Max was giving her every possible opportunity to shine in this high-profile case, and she didn't want to let him down. It was incredibly generous that Max would treat her as an equal partner.

"I'm glad you feel I'm carrying my weight. There's no way I could have gotten this kind of experience if you hadn't opened this door for me." She hesitated, then decided to share what was in her heart. "You know, Max, it's not just a matter of Miguel Vasquez's legal right to bail. It's a matter of what's morally right. He's innocent, and he's already been in jail a year."

Max nodded. "I agree. And if I didn't have complete confidence in you, I'd go to the hearing myself. I told you at our first meeting that Dave thought you were one of the brightest young attorneys on staff. He was right; you've more than measured up to your billing." Max's face became serious. "He admired and respected you . . . and so do I."

Angelica busied herself, gathering up her papers and files that were spread out across Max's desk. His words made her feel that he was moving their working relationship to the next level. Yet the closed office door, the confidentiality of what they were saying, their common cause, somehow gave an intimacy to the moment that made her uncomfortable. "I'll finish this up in my office and then get to my doctor's appointment." She stepped toward the door. "I'll talk to you this afternoon and let you know what happened at the hearing."

"I should be back here by the time it's over."

Angelica went to her office. She did little more than get organized before she had to leave for her doctor's appointment. She wished Antonio were going with her, but when she'd checked with the nurse the day before, she'd been told the AFP results still weren't in, and she and Antonio had decided there was no reason to interrupt his work and study for her routine appointment.

She suddenly missed him. She looked at her watch. It was early for him to be home for lunch, but maybe . . . She picked up the phone and dialed. The machine answered.

"Hi, honey. I'm going to the doctor now. Then I'll be coming back to work. I'll call you later. Love you." As she hung up the phone, she felt tears prick her eyes. "What's the matter with me? I'm acting like a child. Everything's working out just fine."

She rubbed her arm where the pebble and tape had been until a few days before. Her morning sickness had almost disappeared. *Praise You, Lord.* Max had reassigned most of her cases, making her workload manageable. *Thank You.* And Antonio had picked up two new accounts, replacing two he'd lost. *God, You are so good.* Thoughts of Antonio's job brought Bill to mind, and her promise to pray for him. *Please bless Bill's business.* She remembered Jan Wilcox's plea for his salvation. *And more important, Lord, send someone across his path to show him Your love.*

As Angelica drove to Dr. Gremian's office, her thoughts turned to her child . . . Ben. Antonio was so sure it was a boy, they'd started calling him Baby Ben. It delighted her parents. Most of the family get-togethers ended up being about plans for Ben's future. She giggled, remembering how heated the discussion had become over whether he would be an attorney, or a heart surgeon like her father. Benito had finally stamped his foot and declared that funds would be available to finance a medical career. Law school would be up to the Perez family. As silence settled over his declaration and his scowl grew deeper, she'd burst out laughing. That had given the moment perspective, and her father had begun to chuckle. Both knew Ben would choose his own career, and they would support it. It wasn't about them; it was about him.

Angelica checked in with the nurse and took a seat in the busy waiting room. She found an empty spot next to a professional-looking woman reading *People*. As Angelica tucked her purse between her thigh and the side of the chair, she noticed the woman's arms. There were blue bands above each of her wrists. She looked at the woman's face, wondering if she was Mexican.

Angelica shifted in her chair, toward her. "Excuse me."

The woman put down the magazine and smiled.

"I noticed those bands on your arms. Would you mind telling me what they are?"

The woman's pleasant smile widened. "I think they're the greatest. They're called travel bands. They're for motion sickness." She held one arm out and turned her palm up. "See that button? You put it three finger widths above the wrist." She slipped the band down and pointed to a spot between the two tendons of her hand. "Right there is the Nei-Kuan-Point. They're for motion sickness, but they've really helped me with morning sickness."

"You're kidding. I never heard of them." Angelica lowered her voice. "My husband's grandmother is from Mexico, and she taped a pebble on my arm in the same spot."

"Did it help?" The woman slipped the band back in place.

"It did. But I thought maybe it was a coincidence. I'm over morning sickness now."

"There are lots of old-fashioned remedies that work better than new ones. Is this your first child?"

"Yes. Are you here to see Dr. Gremian?"

"No, just one of the nurses this time."

"Angelica Perez." The nurse's voice interrupted them.

Angelica rose and followed the nurse to the scale, then to an exam room.

The nurse performed the standard routine, including taking Angelica's blood pressure and temperature, then she made notes in Angelica's file. "You're doing great." She looked up at Angelica. "Any problems? Anything you need to talk to the doctor about?"

"No, I'm just waiting for my AFP test results."

The nurse smiled at her. "Here's a gown. Dr. Gremian will be in soon."

Angelica slipped out of her clothes and into the gown. She'd just scooted onto the table when she heard a knock and the door opened.

"Good morning, Angelica." Dr. Gremian took her hand and helped her lie back. "How have you been feeling?"

"Thank the Lord I haven't had any morning sickness for a week."

"Have you felt the baby kicking?" Dr. Gremian placed the tip of the measuring tape at her pubic bone and measured to her belly button.

"Not yet." Angelica thought for a moment. "Do you think that's because the baby's small?"

Dr. Gremian seemed pensive as he rubbed gel on her stomach and listened to the baby's heartbeat. He made a note in her file and then helped her sit up. "The lab called me this morning about your AFP test, and I just got the faxed results." He sat on a stool next to the exam table.

She stiffened. "And?"

"It showed a lower than normal level of alpha-feto-protein."

Angelica anxiously searched the doctor's face for the meaning behind his words. "What does this mean? Is my baby all right?"

"What it means is that there is an increased chance that your child could have a chromosome abnormality. About one in two hundred and thirty."

Angelica felt overrun by conflicting emotions. Relief that the chances sounded very small that anything was wrong. Fear that one chance was all that was needed to turn conjecture into certainty. "What kind of chromosome abnormality?"

"Such as Turner's, Klinefelter's, or Down syndromes . . ."

"Dr. Gremian, this is scaring me." She took an unsteady breath and tried to focus on what the doctor was saying.

He put his hand on her arm. "I saw no physical markers for any of these syndromes on the ultrasound. The baby is a little small. But these tests are only sixty percent accurate. I suggest that you see a genetic counselor, and we'll schedule a level two ultrasound. We'll be able to check all of the bone lengths, the heart, the brain, and lots of other things. That will give us a complete picture."

Angelica struggled to keep control of her emotions. "If everything shows that my baby has one of these birth defects, is there anything that can be done?"

"There is nothing that can be done to change the outcome if you decide to have the baby. But it's premature to talk about that. Let's do some additional testing and schedule an appointment with a genetic counselor for you and your husband."

Her husband.

Suddenly, the reality of her situation gripped her. Antonio had not wanted any testing done at all. She'd made a point of telling him *her* blood was being tested for the alpha-feto-protein. Now the doctor was suggesting additional testing. Testing to find out if the baby had birth defects.

Dr. Gremian stood. "When you stop at the front desk, the nurse will make your appointments. I recommend The Genetic Institute in Santa Rosa. I've referred to them often."

"Thank you, Dr. Gremian." Angelica watched the door close behind him.

Alone, she suddenly became aware of the sterile coldness of the room, the faint smell of rubbing alcohol, the gray linoleum tiles on the floor. She put her hand on her stomach. *Dear God, make everything all right. Don't ruin our lives.*

She must stay positive. Dwelling on the worst case scenario would accomplish nothing. Instead, she would hope and pray for the best case, pursuing the facts and dealing with whatever they revealed. She began to dress.

She picked up her purse, then stopped and looked in the small mirror on the back of the exam room door. She ran her fingers through her hair, pulling it away from her face. The gold of her simple wedding band caught the light. Antonio.

As she walked to the office counter, the memory of the drive to the airport to pick up Maclovia came to her. Antonio sitting next to her in the car. "Why would we want to test our son? He's just a baby."

"I have your file right here." The nurse behind the counter interrupted her thoughts. "Now you want to see a genetic counselor. Is that right?"

Angelica hesitated. As clear as if he were standing next to her, she heard Antonio's voice. "Why would we want to test our son?"

The bail hearing had been a disaster.

Angelica picked up the phone and pressed the button to ring Max at his desk. No answer. She looked at her watch. His meeting with the commissioners must be running long. Couldn't anything go right today?

After the upsetting news from Dr. Gremian, traffic had been heavy, and she'd barely made it to the courthouse on time. When she'd gotten inside, she'd realized she'd forgotten the file that contained the letters of support for Miguel Vasquez that they'd received from members of the community. She'd felt completely rattled and had had to talk about them from memory. Then the DA had dropped a bombshell. She picked up the phone and tried to ring Max again. No answer.

She turned back to her computer screen and clicked on the next site listed in the search results for alpha-fetoprotein. Information. That's what she needed. Knowledge was power. She wasn't going to let fear stalk her for the rest of her pregnancy. Everything she was reading confirmed that the AFP test was only an indicator. There *might* be a problem. That's what Dr. Gremian had said.

She walked over to her window and looked out at the beautiful summer day. There was additional testing she could have that would be definitive . . . but then what? Why did she even have to think about this? Why couldn't her pregnancy be normal, her baby perfect? *God, where are You?*

She felt a flutter in her tummy. A movement.

"Angelica?"

She whirled around. "Max."

"You should see the look on your face." He stepped toward her. "You okay?"

"I . . ." She put her hand on her tummy. "I think I just felt my baby move!"

Max tilted his head, his eyes tender, his smile sweet. "I remember when my wife was expecting." He shook his head slowly. "But if you think that's something, wait until they put that baby in your arms."

His words brought everything back to her. Dr. Gremian, the sterile exam room, genetic counseling, chromosomal defects.

She broke down. Biting her lip to control herself, her body shook.

Max stepped toward her. Suddenly, she was in his arms, sobbing into his chest. She felt his hand gently stroking her hair.

"What's wrong?" His voice was a whisper.

Angelica could feel the rough texture of his suit against her cheek, the rapid beat of his heart beneath it. She stepped away from him. She felt an unwelcome blush creep into her cheeks. Her mind began to clear, and she was acutely aware of what had just happened. Nothing. Everything.

She turned away from Max and reached for her purse. Keeping her head down, she dug through it, looking for a tissue.

"Here." Max offered her a handkerchief.

"No, I'm fine." She wiped her eyes with her fingertips. "Sorry." She put her purse down, smoothed her skirt and jacket, and stepped around the desk to her chair, angry with herself for breaking down. Angry that she'd put herself in such an embarrassing situation.

"Do you want to talk about it?" He sat down.

Angelica studied his face. It was filled with kindness. Yes, she did want to talk about it, badly. But this wasn't the place, the time, or the person. She wasn't going to share this with her boss before she told her husband. She wasn't going to do anything that Max could interpret as beyond the scope of their work together.

"It's just that I've had an incredibly upsetting day." She pulled her files in front of her. "The judge increased Vasquez's bail."

Max's eyes narrowed slightly. For a second she thought he was going to call her on her obvious attempt to change the direction of the conversation. But he let it pass. "What happened?"

Angelica opened the Vasquez file and quickly scanned her notes. "Bail was set at forty thousand dollars." She looked at Max, waiting for his response. He nodded.

She sat back in her chair. "That was stated at the arraignment, and it's been widely reported in the papers. In fact, it was rumored that the 'Free Vasquez' people had raised the ten percent necessary to bail him out."

Max nodded again.

"I was prepared to argue that the age of this case and the new evidence certainly justified reducing the bail. With every Hispanic media outlet on the court steps, we figured worst case, the bail would remain at forty thousand dollars."

Max unbuttoned the front of his jacket, leaned back, and folded his arms.

"But the DA argued that the bail schedule was fifty thousand dollars and it should be reinstated at the original amount." She held Max's eye. "I was totally unprepared for that."

"Curse."

Angelica almost smiled. When they'd first started working together, Max had freely punctuated his language with expletives. Finally, she'd told him she found it offensive. To her surprise, the confident, suave, in-control chief public defender had turned red in the face. From then on, he'd stuck with saying only "curse."

"The DA's point was, since there was no proven change in circumstances, and the bail was set below the bail schedule, what was the court's justification?"

"Da . . . Curse."

"The judge set the bail at the bail schedule amount, fifty thousand dollars, and wouldn't allow further argument." Angelica snapped her fingers. "That took care of the court having to justify anything."

Max let out a deep sigh. "It's not your fault. I don't know that I would have handled it any differently."

"I should have researched this more, I should have anticipated it. If I had, I could have asked that the matter be dropped from the calendar, and they wouldn't have had a chance to open their mouths. I feel like I didn't do everything possible for Miguel Vasquez."

"Angelica, it's a risk we took when we set up the hearing."

Angelica lowered her voice. "I have to admit, I didn't fully understand that."

"Look. We're where we are, and we have to go from here." Max looked at his watch. "I hate to ask you to stay late again, but we've got to put our heads together and outline a strategy. Let's meet in the conference room."

Angelica's stomach knotted. She wanted to go home. She wanted to talk to Antonio about their child, about everything that had happened. That was more important than working the case. Surely, they could begin tomorrow.

Max rose and started toward his office. At the door, he

stopped and turned to her. "We'll prove there *has* been a change in circumstances. Not only that, it's compelling evidence." His face was somber. "Will you stay?"

Angelica looked away. How much more did she have to give? She looked back at Max, hoping he'd read her face and would let her leave.

His eyes met hers. "A man's freedom is at stake."

Antonio pulled his mower down the two wooden boards that ran from the truck tailgate to the street. The Catellis' house was the last house of the afternoon. He had planned it that way; he wanted to catch Mr. Catelli at home.

Antonio looked at the truck in the driveway and sounded out the words in the circle on the side of the door. "Ci-ty of Val-le de La-gri-mas." Yes, that was the same truck he'd seen at the park when he'd driven home from school last week. He'd thought it was Mr. Catelli talking to the men who were mowing the park, pointing and walking with them. Maybe Mr. Catelli needed more workers. This was the wonderful thing about America—anyone could ask for work. When he finished today, he would knock on the door.

He looked at his hands. They were dirty and grass stained. Maybe he'd go home and clean up first.

He turned to the lawn and began to walk around the edges to make sure the sprinkler heads were all down. He'd learned all about sprinkler systems at his own house. For some reason, when Angelica got in a hurry backing out of the garage, she'd run over the edge of their lawn. She'd broken those sprinkler heads at least four times since they'd lived there. Thinking about it, his face broke into a smile. She didn't even realize she did it. He'd never told her. His wife had enough on her mind without worrying about sprinklers.

Antonio put his hands on his hips and surveyed the lawn. It didn't look strong and healthy; it needed more water. He could see a brown spot starting near the sidewalk. It was surprising how the look of the yard had declined since his visit the week before.

He steepled his fingers beneath his chin. Maybe the sprinkler timer needed adjusting. He looked toward the garage. . . . He didn't know much about timers. They had lots of written instructions, but not many pictures. Still, his job was to take care of the grass. He strode toward the door on the side of the garage.

He felt around for a light switch. Before he touched it, the lights went on.

"Is that you, Antonio?"

"*Sí*, Mr. Catelli. I need look at the sprinkler box." Antonio wiped his palms on his pants, then walked toward the man, his hand extended.

Mr. Catelli's face was serious. "You're not in here shutting off the timer again, are you?"

"I no shut off timer." Antonio dropped his hand. "Grass needs *more* water."

"I noticed that myself a few days ago and came in here to set the sprinklers to come on more often." He folded his arms across his chest. "The timer was shut off."

Antonio straightened his back. "I no turn timer off."

"Maybe you messed with it and didn't know what you were doing." The man's face was filled with disapproval.

Antonio held his gaze. "I no touch timer. Today I see grass thirsty, I come look."

Antonio saw the quirk at the corner of Mr. Catelli's mouth. The man who hired people for the city didn't believe him.

"Well, the timer's set now. Leave it be." He turned and started back into the house. "I hired you to take care of my

142

lawn. I don't expect to have to do it myself." At the door, he turned back toward Antonio. "My neighbors just hired a man. He's doin' a fine job. Costs him less too." Mr. Catelli put his hands on his hips. "Ya know. Now that I think about it. Why fool around?" He raised his finger, pointing at Antonio. "You're fired." The door shut with a bang.

Antonio stood staring at the closed door.

Deeply saddened, he walked around to the front yard. Not only did Mr. Catelli think he'd done a bad job, the man clearly thought he didn't know the difference between "on" and "off."

He looked up and down the street. All the lawns looked green. It was true. This one yard had become noticeably inferior to the others. He looked at the house next door that Mr. Catelli had spoken about. "Costs him less too." That was the second time he'd heard that.

His thoughts filtered back through his accounts. This was the third one he'd lost. The Jessicks, when B.J., the man he'd somehow offended, targeted him, a client who'd moved, and now Mr. Catelli. His accounts were dwindling.

He grabbed his mower and pushed it up into the truck bed. He would tell Angelica what had happened and ask her to put an ad in the paper. He'd avoided that up until now because he didn't read and write well enough to take ad calls. If people called and gave their names and directions to their houses, he couldn't write them down. If they left messages on the answering machine, Angelica would have to return the calls. He hated to ask her to take on part of his job. She was already carrying more than half of the financial load of their marriage. It was important to him that he not become a burden to his wife. It was important to him to take care of her. He shut the tailgate, jumped into the truck, and headed home.

When he walked into the house the tantalizing smell of *mole* greeted him. His steps quickened as he headed to the kitchen.

Maclovia's back was to him. She was standing in front of the stove, pots on every burner. Steam poured from one pot, and Antonio could see a dark brown sauce bubbling next to it. As he approached, she turned.

"Ah. You're home. Good." She wiped her hands on her apron and stepped to the side so Antonio could inspect each pot. "There just wasn't room on the stove outside."

"Oh, boy. Tamales." He sniffed the sauce. "And *mole*." He pinched his grandmother's cheek. "And look at you, young lady, cooking like a *gringa*."

Maclovia beamed. "It's not as good as cooking on my stove outside or the fire at home, but it is good to learn new things." She picked up a wooden spoon and stirred her sauce. "When will your *señora* be home?"

Antonio looked at his watch and shrugged his shoulders. It was past six. "She went to her doctor's appointment today, and that always means she has to stay late." He stepped toward the phone. "I'll call her."

He dialed the number he knew to be the phone on her desk. A man answered.

Antonio hesitated. "Angelica there?"

His wife's voice came over the line. "Hi."

"Who is that man?" He'd never thought about a man being in his wife's office.

"That's Max. We're just finishing up. I'll be home soon."

"You need be home." He hung up the phone.

Why had he said that? Why did he feel angry? He knew his wife was working with her new boss on an important case. She spoke of it freely and often. And about how proud

144

she was to be able to help his people. Yet, suddenly, it didn't seem as simple as when Angelica had talked about it. It seemed personal.

"What's wrong, my son?"

Maclovia's question broke into his thoughts.

"Nothing. Nothing, *Abuela*. I'm going to go clean up, and then I'll help you finish making dinner. Angelica should be home by then, and we'll eat."

As Antonio showered and dressed, his thoughts kept returning to the man who'd answered the phone. Had it been her boss? He'd known Dave. He'd met him at the Christmas party, and they'd had dinner with him and his wife once. But he'd never met this new boss, or his wife.

Antonio pulled a polo shirt over his head and tucked it into his jeans.

He heard the hum of the garage door. Angelica was home.

When Antonio got to the kitchen, Angelica was setting the table. He walked up behind her and put his arms around her, pulling her to him. He pressed his cheek against hers. "Sorry."

She turned and faced him. "I wish I could have come home sooner."

He could see his wife was tired. Her face was pale and drawn. "You sit. I finish this."

Why had he been so abrupt on the phone? She worked long hours, she helped him with his business, and she was carrying his child. She'd never given him any reason not to trust her. He'd acted like a fool.

He wouldn't ask her to put an ad in the paper. She was doing enough. He'd find a way to get more business on his own. The model homes were almost finished. He would go to the sales office and ask if he could bid for the maintenance of them. He needed to do more for Angelica; he needed to be a help and not a hindrance. He wanted to give his wife what she needed, in every way.

It was unusually quiet at the dinner table. When Maclovia finished her meal, she washed her plate and excused herself, saying she was going to bed.

Antonio noticed Angelica had only picked at her food. "You need eat." He reached over and tilted her chin up. "If you don't, Grandmother will think it's because she cooked on the stove instead of the barbeque."

Angelica gave him a weak smile and then put her fork down. "We need to talk. The doctor got my blood test back today."

Antonio felt a jolt of fear. "You okay?"

Angelica blinked rapidly. "It's not me, it's the baby. They can tell things about the baby when they test my blood."

She had not told him that in the doctor's office.

He tried to recall the memory of that meeting. The doctor had called the baby a "fetus." Then he'd used some other word . . . a long word . . . and the test that they'd discussed was about *her* blood. He was positive she'd said they were not making tests on the baby, but on her blood. Antonio studied his wife's face. She was fighting tears. Was it because she had misled him, or only because she feared for their child?

As he watched her, she would not meet his gaze. His heart sank.

"Angelica." His voice was firm. "What happen, *exactamente*?"

She slowly raised her eyes. "That . . . that day I spotted blood and went to the doctor. Before you came . . ." Her voice faltered. "I was frightened. Dr. Gremian suggested a blood test. You weren't there." Her lips trembled. "I felt like I had to have the test to be sure the baby was all right."

Antonio waited to be sure she was finished. "But the test no make sure the baby all right, and now two things not all right." Her face told him she understood he was referring to her deception.

"It didn't seem wrong at the time." He could hardly make out her words between sobs. "I just wanted to know my baby was okay." She dropped her chin to her chest and covered her face with her hands.

Antonio's heart softened. Her grief was not just from her fear for their child, but also for the wrong she had done him. He stood and walked to her. Reaching down, he pulled her up to him and wrapped his arms around her.

Resting his chin on the top of her head, he whispered, "I forgive, Angel."

He stroked her hair to calm her, and when he felt her trembling subside, he led her to the couch in the front room. Sitting next to her, he pulled her head to his shoulder. "Now, tell me what is wrong with the test."

"It shows that something might be wrong with our baby. He might not be normal. He might be physically or mentally unhealthy." Her tears started again.

As she wept, Antonio stroked her hair. How could blood possibly tell anyone such things? He did not believe it.

His eyes wandered around the room. Seeing the television, he remembered the first time he'd turned one on. Impossible, he'd thought then. He noted the slot where they'd put in a videotape they'd recorded in Mexico. Impossible, he'd thought, until he saw it. His eyes traveled to the thermostat on the wall. Impossible, until he'd felt the warm air rush from the metal grates in the floor.

His gaze returned to his wife. Many things that had

seemed impossible in Mexico, man had made possible in America. Should he be concerned for their baby? Angelica had said the baby might not be normal. Abnormal. *That* was the long word he'd heard Dr. Gremian say.

He turned his eyes to his wife's stomach. A child was hidden there. That too seemed impossible. But, in Mexico or America, God did not make abnormal things. Of that he was sure. He had seen many babies born in the fields of Guadalajara. God always provided what they needed, and if He chose not to, then He returned the child to Himself.

Angelica took an unsteady breath. "Now the doctor thinks we should see a genetic counselor and have another ultrasound."

Antonio turned toward her. "And what will they tell us?"

Her voice steadied. "If the baby has any defects."

"Like what?"

"A chromosomal defect or a physical defect."

He did not completely understand Angelica's words. But her face was filled with worry, and his heart went out to her. She was his wife, but it was more than that. He loved her.

"And?"

Angelica lowered her eyes. "I made the appointments. We have to go to Santa Rosa next week."

Antonio searched his heart. It seemed like what she was suggesting was better left to God and His wisdom. Still, he did not want to put his wife in a position where she felt she had to deceive him. He picked up her hand.

"Angelica. I do not need to know these things now. When our baby born, then we know all there is to know about him. But, if you must do this, I will be with you."

She laid her head on his chest and closed her eyes. "Thank you," she whispered.

As he watched her, she fell asleep. He sat without moving, not wanting to disturb her. *Dios, she too is Your gift to me. Give me wisdom to understand her.* The man's voice answering her phone echoed in his mind. *Help me be everything she needs. Please bring me work.*

He picked Angelica up in his arms and carried her to the bedroom. He laid her gently on the bed and covered her with a blanket. Then he slipped out of the room.

As he walked to the kitchen to help Maclovia clean up the unfinished dinner, he set his jaw. What kind of man was Angelica's new boss?

He would find out.

Maclovia opened her bedroom door and stood listening. There was not a sound in the house. She slipped down the hall and out the front door. The moon moved across the sky as she walked. Finally, she approached the foot of the mountains.

She hiked a short distance to a clear, sloping spot. Valle de Lagrimas stretched before her. She fingered the primitive cross at her neck; thoughts of all Antonio had told her while helping in the kitchen filled her mind. How could these people, who had been blessed with so much, understand so little about God? She turned her back on the city lights and faced the expanse of pastoral mountains.

She climbed farther into the foothills until the trees hid the lights from her. When she found a level spot under a huge oak, she knelt. She had come to petition God.

Her eyes closed, her palms up, resting in her lap, she began to hum a song of praise. How she longed for His presence. She waited.

As time passed, her legs began to ache. But she would

not stand to find comfort and interrupt her call to Him. She would never seek His hands without first seeking His face, and she would wait as long as it took for God to receive her. At last, the things around her began to fade, and the yearning of her heart increased. Her lips began to give utterance to deep emotions of love and adoration for the Creator.

Soon a sweet fragrance filled the air, and a powerful sense of peace and love surrounded her. She put her face to the ground.

There, prostrate before the Lord, she pleaded with Him, speaking out the desire of her heart.

"Let the child who is to be born bring glory to Your name. Let him be perfect in Your eyes, given for Your plans and purposes." She lifted her eyes to the heavens, seeking His answer.

A blade of light split the night sky, arcing over her . . . behind her . . . toward Valle de Lagrimas.

Then it vanished.

9

Antonio frowned at himself in the mirror. He stepped back, took a deep breath, and squared his shoulders. . . . It was still crooked. It needed to be perfect.

For the third time, he undid the silk tie and started over. Two tries later, he was finally satisfied. He ran his hand down the length of the two strips of fabric, making sure they were even. Stepping back again, he examined his reflection . . . hair . . . sideburns . . . shirt collar points . . . tie. Perfect.

He slipped his suit jacket off the doorknob and shrugged into it. Snapping the lapels, he let it fall into place. A flash of silver caught his eye. He smiled as he ran his hand slowly over the shiny sterling buckle, the first gift Angelica had ever given him.

His smile froze. The roughness of his hand next to the beautifully cast buckle brought heat to his cheeks. Even though he'd spent a lot of time scrubbing his hands before he dressed, it hadn't seemed to help. They were still calloused and discolored. He lowered his eyes, staring at the cuts and stains, then put his hands slightly behind his back.

Returning his gaze to the mirror, suddenly he felt ashamed, standing with his hands partially hidden. *Dios, forgive me. I thank You for each and every job You bring to me.* He slowly let his hands drop to his sides.

He took a deep breath, ready as he would ever be to surprise Angelica with flowers . . . and to meet Max.

On his way through the kitchen, he stopped and poured most of the water out of the vase holding the bouquet he'd purchased. Then, after taking it with him and securing it in the truck seat, he backed out of the driveway and headed to Angelica's office.

As he drove, he thought about his visit to the sales site earlier in the morning. He'd learned that the new models would be opening in the fall and that the developer would be taking bids on the landscape maintenance for them. The saleswoman had suggested that he put together a proposal. He didn't know what a "proposal" was, but he would find out. Maybe his English as a Second Language teacher could help him. If it were possible, he wanted to do this without Angelica's knowing. He would get the job and surprise her with his first paycheck. He began to whistle.

He took his foot off the gas and slowed the truck as he neared the Sierra County offices. Scanning the parking lot, he spotted Angelica's red Expedition and pulled into an open space near it. Taking the flowers in one hand and smoothing his hair with the other, he set off for Angelica's office.

"Antonio!" Fronie stood to greet him. "What a wonderful surprise." She leaned across the counter to give him a hug.

"I come to see Angelica." He couldn't help but notice that the other women nearby were staring at him. One woman visibly slowed her steps as she passed, turning her head until she looked like she was walking sideways.

"Mary." Fronie took off her headset. "This is Angelica's husband. Could you cover the phones while I take him back to her office?"

The big woman shuffled to Fronie's chair. "She might still be in Max's office. They were meeting this morning."

Fronie stepped around the counter. "I saw her phone line light up a minute ago. I'm pretty sure she's at her desk."

"Nice meeting you, Mr. Amante," Mary called after them.

Antonio stopped and turned.

The woman, headset perched in her frizzy hair and a chubby hand balled beneath her chin, smiled at him.

"*Igualmente, señorita.*" He flashed her a smile and tipped his head.

As he walked down the long hall behind Fronie, Antonio glanced through the open doors of the offices they passed. Some were empty, one had a long table surrounded by chairs, others were filled with people.

"Look who's here." Fronie turned through an opening and stepped to the side.

Angelica's face lit up. "Antonio!" She stood. "And flowers too?"

It seemed odd seeing Angelica behind a big desk stacked high with papers and books and equipment. She looked so . . . so . . . important. Even though the broad wooden desk was all that separated them, he felt distanced from her. He held out the flowers, reaching across the gap.

"Gotta get back to the front." Fronie slipped out the door.

Angelica walked around the desk, took the flowers from him, and set them on her desk. Then she stepped into his arms. He gave her a peck on the lips.

As he dropped his arms and stepped back, Angelica slid

her hands up his chest and around his neck. Pulling him to her, she kissed him like she hadn't seen him for a year, instead of the few hours since she'd left the house. Her eyes were closed, and she was clearly enjoying him.

Trying not to move, he glanced furtively around the room. This didn't seem like the place for this kind of thing.

Angelica's perfume drifted into his thoughts.

Oh, well.

It was Angelica's office, and she should know. He wrapped his arms around her and lifted her off her feet, returning her kiss . . . and then some.

"Umm. Excuse me?" A voice came from behind him.

His wife gave a little kick, quickly escaping his arms, suddenly assuming an air of propriety. "Max!"

"Should I come back another time?"

Antonio wasn't sure what to make of the cool, mocking look on the man's face. But his wife's crimson cheeks and sporadic smoothing of her dress made the awkwardness of the situation obvious.

With his hand extended, Antonio stepped toward the man who'd answered his wife's phone. "Good morning. I'm Antonio Perez—Angelica's husband." He took Max's hand firmly in his, then exerted a little more pressure.

"Nice to meet you." Max quickly extracted his hand and swung it slightly behind his back, splaying his fingers.

Manicured nails! Perfect, even, white nails. Antonio's eyes traveled up the pressed coat sleeve, to the starched shirt, to the crisp tie knot, to the clean-shaven face, to the narrowed eyes . . . focused on Angelica.

Antonio pursed his lips, his eyes widening slightly as he studied Max's face. The man's eyebrows were plucked. Antonio found himself stifling a smile, suddenly feeling foolish that he'd felt a need to meet Max.

Max handed Angelica a stack of papers. "Here are those copies you wanted for the Vasquez appeal."

No wedding ring.

"Thanks, Max." Angelica set the papers on the desk, then turned to Antonio. "This is for that case I've told you so much about."

"You should be proud of your wife. She's doing a fine job on this case." Max looked Antonio in the eye and folded his arms across his chest. "I personally chose her for it."

Antonio perceived a slight tilt of Max's head, giving Max the appearance of a superior stance, almost territorial. Holding Max's gaze, he said, "Yes, I am very proud of her. She does a fine job as wife too."

A few silent seconds passed, Antonio's gaze never wavering.

"Uh." Max blinked. The annoying tilt of his head vanished.

Angelica cleared her throat. "Yes, Antonio and I are partners in his business. He has a landscape maintenance company."

"Really? Well, the next time the county goes out to bid for upkeep on this complex, perhaps he'd want to submit." Max looked at Angelica.

As Angelica opened her mouth to answer for him, Antonio put his arm around her shoulder and faced Max. "We'll put together a proposal."

"Angelica, maybe you can check and find out when the current contract expires." Max looked at his watch. "Right now I've got to run. Nice meeting you, Antonio."

As soon as Max disappeared around the corner, Angelica shut her office door. She turned toward Antonio and leaned against it. "That was bad timing." Her eyes sparkled with mischief.

Antonio stepped toward her, gathering her in his arms. "Oh, really, *señorita*? I no think so."

Angelica wiggled away from him and sat down at her desk. "A proposal? I had no idea you knew how to write a proposal." Angelica's face was a mixture of confusion and surprise. "In fact, I had no idea you were coming here today. What's this all about?"

Antonio hesitated, considering her question. Seeing his beautiful wife sitting amidst stacks of papers and phones and computers, her face drawn and circles under her eyes, he knew exactly what it was about.

"Come here," he whispered.

She stepped toward him, and he took her hands in his. "I come to say I love you. I no like that you have to work so hard. I want to take care of you and my son. And someday I will."

Angelica lifted his hands to her lips and kissed them. "Antonio, you do take care of me. You give me the things I really need. The things that money can't buy."

Angelica laid her head on his chest. "I've been thinking about the baby all morning." He felt her draw a deep breath. "I want to tell my parents about the tests. I want to talk about everything with them."

He didn't. But Angelica was the one who was concerned, the one carrying the baby. He began stroking her hair, he needed to support her.

"Of course. When?"

She looked up at him. "Maybe tonight. After dinner?"

"I be ready then."

She straightened. "Then I need to get busy. I spent some time this morning looking up genetic counseling on the Internet when I should have been working." She returned to her desk. "I'll call Mom and let her know we're coming. See you tonight."

As Antonio slowly walked through the lobby and out to his truck, his thoughts turned to the *patrón* and Mrs. Amante. What would they say about the tests? They had encouraged Angelica to do everything the doctor suggested. And she had. Now the doctor wanted more tests. What was the purpose in all of this? If Angelica and the baby failed the tests they were given, there was nothing that could be done before the baby was born. . . . Was there?

He slid behind the wheel and started the engine. Preparing to pull out, he glanced around. Just down the row, a man was getting into a black car. Max. Antonio watched him take off his suit jacket and hang it in the back seat.

Several details about the man filtered through Antonio's mind. Max was very careful about his outward appearance. Maybe he wanted to keep people from seeing who he really was. Antonio wasn't sure. There were many things he didn't understand about the Americans. American men seemed to live on the surface of life, seldom revealing what was beneath their words and actions.

He closed his eyes a moment, concentrating, revisiting his sense of the meeting in Angelica's office. Once again he got the distinct impression that as *he* had observed Max . . . Max had been taking measure of *him*. A twinge of uneasiness stirred within him.

"Isn't it about time for you to go home?"

Angelica looked up to see Fronie's sweet face peeking through the crack of her office door. "What time is it?"

"Just after five. I thought I'd check on you before I left." Fronie stepped through the door and closed it behind her, then sat in the chair next to Angelica's desk. "And besides, I'm dying to find out what Antonio was doing here. That's the first time he's ever come to the office. And with flowers no less." Her brown eyes danced. "You guys have a fight?"

Angelica clicked her computer file closed and leaned toward Fronie. "Don't be silly. Nobody was more surprised than I was."

"He looked like a model who just stepped out of *GQ*. So handsome. You should have seen those women up front." Fronie giggled. "Mary called him Mr. Amante."

Angelica grimaced. "What did he do?"

"He answered her as if he didn't notice." Fronie winked at her. "Of course he *did* notice. That guy doesn't miss a thing. What a gentleman."

It was true; Antonio didn't miss a thing. She decided to confide in Fronie. "I have a feeling I know why he came."

Fronie waited for Angelica to continue.

"Yesterday Antonio called me on my private line." She glanced toward the phone on her desk. "And Max answered it."

Fronie's eyebrows went up. "Oops."

"I could tell Antonio was upset about it. I've always kept work and my private life separate. Antonio knew Dave, but he's never met Max."

"That's probably just as well. Max is such a jerk."

Angelica thought a moment. "You know, Fronie, he's not really. I've been working with him on this case for a few weeks now, and he's been great to work with."

"That's probably because you're so professional. He's a player, but he's not stupid. Besides, he wants to win that appeal, and he knows you're the PD who can do it."

Fronie was right about her being the most qualified public

defender to work the case, but even more than that, she felt a burden to see that Miguel Vasquez got justice. "Max is a hard guy to figure out. But really, his personal life is none of my business. He must have his reasons for the way he acts."

"I heard that he was totally in love with his first wife, Angie."

Angie. Suddenly, Max's voice sounded in the back of Angelica's mind. *Angie*. "Is she the one who was killed with their daughter in that car accident?"

"Uh-huh. I never met her, but Mary knew them both in high school; he was the quarterback, and Angie was the cheerleader. In fact she was the homecoming queen, and the valedictorian too. But she had a terrible home life. Her father was an alcoholic." Fronie's face softened. "Max took her away from it. They got married right after graduation. I think they were happily married for over fifteen years."

"How awful for him." She'd never imagined Max as a man of depth and compassion. Her thoughts went to that moment in her office when she'd burst into tears. Suddenly, she saw his spontaneous move to comfort her in a different light. And it felt unsettling. She hadn't been able to put her finger on it at the time, but there had been a familiarity, intenseness, in the way he'd held her.

Angie.

Fronie shrugged her shoulders. "Well, if he was ever a good man, his second wife took care of that." They both knew the story. It had been in all the papers and the topic of endless office gossip while it was going on.

"I thank God every day for Antonio. He's the perfect husband." Angelica glanced at the closed office door. "And I may be testing that very soon."

159

Fronie's face filled with concern. "Why? What's going on?"

Angelica hesitated. The feelings and thoughts she'd been having since her doctor's appointment churned in the pit of her stomach. "Do you promise to keep this between us?"

Her friend's expression grew serious. "I promise. As your sister in the Lord."

Angelica started slowly. "My OB thought the baby seemed small." She closed her eyes for a moment, trying to sort through her feelings. "He did some testing and told me that there's a chance the baby has a birth defect." Angelica opened a drawer and plucked a tissue from the box she'd hidden there.

"How big a chance?"

She twisted her hands together. "I don't know. Enough that he wants us to see a genetic counselor and get a more extensive ultrasound."

"That won't test Antonio one bit." Fronie's voice was firm. "He's totally in love with you. And he'll love the baby the same way."

"I know that. The problem is he doesn't understand why it's important to know everything we can about our baby before he's born, so we can make plans. He seems so fatalistic about everything. Just leave it up to God."

Fronie put her hand on Angelica's arm. "That doesn't sound so bad, does it?"

"You know what I mean. Of course it's *all* in God's hands. But God has blessed us with doctors and knowledge and tools. I don't think we're just supposed to ignore that."

Fronie nodded.

"I love my husband. I want to talk this out with him, share my feelings, but it's hard. There's a language barrier, for one thing. He doesn't really understand the terminology the doctor uses. And there's a naïveté he has about what is possible. In his life experience you *have* to settle for the hand life deals you." She swallowed hard and lifted her chin. "I'm not going to settle for anything less than the best I can do when it comes to my child."

"Do you really think Antonio doesn't want the best for his child?" Fronie's words hung in the air between them.

Angelica lowered her eyes. "Of course not. But there's so much to consider." She looked at Fronie. "I've decided to visit my parents tonight. Since my dad's a doctor, I'd like his take on everything. It is their grandchild after all."

"We'll pray." Fronie's voice was girded with resolve. "I'll get in touch with our prayer group tonight. And every prayer chain that flows from our church. We'll go before the Father nonstop, and we'll storm the gates until we get the assurance that your baby is perfect."

Calm settled over Angelica. It was going to be all right. God would provide her baby with everything he needed. Suddenly, she had complete clarity. God was in control. He would use the people around her, and her circumstances, to bring about His will. She would seek counsel from the people He'd put in her life. She would trust Him.

"Thank you, Fronie." She straightened in her chair. "I feel better already."

Fronie patted her arm. "I'm glad, girl. I'm here for you." Fronie closed her eyes. "Lord, You are knitting together this child. We just praise and thank You for the miracle You are creating."

Angelica whispered, "Amen."

Fronie rose. "Now you get on home and get some rest." She gave her a hug and left.

Angelica began stacking up her most important work next to the computer. *I should stay and catch up.* She glanced at the clock on her screen. It was almost six. If she didn't hurry, she wouldn't get home in time to get a bite to eat before going to her parents' house.

Thirty minutes later, Angelica pulled into the garage. As she stepped out of the car, she smelled the distinct odor of hickory smoke. Antonio was barbequing. Her stomach growled.

Angelica threw her purse on the kitchen table and went out through the slider to the backyard. "*Hola*, you two. What's cooking? It will smell delicious," she said in Spanish.

She'd decided to speak Spanish whenever Maclovia was present. She wanted to get to know her better and learn more about Antonio's culture. She'd tried to include the old woman in various outings, but she either declined the invitation outright or endured it until it was over. There had to be some common ground they shared, something that would allow them to develop a relationship. Angelica was determined to find it, and breaking down the language barrier seemed like the best place to start. Maclovia deserved a more fulfilling life than staring out her bedroom window hour after hour and rocking in her chair.

Antonio and Maclovia were sitting at the patio table, Buddy in Maclovia's lap. She nodded at Angelica. "Good day, *señora*."

"Good day, *Abuela*." Angelica bent over and kissed Maclovia's cheek.

Antonio rose and pulled out a chair for Angelica. "Honey, you said 'will smell.'"

Angelica frowned at him, then laughed, lapsing into English. "Well aren't you smart? Before long you'll be giving me classes in Spanish."

"Welcome to my world." Antonio said each word of the American phrase perfectly, then winked at her.

"You *are* getting good." Angelica put her finger on her lips. "I have a challenge." She pointed at him. "When Maclovia is present, we can only speak Spanish. When it's just us, we only speak English."

"As you wish, *señorita*," he answered her in Spanish, speaking so quickly she could hardly understand him.

"What does she wish?" Maclovia looked at Antonio.

"She wants to speak Spanish with us." Antonio walked to the barbeque and began loading a tray with the food.

Maclovia's face brightened. "I want to speak English."

Angelica could hardly keep her mouth from dropping open. Maclovia's declaration seemed completely at odds with the woman she'd come to know. A woman who had lived off the land in the fields of Guadalajara all her life and showed no desire to embrace the easier life of America. A woman with whom she had nothing in common. "Why you care learn English?"

Antonio rolled his eyes at Angelica. "Bad verb, *señorita*."

"For heavens' sake, Antonio." Angelica broke into English. "When did you get so competitive?" She gave him an appraising look, a smile tugging at her lips. "And so smart?"

He answered her in Spanish, once again speaking so rapidly she couldn't understand a thing he said.

She folded her arms across her chest. Thoughts of where her high school Spanish books might be located suddenly crept into her mind. "Very funny, *señor*. Just you wait. I'll soon be talking to you like a native."

Antonio gave her a look of mock innocence. "And when did you get so competitive?"

Angelica burst out laughing. He knew her so well. "Don't worry about me. You'd better buckle down to your own studies."

"You are speaking English. Breaking your own rule," he answered primly in Spanish as he carried the tray of food to the table.

Angelica shot him a dirty look and turned back to Maclovia. "Why you want learn English?"

Maclovia helped Buddy off her lap and faced Angelica with a broad smile, her wise eyes clear and focused. "So I can talk to you, my daughter."

Angelica drew back as the meaning in Maclovia's words sunk in. She felt like she was sitting naked in front of the old woman. Why had she asked such a stupid, insensitive question? Of course Maclovia would want to talk to the people around her. It was just that . . . well, she hated to admit it, but Maclovia seemed set in her ways, not very curious about the world around her. She was so old. Angelica twisted in her chair, feeling she had somehow exposed herself in an embarrassing way.

"We will help you," Antonio answered for Angelica.

The meal passed with simple Spanish sentences. Angelica was surprised that by speaking slowly and listening carefully, they were able to communicate quite well, though she found it frustrating not to be able to lapse into English when she wanted to get a point across. She glanced at her husband. She felt a new respect for how well he'd done since coming to America.

As they cleaned up the kitchen, Maclovia announced she wanted to join them on the visit to Regalo Grande. The three arrived just as the sun began to set.

Angelica's mother opened the door. "Oh." Her voice was flat.

"Hi, Mom. Isn't it nice, Maclovia decided to come?"

"Do come in." She stepped to the side.

They followed her to a large, tiled patio that overlooked

the valley. There was a cart set up with a silver ice bucket, bottles of wine, a carafe of tea, and various sized glasses.

"Help yourselves." Angelica's father rose from his chair. "Good to see you." He shook Antonio's hand.

Turning to Maclovia, he motioned toward the table. "*Buenas noches*. Sit. Sit."

Maclovia pulled one of the wrought-iron chairs to the side of, and a little behind, the patio table and chairs to a spot sheltered from the cool evening breeze.

Antonio took her a glass of tea.

"So, what have you kids been up to?" Angelica's father sat back down. "Got the nursery finished?"

"Our nursery is coming along nicely. Did you put the crib together?"

"Oh, don't bring that up." Angelica's mother playfully slapped her father's arm. "He's got stuff spread all over your old bedroom. He goes in there and works on it a little every day. It's a mess." She took a seat next to him. "How are you feeling, Angel? How was your appointment yesterday?"

Angelica took a deep breath. This wasn't how she'd imagined the conversation going. It seemed too rushed. She didn't feel ready. "Dr. Gremian ordered some tests."

Her mother set her glass down. "What tests?"

"He thought the baby seemed a little small, so he ordered some testing."

"When will the tests be back?" Her father's question sounded like a demand.

"They came back yesterday. That's one of the reasons I wanted to come up tonight, Dad. I'm hoping you can tell me how serious you think this is."

"What exactly did the doctor tell you?"

As Angelica recounted everything she'd learned, her father's face became somber.

"What does it mean, Ben?"

"The doctor has concerns that the baby may have a birth defect. He's done the right thing advising a more detailed ultrasound. That will tell the story."

"But Dad, does this mean that there *probably* is something wrong? Do we need to brace ourselves?" She looked at Antonio. He took her hand.

"Ben, what does it mean?"

"It means we won't know anything for sure until after further testing." Her father's voice had taken on the tone of a doctor talking to a waiting family after a heart operation. An alarm went off inside Angelica.

"But what do you think, Dad?"

"I think you should listen carefully to your doctor's advice and follow it."

"What's genetic counseling?" Her mother's voice was filled with concern.

"I understand that they kind of translate all the information so we can understand it." Angelica looked at Antonio. He gave her hand a squeeze. "We meet with the counselor. Then I get the ultrasound, and we meet with the counselor again."

Angelica's mother looked at Antonio. "Do you have any birth defects in your family?"

Heat stole into Angelica's face.

"I don't think so."

Why couldn't he give a better answer? Why didn't he know more? She pulled her hand away and sat up in her chair. "His family never had the kind of health care and things we do." She turned to him. "Why not ask Maclovia if all the babies she and your mom had were healthy?"

Antonio spoke to Maclovia in Spanish.

As the minutes passed, Maclovia sat still, not answering.

166

Angelica caught herself starting to lean forward in her chair. "Well?"

Finally, Maclovia spoke.

Antonio translated. "She says she never thought of judging God's gifts. She see many babies in her life. And every child God sent was perfect as far as she knows."

"That doesn't tell us much." Angelica's mother sat back in her chair. "When is your appointment? Dad and I would be glad to come."

Angelica looked at her father. It would be so good to have him there. He would be able to talk to the doctors in their language—know the questions to ask. She looked at Antonio.

"Angelica make appointment for next week. We let you know how it is."

"We'll all hold a good thought." Her father reached across the table and patted her shoulder. "How's it going at work?"

"Okay. I'm swamped, but Max has been great about making sure I can take the time I need for my appointments."

The conversation shifted from her work to Antonio's business to Buddy. "He sure loves Maclovia." Angelica smiled, looking in the old woman's direction. "Where'd she go?"

Everyone turned. Her chair was empty, her glass beside it.

Angelica glanced at her mother and said, "She's probably in the bathroom, or maybe she's wandering around the house. She did that last time."

Antonio stood. "It time to go. Angelica work all day and need to rest."

"I'll go get your grandmother, and we'll take off." Angelica turned to her parents. "Talk to you soon." Antonio headed down the hall to the front door.

Angelica walked to the guest bath in the hall. The door was open, and the room was empty. She quickly walked down the hall looking in the rooms that adjoined it. Maclovia was nowhere to be found. She stopped, listening. The floor creaked above her. She bounded up the stairs. At the top, she listened again. She moved through the dim light to her old bedroom.

"There you are, *Abuela*."

Maclovia was looking at the pieces of the white crib laid all around the room.

Angelica turned on the lights.

Memories flooded over her. This had been her room when she was growing up. The queen-sized bed, topped by a big canopy, was still made up with a thick white comforter and overstuffed pillows. Sheer drapes fell from the twelve-foot ceiling to a casual gathering on the tiled floors, framing a huge glass sliding door that opened to a private redwood deck overlooking the Sonoma Valley.

Her desk and bookcases were gone from the far end of the room near the bay window, and she guessed that was where her mother was planning to set up the crib and armoire. She stepped through the crib parts until she reached the big glass bay. It faced the rolling hills and pastures of Regalo Grande.

Cranking the window open, she felt a breeze filter in, carrying voices from the patio below. She heard the word "baby."

Leaning closer, she recognized her father's voice. "I didn't want to frighten her."

Her mother's shrill voice followed. "I'll be devastated if there's anything wrong with my grandchild."

"Let's wait and see what the doctors say. They'll give her choices, options."

What was her father talking about? What choices . . . options? Her mind raced.

"I guess we'd better wait on the nursery."

She didn't want to hear any more. She began cranking the window shut, closing out her mother's voice. Tears stung her eyes. She pressed the window lock down.

Turning, she found Maclovia directly behind her. The old woman, leathery hands clasped in front of her, worn shawl wrapped around her shoulders, stood in the beautiful, perfect, crisp white room. The room that indulgent parents had prepared for *their* perfect child.

Maclovia reached up and wiped a tear from Angelica's cheek. "Believe." Her voice was strong.

Angelica reached out, and the two women embraced. Alone in the room. Standing on common ground.

10

IT ALL MADE sense.

Max set his coffee down, swiveled his chair to the computer screen, and typed three letters into the box on the Explorer toolbar. Pointing to "Search," he clicked, eyes locked on the screen, waiting.

Finally, the list of search results materialized. Statue still, Max silently reviewed the entries, eyes stopping on the fourth one down.

"The AFP [alpha-fetoprotein] level in conjunction with an abnormal ultrasound scan indicates increased probability that the baby will have one of the four most common birth defects." His throat constricted.

With disquieting clarity, the day Angelica had broken down in her office came back to him. That's when he'd glimpsed the letters on her computer monitor. It hadn't registered then. He'd thought her outburst was just a pregnant woman's overemotional response to the stressful day she'd been having. Angie had done that when she'd been expecting their little girl. The dull ache in his chest started.

They'd thought they couldn't have children. He still couldn't think about his wife and child without some remnant of the devastating grief he'd felt over their deaths surfacing. If only he'd been a better husband. If only he'd been a better father. If only . . .

But the day he'd met Angelica's husband, he'd seen information about genetic counseling on her computer screen. That's when he'd begun to put it together . . . the day she'd left the office so unexpectedly, the numerous doctor's appointments, and she seemed to be losing weight. Something was going on in Angelica's life. And now he knew what it was.

He steepled his fingers under his chin, thoughts turning to Antonio. Who would have guessed that the girl who should have everything was strapped with a gigolo husband? Young, handsome, and strong was about all he had to offer her. He mowed lawns for a living. Trying to spin that into a "landscape maintenance company" didn't fool Max for a minute. How did a woman like her get mixed up with a guy like that? She deserved better. A whole lot better.

Max's eyes drifted to the window. A beautiful, bright, good woman. Trapped. First with a loser husband, and now the uncertain outcome of her pregnancy.

He turned back to the computer screen and clicked on "Genetic Counseling."

"A genetic counseling session will communicate complex medical information to the patient. The challenge is to help families cope with the emotional, psychological, medical, social, and economic consequences of genetic disease."

Max slowly shook his head. She hadn't said a word about any of this to anyone. If she had, he was sure he would have heard about it. It was obviously something she considered a very private matter.

He closed his eyes for a moment, bringing her beautiful

face to mind. How many times had he seen her at her desk late at night, lost in thought, fighting for justice for Miguel Vasquez, with her own life in chaos? He'd only known one other woman with that kind of courage and inner strength. Something stirred within him.

Max drummed his fingers on the desk. He would help her. She wouldn't know anything about it. He'd already cut back her workload so she could devote more time to the Vasquez case. He'd tell her that he was going to be giving her more responsibilities with the Vasquez appeal and reassign the cases she hadn't finished.

Maybe he'd check and find out when the landscape contract came up for the Sierra County offices. He picked up the phone . . . maybe not.

Why help her husband? Would that really be helping Angelica?

As he thought about it, he realized that it would just perpetuate the myth that the Latin gigolo was capable of more than mowing lawns. You couldn't help those kind of people. Look at his loser brother. How many times had he tried to help him? He put the phone back in its cradle. Let Mr. Perez fight his own battle.

His office door slammed, jerking Max back to the present.

"I've been over at that sewer of a jail." Angelica's dark eyes smoldered with fire as she yanked a chair around to face him. "It just makes me more determined than ever to see this through." She sat down and crossed her arms. "Having to sit across from Miguel and explain to him that his bail amount has been raised, that Immigration is now putting a hold on him . . ."

He heard her swallow.

"To sit across from an innocent man and know the system is against him . . ."

She stood. Seconds passed. Blinking rapidly, she turned on her heel.

Swinging the door of his office open, she faced Max. "This fight is just beginning. Miguel Vasquez *will* be vindicated. I'll never give up." The door slammed shut behind her.

A trace of her perfume lingered in the air. Max closed his eyes.

Passionate, caring, dynamic. He couldn't deny it. He was drawn to her.

Angelica Amante was so like the woman he'd fallen in love with and married. The kind of woman who only came along once in a lifetime.

At least that's what he'd thought . . . until now.

Angelica locked the bathroom door and leaned against it. She needed a few moments to herself before returning to her office and tackling all the work she had to do before she left for the genetic counseling appointment. She drew a jagged breath. At least she'd managed to keep it together in front of Max.

Oh, God, I feel so overwhelmed. I need You with me today. I need to be strong. She closed her eyes, waiting. Wanting to feel His presence.

Immediately, thoughts of unreturned phone calls and stacks of files intruded. She bit her lip. She shouldn't be taking time for herself right now. She should get back to her desk and give Miguel's case the focus it deserved. Tomorrow was Bible study. She'd set aside time for God tomorrow night.

She stopped at the vending machine on her way to her

office and bought four bottles of water to force down before the ultrasound. She set them on her desk in easy reach of her work area, swiveled around, kicked the office door shut with her toe, and spent the next three hours plowing through files and doing research on the Internet.

Angelica stopped at the front counter on her way to the parking lot. "Fronie, I'm leaving now."

Fronie gave Angelica a knowing look and slipped her headset off. "Mary, could you cover a sec? I'll be right back."

Fronie stepped away from her desk and walked with Angelica to her car. "I'll be thinking about you and praying for you, girl." Fronie put her arm around Angelica's waist as they walked.

"I'm so scared. I just want everything to be okay." Once again, Angelica felt her emotions bubbling up.

"Don't you worry, sweetie, everything's going to work out. Forget about everything else and take the time you need."

"The timing couldn't be worse. We're right in the middle of the Vasquez appeal."

They stopped at Angelica's car.

"Shhh, now. Max is perfectly capable of taking care of things."

Angelica turned to her friend. "You're right. He's been totally supportive and understanding." She unlocked her SUV and got in. "And a complete gentleman too." She started the car. "I'm so thankful for that."

"Just think, a few hours from now you'll know *officially* if it's a boy or a girl. I can't wait to hear."

"Antonio's positive it's a boy. We've already started decorating the nursery in blue."

She glimpsed Fronie in the rearview mirror, waving at

her as she drove out of the parking lot and headed home to pick up Antonio.

Alone in the car, she tried to mentally prepare herself for the meeting. There was so much at stake. The next few hours could turn her life upside down. Her father's words floated through her mind. "I didn't want to frighten her." A blade of panic cut through her chest.

No. I'm not going to think the worst. People are praying for me. She made a mental list of all the reasons why her baby would be fine. She was young, there was no history of genetic defects in her family, or Antonio's as far as they knew, and statistically the odds were in her favor. Above all . . . God wouldn't allow anything bad to happen to her baby. "I'm trusting You, Lord."

Her shoulders relaxed. God was in control. She was counting on it. She drummed her fingers on the steering wheel. In fact, she didn't even know anybody who had a baby with a birth defect. There was no reason it should happen to her.

The garage door opened as she pulled into the drive, and Antonio jogged out to the car.

Angelica's face fell. "Didn't you have time to clean up?"

"I have trouble with my mower today. It make me go behind." He shut the passenger door.

Angelica huffed a sigh.

"I changed my shirt and washed my hands." He winked at her, and his face broke into a smile.

The words were clearly a peace offering.

"I'm sorry, Antonio. I'm just worried about this appointment."

He reached across the front seat and put his hand on her knee. "No worry. What will happen, will happen."

Anger flashed through her. Why had she married a man

who was so ignorant? "How can you be that fatalistic? Especially about something as important as the health of our baby. You don't have to accept everything that happens in life."

She looked at him, her mind racing ahead, preparing a quick retort to the foolish answer he was bound to give her.

His eyes met hers, his face filled with compassion. "That is true, Angelica. You only have to accept the things you cannot change."

She looked away from him. The firm tone of his voice, the quiet acquiescence to a universal truth—this was wisdom. This was his way of correcting her.

"I just want everything to be okay."

He lifted his hand from her knee and tilted her chin toward him. "I know."

A tapping on the car window startled them.

It was Maclovia, her white hair pulled into a ponytail at the nape of her neck, shawl around her shoulders, and Buddy at her side, his rope knotted in her hand. "I want to come," she spoke through the window.

Angelica looked at Antonio. "Why?"

He shrugged his shoulders.

"She wouldn't be able to understand anything, bless her heart." Since the evening at the ranch the week before, when Maclovia had been such a source of comfort, Angelica had begun to spend a little time talking with her each night, just before going to bed. They talked mostly about the baby. Out of the corner of her eye she could see Maclovia's expectant face. "She knows we're going to the appointment about the tests, doesn't she?"

He nodded.

"I hate to have her come and have to sit in the waiting room for who knows how long. Think of something."

Angelica rolled the window down, and Antonio leaned across the seat. "*Abuela*, the appointment is only for the two of us. We will be back soon and tell you all about it."

Maclovia opened the door to the backseat and followed Buddy in, speaking Spanish so quickly that Angelica couldn't understand a word, except "God."

"What on earth did she say?"

Antonio sat, thinking. "Um. She said God has called her. Er, told her." He looked at his grandmother. "She feels like she should come."

Though she didn't know Maclovia well, Angelica did know the old woman spent hours in prayer in her bedroom. If Maclovia thought God was leading her to go with them, He probably was. "I'm not going to argue with that."

They talked about everything but the appointment as they drove over the Sonoma Mountains to Santa Rosa. Angelica had been to Santa Rosa many times over the years and easily followed the directions the nurse had given her. Finally, she turned off Petaluma Hill Road onto Appleway, where the large complex of medical offices was located.

"What's that?" Antonio pointed to a crowd of people standing in a park across from the buildings, holding signs.

Angelica braked, slowing down with the rest of the traffic. "Oh great. It looks like some kind of a protest." She glanced at her watch. "Good thing we've got plenty of time."

"God hates aboorrr . . ." Antonio tried several times to sound out the word on the signs. "What they protest?"

Angelica looked at her husband. They had never talked about abortion. It had never come up. She didn't even know if he knew what it was. She glanced in the rearview mirror at Maclovia, who was looking out the window at the

177

crowd. For two people who found testing a baby before it was born difficult to accept, a casual conversation in the car using broken Spanish wasn't the way to explain why a mother would kill her unborn child. *God, forgive them. How could they ever even consider such a thing?* She looked at the building across the street from where the crowd stood.

"That's a clinic where women go who don't want their children."

She saw Antonio glance up and down the street. "I no see any children."

"I'll explain later. The address we want is on the next block." She wove her way through the traffic. "Help me watch for it."

Angelica swung the car into the big parking lot. "Would you tell Maclovia that Buddy can't come in? He'll have to stay in the car."

Antonio translated.

A lengthy discussion ensued as Angelica cruised through the rows, looking for a parking space. Finally, Antonio gave Angelica a helpless look and said, "Grandmother *prefiere* wait in the car then."

Angelica rolled her eyes. "Well, it's her choice. Thank the Lord, it's a beautiful day."

She finally found an empty space sheltered by the shade from the trees lining the street. "They'll be comfortable here." She pulled in, rolled down the windows, and turned off the engine. "I'm so full of water, I can hardly walk."

Before she could open her door, Antonio was around the car helping her out. He pushed her door shut with his back and gently swept her into his arms, cradling her like a baby.

"Put me down." She began to giggle. "And whatever you do, don't make me laugh."

"I put you down inside, so you no have to walk." He pressed his rough cheek lightly to hers, as if she were a child, and carried her into the office building.

Angelica closed her eyes, feeling him—the solid strength of his arms, the gentleness of his touch, the steady, even sound of his breath. She melted into him. For the moment, for the first time in a long time, everything was right in her world. If only she could stay in his arms forever.

She felt herself falling.

Antonio set her on her feet in the lobby of The Genetic Institute.

Gripping his hand, she walked to the office directory that was fastened to the wall and scanned the list of names. "It's this way." She led him down a long hall.

They checked in, and the receptionist handed them a huge questionnaire. "When you've finished filling this out, the counselor will see you." The sentence sounded practiced and sterile.

Angelica and Antonio sat down and went over each question together. Every detail of their and their families' histories was probed. Besides health questions, there were questions asking if they'd ever been exposed to toxic substances and did they take any medicines, drink, or smoke. It was almost an hour before they finished.

Angelica returned the forms to the receptionist. "Have a seat, you'll be called soon." She put the paperwork in a yellow file and laid it on the counter.

Angelica returned to her seat next to Antonio. Perched on the edge of the chair, she knotted her hands in her lap, took a deep breath, and locked her eyes on the closed door that led to the private offices where the course of the rest of her life would be disclosed. She stopped the thought. She would not think, she would not feel; she would wait until she had information. The minutes dragged by.

"Antonio, maybe you should go check on Maclovia. We've been in here over an hour."

Suddenly, the door she'd been staring at opened.

A man ushered a smiling young couple out.

Angelica felt herself breathe. They looked happy. They had come here for genetic counseling, and they were smiling. Their doctor must have had reason to send them. Angelica looked at the girl, she wasn't showing at all. Maybe their baby was small too.

She reached over and took Antonio's hand. It felt warm and relaxed. He stroked her forearm.

The young woman spoke. "Thanks so much, Mr. Dunteman." She stood on her toes and hugged him.

"Thanks, again." The young man pumped the counselor's hand with enthusiasm.

"You're most welcome."

As the couple left, Mr. Dunteman stepped to the counter and picked up the yellow file. "Mr. and Mrs. Perez?"

"Yes." Angelica rose.

They followed him down a short corridor, into a room with a round table.

"Have a seat." He shut the door. "I'm Barry."

He explained that his role was to translate the technical scientific information so they could make informed choices about the pregnancy. For the next hour he went over the questionnaire, item by item, with them. The counselor's manner was professional, yet not aloof. He was patient as they asked questions and thorough in answering them, explaining how the details of their life histories could impact the pregnancy.

He pointed out how the score from her AFP test was plotted on a bell curve, showing her results compared to others in her age and risk group. He went carefully through the error rates, and false positives, and inaccuracies of the test.

The information that had once filled her with fear now seemed less threatening. The test truly was only a measure of probability, not certainty.

"When you add the results of the ultrasound to this, will you be able to tell us if our baby is all right?"

"The only way we can be positive is if you have an amniocentesis done."

From her time on the Internet, Angelica knew that test had risks of its own. She looked at Antonio. His eyes were focused on the counselor, dark and penetrating, as if he were evaluating the man, rather than the information he offered.

"Let's wait and see what the ultrasound shows."

Mr. Dunteman smiled benignly. "The amniocentesis would be conclusive."

Angelica looked at her husband again.

"No more tests." He delivered the words with uncompromising clarity.

The counselor flinched.

"Angelica, we have Spanish-speaking counselors here. Would you like one of them to meet with your husband? Perhaps Mr. Perez would benefit by getting a fuller picture in his own language."

"I think he has the picture, Mr. Dunteman."

The counselor raised his eyebrows. "Very well."

He closed the file.

They went back to the waiting room and were directed down the hall where Angelica changed into a gown. Then a nurse took them to an exam room. She helped Angelica onto the exam table and offered Antonio a stool beside it.

A man in a green smock appeared. "Hi. I'm Ted. How are you two today?"

"Nervous." Angelica gave him a weak smile.

The sonographer began to rub gel on her abdomen, the cold wetness making her shiver. Antonio rose from the stool and took her hand.

"Don't be nervous. I'm just going to take some measurements."

"How long will this take? I feel like my back teeth are floating."

"It won't be long now. About twenty minutes." He began to move the transducer slowly along her abdomen, his eyes on the monitor. "Have you named your baby yet?"

"We think it's a boy. If it is, we're going to call him Benito Crecencio."

Ted smiled. "Do you want to know the sex of the baby?"

"My baby is a boy." Antonio's voice was firm.

The tech gave him an amused look and glanced at Angelica. She nodded her head.

"You're right, watch the monitor." He smiled. "You're looking at Benito."

A surge of happiness welled within her. For all the assurances Antonio had given her that it was a boy, it wasn't until this moment that it became real. She pressed her head back to see her husband. "That's our Ben."

But Antonio didn't respond. His eyes were fixed on the monitor. He seemed deaf to her voice, removed from her presence, his lips parted slightly in reverential awe. She squeezed his hand.

He turned to her. His eyes filled with tears, he bent down

and kissed her forehead. "Thank you," he whispered, his voice husky.

Angelica watched the shadows and outlines on the screen. "Do you see anything that doesn't look right?"

"The genetic counselor will go over the results with you."

As the time passed, it seemed to Angelica that the tech's voice lost some of its easy friendliness and became more reserved.

Angelica continued to pepper the sonographer with questions as he performed the exam. "Why do you keep looking at his head?" Angelica eyed the clock. It had been over thirty minutes.

"I just want to be sure I'm getting good, clear pictures." He didn't look at her.

Finally, he stepped back. "Okay, we're finished. Go ahead and get dressed."

"I've got to get to a bathroom."

"There's one right next to the dressing room."

As Angelica dressed to meet with Barry Dunteman and go over the results, she realized she'd learned nothing more than her baby was a boy. *He's probably not allowed to tell me anything. There's probably some law about it.*

She took a slow, deep breath, opened the door of the dressing room, and began the walk down the long hall to the room, to the man who held the key to the rest of her life.

When she arrived, Antonio and the counselor were sitting at the table. She noticed pictures from the sonogram were stacked on top of the yellow file. She sat in the chair next to her husband.

"Does everything look okay?" *Say yes. Please, God. Say yes.*

The counselor lifted some of the sonogram pictures from

183

the stack and laid them on the table. "Well, let's take a look."

She leaned forward in her chair.

Running his pen over one of the pictures, he began to explain, "This is the femur, and this is the humerus bone. They are a little shorter than they should be."

A fiery dart of fear hit the pit of her stomach. Her eyes flew to the counselor's face. "Why?"

Maclovia watched her grandson and his wife disappear into the big building. She settled back into the seat and patted her leg.

Buddy obliged her and laid his nose on her knee. As she stroked his head, she looked out the open car window toward the park. She could see the big letters on one of the signs. "G-O-D."

She knew that word. Her grandson had written it on a piece of paper for her once, shortly after she'd come to America. She often laid the paper on her lap during her prayer time, speaking the English word in tribute to the Creator. She closed her eyes. "God, you have brought me here today." She sat quietly, listening, trying to discern His will for her.

After a few minutes, she opened her eyes and looked down the street to the park again. Now, two signs were clearly visible . . . G-O-D.

She picked up Buddy's rope and opened the car door. After straightening her skirt and shawl, she wrapped the rope around her hand and set off to the park to see why God had called her to Santa Rosa.

As she approached the crowd, she sensed a current of

hostility. She slowed her steps, stopping a short distance from the group.

Many held Bibles in their hands, and some shook their Bibles in the air, shouting across the street. Others held their Bibles to their chests and stood with their heads bowed.

Maclovia looked where they were directing their attention and watched.

Every once in a while, a woman would go in, or come out of, the building. Then the crowd would become loud. She heard the words "God" and "*Dios*" dispersed among the many words that were hurled through the air.

Why didn't they just walk across the street and talk to the women? Why did they stand shouting? Why were they lifting the name of the Creator for everyone to see? She did not feel God's presence. Slowly scanning the faces of the men and women, she studied them, one by one.

One man on the edge of the crowd had black hair and dark brown skin. "Come, Buddy."

She came up quietly next to him and tapped his arm. "I have a question."

"*Sí, señora.*" He had a slight American accent.

"What is going on here? Why is everyone so angry at the women across the street?"

The man tilted his head and looked at her for a moment. "We're not angry, *señora*. We just want to have a chance to talk to those women, pray with them. Explain that God loves them, we love them, and they shouldn't go to that clinic."

Maclovia didn't feel the balm of peace that was the vehicle of God's love nor sense the shield of faith that insured the path of prayers to the Creator. Instead, she felt an icy chill.

"Why don't you want the women to go there?"

185

The man spoke slowly, enunciating each word. "That is an abortion clinic."

She stared at him, waiting for him to continue.

"They are going there to end their pregnancies. The law says we must stay here. We can only pray they will come to us."

The crowd's voice began to rise, and the man moved away from her, lifting his sign above his head.

As the meaning of the man's words became clear, Maclovia dropped Buddy's leash, her heart began to pound, and she clenched her fists into her chest. *No. No. No!*

With Buddy at her heels, she hurried a little distance to the side to get a better view of the women going into the clinic. Some of the women looked frightened, one woman was crying, many kept their heads down, faces hidden. As she observed them, she began to discern shame, fear, and despair. Not one, but two victims.

Each time a woman approached the door, Maclovia silently spoke, "God loves you," and prayed, "Lord, touch her with Your love." But each time, the woman continued into the building.

Finally, a very young woman walked toward the building. Beneath her bright orange top, the soft, round swell of her belly was clearly visible. That image, the reality of what she was witnessing, the enormity of it, inflamed Maclovia's spirit and wounded her soul. For the sake of the unborn child, for the sake of its mother, this must be stopped.

Standing with her feet apart, her eyes on heaven, raising her fists, she demanded of the Creator, "Mountain, move."

As her words left her lips, imbued with the passion of grief, they became living things, spiraling heavenward to the throne of God.

A blade of light cut through the air above the building. The power of His might breaching the dimension separating the physical and spiritual world. Unrolling a scroll. Revealing a battle. Not of flesh and blood, but against powers, against spiritual wickedness in high places, against the rulers of the darkness of this world.

She began to tremble but would not move, claiming the ground, persevering, praying fervently in the Spirit that the victory would be won. That the love of God would pierce the darkness.

Within moments, the light vanished, and she was once again present in the park.

Maclovia fell to the ground, prostrate before the Lord, begging His mercy and forgiveness for them all.

Before the counselor could answer her question, Angelica asked him again. "Why would our baby have these short-ened bones?"

"Well, the fetus is small for its gestational age."

She heard Antonio shift in his chair.

"So, it isn't that unusual?"

"By itself, no. But . . ." He looked through the pictures and laid one down between them.

"Here." He pointed to the baby's neck. "The measure-ments indicate the nuchal fold is thickened."

"What does that mean? Is that considered abnormal?"

"It's the totality of the information that will indicate the probability of a chromosomal abnormality. Let's finish going over the information. Then we can talk about what it means and what your options are."

The counselor's words sounded rehearsed. How many other times had he said them? What did he already know from his years of experience? As a public defender, she talked to people every day who had something to hide. The careful choice of words, reserved tone, masked face, everything about the counselor suggested to her he suspected more than he was saying. Why had he used the term "chromosomal abnormality"?

"Does our baby have a birth defect?"

"Amniocentesis is the most conclusive way to determine the presence of birth defects."

"That isn't what I asked." She felt a rush of anger.

Angelica folded her arms across her chest. She wasn't going to let this man ruin her child's life. "So far I've heard two . . . issues. Are there more?"

The counselor thumbed through the pictures. "Here's the nasal bone scan." He laid it on top of the previous picture.

She saw the clear outline of her child's chin, the plumb rise of his lips . . . a flat black space . . . above his lips . . . nothing, where his nose should be. She squinted. Staring. Her hands fell to her lap. She felt like she was being stripped of any power to keep Dunteman's words at bay.

"Exactly what chromosome abnormality would cause that?"

"Considering everything we see here, and the results of your AFP test, there's a high probability of Down syndrome."

She gasped.

"Nearly two-thirds of fifteen- to twenty-two-week-old fetuses with Down syndrome lack a nasal bone. For normal fetuses, the figure is one percent."

Everything became surreal. She felt like she was sitting in a bubble. All of the words were in the air just beyond the bubble. She couldn't breathe. She had to breathe. But then the bubble would dissolve and all the words would be breathed in. Bile rose in her throat. Her hand flew to her mouth.

Antonio's arms were around her, pulling her to his chest.

She breathed in.

"How can we help our baby?" His voice, strangely loud next to her ear, was calm.

"Well, there are several positive markers here for Down syndrome. You can have an amniocentesis. That will be definitive. There is still plenty of time to consider all options."

"What are options?" Antonio asked.

"For the pregnancy?"

Angelica found her voice. "No, he's asking what the word means. Options."

"You could decide to abort the fetus."

"No fetus." Angelica could hear frustration in Antonio's voice. "This my son. What this means, abort the fetus? What it mean to my son?"

The counselor seemed at a loss for words. He looked at Angelica. "Should I see if Ms. Torres is still here? She can translate."

Angelica knew no translation was necessary. The only option her husband would consider was having the baby and loving him. She had to pull herself together. Take control.

Suddenly, she didn't want anything more explained to Antonio. This was too complex. There was too much to consider. What kind of life would the child have? What were the consequences of bringing this life into the world? She felt like everything she'd ever believed was being challenged—who she was . . . who she should be.

"Do you have more questions?" The counselor's voice broke into her thoughts.

Angelica moved away from Antonio into her own chair.

"You've seen hundreds of these images. In your judgment, is our baby going to have Down syndrome? Is there any chance he'll be normal?"

"There is always a chance. Only an amnio can remove all doubt."

Angelica rose. "We appreciate your time."

"I'll send these reports to your doctor."

The counselor led them to the waiting room.

Angelica walked past him without a word, through the office, out into a world that suddenly seemed unpredictable and hostile. She could hear Antonio's steps beside her. Barry Dunteman had said there was a chance. A chance. *Oh, God. A chance is enough for You. More than enough. All things are possible with You.* A fiery dart of doubt pricked at her.

As they approached the car, Angelica could see that Maclovia wasn't in the backseat. What now? "Where's your grandmother?"

Antonio looked at his watch. "We gone over three hours." He stepped onto the sidewalk, looking up and down the street. "There she is. Over there, leaving the park."

"She must have taken Buddy for a walk." Angelica looked past her, to the protesters, their signs, and their Bibles waving in the air. Her thoughts went to the women who were going to the clinic. Some probably had good reason. She got in the car and started it.

Antonio helped Maclovia and Buddy into the backseat. "I'm sorry we were gone so long, *Abuela*, but the tests were not good. We needed . . ."

"Antonio, I don't want to talk about it any more right now. Please." But she did want to talk about it . . . to people who would understand, people who spoke the language, people who would weigh the options.

Antonio got in the car, and she backed out of the parking space. As they drove past the protesters, they passed a van with the local NBC affiliate's logo on it. She glanced at the clinic. *Can't they leave those women alone?* Something clicked . . . turning tumblers of a locked vault. For the first time in her life, she understood why women fought for the right to choose.

No one spoke on the way back to Valle de Lagrimas. Angelica could see in the rearview mirror that Maclovia was visibly upset, staring out the window, her face grief stricken. How much could the old woman possibly understand about what had happened? Perhaps she sensed it.

When they arrived home, Angelica dropped her purse and keys on the kitchen counter and went straight to her bedroom.

She shut the door behind her, locked it, and fell against it. This was not going to happen to her baby. She would fight. The counselor had said there was a chance her baby would be normal. A chance was enough to fight for.

Shortened femur . . . nuchal fold . . . lack a nasal bone. A barrage of words pelted her. She began to tremble.

Was it her fault? Had she done something wrong? Not eaten right? Not exercised enough? The spotting! She should have rested, like the doctor had told her to. Was she being punished now?

She slid down the door, burying her face in her knees. Folding her arms over the top of her head, she wept. . . .

A faint *tap, tap, tap* opened her eyes to darkness.

"Angel?"

It was Antonio's voice.

"Angel?"

She felt for the doorknob, grabbing it and pulling herself up. Turning the knob, she cracked the door open. The hall light behind Antonio hurt her eyes. She turned her head and stepped back into the moonlit darkness of their bedroom.

Antonio slipped through the door and pushed it closed.

His arms were around her, his hand pressing her head into his chest. "Don't shut me out." His voice thick, urgent. "I love you. I understand."

"No, you don't understand. You don't understand anything. You don't even read and write. This is devastating. This is wrong. This is unfair. It shouldn't happen to us. It shouldn't happen to anybody. Ever." She began sobbing.

Her anger and her tears only drew his arms more firmly and lovingly around her. He neither moved nor spoke as she railed against a reality she could not accept.

Finally, she was spent. Her rage replaced by a dulling numbness. She stood still, suddenly realizing the cutting, wounding words that had somehow seemed permissible in the midst of her pain had been heard . . . and understood.

She felt ashamed.

"Antonio. I'm sorry." She looked up into his face. "I'm so sorry."

But he didn't meet her gaze. Instead, he closed his eyes, his jaw set and his face void of emotion. Only the watery tracks on his cheeks, shiny gashes in the dim light, gave a glimpse of what he had endured . . . for love.

He pulled her roughly to him. His voice low. "You are my life, Angelica. And if you can't love our son, I will. If you can't care for him, I will."

The simple, honest words, spoken from his heart, broke through to her. No matter what else changed, Antonio would not change. No matter what happened, she would not be alone. He was giving her a safe place. A place to start. A place where she felt supported and strong enough to face the future, whatever that was. A place that did not come from understanding how to read and write, but came from understanding her.

She stood on her toes, kissed the tears on his face, and wrapped her arms around his neck. "Oh, Antonio. I want every good thing for our baby. I want him to be born perfect. I want his life to be meaningful, to have purpose."

Antonio stroked her hair. "He be born perfect for God's plans. And his life have purpose."

"Do you really think so?" She searched his face.

"I promise."

She rested her head on his chest. She wanted to believe him. . . . She needed to believe him.

But she didn't.

11

THE MORNING SUN began to light the sky; a new day was beginning. As if nothing had changed. Angelica turned her back on the bedroom window.

Her gaze rested on the nightstand. Two roses. "One for you, one for the baby," Antonio had whispered to her when he'd kissed her good-bye and left for work.

The baby. Tears sprang to her eyes, yesterday's devastating news still painfully fresh. She took a shaky breath and bit her lip.

She'd promised herself sometime in the middle of the long night that she would be positive. She wasn't going to become a victim. She would take control. She would learn everything she could about Down syndrome. How it would affect her baby, her family, herself. What her options were. She would even be open to an amniocentesis. And, of course, she would seek God's counsel.

A glance at the clock next to the lamp told her it was 5:36 a.m. She needed to get up and get to the office. All the work she'd missed yesterday was waiting for her on her desk. This was her personal burden and had no place in the office. The income from her job paid the bills. She had to stay professional. Of course, eventually people would find out. The thought of sympathetic glances being exchanged behind her back made her stomach turn. The only thing worse than that would be not working and depending on her parents for income. She steeled herself and rose from the bed.

As she stepped into the hall, she noticed Maclovia's door was still closed. Let her rest. She'd certainly seemed upset about the whole thing. How she had picked up on the seriousness of the situation without anyone explaining it was beyond Angelica.

The telephone rang.

Angelica quickened her steps. Now what? Just as she reached for the phone, the machine picked up.

"Angelica, dear . . ."

Her mother.

She withdrew her hand and stared at the machine.

"I'm *so* concerned. I called last night to see how the appointment went, and no one answered. I left a message, and you didn't return the call. I tried your cell too. I'm going to stay close to the phone now, and if I don't hear from you this morning, I'll come to the house. We love you, Angel."

She'd heard the phone ringing last night when she was in her bedroom and presumed Antonio had answered. She'd forgotten all about it. Looking at the little window on the face of the machine, she saw there was another message. She pressed "Play."

"Hey, girl. It's Fronie." A tired smile tugged at Angelica's lips. "Thinking about you. Hope everything is okay. Call when you can."

Fronie. God bless her. The one person, outside her family, who would understand. A sense of relief flooded over

Angelica at the thought of being able to talk to another woman about her feelings. She looked at the clock on the stove. It was too early to call her now.

Angelica poured herself a cup of coffee, then went into the living room and plopped down on the couch. Thoughts of the day ahead crowded into her mind. She reached for the remote and aimed it at the television. She would allow herself a few minutes to wake up and catch the morning news; the day would start soon enough. The television flickered on.

Angelica sat up, leaning forward. A wide shot of the park in Santa Rosa, and the protesters she'd seen the day before, filled the screen. The camera zoomed to a close-up of the reporter standing in front of the clinic. Angelica nudged the volume up. ". . . was shut down for the rest of the afternoon."

The shot cut to two women, their backs to the camera. One was speaking.

"I had this appointment for a week. I wanted to get it over with. I even came early. As I was walking here from the bus, I suddenly realized I couldn't do it."

An abrupt change in scene showed the reporter speaking to a woman in a bright orange top.

"Did you see anything suspicious?"

The woman shook her head slowly. "I swear I heard thunder, it was very confusing. There wasn't a cloud in the sky. And then I felt something."

The scene switched to a tight shot of a man at a desk. "The power went out this afternoon. We have no idea why, and it still hasn't been fixed."

The reporter pressed him. "Do you think it was sabotage? Part of the protest?"

"We're investigating. There is no evidence of it at this time, but God only knows what those zealots are capable of. Unfortunately, they may have intimidated some of the women. No one came in for our services after the outage. We'll be up and running by tomorrow, I'm sure."

The camera pulled back and panned the park. Many of the protesters had their hands raised, singing. Angelica listened to the voice-over as the piece closed. "The clinic reported not one abortion was performed here this afternoon. A power outage was apparently able to do what the protesters could not."

Angelica frowned at the television. The women hadn't sounded like they were talking about a power outage. Their voices seemed reserved, measured, uncertain. She tilted her head, staring at the screen.

Her eyes widened as the camera again panned the protesters. Behind the crowd just to the side was a dog, a sheltie, standing, tail up, ears forward. Angelica leaned closer to the television. Right next to him was a figure, kneeling, black shawl . . . Maclovia. It was Maclovia kneeling. The same way Angelica had seen her kneel in her bedroom, face to the ground.

This explained why she'd been so upset in the car. It wasn't about the appointment, it was about the protest. Somehow Maclovia had found out what the protest was about, and she'd prayed. Those women, their voices, there *was* more to it. The reporter had said not one abortion had been performed that afternoon. Maclovia had prayed. She had prayed, and God had answered.

Angelica's heart began to pound. She would ask Maclovia to pray for her baby, pray her baby would be born healthy. And she would pray too. She hadn't been faithful about her prayer time. There'd just been too much going on. She'd had to miss Bible study because of work, and, yes, she hadn't been to church in awhile. She hadn't felt well. But she would change. She would give God the time He deserved by putting Him first in her life. Surely, He would honor that. If God was with her, who could be against her? It said in Luke, "Men always ought to pray and not lose heart." This was a test. And she would pass.

Her eyes wandered to the entry table. Her Bible. Still lying where she had dropped it when she'd returned home the last time she'd gone to church. She would put it next to her bed, where she could read it every night.

Suddenly, the front door opened.

"Maclovia!"

A sign from God. Confirmation. She would focus more on learning Spanish so she could understand all that Maclovia could teach her about prayer. "I thought you in your room."

"I was on a walk. Talking to God." Buddy pushed past her and greeted Angelica.

Maclovia handed Angelica the newspaper. "This was out front."

"Did you know you on the news?" Angelica took the paper and unrolled it.

"News?"

Angelica broke into English. "The television news. Here, I bet it's in the paper." She sat on the couch, shaking the paper out. Maclovia sat next to her.

Angelica scanned the front page of the *Press Democrat*. Nothing. She turned to page two. Nothing.

She continued to look through the paper. "Here it is on the back of first section." She pointed to a small headline at the bottom of the page. POWER GOES OUT AT CLINIC.

Maclovia looked at her, questioning.

Angelica quickly read the paragraph to herself. The focus

was on the investigation into criminal activity by the protesters.

Angelica folded up the paper. "You on television, at the
clinic."

Maclovia's eyes sharpened. "Yes?"

"How you do that?" The words slipped out. That wasn't
what she'd meant to ask. Suddenly, Angelica felt bold and
intrusive, like she was trivializing something that was profoundly serious. Not being fluent in the language only made
it worse.

"Do what?"

If only Angelica spoke better Spanish. The old woman
didn't understand what Angelica was talking about.

"You prayed. And women didn't go into the clinic. How
you pray?"

Maclovia's eyes held hers. "From here." Maclovia brushed
her fingertips on her shawl, over her heart.

The simple gesture touched Angelica. She broke down,
sobbing and pouring out her fears in a jumbled mix of
English and Spanish, telling as best she could what she'd
found out about the baby. Maclovia put her arms around
Angelica and held her.

Finally, Angelica pulled away. "I'm sorry. I'm just so
upset."

"I understand." Her simple words settled like a balm over
Angelica. "My grandson spoke to me of this, and so I went
for a walk this morning to encounter God."

"Oh, Maclovia. I want so to encounter God." She'd
blurted the words out in English.

Maclovia sat patiently, observing her.

She took a deep breath. "Maclovia. I . . . want . . . to . . .
learn . . . to . . . pray . . . like . . . you." She pronounced each
word in Spanish, slowly.

"I know, child." Maclovia gave a slight nod of her head and then continued with a sweet smile. "When I encountered God this morning, that is what He told me."

Maclovia reached for her hand.

"Oh, *Abuela*, thank you." She patted Maclovia's hand. "If only we could start now, but I can't, I have to get to work. Tonight. I'll see you tonight."

Angelica wished she hadn't used the drive to work as time to return her mother's call. It had ended with Angelica hanging up at her mother's suggestion that she should consider all her options. Why hadn't her mother just said, "Get an abortion"?

Angelica fumbled in her purse for the office door key. At seven o'clock in the morning, the front door would be locked.

She slammed her purse down on the console. Abortion. That's what everybody was thinking and nobody said. An anchor of guilt fastened itself around her neck. Last night, in the darkened bedroom, staring at the ceiling . . . She crossed her arms on the steering wheel and pressed her forehead into them, helpless against the weight of the memory. *God, forgive me.*

She felt the car shift. Startled, she lifted her head.

"Max!" Right at her elbow, on the other side of the driver's window, hand on the door latch. How long had he been standing there? Angelica grabbed her purse and opened the door.

Max stepped up close to her and took her upper arm, helping her from the car. "You okay?" She heard real concern in his voice, his face just inches from hers.

"Uh, yes, I'm fine." She stepped away from him with a

false casualness and shut the car door. There was a faint smell of liquor just beneath the aftershave. "Sorry I didn't make it back yesterday. The appointment went longer than I thought it would." Max's gaze was penetrating and made her uneasy. He'd never taken more than a passing interest in her personal life, but now she sensed a subtle undercurrent.

He was the chief public defender, with the responsibilities of the whole department. He'd chosen her to work with him on the Vasquez case because he needed someone capable and committed enough to take the bulk of the workload. Maybe he was beginning to wonder if she was up to it. Her stomach knotted. She had to call Dr. Gremian today and find out if he wanted to see her after reviewing the ultrasound results. But she just couldn't take more time off work. Max had done everything in his power to keep her freed up from other cases so she could devote all her time to the appeal, not so she could spend hours away from the office. She couldn't let him down now. There wasn't a thing Dr. Gremian could tell her that she didn't already know.

They walked side by side across the parking lot. She broke the awkward silence. "What are you doing here so early?"

"Things have been backing up. I've been here since five. I serve at the pleasure of the board of supervisors and the county administrator." He gave her a conspiratorial smile, changing the atmosphere between them back to the amiable work relationship she'd come to enjoy. "That's a lot of bosses. Glad I've got you backing me up on the Vasquez case. By the way, I'm through with those depositions you've been bugging me for. You can have the files back." He took a key out of his pocket and opened the office door. "I've got to prepare for a meeting. I'll catch you later." He gave her a wicked smile. "The media's been calling about Vasquez."

She stopped in her tracks as he sauntered down the hall to his office. The media. That could be a blessing or a curse. Fortunately, the media bias had favored them . . . so far.

Angelica stopped and got a bottle of water from the vending machine, then continued to her office. As she stepped through the door, she caught her breath. Flowers. A small bouquet of baby roses in an exquisite glass basket. She looked for a card. There wasn't one.

She turned the basket slowly, in a circle. Whoever had bought it knew her well. She loved it. On the back was a gold sticker with a silver border. "Crossley's." The expensive gift store across town was a place she'd visited often to find special gifts for special friends. Her mouth curved with tenderness. Fronie.

"Hey, girlfriend."

Angelica whirled around. "They're beautiful."

Fronie's lips parted in surprise. "Oh my, they are." She stepped beside Angelica and examined the gift.

"I just love that store. Thank you so much." Angelica felt herself tearing up.

"Me?"

"Yes, *you*. For the flowers."

Fronie stared at her blankly.

"Did this come while I was gone yesterday?"

Fronie thought a moment. "Not while I was at the front desk. And besides, when you didn't come back yesterday, I looked in here just before I left to be sure your lights were off. I didn't see them then."

Angelica frowned. "It couldn't have been Antonio. Even if he'd managed to buy these without me knowing, he couldn't have gotten them on my desk this morning."

"Not unless he came by and someone happened to be here and let him in."

"Well, I did run into Max in the parking lot, and he said he's been here since five."

Fronie smiled. "I bet that's it." Her face grew serious. "I just wanted to see if you're doing okay. You didn't call me back last night." Fronie ignored the vacant chair by the desk. Instead, she remained standing.

A simple "I'm okay" would send Fronie down the hall, respecting her wishes not to discuss the matter.

Angelica looked at the clock on her computer. She should get to work; there was so much to do. But she might not get a break for the rest of the day, and she did want to talk about it. "Sit a minute." She reached out and pushed the door shut with her toe.

Turning to Fronie, she opened her mouth to speak. But every time she tried to form a word, her chin began to tremble. She pressed her lips together. She must stay in control.

Fronie put her hand on Angelica's arm, gently rubbing it. "It's okay."

Angelica silently shook her head.

It wasn't okay. It would never be okay again. But she had to keep it together. What if the phone rang, what if a client came in, what if Max stopped by? She must not cry here, in the office.

She broke down.

Fronie's arms were around her, holding her, comforting her.

But rather than allow herself to feel her pain, she fought it. This wasn't the time or place. She swallowed hard, choking down her grief. With a force of will, she managed to steady her breathing. Pulling herself up, she composed herself. She opened her drawer and took out some tissues.

"Oh, Fronie, I'm so scared and confused." She wiped her

nose. "The ultrasound showed three indicators of Down syndrome."

Fronie's shoulders slumped, and she closed her eyes for a moment.

All the things Angelica had not allowed herself to voice were suddenly on her lips. "What does this mean? Will I have to quit my job? What happens if the baby never walks or talks . . ." She could feel her throat closing up again. ". . . or knows who I am?"

Her friend seemed at a loss for words.

"I've gone over everything a hundred times. What did I do to cause this? What could I have done differently? Why am I bringing all of this onto my family? What's wrong with me that God would allow this?"

Fronie shook her head. "It's not your fault. These things just happen."

"But why is it happening to me?"

"Hon, try not to think the worst. Did the doctor say your baby definitely has Down syndrome?"

Angelica hesitated. "No." She wiped her eyes. "But everything is pointing to that."

"Can't they give you a test that would tell you for sure?"

"They can, and I'm totally open to it. But Antonio is really against it. He didn't even like it that I had this testing done that we just went through."

"Why?"

"He says this is the baby God is giving us and feels the tests are pointless. He says we'll find out all we need to know when the baby's born."

Fronie sat back in her chair and put her hands in her lap, searching Angelica's face. "He's right, you know. God is in control."

Angelica stared at Fronie, the words somehow penetrating the wall of fear that hung between her and the real world. "God *is* in control," she whispered back.

Fronie took her hand with gentle authority. "He'll never leave you or forsake you, Angelica."

Fronie said it with such confidence, Angelica felt her spirits lift.

"Bible study is tonight. Come, and we'll pray for you." Fronie gave her a sweet smile.

It was true. God was in control, and hadn't she just made a promise that morning that she would pray more? Maybe this was God, acknowledging he'd heard her, using Fronie to reach out to her. "I've missed the last few, but I'll be there tonight. Those women are such a blessing."

"That's for sure." Fronie rose. "Guess we should both get to work. I'll see you later."

She shut the door behind her as she left. Angelica turned back to her desk.

The basket.

Antonio had never been to Crossley's as far as she knew. She picked up the basket, looking at it more carefully.

It wasn't glass, it was crystal. Heavy and expensive. An unsettling thought formed in her mind. Max.

The more she thought about it, the more uneasy she became. It was critical that she and Max maintain a strictly professional relationship.

The fragrance of the roses had begun to sweeten the air. Angelica frowned. Better to confront the issue. She thought for a moment, then stood. Max had said he'd finally finished reviewing the depositions. She'd go pick up the files, and if he wasn't in the middle of something, she'd ask about the flowers. She turned and walked to Max's office.

His door was open, but the office was empty.

Angelica took a few steps toward his desk, looking at the stacks of documents, but she didn't see the deposition files. She stepped around the edge of the desk and sat in Max's chair, leaning over the desk, scanning the papers, envelopes, and files, carefully picking through them, hoping to find what she was looking for. But she didn't.

It wouldn't be appropriate for her to go through everything on his desk, even though she did need the information for reference. She sat back in his chair.

Something jabbed her.

Arching her back, she leaned forward, then reached around, pressing her hand against the soft chair cushion. There was definitely something hard behind the fabric.

Angelica stood up and faced the chair back. Pressing her hand near the base of the cushion, she tried to relocate the hard spot.

Just above where the seat and back cushion met, she found it. She stepped back; there wasn't any telltale bulge. She pressed the spot again.

Feeling her way to the side of the chair, she ran her fingers down the seams. Near the arm she felt an irregularity. A flicker of apprehension fluttered in her stomach. She pulled her hand away, looking anxiously toward the door.

Quickly bending down, she saw the seam had been closed with Velcro. Giving it a tug, it opened easily, the strips well worn. Her heart began to pound.

She slipped her hand into the cushion and immediately felt a slick surface. Grasping it, she pulled.

She turned the bottle's face so she could read it.

"Jose Cuervo Tequila."

By the time Angelica arrived at the Faith Community Church parking lot, she felt completely overwhelmed.

When she'd called Dr. Gremian, he'd insisted she come in. But she'd already made up her mind; she was going to put her faith in God. She wouldn't be seeing Dr. Gremian for another four weeks.

Then Max had come into her office. She hadn't mentioned the basket, and neither had he. She should have. When she'd talked to Antonio at dinner about his day, it was clear he knew nothing of the flowers. A twinge of guilt pricked her. She felt like she was hiding something from her husband. Still, there was no reason to upset him, when she didn't know for sure who'd given the gift to her. She pulled into a parking space.

The worst part of the day had been when she'd allowed herself a break from the Vasquez case and started searching the Internet to find information about Down syndrome. The details about the defects the ultrasound had shown hadn't made her feel any better. The defects were called "markers." She knew that now. She also knew the statistics were against her. She needed a miracle, and she'd come to Faith Church to get one. This wasn't going to happen to her or her baby.

Angelica shut off the engine and got out of the car.

"Wait up."

Angelica stopped and turned. It was Fronie. They picked their way through the cars, toward the church.

Natalya greeted them as they walked into the sanctuary. The lights were dimmed. Some people were kneeling at the altar. There were more women than usual, and Angelica didn't recognize some of the ladies.

"We love you so much." Natalya wrapped her arms around Angelica and hugged her. "When Fronie called and said you needed prayer and were coming tonight, I called our prayer chain and let people know."

"Oh, thank you," Angelica whispered.

"I told Pastor Bob we were skipping Bible study tonight and devoting the evening to prayer. He said we could use the sanctuary."

Angelica and Fronie followed Natalya to the front of the church. Angelica seated herself while Natalya and Fronie sat on either side of her. Angelica bowed her head. Fronie took her hand, and Natalya put her arm around Angelica's shoulder. They prayed silently with her.

Soon another woman joined them. Fronie let go of Angelica's hand and slipped away.

One by one, the women present came and sat by her and prayed with her. Some Angelica knew, some she recognized, some she'd never seen before. She felt their love and concern. It touched her deeply.

She had no idea how much time had passed when Natalya got up. "Everyone, let's make a circle around Angelica. It's time to close."

Angelica stood and walked to the open space between the pews and the steps that led to the elevated platform from which the pastor gave his sermons. The women gathered around her.

One woman near the back spoke out. "We pray *to You*, O Lord, believing You for a miracle."

Angelica heard the woman next to her whisper, "Yes, Jesus."

Some gave long prayers, holding God to account with His own words. Others prayed fervently, calling on God's greatness to do all things, asking God to give Angelica and her husband a child whose life He could prosper to serve Him.

One woman humbly reminded God He was a God of mercy and love. Another quoted from the book of Job, a subtle reminder that God sometimes tries those He loves.

Finally, Natalya spoke. "Dear Lord, we know with You all things are possible. We ask that Your will be done in Angelica's life and the life of her child. Amen." She looked at Angelica.

Angelica slowly scanned the group of women. "Thank you all, so much. Please keep me in your prayers." The circle began to break up.

By the time Angelica got on the road home, it was after eleven o'clock. She'd told Antonio when she'd left not to wait up for her. Undoubtedly, Maclovia would have retired for the night. She was usually in her room with the door shut by seven. Angelica had hoped to meet with Maclovia, but the time she'd just spent with the ladies at church, hearing their prayers and being reminded of God's promises, gave her a sense of peace that she hadn't felt in days. Talking with Maclovia didn't seem so important now.

The house was dark when Angelica pulled in. She went through the garage, then into the house through the utility room. Buddy opened one eye as she stepped over him.

After laying her purse and keys on the table, she kicked off her shoes, then tiptoed through the kitchen and down the hall. Maclovia's door was cracked open. Angelica peeked in.

"Come in, my child."

Angelica was so startled she didn't move. Maclovia was sitting by the window in her rocker, hands folded in her lap. Waiting for her.

"Come," she said gently. Rising, she extended her gnarled

hand to Angelica. Even in the dim light Angelica could see the tremor of old age.

Angelica grasped Maclovia's crooked fingers and stepped closer, stopping in front of her.

"You want to learn to pray, child?"

She did want to learn to pray. But she was so tired. The time at the church had been emotionally draining. She couldn't quite recall why it had seemed so important this morning.

Maclovia began to hum.

Angelica suddenly felt a drawing. The tremulous grip of Maclovia's hand became strong and firm, like that of a much younger woman.

Angelica felt the baby move.

"Can you teach me to pray like you do?"

Maclovia knelt, and Angelica followed. Moments passed. Maclovia did not speak; she only hummed softly.

Perhaps she was waiting for Angelica to start. Angelica closed her eyes and began, "Oh, dear God."

The humming stopped.

Angelica looked at Maclovia, searching her face. "What's wrong?"

Maclovia spoke softly. "He is not here."

"Of course He's here. God is everywhere, all the time."

"We must wait on Him."

Angelica's heart sank. She was too tired to wait. Why would God make her wait? What was Maclovia talking about? He wanted to hear her prayers, didn't He?

"Why?"

"He is God."

Angelica felt a flash of anger and dropped Maclovia's hand. "I know that." She immediately regretted her words. "I'm sorry, *Abuela*. I am very tired tonight." She rose. "Maybe tomorrow night."

210

Maclovia stood, listening. She heard Angelica shut the bedroom door. This *was* a serious matter.

Antonio had told her all the doctor had said about the baby. How there was something wrong with him. How he was not acceptable in some way. How Angelica had believed it.

Maclovia's heart was heavy. Man's truth. That's what it was. Not God's truth. The two things as different as God and man. Only God could reveal *His* truth. Man could not discover it with machines and tests.

Maclovia sat in her chair and began to rock. She closed her eyes, revisiting each moment she'd just spent with her grandson's wife.

Angelica had begun by praying *to* God, apparently unaware that she could pray in His presence. Perhaps she only knew the Lord and had never experienced Him. It was only when one was dealt with by God that one came to a true knowledge of Him.

She began to hum, wanting to discern the unspoken words, the nuances, the purpose of the meeting God had called her to.

A beautiful, high voice began to fill the air around her. She lifted her hands, trembling. Not with the palsied shaking of old age, but the holy tremor of the Spirit.

Suddenly, a certain knowledge came to her. The child was special. The child had something extra. Something God would use to reveal His truth.

12

WHAT A WAY to spend a beautiful Saturday morning in July. Angelica dropped her pen and leaned back in her office chair, she'd been working nonstop since seven. As much as she hated coming in on the weekend, these Saturday mornings spent in the office kept her head above water during the week.

She kicked off her sandals and threw her feet up on the desk. At least she didn't have to dress up. Nobody was around. She looked at her legs sticking out of her cuffed shorts. Not a bit of color to them. She promised herself that she'd make time to sit out in the backyard when she got home. Antonio would be there. Some time with him sounded wonderful.

She smoothed the fabric over her stomach. Her pregnancy barely showed. She'd thought about buying a few maternity outfits, after seeing a sale advertised on television. She'd actually gone to the store and admired a darling yellow summer shift with an empire waist and smocked bodice. But when she'd tried on a size 8 and it had hung on her, she'd abruptly left the store. Too many weeks of morning sickness. Too many sleepless nights. She leaned her head against the back of the chair.

It had been over three weeks since the wrenching visit with the genetic counselor. She'd managed to avoid her parents. Her mother had called several times, and their conversations had been cordial, but short. It was awkward to talk about everything but the baby. Yet the minute the conversation started in that direction, Angelica found herself becoming defensive. *When is your next doctor's appointment, why haven't you been up to see us, have you considered the options . . .* were all woven into casual conversation, disguised as *what are your plans this week, been working late,* and *we love you and want what's best for you.*

Her eyes wandered to the little credenza under the window, across from her desk. A picture of her parents, broad smiles, faces full of pride, standing beside her the day she graduated from law school, stared back at her in silent condemnation. Her parents *had* been good to her. They'd given her the best of everything, and they loved her. She knew that. But suddenly, for the first time in her life, she felt like she was failing them.

A sparkle of sunlight glinted off the crystal basket next to the picture. She stared at it, frowning.

She threw her feet down and walked over to it. Picking it up, she watched the sun play in the crystal. She hadn't known what to do with it when the flowers died. It was such a pretty piece. It looked much too expensive to throw away. Yet she felt like she didn't have any business keeping it. She held it a little higher, watching the light dance through it.

Over the past few weeks, Max had seemed to involve himself more and more with the Vasquez case. Things she could do, he took on; things they'd discussed required a second meeting. He even asked her on occasion if she was feeling ill and wanted to go home. In a way, she felt supported and secure by his sensitivity to her situation. In another way, she felt uneasy. He asked her about a lot of things, but he never asked her about her husband.

She sighed. Monday she would ask one of the girls up front if they would like to take the basket home.

"Beautiful, isn't it."

Angelica jumped. "Max!" She felt heat crawling up her neck as she turned to face him.

He stood so close to her she could see the stubble of his beard. As she stepped away from him, his eyes traveled to her legs.

Angelica put the basket down and hastily maneuvered around him. She sat down in her chair and walked it tight under her desk.

"What are you doing here?" His clothes were wrinkled, and his hair looked like he'd combed it with his fingers.

"I was driving by and saw your car."

The residential area down the street from the office was nowhere near where Max lived. But from the looks of him, she concluded there must have been one colossal party in that nearby neighborhood the night before.

He picked up the basket, admiring it as he stepped to the chair next to her desk. "I thought it would cheer you up."

So it had been Max. She felt a twinge in the pit of her stomach. "That was very kind of you." She avoided his gaze. "I need to get to work now."

"You shouldn't be working so hard." He set the basket on the desk, between them.

The clink of the glass against the desk seemed oddly loud on this quiet Saturday morning.

He sat down.

Angelica picked up her pen and tapped it on the legal pad

in front of her. "It's my job." She gave him a guarded smile and turned back to her work.

He didn't move, seizing her dismissive words and turning them into a cumbersome silence, creating an undercurrent of tension. She felt heat stealing into her face.

He placed his hand on her arm.

Angelica pulled away, leaning back in her chair and facing him. Her lips set in a firm line.

"It's okay, Angelica. You don't have to pretend with me."

"Pretend what?" She leveled her eyes at him, her voice demanding.

"I know." His gaze was calm, his voice steady.

She didn't move, searching her memory for some clue as to what he was talking about.

"The baby."

Stunned, she watched him warily, waiting for him to continue.

"I've seen the websites on your computer screen. All the doctor's appointments, all the time you've taken off."

She looked away. "It's not something I want to talk about. It's none of your business."

He leaned toward her. "I care about you. It *is* my business."

There was a territorial possessiveness to his voice. Suddenly, she felt like she was standing in a minefield. She picked up her pen and adjusted the pad. "I've got to get busy, Max. I want to spend some time with my husband this afternoon."

"Fine." He pushed himself out of the chair so abruptly he forced a stack of files onto the basket, tipping it over.

She watched him storm out.

It hit her. He was jealous!

As the door slammed behind him, the basket rolled in a half circle toward the edge of the desk. She reached for

215

it, trying to save it, but it shattered as it hit the edge of the chair where Max had been sitting.

Angelica stood, staring at the beautiful, perfect piece of crystal Max had destroyed.

Antonio gathered up his tools from Mrs. Dupre's yard and put them in his wheelbarrow. He always did her yard on Saturday when he did his own, since it was right next door to his house. He stood with his hands on his hips, surveying his work. She'd been his first account, and he'd worked the first few weeks for free to get her business. He'd underbid the job, and she was paying about half what he would charge now. But a promise was a promise, and he felt bound to keep his word. He looked at his watch. Angelica should be back in the early afternoon. He grabbed the wheelbarrow and rolled it home.

After taking a shower and putting on his good clothes, he kissed Maclovia good-bye and set off to town. He wanted to find the dress store he'd seen on television.

The advertisement for the store had been on the television several times when he and Angelica had been watching. Angelica had mentioned she would like to go to the "specialty shop." Each night when Angelica had worked late, Antonio had watched carefully to catch the name and address of the store, so he could buy her a "specialty dress" and surprise her. But the announcer talked so fast that he could barely follow what was said. The word "First" had been on the television screen, and he was sure that he'd caught "First Street" in the dialogue. The name of the store was a vegetable. He remembered that. What "specialty" meant, he wasn't sure.

When he got to the downtown area of Valle de Lagrimas, he drove to the main street. Most all the stores were on that street or on a cross street. He cruised along, trying to keep his eyes on the road and catch the street names.

He soon found this annoyed the drivers behind him. Several laid on their horns and made rude gestures when they passed him. The Americans had no patience. He'd learned that long ago. Still, it wasn't right for him to make their driving difficult. He pulled into a parallel parking space on the main street. He would walk the rest of the way.

After he turned off the engine, he reached across the seat, opened the glove compartment, and took out a wad of bills from underneath a jumble of sprinkler parts, tape, and papers. He counted it. Forty-three dollars. Straightening his leg out, he stuffed the money into his pants pocket.

He got out of the truck and locked the door.

"Hey, jerk."

Antonio looked around. There was no one else nearby.

"You're blocking my line of sight. I can't see to back out."

Antonio realized that the angry voice was coming from the car parked on the other side of his truck. He walked toward it to see what the problem was.

"You're an idiot. Pulling in like that. I was trying to back out, and now I can't see down the street." The man's face was a deep red, and his hand, hanging out the open window, balled into a fist. He pounded it on the car door. "Stupid Mexican."

Antonio immediately realized he had done something thoughtless. He should have looked more carefully before pulling into the parking space. He would have seen the man was trying to back out. Now, it seemed, the man was looking for a fight.

Antonio hesitated a moment, then stepped toward the

open window of the driver's door. He would turn away the man's wrath.

"No worry. I help you."

He walked backward into the street. Standing behind the car, stopping traffic, he motioned with his hand for the man to back out. Little by little the man did, as Antonio held up traffic.

When the man was completely out of the parking space, Antonio stepped up to the window. "You clear now."

The man's eyes narrowed, and he stared at Antonio, finally speaking. "Sorry I called you a Mexican."

Antonio smiled broadly. "That okay. I am Mexican." He stepped back, whistling as he walked to the sidewalk.

He looked up and down the street, trying to determine where First Street might be. He was reasonably sure that he had not already passed it. He set off down the boulevard looking for a store with the name of a vegetable.

He walked several blocks, then noticed that there were fewer and fewer stores and more and more big buildings with offices in them. He stopped and sat on a bench positioned in front of a low wall that framed the entry to one of the big buildings. He drummed his fingers on his knee. He did so want to buy Angelica a really special present. He frowned. There was so much he couldn't do for her that an American husband would have been able to do, like understanding what had been said on the television and then driving to the store. His shoulders slumped. *Dios, only You know how I love her.*

He stared at his hands, stained and cut, then let them drop to his side. With his chin on his chest and his eyes cast down, he breathed a deep sigh and rose, turning to retrace his steps to the truck.

"Oh, I'm so sorry!"

Antonio jerked his head up in confusion and surprise.

218

"*Lo siento, señorita.*" He extracted his toes from under a baby stroller. "So sorry too."

"I wasn't looking where I was going. The baby was crying. . . ."

"Is okay." He smiled at her, understanding completely.

The young woman picked her baby up out of the stroller. The baby turned toward Antonio. Her almond shaped eyes were barely open, and her tongue protruded slightly from her mouth.

Antonio was immediately transported to his childhood. Margarita. He had not thought of the little girl in years. She was the daughter of one of the families who had lived in the fields of Guadalajara. All the children had loved her and fought over who would get to carry her. The girls had treated her like a living doll, and the boys had protected her from the daily dangers of snakes and animals and swollen streams. She was everyone's child, and everyone grieved that her life had been short. Especially her mother, who never recovered from the loss, and soon after, followed her only daughter to the arms of God.

The woman looked toward the big building. "I'm supposed to meet my husband here. Is that the law office of Genzberger and Grabinski?"

"I don't know." Antonio shrugged his shoulders. "Maybe ask inside."

The pretty girl patted the baby's back, trying to quiet her. *Maybe ask . . .* Of course.

"*Señora*, may I ask you a question?"

She looked at him.

He chose his words carefully and pronounced them clearly. "I am trying to find that store."

"What store?"

219

He bit his lower lip, searching his memory. "It is the name of a *hortaliza*."

She gave him a blank stare.

"Er. Uh. Sorry. I am sorry. Vegetable. It is the name of vegetable."

She raised her eyebrows, then suddenly laughed. "A pea? A pea in a pod?"

He looked at her with a blank stare.

"That's the name of it. A Pea in a Pod. It's a maternity store. I've been there many times."

Antonio beamed. "Where can I find it?"

The young woman turned, pointing across the street, in the direction he'd just come from.

"Walk down there to the light. Turn right. Directly in front of you will be First Street. It runs the same direction as this one. You'll see it. They always have a sandwich sign out front. It has a picture of an open pod with three little baby faces peeking out."

What a "pod" looked like was beyond him. But "three baby faces" he knew, and "sandwich sign" he knew. Since they also sold food, it should be easy to find.

"*Gracias. Gracias* so much." He dashed across the street and didn't slow down until he reached the light and turned right. The very next street sign was "First," and the minute he rounded the corner he saw a sign sitting on the sidewalk with the three baby faces. He glanced around. Nothing about sandwiches though.

He walked the few short yards to the store's windows. The lifelike ladies behind the glass were all expecting babies. Antonio's jaw dropped. So this was the "specialty."

He peered through the open door. There wasn't a man in sight. He took a few tentative steps forward.

"May I help you?"

He turned stiffly toward the friendly, Spanish speaking voice.

"Looking for a gift?"

Just behind the saleslady's right shoulder was a rack of women's underwear. . . . He locked his eyes on the woman's face.

"Yes, for my wife."

"We're having a wonderful sale. Fifty percent off. Did you have something in mind?"

"A dress?"

Reluctant to let his eyes wander around the store, he followed the saleswoman's gaze to several racks of dresses. "And how much did you want to spend?"

Antonio patted his pocket, thankful he'd brought all his savings. "I have forty-three dollars."

"Well, let's see what's on sale." As they moved toward the racks, the saleswoman chatted, and he began to relax. "What size is she?"

"Small." He put his hand horizontal to his chest.

"I meant, what size dress does she wear?" The woman began to slowly turn one of the racks.

Antonio had never heard Angelica speak of the size of her clothes. "I don't know."

The woman selected a dress and held it up. "Does this look like it would fit her?"

Antonio lifted his arms, pretending to put his hands on Angelica's shoulders, then stepped toward the dress, lining them up with the neck. "No, too big."

The saleswoman looked at the distance between his hands, then took a different dress from the rack. "How's this?"

Antonio held the dress in front of him, studying it. Imagining his beautiful Angel standing before him. "Still a little big, I think."

"Oh dear, that was a size 8. We don't have many in size 6. And I doubt there are any on the sale racks." She began to go through the rack, dress by dress.

After searching the rack twice, the woman removed a dress, crammed tight among the sale items. "Here's one." She took it off the hanger and shook it out.

Antonio flashed the woman a smile. "That is *very* beautiful." He took it from her, holding it with his fingertips. The sleeveless, yellow dress was quite elegant, with fancy stitching all across the top.

"How much is it?" He held his breath.

The saleslady fished out the price tag from the back of the neck. She looked at it, then turned it over, then turned it over again. She ran her finger around the neck and armholes. "I'm so sorry. This dress isn't on sale. It isn't marked down at all."

Antonio's face fell.

"That happens sometimes during big sales. People find something, then decide against it and end up sticking it on the sales rack. I'm so sorry. That's probably the only reason it's still here."

"How much is it?" He laid the top gently over one forearm and scooped up the skirt with the other.

The saleslady turned the tag hanging from the dress so he could see it. "Seventy-six dollars."

"Maybe it was supposed to be on sale, and it just hasn't been marked." He took a step back from her, tightening his hold on the dress.

"No, I'm sorry."

"Maybe I could make payments." He would get more work. He could get up earlier and work later into the night.

The woman pursed her lips. "We don't give credit here."

222

He stood silently as she lifted the dress out of his arms and put it back on the hanger.

She hesitated. "You know." She held the dress up, looking at it. "This being on the sale rack was very misleading."

Antonio nodded.

"But there's no way I could mark this down fifty percent. It's part of our summer line."

Antonio didn't take his eyes off her. He felt himself straining with her.

The dress in hand, she tilted her chin toward the front of the store. "Come with me to the cash register."

He followed her, mouthing "thank you, thank you," to the back of her head.

She laid the dress on the counter and picked up a calculator. "Let's see. I think it would be fair to give a twenty-percent discount for the misunderstanding." She pressed several buttons on the calculator. "How much money did you say you have?"

Antonio dug in his pocket and laid the forty-three dollars on the counter. Then he took out his wallet and took all the bills in it, laying them on the counter.

The woman counted the money with him.

"Nineteen dollars?" He looked at her hopefully.

"You were just seventeen dollars and eighty cents short. But—"

Antonio slapped the counter with his hand. "This is great!"

The saleswoman cut her eyes to him. "But. Um."

What could possibly be wrong now?

"Taxes."

He stared at the woman. Moments passed.

Bill by bill, he picked up his money, carefully smoothing

each one and placing it in his wallet. "I'm sorry I made all this work for you. It is not meant for me to have the dress."

"You're only three dollars and sixty cents short."

Antonio shrugged his shoulders. Life had taught him that as a man he was only capable of so much. He had worked hard, and the money he had was all he'd been able to save. "Perhaps I can find something else for her."

The saleswoman reached under the counter. Pulling her purse out, then setting it on the counter, she opened it and took out her wallet.

Antonio's eyes widened. "Oh, no, *señora*. That would not be right."

The lady laid three dollar bills and sixty cents where Antonio's money had been. "I am more than happy to do this. Please let me."

He studied her face. Her eyes were compassionate and kind.

"With a condition, *señora*. You will let me repay this money next week."

Her smile brightened, and she extended her hand. "Deal."

As Antonio carried his package back to the truck, his thoughts returned to Angelica . . . beautiful, loving, kind. He thanked God every day for her. Except for God's mercy, he would never have found her; except for God's grace, she could never have loved him.

And that day in the doctor's office. He had been profoundly moved by the pictures of the child she carried. His son. Reminding him, not only had God blessed him with the woman of his dreams, but now he was being gifted with a life ordained by the Creator Himself.

He opened the door of the truck and gently laid the box on the passenger seat. Then, before starting the engine, he bowed his head and whispered a prayer from a deeply thankful heart.

As Angelica turned the corner onto her street, she saw Antonio pulling into the driveway. She glanced at the clock. It was almost two. She'd left work before she'd finished all the things she'd planned to catch up on because she wanted to be with him . . . in his arms . . . the rest of the world at bay. Thankfully, there was still plenty of time left to have a lazy Saturday afternoon with the man she loved.

Max's behavior earlier that morning had been disturbing. The far-reaching implications of him having an interest in her that went beyond their professional relationship made her shudder. She'd thought of nothing else since he'd stormed out of the office. When she'd first found the flowers on her desk, she'd been suspicious, yet foolishly not pursued it, knowing at some level that confronting Max could compromise her opportunity to help Miguel Vasquez get the justice he deserved. She'd let her commitment to freeing an innocent man cloud her judgment. Looking back, maybe Max had taken that as a signal, her silent agreement to participate in some quiet affair of the heart. Could she continue to work side by side with him? What a mess.

She pulled into the garage next to Antonio's truck. He'd already gone into the house and left the door open for her. She got out of her car, pressing the button to shut the garage door on her way into the house.

When she stepped into the kitchen, Antonio was leaning against the counter waiting for her, holding a big box in front of a bigger smile.

"Ooh. What's that?" The stress and pressure of the day vanished.

"For you, *señorita*." He held the box out to her.

As she stepped toward him, he lifted the box above her head, where she couldn't reach it. She hopped up on her toes, but he stepped sideways. She began to giggle. "Stop it."

"Talk to me in Spanish," he teased her. "I like it when you talk to me in Spanish."

"*Por favor, señor.*"

"I especially like it when you say 'kiss me.'" His dark eyes shone with amusement.

He held the box out in front of him, making an inviting circle between the box and his chest.

Angelica slipped into it, put her arms around his neck, and complied with his request. "Kiss me."

He tossed the box on the table and tightened his arms around her, lifting her off her feet and gazing into her eyes. "I love you."

He was so incredibly strong, yet he held her as if she were weightless. Every kiss with him was like a first kiss. She felt completely at his mercy . . . and it was heavenly. She lapsed into English. "Kiss me again."

He slowly shook his head.

"Kiss me again," she said in Spanish.

He set her down. "I will kiss you later." He flashed her a smile. "Now, open your present."

Angelica sat at the table and pulled the box in front of her. As she was about to open it, Antonio stepped away from her.

"*Abuela*! Here, sit." Antonio pulled a chair away from the table and offered it to his grandmother.

Thinking of everything she'd just said with abandon in Spanish, Angelica felt heat rise in her cheeks. It seemed a little too coincidental that Maclovia happened to appear just after Antonio had set her down.

226

"I was making the baby a hat." She smiled sweetly. "But Buddy said he wanted to go out."

They looked to the slider. Buddy was standing, staring at the handle. Antonio let him out into the backyard.

He took a seat across from them. "Now open it." He nudged the box toward Angelica.

She shook the bottom of the box from the lid, revealing a layer of white tissue paper. She lifted it.

"I don't believe it." She stood, whisking the dress from the box. It looked like the very same dress she'd tried on at A Pea in a Pod. "Oh, this is lovely. But . . ." She held the dress away from her. "I think it's a little too big."

"I don't think so, *señorita*." He rose and walked around the table.

She pulled the dress to her chest. "Do you know I tried on this very dress last week? An 8 was the smallest they had." She huffed a sigh. "I just loved it."

Antonio grinned and stepped toward her, taking the dress and holding it up to her. "I think it will be perfect."

She looked up into her husband's loving eyes. For the first time in a long time she felt a little twinge of excitement about her pregnancy.

"If it's not perfect, I will fix that." Maclovia stooped down and turned up the edge of the dress, looking at the seam.

Buddy started barking in the backyard.

Angelica looked at Antonio. "Was that the doorbell?" She laid the dress on the back of a kitchen chair.

Antonio followed her to the front door, standing beside her as she opened it.

"Mom!"

She looked past her mother and saw her father getting out of their black Jaguar. "Big toys for big boys," he'd said when he'd bought it.

227

Antonio stepped in front of Angelica. "Welcome. Please come in." He pulled the door open and gestured toward the living room couch.

"*Abuela*, come, the *patrón* and Mrs. Amante are here."

They all seated themselves, Maclovia joining them, with Buddy at her heels.

Angelica looked at Antonio.

Her mother looked at her father.

Finally, her father cleared his throat. "The yard looks nice."

"Antonio's roses are certainly blooming," her mother added.

"Do you know that, with all the plants Antonio has planted in our yard and his clients' yards, not one has ever died?" Angelica patted his knee.

Her mother shifted in her seat.

"Have you had to work a lot lately?" Angelica recognized her mother's question as an invitation to explain why Angelica had not been up to visit them.

"I always have a lot of work." The evasive answer should nip that line of questioning in the bud. "You know that."

Her mother stiffened. "Angelica, we've been so concerned about you."

"I'm fine. There's nothing to be concerned about." Angelica folded her hands in her lap.

"You've got to stop isolating yourself, Angelica." Her father's face became stern. "We want to help you."

"I don't need any help. I'm doing fine." She could hear her voice rising.

Her father's voice softened. "You told your mother that the last ultrasound showed some markers for a birth defect. What markers?"

Angelica looked toward Antonio, a morass of emotions

flooding through her. If only he could handle this. If only he could explain to them how she felt.

Antonio straightened and addressed her parents. "Angelica want you to understand."

"Understand what?" Her mother spit the words out.

"Understand she is having our baby."

Suddenly, his simple words cut through to her. She was having *their* baby. Her baby. Of course she had known that, but she hadn't accepted it. Ever since she had seen the devastating ultrasound pictures, she'd distanced herself from her feelings about her unborn child. Thinking privately of him as "the" baby. Even the prayers prayed over her and the prayers she prayed seemed as if they were for some other baby. That somehow a better, changed baby was the one she would be having, instead of the child she carried. It was time to let go of that fantasy. There was a high probability that her child would have Down syndrome. She needed to prepare for the worst and hope for the best.

She straightened in her chair, facing her parents. "The ultrasound showed three markers for Down syndrome. A shortened femur, a thickened nuchal fold, and an undeveloped nasal bone."

Hearing herself speak the terrible words so matter-of-factly severed her fragile hold on her resolve and sent her careening back to despair and denial.

Her parents sat stunned. Visibly shaken.

"That's terrible," her mother breathed out.

"I know it's terrible; it's the terrible truth." She felt the tears stinging her eyes.

Antonio took her hand. "Baby Ben be okay, Angel."

"Let's not say Baby Ben yet." Angelica's father cut in. "That fetus is barely a life-form."

Her mother leaned toward her. "Angelica, he's going to

be retarded. Your lives will be ruined. Listen to reason, you don't have to go through this. You don't have to put that baby through this. You can have other children."

Antonio answered her. "We will have other children. Brothers and sisters for Ben."

"Shut up." Angelica's father stood, lip curling. "This isn't Mexico. Civilized people don't have ten children. If you'd stayed where you belong, none of this would have happened. And stop calling him Ben. You might want to consider reserving that name for one of those other children."

Angelica saw Antonio's hands clench into fists, but he didn't move.

She clenched her jaw. It wasn't Antonio's fault. How dare her father accuse him? And what exactly did her father mean about naming the baby?

"Are you saying you don't want your first grandson named after you? Is that what you're saying?" Tossing her head, she boldly met his eyes. "Are you saying he isn't worthy of the name of a high-and-mighty heart surgeon?"

Her father stood silent in the face of her challenge.

She jumped up. "I'm not going to listen to this." Struggling over Antonio, she stumbled to the front door and swung it open. "Leave. Leave now and stop butting in; stop interfering with our lives. Don't you see, I can't be a perfect daughter anymore. I can't give you a perfect grandson, worthy of your perfect name." Her mother's tears became sobs, condemning Angelica, accusing her. "Get out. I don't want you here."

"Gen, let's go." Her father stormed past Angelica, almost knocking her down.

Her mother stopped at the door and put her hand on Angelica's arm. "We love you, Angelica. Please don't do this."

"Gen. Come on," her father shouted from the street.

Angelica heard the Jaguar's engine roar. Her mother turned and hurried to the car.

Suddenly, Antonio was beside her. "Shhh. Shhh," he whispered, shutting the door and leading her to the couch.

"I didn't mean it. I didn't mean it," Angelica choked out between sobs. "Go stop them. Tell them to come back." But she could see out the front window that the car was gone.

Maclovia sat beside her and handed her some tissues.

"Antonio, I have to go find them. I'm so sorry. I didn't mean it."

"Shhh. Shhh." Antonio's voice was soothing and his eyes filled with compassion. "I know. And their words were not their own. They were the words of frightened people."

Angelica tried to compose herself, but she couldn't stop crying. "Let's go up to the ranch. I'm sure they went straight home."

Antonio stood. "Where are your keys? I'll drive."

Angelica waited for Antonio to back the SUV out of the garage, then got in.

As they drove, she began to realize the enormity of the things she'd said. *Oh, dear God, forgive me. I'm so sorry for what has happened. Please, go before me. Oh please, somehow, work this out. Make things right again.*

When Antonio reached the intersection a few miles from their house, he pulled into a gas station.

"Why are you stopping?"

"You have no gas, *señorita*."

She gave him a faint smile. A perfect ending to a perfect afternoon.

After waiting through the gas line and the check-out line, they finally got back on the road.

As they neared the turnoff that would take them to the ranch, Angelica reached across the front seat. "Antonio,

231

slow down. It looks like a police car up there. I see lights flashing."

Antonio took his foot off the gas. The cars in front of them were slowing to a stop.

"I wonder if my parents are caught up in this." She rolled the window down. The wail of a distant siren drifted through the air, and a helicopter droned overhead. They came to a complete stop.

People farther up the line began to get out of their cars.

"There's no other way up to the ranch, we'll just have to wait it out." Angelica switched on the radio, scanning the stations, hoping to find a traffic report.

After searching the spectrum of stations twice, she looked at her watch. It had been over fifteen minutes, and the traffic hadn't moved. "Let's walk up a ways and see if we can find out what's happened. Maybe we should just try to turn around and go back to the house. I can call my parents."

"Where your cell phone?"

"We left in such a hurry, I didn't even bring my purse."

Antonio got out and walked around to Angelica's side. He helped her out. They began to walk along the shoulder. A few cars up, a group of people were talking.

"It's bad." A young man in shorts shook his head. "They've got the Jaws of Life up there."

Angelica looked at Antonio. "That's a machine they use to cut people out of bad car accidents."

Angelica tapped the young man on the shoulder. "What happened?"

"I'm not sure. Looks like a head-on. The front of the black car was jammed right into its front seat."

Angelica felt an icy grip around her heart. "Black car?"

"And a blue van. Looks like both cars are totaled."

A second man jogged up to the group. "Everybody might

as well relax. We're going to be here awhile. There's at least one fatality. . . ."

Angelica began to run.

"Nooooo." She heard her own voice, from somewhere far away, piercing the air.

As she neared the scene, she ran faster, losing a shoe.

The black car. She could see it. She slowed to a choppy walk.

It looked nothing like her parents' car. She wiped her eyes with the back of her hand. It didn't look like any car. The front end was missing.

Her eyes searched the crumpled mass of metal. The license plate was visible. . . . "TOY4BEN."

Angelica began to tremble uncontrollably. She felt Antonio's arms around her.

"He's dead."

Whose voice was that? Who was dead? She tried to ask, but she couldn't form the words. She couldn't breathe. She fought the blackness. She had to get to her parents, tell them she was sorry.

A dark shadow emerged from the consuming darkness, voicelessly imparting knowledge. Her parents wouldn't be interfering anymore.

Max emptied the bottle of Scotch into the tumbler.

Walking out to his patio, he stirred the drink with his finger, then stuck it in his mouth and sucked off the tart liquid. He kicked one of the plastic lounge chairs around toward the sun and managed to drop into it without spilling the drink.

Angelica. He hadn't stopped thinking about her since he'd walked out on her at the office. Of course she was going to be blindly loyal to her husband. She was a good woman.

But somehow he had to make her see that she'd married the wrong man. She needed *him*, Max Jaeger. Someone who would take care of her and her baby. Someone who would give her the kind of life a beautiful woman deserved.

It pained him to watch her struggle through each day. But clearly, the more overwhelming her life was, the more likely she would see the error of her ways. As a defense attorney, he prided himself in being a shrewd student of human behavior. It was just a matter of time. The signs were all there. Loss of weight, frantically trying to stay on top of her workload, dark circles under her eyes. She was breaking.

Max took a sip of his drink. He'd seen her in her office reading her Bible. As the pressure mounted she was turning to God. That was one of the things about her that charmed him. She was tough as nails in her professional life, but an idealist at heart. That's how he'd known the Vasquez case would captivate her, binding her to him for the years it would take to process the appeal. Max swirled the drink in his glass. Turning to God was a good sign. She'd find out, just like he had when his wife and daughter had been killed, there is no God. And that's when he'd step in.

He laughed, holding his glass up to the sun, as if making a toast. "Hey, God. You probably sent her that loser husband." He smirked. "Well, You just bring her all the trouble You want, buddy. 'Cause that's going to put her right where I want her."

Angelica. He closed his eyes, bringing her to him. He took a slow, deep breath, letting the warmth of the Scotch and the sun erase any distance between them.

He drifted off to the place where thoughts of her were hidden. She was with him again, as she was every evening.

A little smile tugged at his lips. Alone at last, with the woman he loved.

13

THE LAST TEN days had been a maze of police reports, insurance claims, and unsettling discussions with doctors. The drunk who'd hit her parents head-on, Gerald Levine, had walked away from the accident. When the police had escorted her and Antonio back to their vehicle, she'd observed the drunkard sitting in the police car without a single visible mark on him. The irony of that made her furious. Fortunately, her mother's only serious injury was a mild concussion, and she'd been released from Memorial General after a week. But her father remained there in a deep coma; with preliminary tests showing him paralyzed from the waist down, his prognosis was unclear.

Angelica could not escape the wrenching guilt that shadowed her through the stressful days and sleepless nights. She spent every free moment sitting by her father's bedside, praying for some small sign of recovery. But each night her prayers went unanswered, reminding her how undeserving she was, and finally convincing her it was a useless effort and better left to others.

She desperately wanted to talk to her mother about the terrible things she'd said to them. She needed to ask her forgiveness, but even more than that, she needed to receive it. She'd agonized over reopening the wound, and the fact that her mother hadn't brought it up only added to Angelica's burden. Angelica was the one who had avoided her parents, forcing them to seek her out that afternoon. She was the one who had blown up and told them to leave, sending them out on the road and in the path of Gerald Levine. She hoped he was punished to the fullest extent the law allowed. She would do everything in her power to make sure that happened.

The doctors had warned Angelica that her mother would be emotionally fragile for months, that her concussion, though mild, was still serious. She'd been little help to the police, remembering only bits and pieces of the accident. With all the trauma her mother had suffered, Angelica was loath to rehash the events of that Saturday afternoon, but holding it inside was killing her. She had been wrong, so steeped in her own self-pity about the pregnancy she couldn't even consider her parents' pain.

But after sleepless hours in the dark of night, she'd had time to do some deep soul-searching. There, in the safety of Antonio's arms, comforted with the knowledge that he would face the future with her, she had dared to look at her life through the uncompromising lens of reality. She was the mother of a child growing in her womb. Whatever the consequences of that were, she would have to deal with them. She was not going to abort her child . . . Antonio's son.

Her parents were precious to her, and she loved them. No matter how misguided their thoughts, she would treat them with respect. Her mother needed her, especially now. And she needed her mother. She would go to the ranch and repent of what she had done. They would put everything that had happened behind them.

Angelica stood and leaned over her father, kissing his forehead. "I've got to leave now, Dad. I'm going to run up and check on Mom. Don't worry about her. I'm taking good care of her." She waited a moment, hoping for some response, then quietly turned and left the room.

As Angelica drove to the ranch, she rehearsed her speech again. "Mother, I'm sorry. I was wrong." Doubt pricked at her. Maybe her mother wouldn't want her to bring it up. Maybe she should start with, "Mom, I need to talk to you," or "Do you feel like talking?" . . . or maybe nothing at all.

By the time Angelica pulled up in front of the massive, arched portico, her stomach was in a knot. She could see Martha, the woman she'd hired to stay with her mother until things settled down, getting into her car. What a blessing the woman had been, arriving every day at eight in the morning, and often staying past eight at night. Angelica looked at the clock on the car dash. It was eight fifteen. She waved at Martha, then parked the car and got out.

Martha backed her car around next to Angelica and rolled down the window. "I'm glad you're here. Your mom's on the back patio. She's had a tough day. She had me drive her down to see your dad this morning, hoping for some sign of progress."

The dull, empty ache in Angelica's heart sharpened. "We're all hoping for that."

"I'll be back tomorrow morning at eight." Martha rolled up her window and headed down the drive.

Angelica walked through the entry, down the hall, through the kitchen, and out the door to the back patio.

"Hi, Mom." She bent down and kissed her mother's cheek. "What a beautiful sunset."

"Yes it is, dear." Her mother looked at her, dark circles under her red-rimmed eyes. "Just wish your dad was here to enjoy it with us. You know, we used to sit out here every night and watch the stars come out."

"I know, Mom." Angelica felt the sting of tears, her mother's innocent words accusing her.

Angelica pulled a chair away from the wrought-iron table and seated herself.

With her eyes still on the sunset, her mother spoke. "How you feeling? When are you having another ultrasound?"

This was the first time her mother had mentioned the baby since the accident. Was it a sign? A signal? Was she ready to talk about what had happened? Maybe God *had* heard Angelica's prayers and finally decided she'd suffered enough. "Mom, I'm so sorry about what happened." The words tumbled out.

Her mother reached across the table and patted her arm. "Of course you are. You've been so wonderful. Your strength has been such a comfort to me."

"It's all my fault. I shouldn't—"

"Angelica, that's a ridiculous thing to say. It's no more your fault than it is mine. I'm the one who insisted we go down to your house." She gripped Angelica's hand. "I've gone over and over it in my mind. I'd been badgering your father for days. He said we should stay out of it . . . about the baby and everything." She pulled a crumpled tissue from the sleeve of her blouse and wiped her eyes. "His last words to me, right before we left the house, were, 'No matter how things turn out, she's our only child, and we'll support her no matter what she decides.'" Her mother took a shaky breath. "You know, I don't even remember the drive to your

238

house that afternoon or much of anything until I woke up in the hospital, but it's been such a blessing knowing that was why we were there that day. That your father was able to accomplish the one thing he wanted most, to draw you back to us, make us a family again."

Angelica sat in stunned silence, trying to process her mother's words. Clearly, her mother didn't remember what had happened at the house. She thought they had reconciled and had viewed all of Angelica's actions since the accident from that perspective. But that wasn't what had happened, and her thinking so didn't change anything. But what purpose would it serve to bring it all up now, tearing a scab off a healing wound? What purpose . . . other than releasing Angelica from her terrible guilt, at the expense of her mother's peace of mind?

Angelica felt trapped, unable to forgive herself. A prisoner of the truth.

"Creator of heaven and earth, draw Angelica to You."

Maclovia had been on her knees before God all morning. Her family was in deep and terrible trouble.

When Angelica had returned from her mother's house the night before, she had been very upset. Maclovia had heard her talking to Antonio late into the night. Maclovia had understood little of what was said. But she didn't need to understand a single word to know the young woman was grieving . . . for her child, for her father, for herself.

The grief was powerful and dangerous. It had been what remained after the doctors had robbed Angelica, first of her joy, and finally of her hope for the new life she carried. And now it had spawned unbelief, the first sign of spiritual death. A moan escaped Maclovia's lips as she prayed against the darkness that hovered over the family of her grandson. She petitioned God with silent lamentations spoken by the Spirit.

The doctors knew something about the baby, but they did not know everything. They were not able to comprehend the things of the Spirit. How much better to be known by God, the only One who could bring the healing Angelica and her family so desperately needed.

When Maclovia had first perceived the terrible, tragic imperfection brought to light by the unborn child, she had begun to speak to God, asking for His mercy and grace. As the weeks had passed, Maclovia had realized from Angelica's alarming reports about her child and the reactions of her parents that nothing had changed. Maclovia had searched herself, asking God to reveal to her anything hidden in her heart that did not please Him and might keep her prayers from taking flight. But even this total surrender of the flesh brought no evidence that God had heard her and moved.

As more time passed, she perceived she had been set against a powerful enemy, bitterness taken root, and so she began to fast. Finally, she was brought to this day, prostrate before Him, vowing she would not rise until she received a word, a sign, an acknowledgment that He had heard her. Her joints ached and her knees were raw, but she would not give in, confident if she did not fail Him, He would not fail her. He would send His healing power.

Still, time was short. The baby would be born soon. She desperately wanted God to perform the miracle she requested. The healing that Angelica and her father and her mother needed. The healing that would let them receive the child born perfect for God's plans and purposes . . . the healing of their hearts.

Maclovia felt a breeze pass over her. She raised her head,

aware of His presence. Sitting quietly, she listened, waiting. Once again she felt the breeze, a transparent band of light, moving faster and faster, forming a circle around her. The light became brighter and brighter, until Maclovia had to close her eyes and turn her head, unable to look upon it. Then as quickly as it had come, it disappeared, leaving no evidence of its presence, other than the unmistakable impression that she was to walk to the mountains, to the wildflowers and mossy oaks. Where God was waiting for her.

Angelica rushed through the parking lot of the Women's Health Center to her car. Breathe in. One more step. Breathe out. One more step. Put the key in the lock.

She got the door open, slid behind the wheel, and pulled the door shut. She sat staring through the windshield, seeing nothing, dazed, angry, frightened.

The night before, when her mother had asked her when she was having another ultrasound, she hadn't told her that she'd just had one and would be meeting Dr. Gremian today to discuss it. And she would not be telling her mother what Dr. Gremian had just told her. How he'd said the baby's weight was below the tenth percentile for his gestational age and the diagnosis was intrauterine growth restriction, for which he'd advised bed rest during the remainder of her pregnancy.

When Angelica had explained to him there was no possible way she could quit her job, he'd finally agreed that she could cut back to half days and then they would reevaluate after the next ultrasound at thirty weeks. Thankfully, she only had the Vasquez case to deal with. But still, it was a full-time job.

There was no way around it. She was going to have to

talk to Max about her situation, and no matter how she presented it, it would mean he'd have to take on more of the load himself.

A barbed wire of pain started deep in her gut . . . *she didn't want to have to confide in Max, beg him for a favor* . . . working its way out . . . *she didn't want to give up fighting for Miguel Vasquez* . . . tearing through her in serrated, spiked bursts . . . *she didn't want her baby to have Down syndrome.* . . .

Angelica made no attempt to stop the raw, ragged wail that erupted from her lips. She cursed the darkness, pounding her fists on the steering wheel. As her cries became sobs, she slowly lowered her chin to her chest, weeping, lost in a fog of grief.

Oh, God, where are You? The more I need You, the more distant You seem. A fiery dart pricked her, its spark igniting a thought. *Maybe there is no God.*

She had no idea how much time had passed when she heard her cell phone ringing. She reached for her purse, feeling through it, finally locating the phone and flipping it open.

Angelica took a steadying breath, hoping her voice wouldn't give her away. "Hello."

"Hi, girl. It's Fronie. I hate to call you; I know you had that doctor's appointment. But Max has asked me three times if you're back. Made a comment about you taking too much time off."

"I'm on my way. Would you buzz him and tell him I'll be there in twenty minutes? And that I'd like to meet with him."

"Sure will. I'm not afraid of the big, bad wolf."

Fronie's teasing tone and sweet voice felt like a lifeline. "Thanks." Angelica closed the phone.

Max had continued to be considerate and supportive, even after that awkward and embarrassing moment in her office, acting as though nothing unusual had happened and encouraging her to take all the time she needed for personal business. She started the car and backed out of the parking space. She'd been scrupulously careful not to take advantage of his generosity, wanting to keep things on a professional level. But she *had* been gone from the office a lot, first with doctor's appointments and then her parents' accident. Still, he'd constantly reassured her that her work was satisfactory, more than satisfactory.

She hadn't confided in anyone but Fronie about how serious the car accident had been, and she'd been relieved to see the newspaper had not reported any details, since it was still under investigation. She blinked rapidly. *God, why are You allowing all this to happen to me? Why me? What have I done to deserve this?*

By the time she arrived at the office, Angelica had decided not to tell Max that she could only work half days. She didn't want to ask him for any more favors, and having only the Vasquez case to litigate was far easier than the job she would have if she went back to a regular caseload. Besides that, she cared about what happened to Miguel Vasquez. Dr. Gremian hadn't been happy about her wanting to continue to work, but he hadn't forbidden it. She had the distinct impression that the lighter workload was for her sake, more than the baby's. She would put in full days, but she promised herself she would not continue to work nights and weekends.

Angelica put on some lipstick and ran the little brush she kept in her purse through her hair. Before getting out of the car, she lifted her chin and managed a smile. Her father would be proud of her. He'd always held her to a high standard and expected her to rise to it. "You're an Amante," he always said. She certainly wasn't going to fail him now.

Angelica stopped at the front desk. "Is Max in his office?"

Fronie put her hand over her headset microphone and mouthed, "He's expecting you."

Angelica stopped at her desk, set her purse down, picked up a yellow legal pad, and walked to Max's office.

"Sorry I'm late, Max." She took the chair across from his desk. "I know you were looking for me. I'm here now, for the rest of the day and half the night if needed." She crossed her legs and settled into her chair.

Max folded his arms on the desk. "I was looking for you, because I was concerned about you. Over the past few weeks your work's been slopp . . ." He hesitated. "Not what you're capable of."

Angelica stared at him, her mind racing. She wasn't prepared for this conversation. She didn't want this conversation. But he was forcing the issue. "I know I've been a little distracted lately, but there's a lot going on in my life. What exactly are you talking about?"

She saw him steal a glance at the open door. Was he going to say things she wouldn't want other people to hear? He knew about the baby. What else did he know? She'd sacrificed so much to keep everything at work on an even keel. She needed this job. She couldn't let it all slip away. Better to get things out on the table.

She rose and shut the door, then turned and faced him. "Exactly what are you talking about?"

"Sit down and I'll tell you."

She took her seat.

"First, I want to apologize for what happened in your office last week. I was out of line."

Angelica felt herself begin to relax. Was that what this was all about? "Apology accepted."

"It's just that I'm concerned about you. You look tired, you've lost weight, and it does seem that you're struggling to get your work done."

Max's eyes were focused on hers, but they were reserved and polite.

Part of her wanted to tell him everything. Share her burden with someone who could help her. But somehow that seemed like it would be crossing a line, giving him permission, making him privy to her deepest feelings. No. She needed to keep her personal life out of the office. "It has been hard, Max. But when I think about Miguel Vasquez sitting in prison every day for a crime he didn't commit, it hasn't been that hard."

Max slowly shook his head. "That's vintage Angelica Amante, always thinking about other people. Sometimes you have to think of yourself."

"There's time for that after work."

"Angelica, you're not a machine." His face grew serious. "I know what you're going through. I know what it's like to watch your dreams die."

His eyes didn't leave her face as he waited for her response.

She looked away from him. Maybe it would be all right to open up a little bit. She looked at him again. She sensed nothing improper about his demeanor or his voice. He looked as vulnerable as she felt.

He reached in his jacket pocket and took out his wallet. He opened it and handed it to her. "That's *my* Angel."

Angelica looked at the photo of a younger Max, holding a little girl, curly blonde locks askew, her arms locked around his neck, her cheek next to his.

Angelica's gaze returned to his face. There were tears in his eyes. Somehow, the way he'd said the words "my Angel" touched her deeply. It was as if she were looking through a window to his soul.

Suddenly, everything that had happened over the past months welled up in her. There was so much pain in this world. Max was right. He'd suffered plenty. He did know what she was going through, probably better than anyone else she knew. Her heart went out to him. "I'm so sorry, Max." She felt the tears roll down her cheeks, her eyes still on his.

"You can talk to me," he whispered. "Let me help you."

Angelica tried to get ahold of herself. She could feel the wall she'd been hiding behind begin to crumble under waves of conflicting emotions. Maybe it would be all right to confide in Max. He could help her figure out how to manage her hours. He might even bring in another attorney to help them. If she leveled with him, life wouldn't be so hard. He was right, she wasn't a machine.

Max reached across the desk and laid his open hand in front of her. She set the wallet in it.

His hand closed quickly, catching her fingers in his grasp, sending the wallet tumbling to the desk. "Angelica, I can give you what you need. I can take care of you."

Angelica gasped. A shadowy haze lifted from her, and her thoughts became focused and clear. She jerked her hand away from him. "What are you talking about?"

He rose. "Angelica, let me help you. No one has to know."

Angelica stood, her composure fragile. Was he serious? Was he propositioning her? Had his concern been staged so he could get close to her? She could hardly process everything that was cascading through her mind. "I hope you didn't say what I thought you said."

He stepped toward her. He seemed humbled, his face anxious, his eyes pleading. "I said exactly what you thought I said. And I meant it."

His voice was full of emotion, his manner intimate. She felt disoriented. "Are you drunk?"

He flinched, as if she'd slapped him. "No. And if you ask me to, I'll never take another drink."

Angelica wanted to run out of the office, get in her car, drive home to Antonio's arms, and never come back. But that wasn't possible. Max was effectively putting her career in jeopardy. She was a woman in a man's world, and how she handled the next few minutes would affect the course of the rest of her professional life. She'd learned that lesson the hard way in New York. Anxiety spurted through her.

She steeled herself. "Max, I'm in love with my husband, and we're expecting our first child. You're way out of line."

"Can't you see he has nothing to offer you? He's just along for the free ride."

She clenched her jaw, fighting to keep control of her emotions, her anxiety turning to anger. She had to turn the tables on him. "I'm not going to dignify that remark with an answer."

She saw a flicker of uncertainty in his eyes. Her mind raced.

"Instead, I've got a question for you. How many times have you had sexual harassment charges filed against you?"

Max rocked back on his heels, his face a mixture of bewilderment and hurt. "You're too smart for that, Angelica. You know how the game's played. You start down that road, and you'll end up on the outside looking in. I've never touched you . . . though God knows, I've wanted to." His eyes went over her. "But this isn't like that. I can have any woman I want." He stepped toward her. "You're beautiful and smart. You deserve the best in life. Better than what you've got. He's just another Mexican."

Angelica fought the urge to take a step back. She couldn't show any weakness. She had to get the upper hand.

Suddenly, she stepped past him and around to the back of his desk. "Excuse me, Mr. Jaeger." She reached into the pocket of the chair cushion and pulled out a bottle of tequila. "I'd say you're married to a Mexican of your own." She slammed the bottle down in the middle of his desk.

Max's eyes widened, and his face drained of color.

"I know more about you than you think, Max." From the look on his face, Angelica realized she'd struck a nerve. Apparently, there *was* more to know. Following her intuition, she seized the inch she'd taken. "I could make it my business to find out every detail of your life in this office over the past few years . . ." She let her words sink in. ". . . or you could decide to clean up your act."

Max stood, speechless.

"I'll be watching." She raised her hand and gave Max a slight push in the chest, then walked past him to the door. Opening it, she turned.

She had no choice.

"I won't be working on the Vasquez case with you any longer." She felt a sinking in the pit of her stomach. "I'll work closely with whomever you assign to make the transition as seamless as possible. Miguel Vasquez shouldn't suffer for any of this. He's been victimized once by the system, and I'm not going to be the cause of it happening to him again."

Max stared at her.

"I'll expect to get some new assignments tomorrow."

She took a step into the hall. Looking back at him she added, "Since I don't have any cases right now, I'm taking the rest of the day off. In fact, my doctor doesn't want me working more than half days. So, starting tomorrow, I'll be working from home in the afternoons."

It wasn't until she was back in her office that she began to tremble. She pushed her door shut and walked over to the window, pressing her forehead against it. She took some deep breaths and let the warmth of the sun bathe her.

Finally, she lifted her head, raising her eyes to the clear, cloudless sky. She'd told Max she was leaving, and she was going to. She needed to get away. She hadn't had a moment to herself in months. She glanced at her watch. It was just past noon.

Picking up her purse from her crowded desk, she couldn't help but think of the months of work she'd put into the Vasquez case. Now, all of that would be turned over to someone else. Someone who wouldn't agonize over the terrible injustice of the situation. Someone who would just be doing a job. She sighed. Maybe it was better that way.

Tucking her purse under her arm, Angelica picked up the phone and buzzed Fronie.

"Hi." The familiar sound of her friend's voice lifted her spirits.

"Hi. I'm leaving now, and I won't be back today."

There was a pause. "You just got here. What's Max going to say?"

"Don't worry. He's not going to say a thing. I'll tell you all about it later."

Angelica hung up the phone, then slipped down the hall and out the fire exit. She didn't want to see anybody or talk to anybody. She wanted to be alone.

After starting her car, she sat back for a moment, trying to sort out her feelings. Her eyes wandered to the surrounding hills. Memories stirred. She and Antonio had spent many afternoons riding in those hills—she on Pasha, he on Serif. Life had been so simple then. It would be wonderful to drive to the ranch, saddle Pasha, and take a ride for the rest of the afternoon. She huffed a sigh. Throwing a heavy saddle on the back of a horse was out of the question. She put the car in gear.

As she began to back the car out, her thoughts returned to the mountains. She felt a drawing she couldn't ignore— almost a yearning to be there.

Pulling onto the street, she turned toward the road that would take her to the edge of town and the foot of the Sonoma Mountains. Suddenly there was no place on earth where she would rather be than among the wildflowers and the mossy oaks.

As Angelica drove, her thoughts returned to what Dr. Gremian had told her. Only about twenty percent of intrauterine growth restriction was caused by the fetus. But considered with her AFP results and ultrasound information, this was most likely a result of the baby having Down syndrome. She felt her stomach turn over. One more indicator, one more weapon to put in the arsenal that threatened to destroy her hopes and dreams. One more fact to work against the prayers of her church and friends. Her grip tightened on the steering wheel. Maybe she should have had the amnio test done. Even if it had been positive for Downs, at least it would have removed all doubt and she could have begun to prepare, instead of leaving her in this hellish limbo of uncertainty. But she hadn't. She'd felt it was an act of faith. Allowing God to work.

Her conscience pricked her. That wasn't the truth.

The truth was the amnio *would* have removed all doubt,

and somehow it seemed like a miracle would be easier if there were no scientific facts to work against it. She felt a flicker of hope. No one knew for sure the baby had Downs. Maybe she didn't need a miracle.

She tossed her head. Maybe a miracle wasn't even possible. Maybe the miracles she read about in the Bible were just stories. Her father had often told her that.

Angelica followed the curve of the road to the west and was soon driving along the foot of the mountains. Rolling down her window, she breathed deeply, savoring the smell of the wildflowers carried on the breeze.

The sweet scent filled her with nostalgia, transporting her to the happy, uncomplicated days on the ranch where her biggest problem had been hiding her interest in the handsome stable boy who worked for her father. Another gust of wind puffed through the window, drawing her to the mountains.

Just ahead, there was a wide spot on the shoulder of the road. She took her foot off the accelerator and pulled over.

After driving the SUV well off the pavement, she pulled the brake and hopped out. Taking only her keys, she locked the car, then dropped the keys in her pocket.

Angelica threw her head back, raising her face to the sun. She stretched her arms out. It felt so good to stand there, no briefcase, no purse, no phone to ring. She felt free.

After a few moments she began to walk along the grassy edge of the hill, then stopped. She'd heard something. Voices? She tilted her head. Nothing.

Silly. Who would be here, miles outside of town? She took a few more steps.

There it was again. She held her breath, listening.

A voice. A high, beautiful voice, singing. Angelica scanned the area around her.

A few steps ahead of her she noticed a small trail, rising up into the mountain. She walked to it, craning her neck to see where it led. A breeze whipped up, surrounding her with the scent of wild roses and carrying the pure, high vibrato of the unseen singer.

Angelica stepped out of her flats, took off her knee-highs, and stuck them into her shoes. She rolled up the bottom of her slacks and stepped onto the trail.

Walking slowly, she followed it and soon found herself standing in a clearing. Valle de Lagrimas stretched before her. It was beautiful.

She listened. The singing had stopped. She frowned. Maybe it had carried across the mountains in the clear air from some faraway place. Oh well, it had brought her here. She marveled at the expansive view. It was nearly as magnificent as the views from Regalo Grande. She turned in a slow circle, taking in the hills and valleys. The oaks and rocks and wildflowers scattered across the canvas of the mountains.

She started and caught her breath. Not more than thirty yards from her, a woman was kneeling beneath an old oak, her back to Angelica.

Angelica took a few tentative steps. Yes, it was a woman . . . a black shawl around her shoulders.

Angelica's mouth dropped. Maclovia!

What was she doing here? Angelica knew that the old woman was always taking long walks and was often gone for hours. But she never dreamed she walked this distance. And for what purpose? It was much too far to be enjoyable.

As Angelica walked toward her, it appeared Maclovia was sitting in a circle of light. Angelica stopped, observing how the sun filtered through the branches of the ancient tree, creating the unusual effect.

Angelica called out to her. But the old woman didn't move.

A gust of wind blew through the oak. As the branches swayed, the circle of light remained steady, then seemed to expand. Angelica's fingers flew to her lips.

The wind gusted again. The circle of light widened, stopping just in front of her feet.

"Maclovia?"

The woman, though only twenty feet away, didn't turn.

Angelica extended her hand across the ring of light, waving it back and forth, half expecting to hit an invisible wall. But she felt nothing.

She lifted her foot and slowly placed it inside the ring. Straddling the edge of light, she debated whether or not to step fully into it.

This is ridiculous. She straightened and brought her feet together inside the circle.

Immediately, she was filled with a peace that passed her understanding.

"Maclovia?" she whispered.

The old woman turned her head, then stood. "I've been waiting for you." She held her hand out to Angelica.

As soon as Angelica touched Maclovia's hand, she felt a tremor. "We're in His presence, aren't we?" Angelica could hardly hear her own voice.

The old woman nodded and knelt. Angelica followed her to her knees.

"He wants to know you. He's been waiting for you."

Angelica couldn't speak. She felt overwhelmed by a powerful sense of love . . . of being loved. A feeling so intense it consumed her. She could not feel her heart beat or feel herself breathing. It was as if she had no need of the physical necessities that sustained life. As if the presence of God's love alone would sustain her.

The feeling ebbed, and Maclovia spoke. "Do you want to pray?"

Angelica opened her mouth and, though her lips formed words, she couldn't speak. She couldn't gather her thoughts. Her mind was reeling from the truth revealed to her. There was a God.

She'd thought she believed in God, but she hadn't. Not like this. She had known about Him, but she had not known Him. She had known of His self-sacrificing love, but she had never felt it. She believed that Jesus Christ was His son and the Savior of the world who'd made the ultimate sacrifice. . . . Something stirred in her. A knowing, a conviction. He wasn't *the* Savior. . . . He was *her* Savior.

Suddenly, it seemed wrong to seek only His hands and never His face. Suddenly, it seemed wrong to start spouting a litany of directives after never having time for Him unless she needed Him, and lately . . . not even then. Suddenly, she felt ashamed. Who He was and who she was separated themselves in her thinking.

"God, forgive me."

She felt a quickening in her heart, followed by a sensation that started at the tips of her toes and traveled to the top of her head. Then the circle of light vanished.

"No. No. Come back." Angelica reached out.

Maclovia's hands were on her face, cradling it. "Daughter, He will come back if you seek Him with all your heart."

Angelica slowly nodded.

Maclovia took her hand, and the two of them walked silently back down the trail to the car.

Angelica helped Maclovia in, then got in the SUV and

started it. The sound of the engine, a car speeding past, the ordinary world functioning around her brought an avalanche of thoughts crowding into her mind. Max, her father, the baby. Would things be different now? She closed her eyes, trying to recapture the essence of the moments under the oaks. But she couldn't.

She glanced at Maclovia. The woman's wise eyes met hers. "Believe."

Max glanced at the woman sitting on the barstool next to him. Perfectly applied lipstick, messy blonde hair, bright red, manicured nails occasionally tapping her empty glass. Everything but a sign that read, "Buy me a drink, and then, maybe . . ."

He turned back to his drink.

So Angelica thought she'd made a real catch with her Mexican gigolo. *"I'm in love with my husband. You're way out of line."* Max downed the shot. She was no better than his second wife, who'd thought his loser brother was such a great catch. He sucked his tongue, clinging to the last of the tequila.

He wouldn't give her another chance; she'd made it plain she wasn't interested. He'd been down this road before, and his ex-wife had made a fool of him. This time he wouldn't be so stupid. He clenched his jaw.

Max snapped his fingers to get the bartender's attention, then jabbed his finger at the shot glass. No matter which shift it was, the bartenders knew Max and what he liked to drink. The quiet drumbeat of the tapping red nails next to him started again.

Angelica hadn't said a word to anyone about that accident her parents had been in, but he knew all about it. A few calls

255

to some well-placed friends had revealed that a drunk driver had hit her parents head-on and her father was in critical condition at Memorial General in a coma. He'd even found out something Angelica didn't know. The drunk who'd hit them was a man whose son had committed suicide, leaving a child and a pregnant wife behind. Mr. Levine had apparently left his son's funeral and gone straight to a bar.

Really too bad. If you couldn't hold your liquor, you shouldn't drink and drive. Max was very careful about that. But then . . . going to your own child's funeral . . . Max ground his teeth. He understood Gerald Levine's pain.

Max thought about the new case sitting on his desk waiting to be assigned. Another drunk driver, arrested just today in fact. Pedro Navarro, whose address was some trailer at one of the vineyards, was driving drunk without a license. Things were going to get real simple. Angelica was going to realize she'd made a big mistake, turning on him like that. Miss Holier than Thou, I love my husband. Miss High and Mighty, we have to get justice for Miguel Vasquez. His mouth quirked. She'd dumped Vasquez too. Vasquez didn't deserve that. . . . No one did.

He ran his finger around the top of the shot glass. Well, now she could get justice for Pedro Navarro. The man was entitled to the best defense possible. Angelica knew that. And if Max had it figured right, she'd also know she couldn't defend him. She'd never be able to put aside what had just happened to her parents. Her inflated sense of ethical purity would force her to decline the case, and then she'd have to come crawling to him. She'd have to ask him to reassign it to someone else.

Then, in the coming weeks, he'd start entering notes in her personnel file. Some he'd have to back-date, but they would document every time she came in late, took extended unauthorized time away during business hours, or left early. They would have to be very detailed so no one could accuse him of going after her because of her pregnancy. In fact, from now on, whenever she wanted to speak to him, he would ask a chief trial deputy or assistant public defender to sit in on the meetings.

When the time came, anyone reviewing the notes would understand his reluctance to bring it up. They would understand she was a troubled young woman whose personal life had overwhelmed her. They would also be able to understand he *might* have made some innocent gesture that she misconstrued as sexual harassment.

He hated doing it, but she'd given him no choice. Max snapped his fingers at the bartender again. He had to get her out of his life.

The drumbeat of the red nails broke into his thoughts.

Max turned to the woman next to him. "Can I buy you a drink?"

14

His son would be named Manuel. They had talked about it late into the night. Remembering Angelica's tears, Antonio's heart ached. She'd gone over and over every word the *patrón* had said that last time they'd spoken. And it always came back to the anger in his voice. "Stop calling him Ben." Antonio understood her pain. Blinking rapidly, he focused on the road.

He turned his truck into the long drive that led to Regalo Grande. Though it saddened him deeply that the *patrón* didn't want his first grandchild to carry his name, Antonio would respect his father-in-law's wishes. Still, the problem remained of how to bring it up to Angelica's mother without explaining why the change was being made. Angelica said her mother remembered nothing of the terrible scene that had led to the accident and to bring it all up might damage the closer relationship they had begun to forge. His wife was deeply troubled by her dilemma, and Antonio's reassurance that God would make a way had been answered with, "How?"

He was about to find out.

Passing through the wrought-iron gates that marked the entry to Regalo Grande, Antonio began to look at the grounds with a critical eye. There hadn't been a man on the ranch in almost two weeks. A ranch needed a man's hand, and Antonio had decided that that responsibility would fall to him as long as the *patrón* was not able to oversee his property. And beyond that, there were probably things Mrs. Amante needed to have done that the *patrón* would have taken care of.

Antonio pulled in front of the big hacienda and got out of the truck. The flowerbeds that surrounded the flat parking area needed weeding, and there was an oil stain on the pavers near the front steps. Antonio shook his head. It was clear that the gardener had realized the *patrón* wasn't home.

Antonio turned, walked through the arched entry, and knocked on the front door.

No one answered.

He cracked the door open. "*Señora* Amante."

There was no answer. He frowned. Where was the woman who was taking care of her? He stepped into the hall and called out again.

The house seemed empty. He shrugged; maybe they'd gone to the hospital.

Antonio walked down the hall, through the kitchen, and out to the patio. Walking to the edge of the tile, he scanned the property, down the grassy slope, to the arena and horse facilities. He could see a board down on Pasha's fence, and the area between the barn and the bunkhouse needed weed-eating. He jogged down the hill.

As he neared the barn, he stopped.

"Here."

Antonio tilted his head, listening.

259

"Here. I'm over here."

He turned toward the sound, stepping forward, surveying the area around him.

"Here."

He quickened his steps toward the shed where the *patrón* stored extra patio chairs, golf clubs, and other miscellaneous things.

"Antonio."

He could see the *señora*, propped up against the wall of the shed, her right leg extended in front of her.

"*Qué pasa, señora?*" Antonio knelt beside her, glancing at the fishing pole and baseball mitt scattered nearby. The image of the *patrón* explaining how he'd dug through the shed to find them filtered through Antonio's mind. The *patrón* had insisted they be kept in the house, now that he was expecting a grandson.

"I was just trying to put away a few things, and I slipped." He saw color creep into her cheeks. "I should have waited until Martha got back from the grocery store."

"You hurt?" He placed his hand gently on her shoulder.

"I've turned my ankle. I think I heard something pop."

Antonio stood, picked up the mitt and fishing pole, and set them inside the shed. Then he stooped down and gathered the woman into his arms. Rising, he lifted her. "No worry, I help you."

Back in the kitchen, he set her on a chair and took off her sandals. Then, kneeling in front of her, he examined her foot. It was smudged with dirt, and there were several small abrasions near her toes. In Mexico, he'd seen many sprained ankles and even some broken ones. He ran his fingers lightly over the joint. It was swollen, but she would be fine.

He stood and turned to the kitchen sink, opening the

cabinet under it. When he'd first come to work on the ranch, he'd often helped the cook clean the kitchen. He bent down, looking in the back; the cleaning bucket was still there. He took it out and filled it with warm water. He grabbed two clean dishtowels and turned to Mrs. Amante.

She looked concerned. "What are you doing?"

"I take care of you." He stood quietly, waiting for permission.

"Oh."

Antonio knelt in front of her and spread a towel on the floor. He dipped the other towel in the warm water and squeezed it out. Then he gently lifted her foot and began to wash it. As gentle as the brush of an angel's wing, a thought occurred to him.

"*Señora?*"

"Yes."

He sensed her stiffen. "I like to ask you a question."

"What is that?"

"In my country, the man choose the name of his first son."

She didn't answer.

He set her foot on the dry towel and picked up her other one. "Do you think Manuel would be a good name for my boy?"

Still, she was silent.

Antonio glanced at her. Her face was a mixture of surprise and confusion.

She looked down. "I think that's a fine name."

He looked back to her foot, not wanting her to feel uncomfortable.

She continued. "And I think you are a fine father."

Praise to You, Dios. Antonio patted her foot dry and stood. "You need stay off the foot." He lifted her again and

261

carried her to the living room. Setting her on the couch, he propped her foot up on pillows.

"What on earth happened?"

Antonio turned at the voice behind him.

"Oh, Martha, I fell. Luckily, Antonio happened to come by."

"I shouldn't have left you." Martha hurried toward her, arms full of groceries.

Antonio took the groceries from Martha and carried them to the kitchen. After putting away the bucket and towels, he headed down the hall to the entry. He needed to get back to work.

He stopped in the living room. "I see some things outside need doing. I come back soon."

"Thank you, Antonio." The *señora* raised her head. "I look forward to seeing you again."

He heard the sincerity in her voice. Humbled, he nodded toward the women. "You are welcome." Then he turned and left.

As Antonio drove out the gates of Regalo Grande, his heart was full. He would have the honor of helping his wife's family, and best of all, his son would be named Manuel.

He had not told Angelica, or anyone, why he had chosen that name—the name esteemed by his people because of its special meaning . . . God is with us.

Angelica looked in her closet. The yellow dress. She'd never worn it. Somehow it seemed to mark the end of her life as she'd known it. Life before her father was in a coma, paralyzed from the waist down. Life before her job had become a place she had to go, instead of a place she wanted to go. She took the dress out and looked at it, fingering the fabric, remembering how sweet the moment was when Antonio had given it to her.

She sighed. Her life was what it was, and it was time to get on with it. She took the dress off the hanger and slipped it on.

She hesitated, then stepped in front of the mirror. She tilted her head, observing her reflection. The dress definitely accented her pregnancy. Antonio would love it on her. That thought made her smile. She hummed as she finished dressing.

Driving to work, she reflected on the mysterious and beautiful moments she'd spent with Maclovia the afternoon before. Even now, remembering, the same sense of peace brushed over her. So near and yet so far. If only she could capture God's presence and walk in it.

When she'd awakened she'd tried lying still and focusing on Him. Maclovia had said He wanted to know her, but somehow the idea of God really wanting to know *her*, really caring about *her* seemed hard to believe. Yet she couldn't deny the overwhelming sense of love she'd felt in the circle of light beneath the oak. Still, no matter how she tried to concentrate while lying in bed, she couldn't recapture the experience. Other things had crowded into her mind, the baby, her job, the accident . . . her anger at Gerald Levine. Finally, she'd given up.

A whisper, still and small, passed through her thoughts. "Believe." That's what Maclovia had said. Angelica wanted to believe with the faith Maclovia seemed able to summon at will. But somehow it eluded her.

She pulled into a parking spot, turned off the engine, and climbed out of the Expedition. Shouldering her purse and briefcase, she straightened and took a deep breath. There should be some new cases in her in-box. This was a new day and a fresh start.

Passing through the entry, Angelica saw Fronie was busy on the phones. But Fronie acknowledged the new dress with a quick smile and raised brows as she transferred the calls.

Angelica stopped and grabbed the contents of her in-box. A single file marked "Navarro." She hesitated before picking it up. Considering the workload the office carried, she'd expected Max to assign her eight to ten cases to start. Maybe he was waiting until she had someone up to speed on Vasquez. She shrugged and proceeded to her office. It was going to be a good day, another Hispanic client, another chance to help the Mexican people.

She spent the first few hours gathering all the documents pertaining to the Vasquez case and organizing them for whomever Max had decided to assign the case.

Glancing at the clock on her computer screen, she saw it was nearing noon. She decided to move on to the Navarro file. She picked it up.

"Hey, girl."

"Fronie. Come in."

"I wanted to catch you before I left for lunch." She stepped through the door and shut it behind her. "What's up with sharing your office?"

"What are you talking about?" Angelica laid the file on the desk.

"I heard Max talking to one of the interns, Commissioner Jackson's daughter. I was in the resource room, and I could hear everything he said."

Angelica sat back in her chair and folded her arms across her chest. "And?"

"He said you were only going to be working half days and your office would be available to her afternoons starting next week."

Angelica pursed her lips. "Really?"

264

"Didn't he talk to you about it? He told her when you go on maternity leave she can have the office."

"I had no idea." Angelica stared at Fronie. "Thanks for telling me."

"I've got to run. I have a million things to do." Fronie rose.

"Is Max in his office?"

"No, but he's got some appointments here later." Fronie opened the office door. "Love your dress."

Fronie stepped into the hall. Turning, she whispered, "Good luck," then closed the door.

What was Max up to? There was really nothing wrong with allowing an intern to use her office when she wasn't there. It just seemed so sudden. It had only been yesterday she'd told him she'd be working half days. She looked at the lone file that had been in her box, and a wave of uneasiness washed through her. She'd wait and see what he had to say.

Angelica reached for the Navarro file. She wasn't going to let Max stop her from advocating for the people she felt God had called her to help.

She opened the file and read the complaint.

"Said Defendant Pedro Navarro did on or about the 3rd day of August, commit the crime of **DRIVING WHILE UNDER INFLUENCE: VEHICULAR MANSLAUGHTER WITHOUT GROSS NEGLIGENCE,** a FELONY violation of Section 192(c)(3) of the California Penal Code, in that said defendant did unlawfully kill a human being, to wit . . ."

Memories of her parents' accident seized her—the mangled Jaguar, the sound of the ambulance siren, the smell of the hospital. Clenching her jaw, she picked up the police report and continued to read.

Navarro had been arrested after swerving into oncoming

traffic on the interstate. He'd had a blood alcohol level of .19. It was a wonder he'd even been able to get behind the wheel.

He'd hit a minivan, killing a father and his three children. Only the mother had survived. Shock yielded to cold anger. Angelica slammed the file shut and threw it across the room. He should burn in hell.

Heart racing and adrenaline pumping, she shot out of her chair. She paced around her office, then finally stopped in front of the window. But instead of seeing the manicured grounds, she was looking through the glass of her father's hospital room in the ICU. She blinked away the image, and her eyes focused across the lawns to the parking lot. A black Lexus was pulling in. Max. She felt her chest tighten.

Suddenly, it was as clear as if she'd read it in the file. Max had set her up. The intern—now this. It was a power play. She felt it in her gut.

He must have made it his business to find out the details of her parents' accident, just like he'd found out about her unborn child. He could have assigned the Navarro case to anyone, but he'd given it to her. And he'd underscored his point by giving her just the one file. A single statement of what she could expect in the future.

She picked the file up off the floor. Fighting tears, she slapped it against her leg. *Jerk.*

As the moments passed, the reality of what she was facing began to crystallize in her mind. She was a public defender, and it was her duty to give every client assigned to her a vigorous defense. That was the system of justice the country was built on. Every human being, no matter whether they'd committed a crime or not, deserved representation in court, deserved to have their story told. The Bill of Rights guaranteed that process, and up until this moment she had never questioned those principles. But suddenly it wasn't black and white. It was personal. For Angelica, Pedro Navarro wasn't a drunk driver entitled to a defense; he was the demon brother of Gerald Levine. And she was being asked to defend him.

The thought of delving into the details of the case turned her stomach. It was too soon. Somehow defending Pedro Navarro seemed like a betrayal of her father, making the terrible wrong he had suffered nothing more than an offense to be routinely handled with the cool, dispassionate hand of the law. Her thoughts went to the family in the minivan. The mother left with a shattered life.

Another shattered life.

Maybe she should be able to set aside her personal feelings. During the entire time she'd worked as a public defender, she'd never known anyone to refuse to represent a client, no matter how horrific the crime. But she couldn't. There was no way she could honestly keep an open mind and aggressively defend the accused . . . and Max knew it.

Angelica took a deep, steadying breath. She wasn't going to play this game. And she would put Max on notice to that effect, now. She opened her office door. Stepping into the hall, she heard a faint ringing.

Her cell phone.

She rushed to her desk, grabbed her purse, and opened it. Feeling around, she finally located the phone halfway through the fourth trill.

"Hello?"

"Angelica . . ."

Her mother's sobs prevented Angelica from understanding what she was saying. "Yes, Mom. What's wrong?"

"I'm at the hospital. . . . It's your father."

Maclovia followed Antonio down the hall of the hospital to the *señor*'s room.

As they entered she saw the *señora* sitting by the *patrón*'s bed. Antonio spoke to her in hushed tones.

When Antonio had received the *señora*'s call to come to the hospital right away, Maclovia had asked to come too. She had not seen the *señor* since the accident. Looking at him now, with tubes and hoses and lights everywhere, she marveled that the man had survived with so many intrusions. How could the body heal with such interference? She tapped Antonio's elbow. "Are you sure he's alive?"

"Yes, *Abuela*. The nurse told the *señora* that he opened his eyes, and she is waiting for him to open his eyes again."

Maclovia noticed, though the *señora*'s face was drawn, it was flush with color, and her eyes were bright. She began speaking to Antonio.

Maclovia didn't understand a word being said, except the clear mention of her name.

"Grandmother, let me find you a place to sit in the waiting room. When Angelica comes, we can't all be in here. I'll sit with you."

Maclovia followed Antonio to a little room with gray chairs. He helped her into a seat, then sat next to her.

"Son, go sit with the *señora*. That is where you are needed."

Antonio nodded in agreement, then disappeared around the corner. Maclovia offered a silent prayer for the *patrón*. She knew he had been injured seriously, yet seeing him, and his wife anxiously sitting by his side, moved Maclovia deeply. She prayed his life would be restored to him and that God would bless him greatly. God's goodness was sometimes a mystery, still she prayed with an abiding faith that God's workings in the Amantes' lives were for their good.

From her chair Maclovia could see many people passing back and forth in front of the door. She stood and walked out into the hall, looking up and down the long walkway. Many rooms lay beyond the one she was in.

Curious, she shuffled along, casually looking into the rooms. Most had beds separated by curtains, with people of all ages in the beds. The sound of voices drifted to her as she walked and, every once in awhile, she heard her own language. When she reached the end of the hall, she turned around and began to retrace her steps. After passing a few doors she heard the words, "There is no hope."

She stopped, listening, then moved in the direction of the words spoken in her native tongue.

She peered through a door. A child was lying in a bed, surrounded by machines. There were several people around the bed.

She stepped just inside the room, but no one took notice of her. A woman, deeply grieved, smoothed the child's forehead. A man sat nearby, his head buried in his hands, his shoulders shaking. Another man holding a big, black book read from it, "Yea, though I walk through the valley of the shadow of death, I will fear no evil; for You are with me; Your rod and Your staff, they comfort me."

Maclovia recognized the words. She had heard the missionaries read them, but now she felt great concern, hearing them. The man was reading them as though they had no meaning. He seemed to be reciting the words, rendering them powerless. She continued to listen.

After reading awhile longer the man closed the book and said, "Thanks be to God, who gives us the victory through our Lord Jesus Christ."

Maclovia lifted her head, straightening. The man had spoken the name of Jesus. God's love become man. The power of all prayer, the evidence of things unseen.

Maclovia closed her eyes, waiting, knowing when God's glory fell upon the child she should not look upon it. Whether God would take the child to Himself or restore the child to the parents, she did not know. She only knew that His will would be done.

But as the moments passed, nothing happened, and she discerned God was not moving. Though the man had spoken the great Truth, he had said it without conviction. The words were upon the man's lips, but not in his heart.

Feeling a tremor in her hands, she lifted them. "Your will be done," she whispered, believing. Then a brush of air, as light as the hem of a robe, crossed her feet.

Maclovia turned and left. As she walked she continued to pray for the child.

"*Abuela*, there you are."

The sound of her grandson's voice drew her out of her thoughts.

"Angelica is here now with her mother. We're going to go home. Buddy needs to go out, and I'm meeting with my teacher who's helping me with the plan for the models."

As they walked down the hall, Maclovia felt a release and recognized the scent of a sweet fragrance. Her heart rejoiced, filled with certainty. Soon the parents' tears would become tears of joy.

It was after nine o'clock by the time Angelica left Regalo Grande. She'd taken her mother home from the hospital, and for the first time since the accident, they had talked about the future.

Her father had opened his eyes again when Angelica arrived. Her mother had said he was responding to the sound of Angelica's voice, but Angelica wasn't so sure. She wasn't even sure he recognized her, or her mother. Though his eyes were open, there was no depth to them. Still, this was the first sign of hope, and they were embracing it. The doctors had warned them it could be a week, a month, or a year before her father stabilized to the point that they could make an accurate prognosis. Angelica and her mother chose to think it would be soon, and when they had returned to the ranch from the hospital, they'd sat on the patio drinking iced tea and discussing modifications they would make to the house to accommodate his paralysis, should it prove to be permanent.

As Angelica skirted town, she noticed her gas gauge was almost on empty. She pulled into a service station.

As she stood pumping gas, her thoughts turned to the scene in her father's room when she'd arrived, Antonio sitting with her mother, holding her hand. Angelica swallowed the lump in her throat.

After topping off the tank, she took the receipt and got back into the Expedition.

Seeing that an RV was blocking the exit to the street, Angelica headed across the parking lot of the bar next door, to reach a side street.

As she neared the exit of The Wine Rack she slowed, waiting as the car in front of her stopped. She could see it was two people who obviously hated to part. She thought about laying on the horn to break up the passionate scene. The man finally got out of the car, and the woman drove off.

The man crossed through her headlights, putting one foot uncertainly in front of the other. Angelica caught her breath. Max.

She silently watched him make his way back to the bar. All the anger she'd felt that morning returned. She glared at the figure in the dark business suit. As she lifted her foot from the brake, Max veered off the aisle leading to the front of the bar and stepped between two cars.

Angelica pressed her foot back on the brake pedal. He wasn't going into the bar, he was leaving. He had no business driving.

She saw him get in his car and start it.

Her anger rose. This wasn't her problem. She didn't want to get involved. She didn't want to deal with him, especially not in this condition.

She thought a moment, then reached for her cell phone. She could call the police and report an erratic driver.

She hesitated. What if it got in the papers and cost him his job?

So what, if it did? Better that than hitting somebody.

Max pulled out of his parking space, slowly heading down the lane toward her. Her car blocked his path.

She wanted to drive away. No one would know. He'd probably get home safely, just like he had for years. She took her foot off the brake.

She couldn't do it. She couldn't let him drive away. Angry at herself and at him, she threw the cell phone down and jammed the gearshift into park. His car stopped a few feet from her door. As she stepped down, she saw him get out.

"Hey, you're blocking . . ."

She saw his face fill with recognition.

Angelica reached into her car and picked up the phone. "You need to call a cab, Max." Her words were clipped.

"Angelica!" A grin spread across his face. "You come lookin' for me? Change your mind?" He stumbled toward her.

Angelica stepped around him and took a few steps toward the open door of his car. Maybe she could grab the keys and leave them with the bartender or the manager. They could decide what to do with him. They had liability for his actions.

Max pushed himself between her and the car door, shutting it. "Whadda you doin'?"

"Give me your keys."

He reached out and stroked her hair. "You wanna drive me home?"

"Give me your keys. You're drunk." Angelica slapped his hand away.

He grabbed her wrist. "Hey, what's that supposed to mean?"

She struggled, trying to loosen his hold. "Let go of me."

He tightened his grip and circled his other arm around her neck, pulling her into him, kissing her. Hard.

She took her free hand and pushed it against his face. Her fingernails dug into his flesh. He released her, pushing her backward into her own car.

Hitting her head on the side mirror, she stumbled, twisting, falling. She glimpsed the edge of the running board as it slammed into the side of her face.

Max stood in front of the double glass doors, holding a small valise.

He looked at the smudge of blood on his right shirt cuff. He'd held her, begging her to forgive him. Begging her to live.

The manager, Brix, had understood. It had been an accident. He and Brix knew each other . . . well. There'd been a few times over the years when she had needed a little help with the commissioners. There'd been a few times when Max had needed a little help with his bar tab.

Brix had thought it would be better for Max to leave and let her handle it. Then she'd called an ambulance. But Max hadn't left. Instead, he'd parked his car a few rows away and watched. He'd felt like a common criminal, slouched behind his steering wheel, window cracked, trying to hear what the paramedics were saying. Hoping Angelica might suddenly speak or sit up. But she didn't.

He closed his eyes and shook his head. The dress. The yellow dress. It was the first time he'd seen her wear a maternity smock. There had been something about it. Maybe it was the bright yellow against the asphalt. Maybe it was the way she had fallen, the dress billowing out, then settling around her, covering her legs and feet. Maybe it had just been the booze. But there was something about the way the dress had clung to her, to the rise in her stomach, as though cradling the unborn child, that had caused him to step away from her. That had caused him to see how far he had fallen.

God help me. Max grasped the handle of the glass door, pulled it open, and stepped into the lobby of the Mountain Ridge Substance Abuse Treatment Center.

15

ANGELICA PROPPED HERSELF up on her elbow. From the window next to her bed, she could see the manicured grounds of the hospital.

It had been five weeks since she'd been admitted with a mild concussion and a gash behind her ear that had required stitches. But that wasn't the reason she was being kept under observation now.

Even though it had been an accident, she'd been ready to leave the hospital and see about filing assault charges against Max the night it had happened. But when the doctors had insisted she stay until Dr. Gremian could see her the following day, she'd put her anger aside and chosen to do what was best for the baby. Unfortunately, Dr. Gremian arrived to see her at the same time as Antonio came to visit. As Dr. Gremian discussed the results of her last ultrasound, her continued lack of weight gain, and his concerns for the baby, Antonio had become convinced that she should follow the doctor's orders to the letter and stay at home, getting complete bed rest until the baby was born. So, instead of returning to work, she'd reluctantly filed for worker's compensation.

Kit Elliot had taken over the Vasquez case, and other than a few weekly conversations with her, Angelica had been confined to the house. She'd also learned from Kit that Max had admitted himself to rehab. Though still angry, she'd decided not to pursue any action against him.

Without the constant pressure of her job, she'd begun to read her Bible, and she and Maclovia had fallen into a routine of meeting together after Antonio finished his lunch and went back to work. Angelica read to Maclovia from a *Nuevo Testamento*, and Maclovia led them in prayer afterward. The daily exchange had resulted in Angelica becoming fluent in conversational and "King James" Spanish. It had also resulted in a dramatic change in Angelica's prayer life. She could not say exactly how it had happened, but she had learned how to "wait" on the Lord, and when she felt His presence, to praise Him. She found herself hungering for that time with Him.

After she'd begun the bed rest, Dr. Gremian had ordered ultrasounds to be done every week. The results of the ultrasound the day before had led to her being admitted to the hospital.

Angelica rolled over on her back. Though she was only thirty-two weeks into her pregnancy, not only did Dr. Gremian want her to have strict bed rest, he'd ordered she have an ultrasound every six hours . . . and he'd ordered an amniocentesis.

After he'd explained to her that it was critical they determine the baby's lung maturity because it was an important component of survival should Manuel be born prematurely, she'd agreed. Dr. Gremian had received the results regarding lung development within an hour of drawing the amniotic fluid, but the full spectrum of results would not be available for at least two weeks. Her stomach knotted.

The ultrasounds were monitoring the baby on a point system. Normal amniotic fluid volume equaled four points. Non-stress test positive equaled three points. Fetal breathing movements active equaled two points. Fetal extremity and trunk movements active equaled one point. Ten possible points. At the end of each day the scores were compared to the scores of the previous day.

"How's my girl?"

Startled by the voice, Angelica looked toward the door.

"Hi, Mom and Dad." Angelica pressed the button to raise the head of her bed. "Is it already after three?"

Standing behind her father's wheelchair, Angelica's mother pushed it to the foot of the bed, then swiveled it so Angelica and her father faced each other. "Not quite. Dad finished his physical therapy early today."

Angelica's mother had made a full recovery, and now she was focused on helping her husband. Angelica debated whether or not to ask how it was going. Her father hadn't risen to the challenge of his recovery. He'd told her and her mother that life in a wheelchair wasn't worth the fight. As far as he was concerned, his life was over. "Well, now that I have to stay here, maybe we can spend more time together, Dad. I'd like that."

"Can't do much but sit." His voice was flat.

Her mother rolled her eyes and took a seat in a nearby chair. "How's Antonio? Has he been in?"

"Antonio probably won't come to see me until later. He's been working late every night. After he does his regular jobs, he goes door to door looking for new accounts. He picks out a neighborhood, parks his truck, and starts walking."

Her father shook his head. "He's been trying to build that business all summer, what's the problem?"

"The problem is, for some reason, he keeps losing clients, particularly in our neighborhood. There are over three hundred houses in our subdivision. If he got only a tenth of those as accounts he'd be making a decent living."

"If he can't hold on to his clients that's a bad sign."

"I don't look at it that way, Dad. There always seems to be a reason that's out of his control. Bad luck, really."

"Angelica, you make your own luck. You know that."

"It's not just him. There's a man, Bill, whose name I got from my Bible study, who I pray for. He's in the same business and really struggling too. It's been terribly hard on his family. The financial strain has nearly broken up his marriage. He's finally starting to turn the corner though."

Angelica thought about her prayer time with Maclovia the day before. Angelica had prayed that not only would God prosper Bill's business, but that He would send a laborer into his path who would soften his heart. The unbelieving man blamed God for his circumstances, and it continued to be a source of constant friction between him and his Christian wife. But yesterday, during prayer, as she'd finished putting Bill's name and situation before the Lord, she'd felt something. A knowing. She'd never experienced the sensation before, but with it came an absolute certainty that her prayer was heard, and she believed it would be answered. She was so sure, she'd even called Natalya and told her about it.

"Sitting around praying doesn't solve problems. You've got to take, take . . . control."

Angelica felt like answering, "And why don't you do just that at your next physical therapy session?" But she didn't. There was no fire in his voice, and his stumbling to find the word "control" only underlined how serious his condition was. "Antonio's been working with someone on a proposal for the models for the next phase of houses they're building in our subdivision. The builder is going to start taking bids next month. Antonio's planning to mail his bid soon. He's hoping if he gets it, it could lead to other jobs with the builder. Even commercial accounts."

"Excuse me." The nurse stepped into the room. "Time for your ultrasound, Mrs. Perez."

"She's an attorney. She uses her maiden name, Amante," Angelica's mother corrected the nurse. "We're her parents."

"Actually, Mom, it's okay. I've been thinking about that a lot lately. When our son is born, his name will be Manuel Perez. I think it will be much better for him if his mother is known as Mrs. Perez. I've decided to start using my married name both privately and professionally."

Angelica closed her eyes against the morning sun. The last ten days had seemed like ten years.

When she'd checked into the hospital, she'd known she was committing to complete bed rest. But she hadn't realized that meant she couldn't even take a shower without someone taking her to it in a wheelchair, or that she'd have to ask permission to go to the bathroom. She didn't know it meant four-hour intervals strung together in endless succession, punctuated by a nurse, smile pasted to her face, asking the same questions, "How much have you eaten? Do you have pain in your legs? Do you want more water?" Twenty-four hours a day, every four hours, in the middle of the night and the middle of the morning, "Let me get your blood pressure." "Just a moment, while I take your temp." And when she wasn't being tormented by the monotonous intrusions of the nurses, she was tortured by her own thoughts. Did her child have a birth defect? What did the future hold for him . . . and for her?

As her pregnancy had progressed, she'd refused to allow herself to dwell on the possibility that her child had Down syndrome. Yes, the baby was small, and there were markers, but there was no scientific proof. A wave of apprehension washed through her. Tomorrow the test results would be in.

Still, no matter what the results showed, there was a chance the baby did not have Downs. Angelica went over in her mind for the thousandth time the story she'd heard at Bible study about a woman who was told her child would have Down syndrome, and the baby had been born perfect. It could happen. It would happen. She had to believe that. Any other outcome would be devastating, not only to her but to her family. "Stop calling him Ben," her father's angry voice whispered in her ear. Her parents would never accept him. Nothing good could possibly come from so much heartache.

The sound of a baby crying broke into her thoughts. Of all the things she'd had to endure over the last ten days, that had been the worst. Listening to healthy newborns crying for their mothers and watching the new moms, babies cradled in their arms, their faces full of love and pride, passing in front of her door. She wiped her eyes with the back of her hand. The first ultrasound she'd been given had yielded a score of seven . . . the last one, a five. For the hundredth time she wondered, would she ever hear *her* baby cry? She bit her lip. For the hundredth time she pushed away the thought that always followed. Would it be better if he never did? Would it be better if Manuel died? Better for him . . . for everyone. *God, forgive me.* She turned her face into her pillow, sobbing.

Firm, strong and sure, someone lifting her. The tender touch of a loving hand on her face, wiping her tears.

"I love you, my precious Angel."

Antonio.

She felt his words more than she heard them, and for a moment she closed her eyes just to feel him, to draw strength from him, to be in the presence of his beautiful spirit, to be nurtured by his love for her.

"Oh, Antonio, you're here." She clutched his shirt. "I'm so scared."

He didn't speak, he held her. And in a way she could not explain, in a way that was so profoundly intimate it made her weep, there in his arms the darkness that gripped her faded. And in its place came understanding. Whatever her future held, she was not alone, she would be provided whatever was required of her.

"Oh!" Angelica's mother wheeled her father into the room.

Angelica saw the surprise and concern on her parents' faces. Extracting herself from Antonio's arms, she smoothed her hair.

"Is something wrong?" Her father looked from one to the other.

"No, Dad. Nothing really. Antonio happened to stop by when I was having a bad moment." She straightened the sheet across her stomach. "It's just hard being confined to this bed."

"Honey, I know it is. Dad and I try to visit you as much as possible to help pass the time. What are the doctors telling you?"

"I have four of them now." Angelica managed a weak smile. "They're watching the baby's growth, especially his head. Also his heart movement and the blood flow through the umbilical cord."

Her father's face was expressionless. "Have things improved since you've been here?"

Seeing him sitting stiffly, hands resting on his lifeless legs, she wanted desperately to tell him that things were improving, that things were going to work out, that soon he would have a grandson to live for. But she couldn't.

"The doctors say every day I carry him is a good day."

Her father saw through her dodge. "Angelica, I've performed hundreds of heart operations over the years. And for every patient I ever operated on, I did everything possible to ensure a good outcome. But sometimes, no matter what you do, it's just not meant to be." His eyes didn't leave her face. "Nature is kind. When life cannot be sustained the body shuts down."

Antonio leaned forward. "What this you saying?"

"I'm saying sometimes it's better not to use extraordinary means to prolong life. Sometimes it's wiser to trust nature."

Antonio picked up Angelica's hand and nodded. "Yes, we are trusting."

Antonio looked at the clock on the VCR. It was four o'clock in the morning, and he'd hardly slept. Still fully dressed, he turned onto his stomach, his face to the back of the couch, one hand beneath him, one hand lying awkwardly on the floor.

He'd tried to sleep in their bed. He had every night since Angelica had gone to the hospital. But he'd been no more successful this night than any of the other nights over the past ten days. The lingering scent of her perfume, the communion of their prayer time in each other's arms, and the pure, beautiful intimacy that brought glory to God were palpably present in the room. Not as a refuge, but as a wrenching reminder of the fragility of life. It robbed him of his joy by day and taunted him under cover of night. He closed his eyes, trying not to think, hoping sleep would find him. As the minutes passed, he began to feel himself slipping into the foggy, drowsy place of weary lethargy.

He felt a gentle nudge in the middle of his back. His eyes flew open, then settled closed. A smile tugged at his lips. "*Sí, señor?*" He wiggled the fingers of his hand lying palm up on the floor, inviting Buddy's chin for a scratch.

But instead of a cold, wet nose, Antonio felt Buddy pulling firmly on the sleeve of his shirt, as if Buddy thought he could pull him off the couch. Antonio rolled over toward the dog. "Hey, want some attention, huh? You miss her too, don't you?" He patted the couch, signaling Buddy, just this once, to join him.

Buddy whined, then backed away from Antonio. The dog stared at him, legs apart, tail up, ears quivering.

"What's wrong, Bud?"

Buddy whined again and darted to the hall that led to the kitchen. Then he bounded back to the couch.

Antonio sat up. "You want to go out?"

Buddy trotted to the hall again and stood looking into the kitchen. He began to growl.

Antonio's heartbeat quickened. He rose quietly, stepping silently toward the hall. Seeing nothing, he crept toward the kitchen, Buddy at his side.

At the entry of the kitchen, Antonio scanned the room. Moonlight, streaming through the sliding glass door that led to the backyard, revealed that everything was just as he and Maclovia had left it after dinner. He began to relax. "What's the matter with you, Bud?" He leaned down and scratched Buddy's ears.

Then he heard it.

He stood, listening. Slowly, he moved toward the utility

room where Buddy slept. Standing next to the washer he stopped, trying to pinpoint the noise.

The razor edge of fear cut through his chest as perception became reality. Someone was in the garage.

He stared at the door leading to the garage. His attention turned to the doorknob, but in the dim light he couldn't see it in any detail. Holding his breath, he rested his fingertips on the top of the knob. If the person on the other side of the door decided to come in, he would know. He tried to gather his thoughts, to reason through his fear.

Slowly, a plan began to form in his mind. He lifted his hand and pressed on the knob. Without making a sound, he turned it to the lock position. Then he edged back.

Ears pointed forward and tail up, Buddy growled.

Antonio dropped down next to the dog and clamped his hand around Buddy's nose. "No," he whispered.

Buddy sat.

Rising silently, Antonio turned and hurried to the living room. Standing at the edge of the big window, he surveyed the front yard and street. He didn't see anyone. He moved to the front door and cautiously opened it. All was quiet. With Buddy at his heels, he sprinted to the corner of the garage and peered around it.

Nothing.

Scanning the street, he caught his breath. In front of the next-door neighbor's house was a blue truck . . . parked . . . with the engine running.

Antonio knew immediately who was in his garage. His concern turned to anger. Every time he saw that truck, trouble followed.

The pieces began to fall into place. His back stiffened as he riffled through his memory. Unexplainable burns after he fertilized the lawns he cared for, trampled plants that owners attributed to his careless feet, unlocked gates that pets escaped from after he left a job, all resulting in him losing work and, worse, his reputation. He clenched his jaw.

Filled with resolve, he walked across the driveway to the side of the house. Rounding the corner, he saw the gate leading to the backyard was open, and beyond it, the side door of the garage was ajar. Slowing his steps, he approached the open door. Standing next to it, he took a deep breath, then, without allowing himself further thought, he swung the door wide open and strode to the light switch, flipping it on and flooding the garage with light.

The man turning the sprinkler clock dial dropped his flashlight and whirled around to face Antonio. "What in the he . . ."

Shock, recognition, confusion, passed across B.J.'s face. "Whadda you doin' here?" His voice was hard, but the fear in his eyes betrayed him.

"I live here." Antonio took in the scene behind B.J. The sprinkler clock was disabled. Mr. Catelli's voice echoed in his mind. *"You're not in here shutting off the timer again, are you?"*

B.J. picked up his flashlight. "You don't live here. You stole this job from me. These people are prob'ly on vacation, and you're watchin' the place."

Antonio glanced at his truck, then met B.J.'s eyes.

Antonio watched the color drain from the man's face.

B.J. tightened his grip on the flashlight, then suddenly charged toward Antonio, swinging the flashlight, narrowly missing Antonio's face. Buddy began barking.

Antonio ducked as B.J. ran past him.

Buddy leaped toward B.J., nipping at his arm.

Lunging through the garage door after the man, Antonio caught him by the shirt and pulled him down. As they

285

struggled, Antonio caught B.J.'s wrists, and straddling him, twisted B.J.'s arm up behind his back, the flashlight still in the man's hand. B.J. cried out, then stopped struggling.

Antonio pulled him up, pushed him against the side of the garage, and held him there. As he tried to catch his breath, he saw the man drop his head. "Please don't call the police."

"Why not? You take my jobs. You make trouble for me." Anger boiled in Antonio's gut, and he tightened his grip. A moan escaped B.J.'s lips. "You come into my house and break the law."

Antonio felt the man's stance change. His shoulders slumped, and he ceased resisting.

"I'm begging you, don't call the cops. Please." Antonio heard the distress in B.J.'s voice.

"You tell me why no call the cops."

"I've got a wife and kids. I need my job."

Antonio heard the man's voice begin to quaver.

"I've failed everybody. Nothing's worked out. I can't feed my family, I can't pay my bills, my wife is threatening to leave me." B.J. let go of the flashlight. "If you call the cops, I'll go to jail. That would end my marriage. How will I face my kids?" His voice trailed off.

Antonio loosened his hold.

Both men stood in silence.

Antonio understood. The man was desperate. He let B.J. turn toward him. He studied the man's face . . . eyes haunted and dark with fear.

It was his own face. He too had been desperate once. His family in Mexico had not had enough food or clothes or money . . . so he had broken the law. He had crossed into the United States illegally.

Antonio dropped his hands to his sides.

And he too had been caught. An immigration officer had stopped him in the driveway of Regalo Grande. But instead of deporting him, the officer had helped him.

"This is very wrong what you have done to me."

"It is wrong." B.J. rubbed his wrist. "But it's no more wrong than all the Mexicans crossing illegally. Coming here and taking jobs from *us*." He picked up his flashlight and stuck it in his back pocket. "I've never been in trouble with the law. I'm not a bad person. Please, don't call the cops."

Antonio frowned. B.J. stealing his jobs was like stealing money from him.

Suddenly, something occurred to him. Was coming to the United States and working the same as stealing from the Americans?

He thought a moment. It didn't seem so. Any American could apply for the jobs the Mexicans took. Just like B.J. could have bid on any of the houses that Antonio bid on. But crossing the border illegally *was* breaking the law.

He felt a wave of shame wash over him. He had been desperate. He had seen no other way. And when he'd realized the enormity of what he'd done, he'd gone before God and asked His forgiveness. Not only had God forgiven him, God had blessed him.

God had forgiven him. Could he do less?

Antonio stepped back. "There is plenty of work for us both. This is not necessary."

B.J. stepped around Antonio and toward the gate. "You won't call the cops, will you?"

"If you don't bother me no more, me or anyone, I no call the cops."

"I won't. I promise." B.J. started across the street, then turned. "Thank you."

Still unable to put away his anger, but believing the man

had learned his lesson, he answered. "Better that you thank God."

For a full minute B.J. stared at Antonio. Then a shudder went through his body. Antonio's eyes narrowed as he watched the man wipe his eyes with the back of his hand. Stammering something, B.J. turned and walked to his truck. Antonio barely caught the odd words, carried on the wings of a night breeze. "She prayed He'd show me His grace."

He watched B.J. drive away.

"Everything okay?"

Antonio looked behind him, toward the mysterious voice.

Mrs. Dupre was leaning on the edge of her office window. "I almost called the police."

Antonio wondered how much she'd heard. "Everything okay. Thank you."

"That guy's a jerk. He tried to get me to switch to his services. I wouldn't do business with B.J.'s Lawn Care if it was the only lawn service in town. And frankly, I think that's what he's after."

Antonio bit his lip. He had plenty of his own opinions he could add. Instead, he said, "I'm sorry I wake you up." Then he turned and walked back to the house.

As he stepped through the front door, he heard the phone ring. He raced to the kitchen. "*Sí?*"

"Antonio. Come. Please hurry." Angelica's voice was frantic. "They can't find Manuel's heartbeat." The phone line went dead.

16

THE NURSE TOOK the phone from Angelica's hand and threw it in the cradle.

"Bring in an ultrasound." Dr. O'Brien, the doctor on duty, shouted the order to a second nurse. "Now."

A third nurse pulled the sheet back.

Dr. O'Brien put both hands on Angelica's stomach and began to shake it, then watched the monitor for the baby's heartbeat.

It seemed like only moments had passed when a second doctor smeared gel over her tummy and pressed a transducer to her abdomen.

The room became silent as all eyes turned toward the ultrasound screen, looking for a heartbeat.

Angelica flashed a look at the doctor. "Is he alive?"

Someone cleared his throat.

No one spoke.

"Why can't I see his heartbeat?" Her mouth felt dry, and her hands sweated.

Angelica returned her focus to the ultrasound, watching

the image of her child on the screen, innocent and helpless. She called out to him silently. *Manuel, Mommy's here.*

She closed her eyes and braced herself. "Is he alive?"

Still, the room was silent.

Please, God.

Suddenly, Angelica felt the tension in the room subside and the pressure of the transducer lighten on her stomach.

Her eyes flew open, and she focused on the screen.

The flickering heartbeat brought a collective sigh.

Someone shouted, "Yes!"

Someone else whispered, "What a little fighter."

The second doctor continued to watch the screen and then exchanged a glance with Dr. O'Brien.

Dr. O'Brien turned to her. "The baby has moved into a transverse breech position, and he's not tolerating the position well. With the umbilical cord severely compromised, the baby's not getting the blood flow he needs." He paused. "His chances are better outside the womb. It would be best for him, and for you, to have a C-section."

"Is he going to live?"

"There are risks. Right now, the odds are against him. The ultrasound scores have been very low, and he's so small, even if he is born alive, he may not be able to survive on his own." The doctor drew a deep breath. "Do you want lifesaving measures to be taken?"

Dr. O'Brien's kind face and gentle voice made the enormity of what he was asking seem surreal.

Angelica felt the baby move. Looking to the monitor, she saw the image of the child clearly outlined on the screen. The flutter in her womb was Manuel raising his arm.

The doctor lifted the transducer. "Hook her back up to the fetal monitor." Manuel disappeared from the screen as the nurses put the band back around her stomach.

Her father's voice crowded into her mind. *"Let nature take its course."*

A whisper, still and small . . . *"We are trusting."*

Antonio. If only he were here. But did he *really* understand what was at stake?

What would he say?

As quickly as that thought crossed her mind, the answer followed.

Angelica touched the doctor's arm. "Dr. O'Brien, do you have a son?"

A startled look crossed the doctor's face. "I do. He's ten."

"Then you'll understand when I ask that you do everything for my son that you would do for yours if you were asked the same question."

"Angelica, I want to be sure you fully understand." Dr. O'Brien's eyes were filled with compassion. "Your baby has less than a twenty percent chance of surviving. He's so small that if he's born alive, he'll probably need a ventilator. If not at birth, within an hour of birth. Because he's micro-preemie status, being on a ventilator will most likely cause brain bleeding. That often results in death or severe brain damage." The doctor's eyes didn't leave her face. "Are you sure about your decision? Do you want us to try to reach your husband?"

Angelica felt the dull, empty ache in her heart start to grow as the doctor's words snatched every shred of hope from her. "My husband has absolute faith that this is the child God has chosen to bless us with. If Antonio were here, he would wonder why the question was even being asked."

Dr. O'Brien's eyes narrowed, his face a mixture of concern and admiration. "I understand." He patted her hand

and turned to the nurse. "Let's get her prepped for the C-section."

As the gurney moved down the hall, Angelica recalled the last time she had prayed with Maclovia. Angelica had read to her from John 14. Upon hearing the words Jesus spoke to his disciples, "And whatever you ask in My name, that I will do," Maclovia had nodded her head and said, "It is so." Then she had taken Angelica's hand and prayed that God would give a healing to the family and had identified Angelica and her mother and father by name. It had been so odd to hear Maclovia speak her parents' given names, Benito and Geniveve, instead of *señor* and *señora*. Angelica hadn't realized Maclovia even knew the first names of her parents. The whole prayer had seemed otherworldly, almost as if it were not Maclovia speaking. But for the same reason, the prayer had been powerful, and Angelica had reasoned, surely God would hear it. Surely God had plans to prosper the child He was bringing into the world. Surely He would give Manuel hope and a future. Suddenly, more than anything else in heaven or earth, she wanted her son to live. She closed her eyes. *Oh, God, I'm begging You, give us the healing Maclovia asked for.*

Someone was touching her arm. She looked up. Antonio was walking beside her.

At the delivery room door, the nurse instructed Antonio to wait until he was called. She gave him some scrubs and told him after the spinal block was completed, she would come for him.

"You can come in." The nurse led Antonio to a chair at the end of the table, behind Angelica's shoulder.

The room was small, and there were four doctors and many nurses surrounding his wife.

He sat down. Something must be very wrong. When his mother had her children, only his father or another woman helped her. And he had never heard of a baby being cut out of its mother's stomach. Dr. Gremian had discussed this with them last week. But he'd said it was only a possibility. Now, it was a certainty.

He looked at Angelica, lying with her arms and legs strapped down. He stroked her cheek with his fingertips. Bending down, he whispered, "I love you."

She reached up for his hand.

He was humbled, witnessing what she was going through to give him a son . . . a testimony of her love for him. He bowed his head. *Dios, I don't understand why this must be as it is. You hold life and death in Your hands. If You judge that now is the time for a life to be returned to You, take mine. Let my wife and child live.*

Immediately, he was filled with an overpowering sense of peace and the knowledge that God's hands were upon all who were present and that what would transpire would be God's will. . . . His son would live.

The doctors worked behind the sheet draped over Angelica's legs. Antonio couldn't see what they were doing. He took a deep breath, he must stay strong. Angelica needed that from him. The minutes dragged by.

One of the doctors at the foot of the bed laid something down on a sheeted table.

Suddenly, an overhead speaker crackled. "Send the NICU team to OR number seven for a resuscitation. Stat."

"Time of delivery 6:12 a.m." The nurse's words startled him.

Antonio stood. He craned his neck, trying to make sense

of the tiny, gray mass, limp on the white sheet. There was no sound, no movement. Nothing but a lifeless piece of flesh, just a little bigger than the palm of his hand.

Angelica's voice filled the room. "Is he alive? Is my baby alive?"

A nurse opened the delivery room door, a doctor handed the nurse the baby, and then they were gone.

"Antonio, what do you see? Why didn't he cry?" She pulled against her straps.

A nurse spoke. "He's been taken to the resuscitation room."

"Antonio, what did you see?" Angelica's voice was rising in panic. "Is he alive?"

Antonio leaned down next to her, pressing his cheek against hers, fighting tears. There had been no sign of life.

He summoned his will and made a conscious choice to believe God. "Don't be afraid. God is with us," he whispered. "He has given us a son."

"Please go to him, Antonio. Go to Manuel. I don't want him to die alone." Angelica's voice was frantic.

A nurse touched his arm. "I'll take you to the resuscitation room."

The nurse led Antonio across the hall, to a small room. When he entered, he saw his son lying on a table. Lifeless.

The doctors spoke in hushed tones to the nurses. Antonio could catch only snatches of the conversation, and many of the words he'd never heard before.

A doctor waved a plastic mask, hooked to a tube of air, back and forth over Manuel's face. Another doctor listened to his heart. Still another doctor was rubbing Manuel's body, hard.

But there was no response.

Suddenly, Antonio saw the room as though he were observing from a distance. Mere men hovered over his child, doing what they could, while his son wavered between life and death in the hand of God. The doctors were helpless. They could not save his son.

At that moment of realization, Antonio believed. God would not fail him.

Dios, breathe on him.

Manuel cried.

Angelica stared out the window next to her hospital bed into the cloudless night as she struggled to awaken from a drugged sleep. Snatches of the hours that had passed since Manuel's birth drifted through her mind. Being wheeled up to the Neonatal Intensive Care Unit on the gurney for her first glimpse of her son, but able to see little more than his silhouette through the incubator before being wheeled back to her room. Antonio sitting next to her while Maclovia held her hand. Her parents smiling lifeless smiles as doctors came and went, one speaking of the little boy's courage, another astonished that he was still breathing on his own. And everyone answering her repeated questions about Manuel with, "He's doing just fine," and, "You should rest." Antonio always adding, "No worry, Angel. Our son is strong."

Fronie had called, but Angelica had waved the phone away. She wasn't ready to talk about everything that had happened, especially not with her parents in the room. She felt like her life was still in limbo. She still didn't know if her child had a serious birth defect. The doctors had told her nothing. And she knew they wouldn't until they received the results of the amnio.

Angelica thought back. She counted on her fingers

calculating the number of days since the fluid had been drawn. . . .

The results should be available now. The results that would show conclusively if something was wrong!

Suddenly awake, she felt for the button to raise the bed, then buzzed for a nurse.

A young woman appeared at the door. "May I help you?"

"Could you send my nurse in, please?"

Within moments, the night nurse, Rebecca, was at her bedside. "Hi Angelica, feeling better?"

During sleepless nights, Angelica had come to know Rebecca well. The nurse had a sweet, quiet way about her and somehow always seemed to come in and check on Angelica just when Angelica was thinking of buzzing for her. "How can I find out if my amnio results came in?"

"If they're in, Dr. Gremian would have them, but he's not on call and won't be making rounds until around six." The nurse checked Angelica's water pitcher.

Angelica frowned. "What time is it now?"

Rebecca gently smoothed Angelica's pillow. "About four o'clock in the morning."

Angelica bit her lower lip. Suddenly, after all the months of wondering . . . the gut-wrenching fear . . . the blind hope . . . she wanted it to be over. She wasn't going to wait for a doctor; she wasn't going to wait for test results; she wasn't going to wait another minute. She wanted to see her son; she wanted to know if he was all right. . . . She wanted to know if he had Down syndrome.

"The doctor said I can go up and see my baby as soon as I can stand on my own."

Rebecca looked directly into Angelica's eyes, as if reading her thoughts, but making no judgment. "Yes, when you can stand, I'll call an aide to take you up in a wheelchair." She smoothed Angelica's forehead.

"Thank you." Angelica lowered her bed.

As soon as Rebecca left, Angelica swung her legs over the edge of the bed. Light-headed, she grabbed the bed railing, steadying herself. She eased out of the bed and stood for a moment, trying to get her balance. A wave of nausea passed over her. She stepped toward the window and pressed her forehead against it, still using the bed for support.

Rebecca was behind her. Angelica hadn't heard her footsteps, but she could feel the edge of a wheelchair behind her knees. She sank into it.

Rebecca pulled Angelica's hair back away from her face. The touch of the nurse's hand brought Angelica a sense of peace. In a strange way, though they didn't speak, they seemed to have a shared knowledge. It was time.

An aide wheeled Angelica to the NICU. After she washed her hands at the entry to the unit, they continued to Manuel's incubator.

"Call when you're ready to leave, and I'll come back to get you." The aide left.

Angelica sat staring at the tiny form, mottled gray and pink, veins visible through translucent skin, one eye still fused shut.

"Are you Manuel's mother?"

Angelica started at the voice behind her. *Manuel's mother.* " . . . Yes."

"I'm Ruth, his night nurse." The gray-haired woman's smile was sweet and her manner confident. "Do you want to touch him?"

"Can I?"

"I don't think a few minutes will hurt him." The nurse lifted the top of the isolette.

Angelica reached in and picked up Manuel's tiny hand. She studied him.

The bridge of his nose didn't look *that* broad, and his ears didn't stick out at all. She tilted her head. His eyes only had the slightest slant to them . . . really she wasn't even sure. A smile tugged at her lips. She remembered her baby pictures with Poppy holding her. Manuel looked a little like she had.

She turned her attention to his miniature palm, smoothing it with her forefinger. She caught her breath. It looked normal! Surely if he had Downs there would be the telltale single crease across his palm. Her heart began to pound as she reached for his other hand and opened it.

A single, crimped line, slashing through the thin thread of hope that had woven itself through her thoughts. Still, it was just *one* hand. Maybe . . .

Manuel opened his eye.

A slit of dark sapphire.

Angelica leaned forward, directly in his line of vision, searching his gaze, hoping to meet him there.

But she could not penetrate the deep blue veil before her . . . incognizant, inscrutable . . . unknowing, unaware.

She lowered her eyes.

She knew.

Though conscious of the presence of others around her, aware of the sounds of the machines, aware of the tears silently streaming down her face, somehow it was as if the physical world were now separated from her, cauterized by *her* reality.

Alone with her truth, everything came into question. In the world she'd known, things like this didn't happen to people like her. Had she done something to deserve this?

Her parents were supposed to have a grandchild they

could be proud of. They could never love him now. Would they even accept him?

And what about all the prayers? Hers and Antonio's, Natalya's, Fronie's . . . Maclovia's. Why had God turned away from them? Angelica had truly believed God would give the healing Maclovia had asked for. But now it would never happen. It was too late.

An alarm went off next to her.

Ruth stepped beside her and closed the isolette. "His body temperature is dropping. We've got to keep him warm."

Angelica looked at her, the words barely registering. "Yes, of course." She rolled herself back a few feet.

"He's a handsome young man and doing so well." Ruth straightened the wires leading into the incubator.

"Would you mind calling someone to take me back to my room?"

As Angelica waited for the aide, she kept going over in her mind—why? Why did her dreams have to end this way? Why did her son have to have one extra chromosome? He would never be more than a burden. Her family would never fully heal from all that had happened. And the one thing she had known would give her father a reason to fight for a better quality of life, the one hope she'd held out for him, was now lost.

As the aide wheeled her back to her room, Angelica's thoughts turned to Maclovia, the circle of light beneath the oaks, and the prayer time she'd spent with God since leaving her job. He had seemed so real. A living God who loved her. She had felt it. She closed her eyes, desperate to feel His presence.

The chair rolled to a stop beside her bed. "Thank you." The aide helped her from the chair, switched off the overhead lights, then left.

Angelica looked out the window. The full moon was setting. *Where are You?*

She heard someone sit down in the chair next to her bed. "Oh, Rebecca. I didn't hear you come in."

"How is he?"

Even in the dim light, Angelica could see the genuine interest in Rebecca's face.

"My son has Down syndrome." Angelica rushed on. "I looked at his eyes and hands and nose. All the markers are there. But it was more than that." She paused. "I just knew."

Rebecca stood and took Angelica's hand in hers. "You know, Angelica, one day you're going to look at him, and you're not going to see any of those features. You're just going to see Manuel."

Angelica pulled her hand away and wiped her eyes. "Maybe so. But it's not just about Manuel. It's about me and my husband and my family and our dreams." All that had transpired over the term of her pregnancy pressed down on her. "Why is this happening? What good can ever come from it?" She turned her back to Rebecca. She felt sick to her stomach. She wanted to be alone.

"Believe."

She slowly lifted her head, turning to the nurse who seemed to know and understand her so well.

But Rebecca was gone.

Antonio stepped out on the front porch and sat on the top step, watching the sun edge up over the horizon. Angelica had awakened him with her call, telling him she couldn't sleep, she needed him and wanted him to come to her. Telling him their son had Down syndrome.

Margarita. He closed his eyes and was transported back to his childhood. He had loved the little girl with the perpetual smile, who never noticed she was carried because she couldn't keep up.

She didn't notice a lot of things. He felt a heaviness in his chest, remembering how children from up the river had taunted her. One boy had poked her with a stick, then pushed her down when she'd cried. Antonio pressed the fist of one hand into the palm of the other. He'd made the boy pay.

And her life had been so short. A blessing and a curse.

Manuel.

Antonio hung his head.

For all that was good and all that was wrong. For all that would be and all that would never be. For the unfathomable mind and benevolent mercy of God. He wept.

17

MACLOVIA TOOK THE dresses from her closet and laid them on the bed. Buddy's brown eyes tracked her every move.

It had been over a month since Manuel had been born, God allowing no doubt that He had purposed the child's life. Without Him, Manuel would have died. Even the grandfather had noticed that.

Maclovia huffed a sigh. The grandparents. They continued to strive in endless reasoning about their grandchild. She had faithfully prayed that God would heal their hearts, anointing them with love for their grandson. She had spent much time with God in the days before Manuel's birth fasting and praying for them.

Her mouth curved into a smile. And over the month since the child had been born, she'd realized God had heard her. The little boy had something extra. A life yielded to God. God would use Manuel to bring glory to His name and accomplish His purposes. Maclovia began to hum as she folded the dresses, one by one. What a blessing Manuel would be to his family, especially his mother. He would turn her tears of sorrow to tears of joy.

Angelica. The work of God's mighty hands was so evident in the young woman. He'd created her with a bright mind, deep compassion, and a hunger for Him. But sadly, Angelica had mistaken His favor as a birthright. And worse, she didn't understand He wanted the fruit of His labor. . . . He wanted her.

Maclovia laid the folded clothes in the box by her door. God had a powerful plan for Angelica, and His will would be done. But since the birth of the baby, Angelica had begun to lean on Maclovia and not God for her spiritual needs. This had not been pleasing to the Creator. God was preparing to deal with Angelica Himself.

Maclovia stepped out of her room and looked into the nursery. The blue crocheted blanket was neatly draped over the end of the crib. The wooden shelves Antonio had built were full of knitted booties, hats, and sweaters. The curtains, on which she had helped Angelica embroider bright flowers, hung in the window, and a woolly rocking horse stood by the door waiting to greet his master. Everything was ready.

It had been important to Maclovia that the room be finished by today. Because today was the day her visa expired. Today was the day she was going home. She had finished what God had brought her to America to do, and now He was drawing her back to Mexico.

Returning to her room, she put the last few things in her box, closed it, and tied a rope around it. Then she hurried down the hall, Buddy at her heels, to tell Antonio and Angelica she was ready to go to the airport. Eager to go where she was being called, to do whatever God put before her.

Antonio and Angelica stood in the parking lot of the Sacramento International Airport watching Maclovia's plane rise into the clouds. When it disappeared, Buddy stood, his feet apart, his tail straight up, and his ears pointed forward, as if perhaps he still heard the jet's engines. Finally, he dropped his head and tail and turned soulful eyes to Antonio.

"*Sí, señor*. I know what you mean." Antonio opened the back door of the Expedition and helped Buddy in. Glancing at his watch, he looked toward Angelica. "Who's driving?"

"I will. I'll drop you off at the house so you can get to work, then I'll go on in to the hospital."

They drove in silence with only an occasional whimper from Buddy, sitting in the back of the SUV staring down the road behind them.

"Antonio, I feel like a part of my heart is missing."

"Me too, Angel."

"When I was with her, I felt like I had a direct line to God. I know He heard her prayers."

Antonio turned to her. "Are you saying He doesn't hear *your* prayers?"

Angelica thought a moment. "It's not so much that He doesn't hear me. It's more that I find it hard to pray. Especially for my dad. I just can't concentrate. I try to pray that God will touch him and give him a reason to live." She glanced at Antonio. "But every time I sit down to pray, I can't find the peace I need for my prayer time. I start thinking about the accident. About Gerald Levine and how he ruined *my* life."

Antonio looked at her. The moments passed.

Finally, he added, "And your *mother's and father's* lives too."

Angelica stared straight ahead at the road. "Of course, and their lives too." He saw her grip tighten on the wheel.

Antonio reached across the seat and put his hand on Angelica's shoulder. His heart went out to her. She had never fully forgiven herself for what had happened to her parents, and the birth of their son had been devastating to his smart and driven wife. Her days were consumed with helping care for Manuel in the hospital and learning how to care for him when he came home. They had had no idea what was involved, and now they realized there was a possibility Angelica might not be able to return to work. That thought burdened him greatly. He had to find a way to take care of his wife and son. He looked at his watch. By this afternoon, he might be a lot closer to doing that.

"Be patient, Angel. God is busy with many things. He knows when it is time to answer you."

When they arrived home, he gave Angelica a quick kiss on the cheek, jumped out of the car, and started toward the house.

"Don't forget Buddy," Angelica called after him.

Stopping midstride, he turned around and jogged back to open the car door for the dog. "Come on, boy."

But Buddy didn't move. He sat, staring past Antonio, down the road they'd just traveled.

Antonio reached in, picked up Buddy, then shut the door with his elbow. "See you tonight," he called over his shoulder as he started back to the house.

Once inside, he set Buddy down and checked his watch. He needed to hurry.

He grabbed his keys from the kitchen counter, patted his back pocket for his wallet, and headed to his truck.

Pulling out of his drive, he saw Mrs. Dupre getting into her van and waved at her. She'd shown him her vehicle once. He'd been fascinated by all the gadgets it had that allowed her to drive without the use of her legs. Maybe that would be possible for the *patrón* someday.

A wave of sadness swept over Antonio. It was clear to Antonio that the man had no will to live. The man who had saved so many lives had no desire to save his own. The man who'd so admired his daughter's spirit and achievements, who'd so often reminded her she was an Amante, now seemed to have abandoned all that he once esteemed.

Antonio saw the building a few blocks ahead. Cornerstone Builders. He'd driven by it the week before when he'd received the letter saying that Bryan Tomlinson wanted to meet with him. Antonio's proposal for landscaping and maintaining their new model homes had been reviewed, and he was one of two who had been chosen for personal interviews. His English teacher had translated the letter for him and told him it meant that he and only one other company were being considered. She was as excited as he was at the news.

Antonio smiled, remembering how he'd had to tell Angelica about the proposal. He'd hoped to surprise her if he got the job, but she'd questioned him so aggressively about why he was spending hours with his English teacher that he'd had to tell her about the bid. But she didn't know he was one of the final two and that he was meeting them today.

He parked and checked the time. Six minutes to two. Perfect. He walked to the lobby and stepped to the counter. "I am here for appointment."

The woman smiled at him. "Mr. Perez?"

He nodded.

"Follow me."

306

She directed him to sit on a small couch, facing a room with big glass windows.

Antonio could see two men through the windows. His eyes widened. Anger flashed through him.

B.J.

Antonio watched as the two men rose. B.J. handed the other man a folder of papers.

Antonio chewed his lip. What could they be? He had not brought his proposal with him. The letter had not said he should. He began to agonize over his stupidity. He should have told Angelica about the interview. She would have known what he needed to do. But he wanted to do this on his own. It was his business. He drew a deep breath. He'd just have to do his best and hope that God was with him.

The door opened.

"It was nice meeting you, Bill. We'll be in touch with you."

Antonio stood. He met Bill's eyes and tipped his head.

Bill extended his hand. "Good luck."

"You must be Antonio Perez. I'm Bryan Tomlinson."

Antonio shook the man's hand, then followed him into the room.

"Take a seat." Mr. Tomlinson gestured to the chair Bill had been sitting in. "Do you know Bill?"

Antonio sat down. A barrage of answers crossed his mind. *Yes, he's a liar and a thief. He steals jobs from people. He broke into . . .* but instead, he answered, "Yes."

"He has great references from some of our clients, people we've built for. The Jessicks, the Catellis. To be honest, I don't think I need to look further. The fact he already works in the area and has a good relationship with our clients in that subdivision makes him a perfect fit." Mr. Tomlinson

307

rose and extended his hand. "I'm sorry that I troubled you to come in today."

Antonio felt a nauseating, sinking despair in the pit of his stomach. He stood. The man had already read his proposal and liked it enough to call him in, Antonio reasoned. It seemed that it was B.J.'s references and the fact he was already working there that had impressed Mr. Tomlinson.

"Bill work in the area, but I live in the area."

"Really?" Mr. Tomlinson dropped his hand.

"I live in that subdivision. Down the street from the new models."

"Really?"

Antonio took a seat. "Yes. You know, there have been some problems with vandalism." He hoped that was the right word. He'd only heard Angelica use it once. "In our neighborhood. Even across the street from the models."

"I had no idea." Mr. Tomlinson sat down. "Tell me more."

"Oh, there not much to tell. But I live near the models. It is easy for me to watch them."

Mr. Tomlinson leaned forward in his chair and spent the next few minutes asking Antonio about his experience. He finally ended the interview by asking Antonio why he thought he was the best man for the job.

"I have wife and child. I need to work hard."

"Do you have references?"

"I be glad to bring you some."

"Excuse me." The woman from the front counter interrupted them. "Mr. Tomlinson, Hope is here with the renderings for the models and the layout for the print campaign."

Mr. Tomlinson rose. "Do bring some references by."

Antonio followed him. When they stepped into the lobby, Antonio's eyes widened in amazement.

Mrs. Dupre!

"I'll be with you in a minute, Hope." Mr. Tomlinson nodded toward her.

"*Disculpe*, Mr. Tomlinson. I have reference."

Mr. Tomlinson turned to Antonio.

"Antonio." Mrs. Dupre rolled her wheelchair toward them. "What are you doing here?"

"I give proposal for the new models. I need references."

"Oh, Bryan. Antonio takes care of my yard. I can't say enough about the great job he does. I should have thought of recommending him to you."

Antonio hesitated, weighing his words. *Dios, I hope I'm not doing a wrong thing.*

"Mrs. Dupre, Mr. Tomlinson trying to decide between me and B.J.'s Lawn Care."

Angelica felt like she was living at Valle Medical Center. Between Manuel and her father, it seemed like she was always needed. She stepped into the elevator and looked at the panel of buttons. Who should she see first, Manuel on ten, or her father on four? She noticed the little silver plate next to seven, Maternity.

Rebecca.

Something quickened in Angelica's heart, and she realized she missed the nurse she had come to know during her stay at the hospital. She hadn't really thought about her since she'd left the maternity ward. Angelica looked at her watch. Rebecca probably wasn't even working yet. Still . . . maybe

309

. . . she felt a drawing. It would be so good to see her. Angelica pressed seven.

Everyone at the nurses' station greeted Angelica by name. Angelica asked if Rebecca was working, and to her surprise, Rebecca was there, not working, but visiting one of the patients. They directed Angelica down the east wing.

Looking into the room, she saw Rebecca seated in a chair by the window, talking with a woman who sat on the edge of the hospital bed. "Oh, don't let me interrupt. I just wanted to say hi."

Rebecca jumped up. "Here's Angelica. Come in. Meet my friend Mary."

Rebecca gave Angelica a hug and pulled a chair up next to hers. "Sit. Sit. It's so good to see you."

Mary was holding a little baby boy. His round, brown eyes watched Angelica from the safety of his mother's arms.

Angelica felt a twinge of jealousy. "What's his name?"

Mary smoothed the blue blanket away from his face. "Gerald."

"My, that's a big name for such a little boy." Angelica set her purse down by her feet. "Did you name him after his father?"

"Well, his father and his grandfather." Mary smiled and kissed the baby's plump cheek.

"I bet that makes them proud." *"Stop calling him Ben."* The memory sent a flash of anger through Angelica. She had not thought about those words since Manuel's birth.

Mary tightened her arm around the baby. "His father died before he was born."

Angelica caught her breath. "I'm so sorry."

Mary's voice became a whisper. "There are things worse than death."

The young woman looked at her with eyes so full of sorrow that Angelica looked away.

"Excuse me." Mary rose. "I need to take Gerald to the nursery."

When she was gone, Angelica turned to Rebecca. "Me and my big mouth. I'm sorry I interrupted your visit."

Rebecca didn't speak for a moment, then put her hand on Angelica's arm. "Her husband committed suicide, and she and his father are the ones who found him. She was seven months pregnant at the time."

"How terrible."

"It happened in their home. Her father-in-law was living with them. He had just returned from Sudan where he and his wife were missionaries. She had become very ill there and didn't make it back." Rebecca pressed her lips together, then continued. "Mary opened her home to him. Her husband had had a drug problem for years and had been estranged from his parents since high school. She'd hoped for a reconciliation, a chance for her husband to heal. But tragically that didn't happen. Instead, the tension escalated, and her husband took his life . . . after writing a suicide note that placed the blame directly on his father for all the perceived wrongs of his childhood."

Angelica could hardly comprehend what she was hearing. "I can see why she said there are things worse than death. Her father-in-law must be in a living hell."

Rebecca's face became somber. "In Sudan he lost his wife. After his son's death, he lost his faith."

"I'm so sorry for him." Angelica shook her head. "For them."

"I've known the family for years. Her father-in-law adored his son." Rebecca patted Angelica's arm. "Enough of that. Tell me all about our Manuel."

311

For the next few minutes, Angelica brought Rebecca up to date on Manuel's progress and then was surprised to learn that Rebecca had given notice at the hospital and would be leaving.

"Where are you planning to work?"

Rebecca shrugged her shoulders. "I'm not sure I'll take another position right away." She stood. "Mary might need me." Rebecca gave Angelica a hug. "You know, just before you walked in, I was telling Mary about you. I had a feeling you'd drop by."

"Funny you should say that." Angelica turned away to pick up her purse. "When I got in the elevator, I had the strangest . . ."

Angelica straightened and looked to where Rebecca had been standing. She was alone in the room. She walked quickly to the door and saw Rebecca disappear around the corner.

Angelica hurried after her to the nurses' station. "Did Rebecca come through here?"

None of the staff had seen her.

Angelica put her hands on her hips. Perhaps Rebecca had said good-bye when Angelica had stooped to pick up her purse, and she hadn't heard her. Angelica's thoughts returned to what Rebecca had told her about Mary. For all that had happened to Angelica, it paled when she thought about Mary and her father-in-law.

Angelica wanted to extend her friendship to the young woman. Maybe Mary was still in the nursery. Angelica turned and walked down the hall to find her.

Stepping into the birthing center, Angelica scanned the area. She walked up to one of the nurses. Suddenly, she realized she didn't even know Mary's last name. "I'm looking for Mary, her baby is named Gerald."

The nurse looked across the room. "It looks like Gerald's in his bassinet."

"Oh, which one?"

"The one with the Big Bird balloon tied to it."

Angelica made her way across the floor. As she approached, she saw Gerald was asleep. The thought that he would grow up without a father flitted through her mind. Unexpectedly, she felt tears sting her eyes. *Dear God, please give a special blessing to this baby and his family. Especially his grandfather. Have mercy on him. He served you all his life. Draw him back to you so he can be a father to his grandson.*

She would give the name of the family to her Bible study group, and they could pray for them. Angelica bent down to read the baby's name. She squinted at the card.

Gerald Levine.

Angelica's head was spinning. She didn't even know where she was driving. She'd left the hospital, run to her car, and driven away.

Angry, confused, shocked. She tried to sort through her feelings. There was no doubt that Mary's father-in-law was the man who had hit her parents. And she hated him for it. Because of him, her father's life had been ruined . . . and so had hers.

Snatches of Rebecca's conversation echoed in her mind. *"He committed suicide. His father found him." "They were missionaries." "After his son's death, he lost his faith."*

"I don't care." She pounded her fist on the steering wheel. "Nothing can excuse what he did."

She drove mindlessly through the hills, feeding her anger. But every time she cursed the name of Gerald Levine, she saw the card on the bassinet and the baby sleeping. Innocent, blameless.

Angelica jerked the car into a right turn, onto the road skirting Valle de Lagrimas. Looking down the road ahead of her, she saw a wide spot on the shoulder. Instantly, it snapped her back to the present.

She took her foot off the accelerator and rolled into the open spot. When she opened her door, she smelled the sweet fragrance of the wildflowers and the mossy oaks. She closed her eyes, transported to the moment, months before, when she'd sat in the car at this very spot, with Maclovia.

"Believe," Maclovia had said that day.

Angelica stepped out of the car. If only Maclovia were here to pray with her, to counsel her, to bring her into the presence of God. To set her free from everything that had happened, everything that haunted her.

Angelica looked toward the mountain and saw the little trail she had walked up on that day. She remembered the singing, the high voice. She stood still, listening.

Nothing. Not a sound but the breeze.

She walked along the grassy edge of the hill, then onto the path, climbing up the mountain. Finally, she reached the clearing where Valle de Lagrimas stretched before her. She stood, looking across the valley at the community. She squatted down. Houses, schools, hospitals, and office buildings, each with its own story of tragedy or triumph.

This was how the world was. The reality settled on her . . . all of their lives inextricably intertwined. Any one of them at any time, capable of touching the life of another, for good or bad, by the whim of fate or the hand of God.

She closed her eyes, letting the breeze blow her hair back from her face. If only Maclovia were here.

Angelica stood and turned around.

The oak tree.

She walked toward it, stopping where she had first seen the circle of light. She searched the ground . . . hoping.

Nothing but dirt and rocks.

Angelica continued until she was beneath the big, spreading branches of the ancient tree, then she sat down.

Her thoughts turned to the old woman and the time she'd spent with her.

Believe.

What had Maclovia meant? She knew Angelica believed in God, that she prayed and went to church and Bible study.

Her thoughts went to Rebecca and the night in the hospital when she'd told Rebecca that Manuel had Down syndrome.

Believe.

Rebecca too knew she believed in God, they had spoken about it many times.

Slowly a truth began to reveal itself to Angelica. She believed *in* God. She did not believe God.

Things began to coalesce in Angelica's mind. All of their lives inextricably intertwined. This was not only how the world was, it was how the world was meant to be. It was how *God* had made it.

A gasp escaped her lips. *The God who had made Manuel.*

She had been so focused on the fact that her world was not as she wanted it, she had been unable to see that her world was as God had allowed it. Even her father's accident had first passed through His fingers. For all of her praying and all of her Bible study, in her heart, she had not believed God was in control.

She sat, stunned, trying to grasp the life-changing truth. God's truth, not man's truth.

Slowly, she began to realize the wrongness of her heart before God.

Angelica got on her knees and closed her eyes. Turning her face toward heaven, she lifted her hands and praised His holy name. Thanking Him for the life He had given her, exactly as it was. Asking His forgiveness for her blindness. Choosing to forgive Gerald Levine. For the first time in months, she felt joy. His grace was sufficient for her. Her hands began to tremble as she stretched them upward, receiving His comfort . . . for her father's accident, for her son's disabilities. His strength made perfect in her weakness.

How long she was there, she did not know. But when at last she opened her eyes, she saw the afternoon sun had dimmed. Yet the ground on which she kneeled glowed.

She was surrounded by a circle of light.

18

ANGELICA LIFTED MANUEL from his car seat. "Oh, you're getting so heavy, you good boy." It had been six months since Manuel had come home from the hospital, after spending nine weeks in the NICU.

She swung him above her head, as his daddy liked to do. He gave her an instant smile, fisted hands flailing. Mommy, Daddy, or stranger, it didn't matter, he was flying.

Manuel didn't protest when she put him on her hip. His head rolled back, and he seemed to gaze into the sky. "Pretty day, isn't it, my man." Angelica jostled him up on her shoulder so she could kiss his cheek. "Let's go in and see if your godmother is ready to go to lunch."

It was the first time Angelica had brought Manuel to the public defender's office. She hadn't been ready until now, and still, she dreaded going in alone. It had been hard telling everyone, after Manuel was born, that their worst fears had been realized. It was made worse when the "Thinking of You" cards had outnumbered those that said "Congratulations." As recently as an hour ago, Angelica had considered calling Fronie and telling her she'd meet her at the restaurant. She pushed the car door shut with her free hand.

As she stepped away, she heard a car pull into the open parking spot next to hers. A black Lexus.

A wave of apprehension swept over Angelica. She hadn't seen Max since their confrontation at The Wine Rack. All her dealings with the public defender's office regarding job related issues had been through the human resource department. She'd managed to avoid any contact with him. When Manuel had been born, she'd received a generic card from Max. She knew his signature and recognized the card had been signed by someone else. His assistant, she presumed. She quickened her pace.

"Angelica. Wait."

She could hear his footsteps behind her.

Slowing, she turned. "Hello, Max."

His eyes were focused on Manuel.

"That's a handsome boy you have there." Max's gaze turned to her.

"Thank you."

Each stood silently.

Angelica shifted Manuel to her other hip.

Max slipped his hands in his pockets.

"Angelica." He hesitated. "I'm sorry about what happened." He pulled his hands out of his pockets. "I never meant to hurt you. I was . . ." He grasped for a word. "Impaired. I'm sorry."

Angelica tilted her head, looking at him. He was clearly uncomfortable, his expression concerned, his eyes sincere. Seeing him standing there, she realized she felt no animosity toward him.

"You were drunk, Max."

His cheeks flushed. "And that was the last time."

She hated to admit it, but she enjoyed watching him squirm. "I'm glad."

He shifted on his feet. "Do you mind if I walk with you?"

She turned, and they started toward the front door of the office. "I'm picking Fronie up for lunch. Think you could give her a little extra time off today?"

Max grinned and fell into step beside her. "I think that could be arranged."

Suddenly, Manuel pushed his arm across Angelica's face, leaning toward Max, smile wide.

Max stopped. "May I?"

Before she could answer, he reached out and lifted Manuel from her arms. "Let's go introduce you around the office, *amigo*." Max took Manuel with an ease that startled Angelica.

"Look at him smile at me."

Max's open delight with her son puzzled her.

Midthought it occurred to her that her surprise at Max's immediate acceptance of Manuel said more about her than it did about Max.

She felt quick heat in her cheeks as she realized impairments came in different forms to different people.

Angelica buckled her seat belt and started the car. "Max says you can take all the time you want for our lunch." Angelica winked at Fronie. "I'm glad, because I'm taking you to The Veritable Quandary."

Fronie squealed. "How'd you get us in? Chef Aristo doesn't let just anyone in his restaurant."

Angelica turned out of the parking lot. "My parents have been patrons of his restaurant since it opened. To tell you the truth, I think my dad gave him some of his startup money."

Fronie's voice sobered. "How's your dad doing?"

"He just doesn't have the interest in life he used to have. He spends a lot of time sitting in his living room, staring across the valley. This is the man whose favorite line when I was in law school was, 'You're an Amante. Amantes never quit.'" She glanced at Fronie. "Mom says, as far as he's concerned, his life is over."

"Oh, sweetie, I'm so sorry to hear that." Fronie twisted around in her seat to look at Manuel. "Isn't he doing great?"

Angelica looked in the rearview mirror. "He is, Fronie. But you know, I still feel anxious whenever I take him anywhere. Sometimes people stare or turn away. There's so much prejudice toward people with disabilities."

"Girlfriend, I'm a black woman. You don't have to explain that kind of attitude to me."

Angelica burst out laughing. "Fronie, your father's a senator, and your mother's a doctor, for crying out loud."

"Sweetie, as far as some people are concerned, I'm the color of my skin and nothing else. When we moved into our new house, the following weekend the neighbor planted a hedge of Italian cypress between our walkways."

Angelica frowned at her. "Maybe they'd been planning that for a long time. Maybe that was just a coincidence."

Fronie turned toward Angelica and arched her eyebrow. "Maybe, but they had to tear out their rose garden to get in that second row."

Angelica loved Fronie like a sister, and it made Angelica defensive to hear her talk that way. "Well, those people have problems that are a lot bigger than the color of your skin. We're all one blood, and we all have the same Father. Period."

Fronie settled back in her seat. "How's Antonio making out with that big job he got?"

"Oh!" Angelica slapped the steering wheel. "I forgot to tell you that I called Jan Wilcox. Bryan Tomlinson has been giving him more and more of the company's business, and Antonio said he wants to hire some help. Jan arranged for Bill to come and interview with Antonio."

Fronie's brown eyes sparkled. "God's really worked in Bill's life, hasn't he? What a praise session we had at Bible study when Jan reported that he'd started going to church with his wife."

Angelica grinned at her. "*I* took that prayer request when Jan first made it. I prayed God would put someone in Bill's path."

"Well, He must have. Jan said he did an about-face, with no warning. Like he woke up one day and knew there was a God. Begged his wife's forgiveness for being such a jerk. And now Jan says he's volunteered as a leader for youth group at their church."

"Well, I'll be meeting him later this afternoon. Bill is coming to the models at three to interview with Antonio. He didn't even need directions, knew exactly where they are."

Seeing her co-workers again made Angelica realize how much she had changed since Manuel's birth. Then, her life had been all about her career. Now, it was all about her family.

Angelica pulled up behind Antonio's truck. She turned off the engine and glanced at her watch. She would introduce him to Bill. Then after that, she needed to leave. Manuel had an appointment in thirty minutes for physical therapy, and Angelica had promised her mother that she would stop on the way and pick up her father from his doctor's appointment and then take him to physical therapy when Manuel was finished. Over the months, she and her mother had become close. Sharing each other's joys . . . Benito feeding himself, Manuel holding his head up. And each other's burdens.

Angelica got out of the car and looked over the seat. Manuel was sleeping. She didn't want to disturb him even though she knew Antonio would be disappointed that he wouldn't get to show off his son to Bill. Manuel had missed his nap time in the restaurant and needed to sleep.

"Where's my boy?"

Angelica turned at the familiar voice.

"He's sleeping."

Antonio stepped in front of her and leaned into the backseat. She pulled the back of his shirt. "Get out of there," she whispered. "You'll wake him."

"I know," he said loudly.

Angelica took a firm grip of the back of Antonio's pants and pulled him away from the car. "He has to go to physical therapy in a little while. Let him rest."

Antonio put his hands on his hips, mocking her. "*Sí, señorita.*"

"Stop it. I bet this is Bill." She waved at the blue truck rounding the corner.

Antonio stiffened.

Angelica dropped her voice. "What's the matter?"

He didn't answer.

"That's Bill, Jan's sister's son-in-law I told you about. You've heard me talk about him a hundred times. You thought he'd be perfect to work with you."

322

"*Sí.*"

Bill strode over to them, his hand extended toward Angelica. "You must be Mrs. Perez."

"I am. And this is my husband, Antonio."

Bill extended his hand to Antonio. "We've met. We both bid this job. Looks like the best man got it."

Angelica put her hand on her chest. "You're kidding. Antonio, you never told me that."

"I think maybe Bryan Tomlinson be surprised to see you here." Antonio folded his arms across his chest.

Angelica looked at her husband, wondering what he meant, appalled that he had not shaken Bill's hand. "If he interviewed him for the job, he must think highly of him."

Antonio looked at Bill as if Bill had an answer he might want to give.

Angelica spoke to Antonio in Spanish. "What's the matter with you? This man needs work. He's been through some very rough times with his family, and he's just now going back to church. He needs work, and you need somebody to work for you. He came out here knowing you beat him out of the job. That had to be hard."

Antonio seemed to be sizing the man up. She'd never seen him act this way before. She closed the space between herself and her husband, then dropped her hand behind Antonio, giving him a jab in the back.

Bill looked Antonio in the eye. "I need work. I know you do quite a few private homes. I'll work for you free for one month. You can decide if you like my work. If you do, hire me. If you don't, we'll call it even."

Angelica's jaw dropped. "Even. How could you call that even? That doesn't sound fair at all." She turned to her husband. "Does it, Antonio?"

323

Antonio didn't speak for a moment, then she saw his face soften.

"Yes." Antonio tapped his forefinger on his chin. "Maybe we can work that out."

It was clear to Angelica that there was more going on than she was able to discern. She looked at her watch. She had fifteen minutes to get to Valle Medical Center and pick up her father. "I've got to go to an appointment. I hope you two work out an agreement." She turned to Antonio. "Could I have a word with you?"

Antonio tipped his head toward her.

"Excuse us, Bill." Angelica walked toward the back of the car, Antonio walking beside her. "Antonio, I've prayed for months that God would draw this man to Him and bless his business. Maybe he needs to improve his skills. Maybe that's why he hasn't done well for himself. You're honest, hardworking, and great at what you do. If you hire him, you can be an example to him."

Antonio took a deep breath. "I'm going to hire him, *señorita*. Not because I want to, but because I have to."

Angelica glared at him. "Well, don't do it just because I say so. If you don't think it will work out, then just tell him."

Antonio hesitated, as if considering what he should say. A sparkle came into his eye. "This is between me and the Boss."

Angelica threw her hand up in the air. "What boss? You're your own boss."

Antonio gave her an easy grin. "Let's just say I know what it means to get a second chance." He kissed her cheek, then turned on his heel and joined Bill.

As Angelica drove to pick up her father, she replayed the whole meeting with Bill over in her mind. Antonio's cryptic comments hadn't made any sense at all. The two men had obviously met before, but both had seemed ill at ease. She shrugged. She'd just have to trust that it would work out. *Dear Lord, You have brought these two men together. I pray that You will be glorified as they work together and get to know each other.*

The doctor's office was within walking distance of the physical therapy center. Rather than deal with getting her father in and out of the car, she decided she could push him in his wheelchair and he could hold Manuel in his carrier. She lifted Manuel out of the backseat and hurried up the steps to the office lobby.

Her father was sitting near the door, slumped in his chair.

"Hey, Dad. Looks like you're ready. Hope you didn't have to wait long."

He looked up. "I've got nothing else to do."

"If you'll hold Manuel, we'll go over to the physical therapy offices, and after his appointment, we'll go to yours."

"Fine." His answer was curt, and he made no attempt to take the carrier.

Angelica lifted it and set it gently in his lap, then wheeled him out to the sidewalk.

As she walked, she tried to make conversation with him about the beautiful day, Antonio's growing business, and Manuel's steady progress. But nothing engaged his interest. His only comment was that they could go home early as far as he was concerned. He saw no purpose in him having physical therapy, especially today. His appointment was for upper body work. Now that he had a nurse at home, all he needed his upper body for was to wheel himself around. And he could do that just fine.

Angelica was glad her father couldn't see her face. His attitude made her angry. "Manuel's getting big. As he gets older, I know you're going to want to lift him up into your lap."

But her father didn't answer.

By the time they arrived at Manuel's appointment, she was fighting tears. *Dear God, only You can change the heart of man. Please heal his heart. Not for me, but for Manuel.*

When they were called, Angelica rolled her father's wheelchair into the room and parked it so he could watch as she and the physical therapist, Elizabeth, worked with Manuel.

Angelica put her purse down and slipped her shoes off. She lifted Manuel from his carrier and laid him on the mat, then she sat down next to him.

Elizabeth walked into the room. "Good afternoon, you two." She looked toward Angelica's father and smiled. "I see we have a guest today."

"This is my dad." Angelica turned to her father. "This is Elizabeth."

Elizabeth knelt down beside Angelica. "What have you been working on this past week with him?"

"I've been doing a lot of tummy time. I think he's getting stronger, but he still doesn't seem to be able to bear weight on his arms."

"Okay, let's work on that. I can show you some tricks."

Elizabeth got a towel, rolled it up, and laid it on the mat. "This should help." She sat down behind Manuel and laid him facedown on the mat, his chest on the towel. Next, she pulled his hips up over his heels so his bottom was in the air, but his face was on the mat. Then, she gently moved his hands under his shoulders. Still sitting behind him, holding his thighs together, she began to encourage him to push himself up. "Come on. You can do it, Champ. Push up."

Manuel struggled, managing to lift his upper body about an inch.

Angelica clapped. "Good boy. Look how strong you are."

Manuel sank back to the mat.

"Mom, why don't you get in front of him so he can see you?"

Angelica scooted over in front of Manuel. "Show Mommy how strong you are."

Elizabeth continued to urge him. "You can do it, Manuel."

Angelica rooted him on. "Come on, Manuel." She put her own palms down on the mat, extending her arms.

Manuel struggled, panting, straining. Finally, his right arm straightened, but his left arm gave way. He fell to the mat, rolling to his side. He began to cry.

Angelica reached over and propped him back up on the towel. She looked at Elizabeth. "See what I mean? Bless his heart."

"Let's try again, Manuel." Elizabeth put her hands on his hips, lining them up with his heels. "Come on, Manuel, push."

Manuel tried time and again to raise his upper body off the mat. But time and again he failed.

Finally, Elizabeth looked at her watch. "Time's about up." She positioned Manuel on the mat again. "Come on, Manuel, you can do it. One more try."

The little boy groaned and panted, trying to push himself up.

"You can do it."

Both women turned around and looked at Angelica's father.

"You can do it," he repeated, leaning forward in the

wheelchair. His hands knotted into fists. "Fight, Manuel. You're an Amante. Amantes never quit."

Manuel, for the second time, extended his right arm.

"That's the way, son."

With his little body trembling, Manuel straightened his left arm.

Angelica cheered. Elizabeth started chanting, "Manuel. Manuel."

Angelica's father slapped his knee. "Show 'em what you're made of, Manuel."

Manuel began to rock back and forth on his hands and knees, panting and smiling, gazing at Grandpa.

"Angelica, you watch out. With the right coach, that boy's going to be walking."

Angelica looked at her father. His face was flushed with color, his eyes bright. *Praise Your holy name.*

Elizabeth stood. "That's a perfect place to stop for today."

Angelica rose and picked up Manuel. "Thank you so much for all your help. I'll see you next week." She put her son in his carrier and turned to her father. "Ready to go?"

He picked Manuel's carrier up from next to his chair. "We're ready."

As they started to her father's appointment, Angelica realized she'd forgotten her purse.

She wheeled her father to the side of the hall. "Just a sec, Dad. I've got to run back and get my handbag."

Angelica grabbed her purse from the physical therapy room and returned to the hall. As she approached her father, she could hear him talking to Manuel. She slowed her steps, listening. He had turned the carrier so Manuel faced him.

"It's not fair, is it? You can't do *anything* you want to do either."

Angelica could see that Manuel was smiling at her father.

"But you're a happy fellow in spite of it all, aren't you?" Her father took his finger and tickled Manuel's chest. "Don't you worry, it's all going to work out. You've got a good mom and dad . . . and a grandpa who loves you." He tapped the baby's nose with his finger. "It's your turn to watch me now. I'll show you how it's done."

Angelica slowly backed away, trying to get control of her emotions. Taking a deep breath, she dug in her purse, making sure her keys rattled as she approached her father.

He looked back at her. "Got your purse?"

"Uh-huh. Let's go."

As they started down the hall, she saw a little boy and his mother, looking out one of the windows that faced the street.

"Look, Mommy. It's an angel."

The woman crouched beside him, looking where he was pointing. "Oh my, those clouds do look like an angel. A big angel."

Angelica stopped behind them, looking toward the sky.

The woman turned to her. "Do you see it? What do you think?"

Angelica couldn't see what they were looking at.

She didn't need to.

As Angelica drove home from the ranch, she prayed a prayer of thanksgiving. Something had happened to her father in that room while he watched Manuel. Something mysterious and beautiful.

Coming to a stop at the bottom of the hill, she decided to turn left instead of right. "Manuel, I want to share something with you."

She followed the road that skirted the edge of town and eased the car into the pullout. She took Manuel's carrier from the backseat and jogged up the path until she reached the oak.

She sat down beneath the ancient spreading branches of the old tree. Setting the carrier in front of her, she smoothed Manuel's blanket away from his face. He was sleeping.

"Oh, Manuel," she whispered. "You've taught me so much." She kissed his cheek. "I've learned what humbleness is. I've learned that when life's not fair, you can still smile." She tucked the blanket around his toes. "If it wasn't for you, I would never have taken the time to learn to pray. I was going a hundred miles an hour. You've taught me it's okay to go slow." She smiled to herself. "Sometimes slow is better."

She tilted her head. "And you know what else? God is with us. He understands. He's been where I am." She looked up into the evening sky. "His Son was rejected by the world. He knows what that feels like."

She gazed into her son's little face. So peaceful. His eyes, crescent moons, at rest. Tiny hands, splayed on his chest. Mouth turned upward, waiting to smile. Her baby was perfect. *God's truth, not man's truth.*

"And you're going to teach your grandfather too. Aren't you?"

She dropped her head and wept.

She loved him so much.

Epilogue

A Year Later
Guadalajara, Mexico

THE OLD WOMAN sat in the shade of the jacaranda tree. She held the edge of the paper in her teeth, while she tried to unfold it with her left hand. The twisted, frozen fingers of her right hand were useless, except to use as a brace when she wanted to stand.

An afternoon breeze had come up, threatening to snatch the paper from her. But she would not be deterred. She had just found the lost treasure that morning, in the pocket of a sweater. She patiently worked her finger into the crease. Turn by turn, she managed to get the paper unfolded.

Smoothing it out in her lap, memories flooded through her. Her mouth widened in a toothless smile. How many prayers had she prayed with the paper on her lap, sitting in the white wicker chair? She traced the letters with her finger. G-O-D.

Suddenly, a gust of wind whirled around her, plucking the paper from her, sending it in a spiral, dropping it a few feet away.

"No." The old woman struggled to her feet. "No."

Bent over, her crippled hand clutching her black shawl, she tried to reach the scrap of paper. But just as she touched it, the wind gusted, carrying it into the air. She limped after it.

Floating just out of her reach, the sliver of paper became a sliver of light. Letting go of her shawl, she strained forward with both hands.

The light became larger, and her fingertips touched it. In the twinkling of an eye, her earthly body fell away, and she became one with the light.

Instantly, she understood the mysteries of life. Eternal truths. The alchemy of forgiveness. The resurrecting power of love. Above her the sky opened like a scroll, revealing a kingdom.

Not bound by time, she looked back and saw the beginning. He gathered the waters of the sea together and created a firmament in its midst. She watched Him suspend the expanse above the earth and call it heaven. He spoke, and it was done. He commanded it, and it stood fast.

Then she heard the most beautiful, high voice singing, calling her into the kingdom. Clothed in ethereal brilliance, she approached the gates.

The single voice became a chorus, and she saw God's glory, reflected the color of gold from the hands of the saints as they raised them in thanksgiving. The heavens themselves began shouts of hallelujah, heralding the coming of the newest soul. A living path of light formed, stretching farther than the eye could see. She saw running toward her family members gone so long from her, her husband, sisters, brothers, and ahead of them all, Allegra.

Slowly, a hush fell over eternity, and a single light, brighter than all the others, encircled her and presented her faultless before the presence of His glory.

Maclovia bowed down and worshipped God.

ACKNOWLEDGMENTS

Jesus said, "Apart from me you can do nothing." I have read those words so many times, but writing this book has brought me to a deeper understanding of their truth. Without fail, each time I found myself at a dead end, unable to find the resources I needed, a door would open. Just the people I needed would appear, just when I needed them most.

My deepest thanks to Elizabeth Lindquist, Samantha's mom, who selflessly shared her experiences and her heart with me. Her attention to detail and her intuitive understanding of what I needed from her made it possible for me to write this book.

I will forever be grateful to Michael Cantrall for responding to a desperate email on a Sunday night and taking the time to find an attorney willing to be a resource for me. And thank you, Katharine Elliott, for all your guidance and insights into the public defender's office. Your bright mind and willingness to make time to help me were critical in completing this manuscript.

And Jennifer Leep of Revell, without you this book would not have been published. Also my editors, Carol Craig of The Editing Gallery and Susan Lohrer of The Write Words Editing, who both worked tirelessly with me, I thank you again. Between the three of us, the book was sometimes worked on twenty-four hours a day as deadlines approached.

I also want to acknowledge all the parents of children with Down syndrome who wrote to me openly of their feelings and experiences. Especially Ann Bremer and Jeff Goble.

A special thanks to my husband, mom, dad, and all my family and friends who support and encourage me daily. Sue Callen and Lindsay Murphy deserve special mention.

To Natasha Kern, my agent, you are the perfect companion for my book journey. But if I never wrote another word, I have no doubt we would journey on through life together, hand in hand, pondering the depths of God's love, seeking the wisdom of His Word, and marveling at the beautiful universe He made for mankind.

My prayer partners, Tex Gaynos, Donna and Glenn Wimer, Renae Scott Moore, and Pat and Marvin Miller, thank you for your continual support. This book is very much the fruit of your labor.

And to my audience of one, Jesus Christ, Lord and Savior, who taught me through this process that though I may fail Him, He will never fail me.

Author's Note

I ORIGINALLY DECIDED TO write this book because my husband and I have a son with attention deficit disorder. It has impacted his life and ours in a dramatic way. That got me to thinking of all the parents who have children who are being challenged in extraordinary ways.

I began to research, and the Lord led me into the world of families whose children have Down syndrome. I spoke to many parents, met some of their children, and heard countless stories of how these differently abled kids bless their loved ones daily. Were there difficulties? Yes. Was it sometimes overwhelming? Yes. But the emerging theme, time after time, was that the families of children with Downs found their children had enriched their lives in ways they'd never dreamed of.

It is my desire that readers of this book will consider that every child is born perfect for God's plans and purposes. That sometimes we are called to pray not for the healing of the child, but for the healing of the heart of man.

For support and information about Down syndrome, go to the Association for Children with Down Syndrome (ACDS) website at www.acds.org. Also, please join me this coming year in supporting Buddy Walk and the Special Olympics. If you would like to write to me, my address is: Box 3781, Coeur d'Alene, ID 83816.

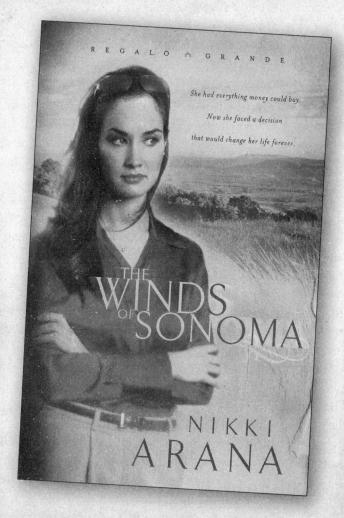